Scent of Lavender

By Margaret W. Miller

Copyright © 2011 Margaret W. Miller
All rights reserved.

ISBN: 1-4611-7674-3
ISBN-13: 9781461176749

Acknowledgments

There are many to be thanked for their influence on this story. First of all, I want to thank Adrien and Michaela Jones. When I retired from teaching school ten years ago, they gave me a notebook and a pen to begin writing the novel that I had promised all of my students I would write. Every time I would see Adrien, he would ask me how the book was coming. He never missed a chance to say, "I want to see that book, and I want to see it now! Where is it?" He made me realize that when you make a promise to that many people, you had better follow through and complete it, so I began to write.

I wish to thank my mother Phyllis Whittaker for reading me all kinds of beautiful books when I was growing up and for leaving me a drop of her writing talent. I took many of Lillian Lewis's good qualities from my grandmother Lillian Page who has always been an inspiration to me. As a tribute to her, I placed her picture on the cover of this book to represent the Lillian in my story.

Next, I would like to thank all of my students over the past 40 years who gave me the inspiration to write the classroom scenes. The children in *A Scent of Lavender* have characteristics of many of my past students, but a special thanks has to go to Adrien Jones, Michaela Jones, Courtney Davis, Nancy Carter, Cherie Hiatt, and my granddaughters, Danielle and Dailey Bradshaw. Their pranks and personalities in a modern classroom setting helped me to write the classroom scenes in 1877 when everything seemed to go out of control.

Mark Dotson, a modern-day mining magnate, took time out of his busy schedule to talk to me for hours about what mining was like in the 1870's. I am thankful to him for giving me valuable information so that I could write the underground scenes in the mine. He also introduced me to the Tommyknockers.

There is no way that I can repay my daughter, Denise Bradshaw; our town librarian, Sherri Yardley; Denise Dewsnup and Suzanne Bettridge for their careful editing of the first manuscript and for their words of encouragement. It always helps to have dedicated readers who cannot only find errors, but can also offer constructive advice on the parts of the book that need improvement.

George A. Horton, Jr. deserves a big thank you for the information that I gained from his book, A Personal View of the History of Milford up to 1914–the Town that Could! From his book I gained valuable information about Frisco itself, classroom routines, and the social activities of the time. Thanks also has to be given to C.J. Brown and her self-published pamphlet, "Someone Should Remember." This pamphlet gave me valuable information about Frisco and the local legends that circulated around about it.

I need to extend a special thanks to Paul Woodbury and David Leppink for their photography skills that brought the cover to life.

My husband Dennis deserves to be recognized for his encouraging words concerning this project. There were times when I would have given up, but his words of encouragement helped me to press forward until the book was completed.

A Scent of Lavender

By Margaret W. Miller

Preface

When I was seven, my father moved our family to Milford, Utah. I have always been a storyteller at heart and spent numerous hours telling stories to my new friends, sometimes in front of the classroom when the teacher needed to leave for a few minutes. They, in turn, told me stories of their own about the ghost town, Frisco, an old mining town just 15 miles west of Milford.

From my very first visit to Frisco, I became fascinated with its history. I spent hours walking its abandoned streets and visiting its graveyard. I grew to love the legends and facts that circulated about the fabulous Horn Silver Mine, one of the richest silver mines in the West. By 1885 over $60,000,000 in zinc, copper, lead, gold and silver had been hauled away by mule train and the Central Railroad. It was a typical mining town in some respects, but when it came to evilness and sin, legend circulated that it was more depraved than Tombstone during its blackest years.

When I decided to write my first book, it was natural for me to place my characters in the midst of this mining town in the year 1877 when the legend was just beginning. There is a great deal of information in *A Scent of Lavender* that is historically accurate. Frisco began with Ryan and Hawkes stopping by an outcropping of rock just as I describe it. The cave-in that I describe in the epilogue was the beginning of the end for one of the richest silver deposits in the West, and the information about this cave-in is taken from an actual newspaper article. The mining strike in the book actually happened, and legend says that a cave-in did result when ladies were taken down into the mine. The fire at Shauntie is based on fact, and the story of the murder at Squaw Springs involving Si and Mary Perkins is a part of Frisco's legend.

It is a historical fact that a sheriff named Sheriff Pearson was hired from Pioche, Nevada to bring law and order to this lawless community. I have patterned the sheriff in this book after Sheriff Pearson, but I have given him a different name, and his actions and thoughts in *A Scent of Lavender* come from my imagination. In reality, no one knows much about him other than he was hired to clean up Frisco, and this he did. What happens to the sheriff in the book is not fact and comes strictly from the mind of the author. In reality, no one knows whether he died in Frisco or left for greener pastures.

Today only a few buildings, coke ovens, and an abandoned mine remain. Only the shifting sands, and the memories whispered by the relentless wind are left to tell the story of Frisco.

Chapter 1

Early August, 1879
100 Miles west of Marysvale, Utah

Every inch of Lillian's body ached each time the freight wagon hit a rock in the rut-encrusted, dusty trail. Her companion, Ned Druthers, the freighter she had been traveling with for the past 5 miles, seemed only interested in holding conversation with his two mules and periodically checking on the grain bags that were jostling about in the back of the wagon.

How did I ever get myself into this predicament? Lillian wondered as she clung tightly to the jolting wagon seat. Of their own volition, her thoughts traveled three days back in time. She found herself in the middle of the dinner hour at the Dalton Mill and Boardinghouse located in Bullion Canyon west of Marysvale, Utah. The boardinghouse provided sleeping accommodations and hot food for mostly single men who sought employment in the gold mines of Bullion Canyon. Laborers, muckers, timber men, car men, and blacksmiths sought the comforts that the Dalton could provide, but due to the roughness of the clientele, there was no daintiness to be found in this eating establishment. Bearded miners grabbed their forks and used them like shovels to move the food into their cavernous mouths. Loud laughter, rude jokes, and utter confusion made the room sound like a hen house at egg-gathering time.

Shouts of "Hey, Lilly, where's the blasted biscuits," and "Lilly, can't a hungry man get some more stew?" filled the air. Running into the kitchen to get the biscuits, she was roughly pulled into a brawny lap and given a wet, bearded kiss by Klauss Peterson, a miner who had given her problems in the past. Lillian didn't have time to stop and think. While Klauss was still reeling from his amorous kiss, she grabbed both of his ears, twisted them as hard as her 110-pound body would allow, and shoved his face into his unfinished dinner plate. Klauss came up sputtering, and the sound that issued from his lips was not human. Lillian jumped off his lap just as he shook his head like a wet dog, spraying food particles over the two men on either side of him.

At this moment war was declared. The two men who had been defiled by the remains of Klauss's dinner swung to hit Klauss at the same time. Since Klauss happened to stoop to retrieve his napkin from the floor just at this moment, the two men hit each other smack in the face, and as they stood up, overturned the table on which they had been eating. Someone yelled, "Fight!" and instantaneously everyone got into the spirit of the disturbance. Metal plates were flying through the air, tables were overturned, and men were slipping and sliding on stew that had now turned to slippery mush as they tried to see who could get in the hardest punch. One man was thrown out the large window at the front of the boardinghouse, and amazingly got up, climbed back through the window, and once again joined the others in the slugging fest.

Lillian ran up the stairs to the safety of her room. She bolted the door and just stood there silently, trying to shut out the cries of the rough men below and the cracking of breaking glass. *There goes the other two windows. It's going to take me hours to clean up this mess. I'll probably get finished just in time to start breakfast,* she agonized.

She sat down on her bed and reached beneath her pillow, drawing out her treasured means for finding peace–the *Book of Mormon*. It was the original book presented to her mother by her father who was acting as a missionary for the Mormon

Church while the Saints were camped at Gainsville, Ohio for the winter. This book had touched her mother's heartstrings, been instrumental in her conversion, and had brought her parents together, resulting in their marriage just weeks after their first meeting. Carefully cherished and guarded, this worn volume had traveled with her parents from Ohio to Salt Lake City in 1850. Help from Brigham Young's Perpetual Emigrating Fund made it possible for them to finally join the Saints in the Salt Lake Valley. The spirit of the book had been infused into the hearts of Lillian and her brother Jesse as they grew up on the family farm in the Salt Lake Valley.

From her earliest remembrance, her memories contained pictures of sweat and heartbreak as her father fought to support the family on a small farm where the bad years far outweighed the good ones, resulting in her family always struggling to make ends meet.

Lillian, her mother, and Jesse had been reading from this very book when with excitement flowing like quicksilver through his veins, her father had thrown open the door of their cabin to tell them of the lucrative gold mines in Bullion Canyon near Marysvale, Utah.

"This is the answer to all of our problems," he had cried as he hugged her mother, assuring her that the gold mines of Marysvale were the answer to all their financial difficulties. And so when Lillian was ten, this very book had traveled with the Lewis family to Marysvale, where they had spent the last eight years living in a claim shanty while her father followed his illusive dream as he worked in the "Canyon of Gold," better known as Bullion Canyon.

Lillian ran her hand gently over the worn cover. Every night before she retired to bed, she read from its pages, and each word brought assurance that the Gospel had been restored in these latter days by a young farm boy named Joseph Smith. As she opened the well-read pages and started to read, she was filled with the peace that always came, and she could no longer hear the ruckus below.

When she closed the book and placed it under her pillow, she fell to her knees to pour out her heart to someone who had become her best friend. "Heavenly Father, thou has brought the gospel into my life. Please show me the path that I need to follow. Direct me to where you want me to go. It's getting impossible to live here, but if it is your desire that I stay, show me how to deal with the problems that I now face. I want to make a difference in other people's lives. Please lead me down a path that will enable me to do so."

The sounds of fighting could still be heard. The cracks in the wooden floor were no detriment to the battle that sounded like it had just reached its peak, making Lillian almost believe that she was right in the middle of the freigh. With a sigh she lay on the bed and gave in to exhaustion. *Just a few minutes of shut eye before I have to start the cleanup,* she reasoned.

As soon as her eyes closed, the dream began. Flames were flicking up the sides of her old shanty in Bullion Canyon. The roof of her home was entirely engulfed, and flames were shooting out the windows which had exploded because of the intensity of the heat. "Mom! Dad! Jesse!" She screamed as she ran towards the inferno.

She could feel the searing heat from the flames that prevented her from entering the house. She fell to her knees at the blazing doorway, knowing that she could go no further, sobbing uncontrollably. Her dream always ended when she raised her tear-stained face to see her father, mother, and twelve-year old Jesse standing in midair amid the flames, their sad eyes accusing her of the crime of helplessness.

Lillian's body was drenched with sweat, and she turned restlessly as she thought back on that fateful morning. She had gone to Mary Smith's shanty to spend the night and had returned in the early morning to find her house and her entire family destroyed, as well as the hillside in back of her home. In her dream, she relived once more the feelings that had taken over her body when at the age of eighteen, she had found herself without a caring family or kin. There was no one here for her now, because both sets of grandparents had disowned her mother and father when they joined the Mormon Church. To her grandparents, the Mormons were a cult more deadly than any plague.

She dreamed of the funeral and how she had dropped wild flowers on the three caskets which held what remained of her precious family. The Marysvale Cemetery was set on a hill, and the harsh Southern Utah winds frequented this lonely place. On the day of the funeral, huge gusts took out their anger on the small group gathered around the coffins. Dirt and rocks pelted the black-clad assembly. It was difficult to sing "Amazing Grace" as the force of the blast threatened to topple over even those with youth and strength in their blood. Amid this sadness and nature's insensitivity, Lillian realized that she was now faced with the task of surviving on her own.

Lillian hugged her pillow tighter as the events that followed the funeral flowed through her mind.

A picture of her friend Mary and her parents slipped into her dreams as she heard them graciously offer to let her stay with them, but the sleeping young woman felt anew the pride and independence that were a vital part of her character, giving her the knowledge that she was a strong, capable person. At that moment of decision in Mary's house, she had known that she was strong and capable of supporting herself, and it was then that she had made the decision to be the master of her own fate no matter how rough the road of life might become.

Flashes of riding in a wagon to the Dalton Boardinghouse up Bullion Canyon now filled her mind. She had heard that there were numerous opportunities for cooks, waitresses, and housekeepers in the boardinghouses which accommodated many of the miners. She remembered waiting on tables on a trial basis, but smiled in her sleep when she recalled the day the permanent cook got sick and she was asked to help with supper. One taste of her fluffy biscuits, and she was promoted on the spot to the position of main cook's helper. That job had expanded into waitressing when needed and being in charge of overall cleanup. Visions of Klauss Peterson entered her dream and how he had made life miserable from the first moment that his eyes met hers. Images of his unwanted attentions for the past three months, as he made her life unbearable, caused her to sit up in her bed as she awakened herself with her own startled cry of alarm.

Wisps of black hair had escaped from the braids she always wound into a bun at the back of her head, and wet tendrils curled on her damp face, which was drenched with cool sweat. The dreams had been so real. Then she realized–silence! She breathed a sigh of relief and rose from the bed to carefully open the door. Everyone was either punched out or had gone home to lick their wounds. She cautiously descended the steep stairs to begin what seemed to be an impossible task. There wasn't one inch of that wooden floor that wasn't covered with something, food, overturned tables, plates, glass, and even some blood here and there. *This is going to take the rest of the night,* an inner voice screamed. Not one to shun hard work, she dug right in and had all the plates stacked in the sink, the tables back in place, and half the floor cleaned when she spied her salvation–a food-spattered newspaper. Her heart leaped in her breast as she turned the pages of *The Frisco Times* and found the answer to her prayers.

Positioned in the "Help Wanted" section and standing out in bold print, she read, "Wanted immediately–a teacher to instruct all grades in the mining community of Frisco, Utah. Need not be experienced, but must be knowledgeable of the three R's. Apply at The Southern Hotel on Frisco's Main Street. Pays $40 a month."

Lillian held her hand over her mouth to suppress a cry of jubilation. Her avenue of escape lay before her. By answering this ad, she could eliminate Klauss and this rough, mining community from her life and pursue a career that had always interested her–teaching. Then she caught sight of her image in the broken mirror, and every ounce of courage seemed to leave her body. *What makes you think you can handle a classroom?*

You're barely 5 feet tall and come just shy of weighting 100 pounds. Why, some of your students will tower over you. How are you going to control them? Your hands are used to work, but they're so small that if you tried to use them to discipline a student, you'd probably get laughed right out of the classroom.

Then the inner strength that had sustained Lillian through the tough times kicked in, and she remembered what her mother had taught her as a little girl when she had problems that seemed too difficult to solve. She could clearly see her mother sitting on the front porch, and feel her arm enclosing her childish body, as she said, "When the trail you're walking gets tough, don't stop and rest. The tough keep hiking."

Could she be a teacher? You bet she could. The family *Book of Mormon* and her school books had been with her at Mary's house and had survived the fire, and they now lay safe and sound in her mother's old carpetbag. She had always loved school, placing in the top of her class, and the teacher had often asked her to help the little ones with their lessons because Lillian always seemed to have a special gift for making learning fun. *I may be small, but when it comes to teaching, I can be mighty,* she told herself. *Thank you, Heavenly Father. Now just help me find a way to get to Frisco, Utah.*

Chapter 2

Breakfast was in full swing when Lillian's prayer was answered. She was serving a third stack of pancakes to Ned Druthers, a freighter who had been in Bullion Canyon just three days. He stood only 5 feet 6 inches, but the bulging muscles in his 200-pound body commanded respect. His gray, grizzled beard and bushy, gray eyebrows lent character to a weathered face that had been tempered by nature's elements. Large, black eyes expressively showed his inner feelings. "I'm gonna be headn' out tomorrow for Frisco, boys. I've enjoyed your company, but I promised my friend Ned Jones that I'd take a load of grain to his father-in-law, Nelson Marshall in Frisco. They're expectn' a hard winter, and they're gonna be needn' plenty of flour. Ned knew I often did freighting, so he's a-paying me to bring the load.

"Besides, my mules, Mabel and Lizzy are getting itchy. They don't like to sit around too long. They've been hankering to take off on one of our journeys all week long. Yes, sir, why when I harnessed old Mabel and Lizzy yesterday, they took off on their own before I could get in the wagon, and it took me pert nigh half the day to get them rounded up. Finally found them at the Witt Tate Mine, just drinking water out of his horse trough like they owned the place. Darned critters! If they weren't so darned lovable, I'd sell them in a minute."

It was difficult for Lillian to bide her time, but she waited until almost everyone had left the boardinghouse before she approached Ned as he was wolfing down his fourth stack of pancakes. As Lillian cleared Ned's plates from the table, she looked into those expressive, black eyes and said, "Mr. Druthers, is there any chance that you would take a passenger with you to Frisco? They are desperate for a teacher there, and I want to apply for the position, but 100 miles is a little too far to travel on foot. I wouldn't be any trouble, and you seem to like my cooking. I have $10 that's yours if you'll agree to get me to Frisco in one piece."

Ned cocked a bushy eyebrow and answered, "Well, Little Missy, it's true that I do enjoy your cooking, but when all is said and done, it's my mules Mabel and Lizzy who'll have to decide. If they take a likin' to you, it's a go. Let's go ask 'em right now, but be careful you don't touch Mabel's tail. Darn critter kicked one drifter through a barn door once because his arm brushed against that tail. Been that way since she was born, so I've learned to give that switching broomstick a wide berth if I don't want to visit the Promised Land before it's my time."

When Lillian stepped outside the boardinghouse, she came face to face with the most adorable, opinionated creatures she had ever seen. They were securely tied to the hitching post in front of the boardinghouse, and all four ears stood at attention when their expressive eyes fell upon Lillian. She confidently approached the mules. She loved animals, and these two were adorable. Their feisty spirit seemed to illuminate from the very depths of their glistening eyes. She felt as though she could drown in the depths of those dark brown orbs. She stepped forward and with one hand on each head, gave them reassuring pats. She was rewarded with loud neighs and the rough feel of wet tongues as they showered her entire face with wet, slobbery kisses.

Ned stood in shocked silence for a couple of minutes then blurted, "Tarnation! I ain't never seen them take on like that about nobody. Little Missy, you be ready at six in the morning, and you got a ride. If you're okay with Mabel and Lizzy, you're okay with me, but pack light cuz the wagon is going to be busting at the seams with all that wheat."

Lillian was jolted back to the present when she heard Ned holler, "Brace yourself! Looks like we have company. By the looks of the lather on their horses, they've been riding something fierce for some time. Look back and tell me if that one with the black beard is that disagreeable heathen who caused a fight two nights ago in the boardinghouse."

Lillian was almost afraid to turn around, but when she turned to view the riders, her worst fears were realized. Klauss Peterson and his brother Red were closing in on them fast.

In a matter of minutes, Klauss and Red were riding beside the wagon. In one fluid motion, Klauss left his horse and transferred himself to Lizzy's back. His big hands pulled on the reins to slow the mules down and bring them to a dead stop.

Dismounting Lizzy, Klauss lost no time in pulling Lillian from the wagon and hauling her into his arms. "Thought you'd get away from me, did you? Nobody runs away from Klauss Peterson–nobody! You're coming back with me to Marysvale right now! I'll make sure that you never leave again. We're going to get hitched as soon as I can get a preacher. Then all thoughts of leaving me will leave that pretty noggin' of yours!"

Lillian struggled to release herself from Klauss' arms, but rippling muscles stronger than any lumberjack's held her fast to his bulky body. "Let me go, you barbarian," she screamed as she struggled with all the energy she had left to avoid the insistent, wet mouth that was inflicting hot kisses on her neck. Just when she thought that all was lost, she saw her salvation out of the corner of her eye. Ned had retrieved his shotgun from the wagon and was taking dead aim at Red who was laughing so hard that he was doubled over with glee.

"Let her go!" Ned hollered "or your brother will be seeing daylight through his forehead. Don't hesitate! I may look old, but I'm not puny. I know how to use this shotgun, and I won't hesitate to unload it on your brother! Let her go, I say!"

Red's laughing stopped, and Klauss loosened his hold on Lillian, enabling her to slowly back away towards Ned.

Klauss was enraged. His face became bright red, and his hands formed two tight fists as he slowly started to move towards the shotgun-toting freighter. "You old geezer! Do you think that sawed-off shotgun is going to make me listen to a wrinkled-up toad frog like you? Throw that gun down now or be prepared to be smunched!" With fire in his eyes, he started to stride towards Ned, his arms in boxer position, ready for a knockout. Without twitching a muscle, Ned now aimed the shotgun at Klauss and was preparing to pull the trigger when Klauss brushed Mabel's tail with his bulky body.

The shrill caterwauling that ensued was loud enough to raise the dead in the Marysvale Cemetery. Mabel turned her tail end to the offending person, and her flying hooves were mere blurs as they kicked in the air. Klauss suddenly found himself airborne as his body flew 6 yards and landed with a sickening thump when it hit an aspen tree. His left leg was crunched beneath his huge body at an odd angle, and he lay with his head resting on his chest, not moving a muscle.

After a few minutes, he shook his head and brought himself back to consciousness. "Ahhhh! You've broken my leg!" he moaned. Then with a muffled cry of pain, his head slumped, and he blacked out entirely.

Ned handed the shotgun to Lillian. "Don't hesitate to drill Red if he makes a wrong move. I'll help him throw Klauss over the saddle so he can get him back to Marysvale to a doctor." Ned turned to Red and warned, "You tell Klauss if he comes after us again, he'll get double what he got today. Nobody messes with my Mabel!"

It was not an easy task for the two men to throw Klauss across his horse, then tie him securely to the saddle, but with this completed, Red had barely mounted his horse when Ned sent it running by giving a hard slap to the horse's behind.

"Better hurry, cause that leg needs attention soon if he's ever going to walk again!" Ned yelled.

When Lillian and Ned could no longer see the two horses in the distance, they relaxed and started to breath normally.

"We don't have to worry about Klauss any more, Little Missy. Did you see that hoof print on his forehead?" chuckled Ned.

"His forehead did look like it had been branded by a hoof-shaped branding iron," Lillian replied as her laughter joined with Ned's.

Ned helped Lillian back into the wagon as he said, "He's got a concussion for sure. When he comes to, he won't want to give you even one thought. It'd be just too painful!"

As they gazed up the rut-covered trail in Clear Creek Canyon where they would soon begin their assent to the top of Tushar Mountain, Ned explained that a freighter could normally travel between 15 or 18 miles each day, but due to the fracas with Klauss and the condition of the mountain trail, they would probably only cover 8 to 9 miles that day.

When they were once more on the trail, Lillian couldn't hold her curiosity in check a minute longer.

"Ned, how did you learn the freighting business? I heard the men at the boardinghouse bragging you up as one of the best freight men in the territory of Utah."

"By golly, it seems like I've been in the freighting business all of my life. You see, I was born in Missouri. When I was twelve, I returned from a hunting trip to find smoke rising from the burned timbers of my house and my entire family massacred in the front yard. Renegade Indians were responsible. All that I loved in this world was gone, so I had to buck up and take responsibility for myself. I was lucky to have a friendly neighbor take me in. He was an old freighter who hauled goods and supplies to Mexico by way of the Santa Fe Trail. He broke me into the freighting business, and for over 30 years I traveled that trail. Can't tell you how many times I hauled freight from Missouri to Santa Fe. For pert neigh 30 years I put up with dust, mud, pesky gnats and mosquitoes, and sometimes sweltering heat, but just when discouragement laid me low, I'd pass through Kansas where the green grasses heaved around like a green ocean. Gloryation! Not many sights are that delightsome to the eye."

Impressed by what she was learning about her traveling companion, Lillian sought to learn more. "Did you ever marry and have a family during those thirty years?"

"Traveling and the time it took in my life is the answer to that question," replied Ned. You see, it took 6 weeks to reach Santa Fe from Missouri and 6 weeks to get back. There was no time for dilly dallying with silly fillies. That doesn't mean there weren't times when I cut a pretty mean rug on the dance floor. It was hard to keep me away from a good jig."

"What brought you as far as Utah?" asked Lillian.

Ned scratched his beard as he reflected for a few seconds. "Now this is the really interesting part of my life. You'd never know it to look at me now, but I joined up with the Pony Express. The year was 1860, and riders were being hired to carry mail from St. Joseph, Missouri to Sacramento. I was one of the 75 men hired, and not one of us weighed over 110 pounds. Each of us rode about 60 miles each day, changing horses every 10 miles. And I can tell you that I rode with the best! Buffalo Bill and Wild Bill Hickok were two of my riding buddies, but two short years later I found myself out of a job when the telegraph and railroad put the Pony Express out of business.

"I went back into the freighting business with lots of freight companies, hauling freight all over Utah. Just last year I became my own boss when I bought Lizzie and Mabel. They were only two years old when I first saw them, but it was love at first sight! Good food at every stopover has added 90 pounds to this old frame. The Express would never hire me now! There's been plenty of freighting business in these parts, and I've traveled to Frisco five times in the past two months."

Lillian was silent for a few seconds as she digested the exciting details of Ned's life. It was now her turn to tell her story, and as the days flew by, they shared the exciting moments of their lives with each other. Frequent laughter filled the mountain air and then the sagebrush plain as their journey progressed, and a warm feeling filled both their hearts. They became lifelong friends on this journey. Lillian became the daughter that Ned never had, and Ned became the father that Lillian had lost. Ties were formed that could not easily be broken.

Chapter 3

On the last day of the journey, Lillian was jolted wide awake when the wagon hit a large rut in the rough trail. *What a journey this has been,* she reminisced. Then she turned to her companion who had become more dear to her than her own father. "Ned, can you believe that we've traveled almost 100 miles and are just 2 miles from Frisco?"

A weathered hand patted Lillian's small one. "Little Missy, got to say that I'm sorry to see this journey end. Why, do you realize that every day we traveled 'tween 8 and 12 miles. That odometer on the wheel will testify to that. That's good time in any freighter's book. It has been pure delight sharing your company for the past two weeks. We've had some adventures, we have."

"Adventures! I guess my favorite would have to be when we were cooking dinner in Clear Creek Canyon at the top of Tushar Mountain and a bear and her cubs decided that they would join us for dinner. Neither one of us gave them an argument on that one. We just hid under the freight wagon and let them fill themselves to the brim. I wasn't disappointed that we didn't get any supper that night. I was just happy that the bears decided to leave, and we got out of that one all in one piece," laughed Lillian.

Ned's eyes twinkled as he scratched his beard trying to think of one that topped the bear story. "Well, Little Missy, my personal favorite was another night when we were camped out on the very top of the mountain. A beaver felled a tree, and it landed right on my bedroll. I got so exasperated that I ran right into the fire and burned a hole in my new buckskins. Mabel and Lizzy started a-kickn' and braying. Scared that beaver so bad that it ran right through my old bow legs and hightailed it off into the trees. That was the last we saw of that buck-toothed rascal!"

Laughter once more filled the sagebrush-covered land, and a warm feeling flowed through both of their hearts. They basked in the warmth of their friendship as the ties between them became stronger.

"You know, Little Missy, I'm gonna be there for you any time you need me. Just because Frisco is in sight, don't mean that I'm ever gonna desert you. I'm even thinking of arranging my freight-hauling schedule so that I can pay you a visit every now and then."

Lillian smiled at the grizzled face that had become so dear to her over the last weeks. "Ned, you, Mabel, and Lizzy will always be part of my family. It's as if you have left your footprints on my heart. Be sure to stop often for some good home cooking."

Disciplining his wayward child, Ned shook the reins so they deliberately hit Mabel on the ear. "Mabel, you scallywag, quit biting Lizzy. One of these days she's going to haul off and really let you have it–you cantankerous critter!"

It was midsummer and the rabbit brush was in bloom, filling the entire prairie with a pungent odor. Lillian watched a herd of antelope off to her right. When they heard the wagon, they bounced off into some cedar trees, then thinking they were safe, peered through the branches. The endless, blue sky ended with the San Francisco Mountains in front of her and the impressive Mineral Mountains with their white granite peaks in back of her. *This country has a strange beauty all its own,* Lillian thought.

She was promptly brought back to the present when the mules, who definitely had minds of their own, broke off into a dead run. With the added speed, the wagon left the road and began bounding over the sagebrush. Lillian gave a cry of alarm and held tightly to the wagon to keep from flying out.

"Mabel, Lizzie! Tarnation! What's gotten into you," hollered Ned as he pulled on the reins to slow down the mules and bring them back onto the rutted road. After what seemed an eternity to Lillian, Ned had the mules under control, and they were back on the road, traveling at a safe speed. Lillian suddenly realized that she had been clenching her teeth so hard that her jaw ached terribly.

"What got into them, Ned?"

"They can smell the water. We're almost to Big Wash Spring, the last good water before we hit Frisco, and they want to wet their whistles. Stay calm, girls; we're almost there," Ned quieted his children.

It wasn't long before Lillian saw a wooden two-story structure on the left side of the road. A stage was stopped there, and horses were drinking their fill at the water trough located on the north side of the building. Lizzie and Mabel didn't have to be coaxed. They rushed towards the trough and noisily began to drink deeply of the cool water. Ned didn't let them dally long, and soon they were once again on the rock-riddled road.

The wagon tracks ahead of them seemed to stretch on forever, but Lillian could see what appeared to be a small dot under the mountains that lay before them. That dot had to be Frisco! She breathed deeply, relieved that their journey was coming to a close. Frisco was only a few miles away. Frisco? Just what did she know about the fastest-growing mining town in the West? With this thought in mind, she turned to Ned.

"Ned, would you mind telling me what you know about Frisco?"

"Well, Little Missy, the town itself is built on the foothills of the San Francisco Mountains that ya see to the north. Two partners by the name of James Ryan and Samuel Hawkes started the whole shebang."

"Seems like I heard something about them stopping for lunch at an outcropping of rock in the mountain each day," said Lillian.

"Ya, got it right, Little Missy. One of them fellers hit at the rock with his pick and broke off a large chunk. By golly, it had a piece of silver in it that was so soft that they could cut it with their knives. As they cut it, the ore curled into the shape of an animal's horn. That's why they called the mine the Horn Silver. They sunk a shaft and struck pay dirt just 10 feet below the surface. Yes, sir, they struck pure silver. After working that darned mine for 6 months, they hit bedrock, and thought their flash of prosperity was through. They sold the mine to some fellers for $25,000. The new owners dug down over 280 feet, and last I heard they were removing thousands of tons of ore each week. They're selling it for $100 a ton and making a fortune."

"Did Ryan and Hawkes ever find out how much money they lost?" asked Lillian.

"You know, Little Missy, those two foolish cahoots were never seen in these parts again. Nobody knows where they went or if they ever learned just how much they twittered away. Why, the town's grown from 300 souls to 1,000 these past three years."

The trail curved around a small hill, and as the clop clop of the mules created a rough symphony, Lillian got her first close view of Frisco. It was indeed a city beneath a hill. Impressive? Her heart sank. Was this where God wanted her to be? Nothing about it was warm or welcoming. Tumbleweeds and dirt raced before them as the relentless wind seemed to tell weary travelers who the real master of this valley really was. Ill-constructed shanties made of wood stood on the hillside near the mine, their rough boards seeming to provide little protection for those sheltered inside. There was very little beauty for the eye to see, probably because the only thing that passed for trees were a few cedars on the northeast side of town. The dirt and dust made it difficult to see the actual buildings in the town itself, but Lillian could see that at least two of the buildings were constructed of stone.

Off to her right Lillian saw the beginnings of a small cemetery. The setting sun cast an eerie light on some small graves outlined with white stones. *Children have died here,* she thought. *Will I have any left to teach? Heavenly Father, am I really supposed to be here?* Lillian asked herself; then she looked at the beautiful sunset. The colors and brilliance of God's ending to this day gave her the answer that she needed. She saw the small town of Frisco, lying below the mine on the mountain, wrapped in a warm glow of vibrant colors and knew that this was where she needed to be. It was here that she could make a difference.

Chapter 4

The day was ending, but life appeared to have just begun in Frisco. As they jolted over the muddy ruts that covered Frisco's Main Street, Lillian counted seven saloons. Lively honkey tonk music drifted from the bustling establishments, and when one of the doors swung open, Lillian could see miners bellied up to the bar, joking, laughing, and guzzling anything that the bartender put in front of them. Ladies in bright-colored dresses sashayed around the miners, vying for their attention.

"Don't look in there, Little Missy," said Ned. It's liable to burn your eyeballs if you catch a gander at what goes on in them places. This is probably the most rip-roaring town in the West. I heard tell that they ain't even got a sheriff or marshal—nobody to stop all this lawlessness."

Just then two miners crashed through a saloon door, fists raised.

"You had that ace up your sleeve, you lily-livered sidewinder!"

"Prove it! Put your gun where your mouth is!"

Gunshots filled the air, shattering the stillness of the evening. One miner slumped and fell to the street. The other miner stood looking at him, holding an injured arm.

"It's the Death Wagon for you tonight. Serves you right for hiding that ace!" the sole survivor yelled.

"Death Wagon," Lillian whispered through tight lips.

Ned's sideward glace gave him a glimpse of the pale face

of his traveling companion. He knew that what she had just seen had shaken her insides something fierce and made her question her decision to venture into this city of sin.

Ned held the reins with one hand while he slipped his right arm around Lillian and gave her a reassuring hug, assuring her that she wasn't alone in this godless city. "Yes, Little Missy, the Death Wagon. When things calm down at night, the mayor has hired Gabby McCarthy to drive his wagon around town and pick up all the dead bodies so that the gentle ladies of the town won't be shocked when they venture out to do their shopping in the morning. Been told that he gets pert nigh to three or four bodies every night."

Ned's arm detected a shudder rippling through the tiny body it surrounded, and he gave Lillian a reassuring pat. He was about to say something comforting when Mabel and Lizzy stopped and reared up on their hind legs as a deafening blast accompanied by flying timber and debris erupted from the bank just a few feet up the road. Ned had to place both hands on the reins and pull hard to bring the mules back under control. Ned and Lillian held their breaths and looked aghast as two rough-clad men, faces concealed by kerchiefs and guns blazing, exited through a gaping hole in the bank's door, clutching their sacks of stolen loot. They jumped on their horses, spurred them into swift action, and in their haste to make a clean getaway, nearly collided with Ned's wagon.

"Now they're using dynamite," muttered Ned. Lillian saw wide-eyed, terrorized eyes peeking from behind calico curtains hanging from the bank's windows as the robbers rode triumphantly down Main Street, shooting, and cussing as they made their get-a-way.

Ned took out his handkerchief and wiped the sweat from his furrowed brow. "That bank gets robbed at least every other day. The new door needs to be steel, at least 6 inches thick."

"Why don't they get a sheriff to keep the peace?"

"They ain't found one who has enough courage to take the job, Little Missy, but they're still a lookin'."

With the gunmen just a speck in the distance and the immediate danger over, the street was suddenly filled with all sorts of curiosity seekers anxious to inspect the latest Frisco calamity. Pale-faced bank employees gingerly exited the gaping hole in the door and were suddenly besieged with curious citizens, anxious to hear a first-hand account of the robbery.

An impressive two-story building with a sign reading, **The Southern** seemed to beckon to Lillian and Ned, offering them safety from the commotion in the street.

"Isn't that where you're supposed to ask about this teacher business?" queried Ned.

"Yes," Lillian gasped with relief. "Thank heavens. We've finally reached our destination, and luckily we're both in one piece."

Ned helped Lillian down from the freight wagon. She realized just how unnerving her entrance into Frisco had been when her legs buckled, refusing to hold her weight, forcing her to grab hold of Ned's shoulder for support.

"Whoa there, Little Missy. Just stand here for a minute until you get over the frights that attack every human who has the nerve to step foot in this water hole of iniquity for the first time."

After a few minutes of giving herself a silent talking to about the importance of bravery and courage, Lillian let go of Ned's shoulders, linked her arm in his, and quietly said, "I'm fine, now. I'll just pretend that bank robbery was Frisco's way of giving me a first-class welcome."

Ned chuckled under his breath, and then emitted a cry of pain as he tried to help Lillian up the steps.

"This blasted rheumatism is goin' to be the death of me," he complained as he gingerly ascended one step at a time, using Lillian's arm for support. On the front porch at last, Lillian shook the dust from her skirt and removed her sunbonnet, placing it in her skirt pocket. After a careful check of the braid that formed a bun in the back of her head, she determined that she was respectable. *I'm glad Ma told me to always wear a bonnet,* she thought. *It helps keep my nose clean of freckles, and protects my hairdo.*

"You look fine, Little Missy, assured Ned. Might as well go inside and see about that job. I heard tell that this here establishment is one of the finest in the West. Let's check it out."

When the door swung open, a calm feeling coursed through Lillian's body. It was as if every item in the room had been especially chosen to put travelers at their ease and give them a strong dose of welcome medicine. Beautifully-crafted, wooden chairs and a love seat were covered with velvet cushions. The mauves and browns in the cushions blended perfectly to give the room a look of elegance. Despite the dust that was blowing outside, the wooden floor shone with a luster that could only signal love, care, and lots of hard work. At the west side of the room was a beautiful bar made of oak and polished to such a shine that guests could see their reflections when they approached it.

Behind the bar stood a man as formidable as the bar on which his hands rested. At first glance Lillian judged him to be in his early thirties. An impressive 6 feet, he towered over her, and the muscles, which threatened to bust loose from his shirt at the least bit of exertion, testified of his excellent physical condition. Sparkling blue eyes, dark auburn hair, which fell to his shoulders, and a well-kept handlebar mustache added character and charm to a rugged face that could have appeared on a poster for a wild west show.

A muscular hand reached across the counter to give both Lillian and Ned a firm hand shake. "Welcome to The Southern. I'm Ben Johnson, the proprietor and elected dentist of this riproaring community. That deafening boom of a few minutes ago leads me to believe that you might need a place of quiet and peace to spend the night. If so, you've come to the right place."

"A room would be wonderful," said Lillian, "But first I have to talk to you about this ad in *The Frisco Times*." She placed the advertisement on the bar and continued, " My name is Lillian Lewis, and I've come to apply for the teaching job in this advertisement. Is it still available?"

A chuckle almost escaped Ben's lips, but was stifled as he pretended to straighten his mustache. "Available? Maybe I shouldn't tell you this, but we can't keep teachers in this lawless town. The students are as unruly as their parents. Why, we haven't had a teacher for the past two months because the last one left without even giving notice or collecting what we owed her. We had a heavy rain that week, and with the rain came a plague of frogs. Those little heathens gathered hundreds of frogs and turned them loose in the schoolhouse. When the teacher came to school, those frogs were jumping everywhere, including her head. The satchel that held her teaching materials was full of the slimy creatures in no time at all. The kids were laughing, screaming, rough housing, and jumping higher than the frogs. It was total pandemonium. Gentle ladies in nearby houses were startled from their morning labors and ran to their front porches to see what could be causing the ruckus. Miss Smith ran screaming from the schoolhouse and has not been seen since by a living soul."

There was silence for a few seconds as The Southern's proprietor examined Lillian's face, trying to determine how his last words had affected her desire to teach.

Somewhat amazed to see that her face remained calm and devoid of any fear, he continued, "Knowing all this, are you sure you want to take on this task? You don't look big enough to discipline a bunch of ruffians. A few of them can match you in height and stare you straight in the eyes."

Lillian swallowed hard. She had never been known to quit when the going got tough. She said to herself, *When life's trail gets tough, the tough keep hiking,* then turned to Mr. Johnson and said, "I might be small, but dynamite is often shipped in small packages. Trust me, I can be explosive if this job requires it. Please give me a chance."

"Well, if you have that much confidence in yourself, it won't hurt to give you a trial period. You'll run away soon enough on your own if you can see that you can't handle the pressure. For right now, let's set you up with a room for the night. It'll be $1 a day, and if you decide to stay, we can offer you a weekly rate of $5. That will include two meals a day—breakfast and dinner. Meals are served in our dining room off to your right there. Lillian swallowed hard as she took a dollar bill from her carpetbag. She would have to look for cheaper lodging. Her meager reserve of $20 was going to have to last her until she got her first paycheck.

Mr. Johnson turned to Ned and asked him if he, too, wanted a room. Ned tipped his ten gallon hat as a thank you and said, "Appreciate your offer, mister, but I'll just go and bed down with my mules at the livery stable. They ain't goin' to be able to sleep a wink lessin' I'm with them. I'll see you in the morning, Little Missy."

Turning to a wooden board in back of him, Mr. Johnson retrieved a key and told Lillian to follow him up the stairs. Lillian was surprised when he picked up a bucket of water from a closet beneath the stairs.

"I'm going to put you in one of our best rooms. Wouldn't want you to get the wrong impression your first day in Frisco," he bragged.

As the door to Room 11 swung open, Lillian was indeed impressed. A comfortable bed with a wooden headboard was topped with a wedding-ring quilt bedspread. Bright calico curtains covered the window, and a maple dresser topped by an oval mirror stood on the east wall. On the dresser was a large enamel bowl for washing and a large pitcher which held water.

"Sorry to tell you your first bad thing about Frisco, Miss Lewis–it's the water. We have to haul all our water for drinking and washing clothes from Milford 12 miles away. The mineral content in Frisco's water makes it unusable for most things. Since each bucket costs us 4 cents, it makes water a precious commodity. That's why we really celebrate when we have a rain storm. Everyone in Frisco has rain barrels to collect the water so we don't have to buy so much. The water in the pitcher is for drinking, but you can use the Frisco water in this bucket for washing up. Use what you absolutely have to, but try to conserve as much as you can."

Always one to get straight to the point, Lillian came right out with the question that had been uppermost in her mind ever since she entered this establishment–"When do you want me to start teaching?"

"Let me show you around the schoolhouse after breakfast tomorrow, and if everything looks fine to you, teaching can start the next day. Try to get a good night's sleep," Ben said as he turned to give her a wide smile before he closed the door.

Lillian undressed and sponged the dust from her body with a wet towel. She would have loved to wash her hair, but maybe tomorrow she could use the remainder of the water in the bucket to do that. She opened her mother's carpetbag to retrieve her flannel nightgown. The minute the bag was opened the familiar smell filled the room. Lavender–it was her mother's favorite scent. Memories of beautiful lavender plants in their Salt Lake yard filled her thoughts. Her mother had often related to her how she had placed some of the precious plants in pots and tended them carefully during their trek from Ohio to the Salt Lake Valley. She had lovingly planted them when they reached their destination. Lillian remembered drying them and hanging them upside down to later be used as sachet in drawers and closets. Her mother had even made cookies and tea from their blossoms, and Lillian had loved gently shaking the plants or carefully touching them to release the beautiful fragrance.

Even though they had left the plants behind when they moved to Marysvale, it seemed strange to Lillian, that ever since her mother had died, the scent of lavender had become part of the bag. It gave her a peaceful, warm feeling every time the bag was opened.

Warm in her flannel nightgown, she reached into the bag to retrieve her *Book of Mormon*. It, too, smelled of lavender. She patted its cover, then held it close to her body. Holding it in front of her, she whispered to it as if it were her dear friend, "We can only be together when we're alone, but that doesn't mean that I love you less." Her mind traveled back to the first day of her journey from Bullion Canyon with Ned.

They had stopped to camp for the night. Following supper, she had retrieved the *Book of Mormon* from her carpetbag and started to read by the fire.

Curious, Ned peeked over her shoulder to see what she was reading. "Tarnation, Little Missy, ya ain't goin' to tell me that you're one of those golden-plate Mormons!"

Lillian raised her head and looked Ned directly in the eye. "Yes, I am, Ned. The Mormon religion has given me a beautiful way of life. I don't know what I'd do without the Gospel."

"Well, I ain't got no objection to you being a Mormon, Little Missy. I've even got a few good friends who joined your church, but ya got to realize that you're plannin' on settling in Frisco."

"Can't Mormons live in Frisco?" Lillian asked.

"There's lots of Mormons in Beaver and Milford, towns nearby, but even though there's a few Mormons in Frisco, people here bouts don't take to them. I guess the town's too lawless to accept talk about angels and gold plates. You better keep that book hidden–at least until Frisco becomes more tolerable towards your faith."

Lillian ran her hands over the worn pages of the book as she began to silently read. On her first turbulent night in Frisco, the words from the book gave her comfort and the reassurance that she could succeed in this new undertaking. After she said her prayers, she slipped into a dreamless sleep.

Chapter 5

The new day brought a breakfast of hot, fluffy biscuits, scrambled eggs, and bacon. When they had finished eating, Mr. Johnson walked with Lillian to the red schoolhouse, which was located at the west end of Frisco's Main Street. A brisk breeze was blowing, and since Lillian hadn't had time to braid her hair this morning, she had pulled the top part away from her face and attached it to the top of her head with a ribbon. Curly wisps of her luxuriant black tresses blew freely across her face, and to anyone watching, it might have appeared that she was a student on her way to school.

Mr. Johnson couldn't refrain from admiring the young lady walking by his side as he commented, "This schoolhouse is used for a church on Sundays. Methodists meet at 9 and Catholics at 11. Those are the two main religions here. Come Monday morning, it's school as usual. You won't have a full schoolroom just yet. There are around 1,000 people in the community, but many of the miners have left their families at home and are waiting to earn some money to transport them here. And then there are some young men who have to work in the mines to help support their families. For some reason that I haven't figured out yet, some mothers choose to keep their real young children at home for home schooling. My guess is that this town is so lawless that they don't want to subject them to all that violence in the street."

When they approached the large, red structure which served as both a church and school, Lillian could readily see that the boards of the school had not been battened. No mud between the cracks of the boards would mean cold drafts in the winter, and as it was early fall, Lillian hugged her arms, trying to drive away the chill. As she entered the small entryway which was attached to the building, her gaze fell on nails protruding from the boards that would come in handy for hanging students' coats and mittens.

As the schoolhouse door swung open, a large room became visible to their view. There was a small table and chair for the teacher at the front of the room. Behind it was a blackboard made of flat wood and painted black. There were four, long tables with benches for the students and a large wood-burning stove and wood box in the upper right hand corner of the room. Lillian could guess that the single stool in the top left hand corner stood there as a stark reminder of what would happen to any student who chose to disobey. The north and south walls each contained three windows which were covered with calico curtains. Since the windows started 2 feet from the bottom of the floor and ended 2 feet from the ceiling, Lillian's unexpressed words were, *I hope these large windows aren't going to be a distraction to the students. I need to be so well prepared that they won't have the time or desire to get side-tracked by anything going on outside.*

A firm hand on her shoulder reminded Lillian of Ben Johnson's presence. "If you don't mind, Miss Lewis, I've got a miner with a bad tooth coming in just a few minutes. I need to get back and get my instruments ready. Being an elected dentist does have its drawbacks, but the extra money comes in handy when it comes to decorating The Southern. I'll just leave you here to get your lessons prepared and to kind of get a feel for the place. I'll have the newspaper man print up some flyers advertising that school will start promptly at nine tomorrow morning and have the young man who works for me deliver them."

Mr. Johnson signaled for Lillian to follow him to the small entryway of the school. "In the morning, pull this rope three times. The bell is the signal that the students have 30 minutes to make it to class on time. When they've had their 30 minutes, you pull it three more times and school begins. If you have any questions, I'll be at The Southern."

Left alone with her thoughts, Lillian's gaze traveled over the room. Discouragement was her visitor as she looked at the small number of books stacked at the front of the room, a homemade eraser on the chalk ledge, and a small amount of chalk on the teacher's desk. *I'm afraid we're going to be short on everything,* Lillian thought, *unless we only have four or five students.*

Her thoughts were interrupted when she sensed that she was not alone. She looked up to see a man with a load of wood in his arms standing in the doorway. His tall, lanky frame was encased in clothing that was so dirt and mud-encrusted that their original colors remained a mystery, and the mining boots that he wore were covered with dried mud which fell off onto the floor and crunched under his feet as he walked towards her. A dirty slouch hat that had seen better days was pulled low on his head and cast a shadow on his entire countenance, making it difficult for Lillian to determine much about his features.

The firm mouth that was surrounded by an unkempt, brown beard, formed in a scowl and a loud voice said, "I don't know what you're doing here, little girl. Students aren't allowed in the schoolroom unless the teacher is present, and we're fresh out of teachers at the present time. Just leave and come back when some stupid idiot accepts the teaching job. Now git!"

His manner was so abrupt and rude that Lillian had a hard time holding back the temper that she frequently had to keep in check. Her deep blue eyes met his dark brown ones as she put her hands on her waist and squared herself for a fight.

The strange man could see that she was going to stand her ground, so he strode towards her, looking determined to throw her bodily out of her own schoolhouse if she didn't leave on her own accord. He stopped about one foot from her and his dark brown eyes flashed. "I said git! Are you hard of hearing? Who do you think you are?"

Lillian was about ready to give him a real tongue thrashing when the scent of lavender brought her to her senses.

The calming scent told her exactly what she must do. As she stretched her 5-foot frame to look up at her 6- foot adversary, she smiled sweetly, and softly but firmly said, "You're talking to the stupid idiot who's going to be teaching in this very room," and with a blazing glare that was hot enough to cause the kerosene lanterns which hung on the walls to light instantly, she hurriedly brushed past him, leaving him standing alone with his mouth wide open, at a loss for words.

Chapter 6

As Lillian stomped out the schoolhouse door, rage boiled up inside of her, threatening to erupt any minute like an active volcano. *The nerve of that creature! How dare he talk to me in that manner? Why, if I'd had a switch, I'd have given him a good thrashing,* she raged. The faces she passed on her way back to The Southern were just blurs. Ingrained in her memory were those piercing, dark eyes and that scowling mouth, and that final word–"git!" The anger that had taken possession of her body was evident in her face as she flung open the front door of The Southern so hard that the force literally rattled the hinges. Her red cheeks and flashing eyes were a signal to Mr. Johnson that all was not right in Miss Lewis's world.

"Is there a problem at the school, Miss Lewis?" he asked.

"Problem! You could say there is a problem. A 6-foot problem who looked like he just came out of a dust storm just told me to get out of my own schoolhouse. I have never met such a rude, obnoxious man in my entire life!"

Mr. Johnson tried not to smile, but he could not suppress a small chuckle. "I see you've met Charles Anderson. He's quite a critter all right. That one doesn't care much about people. He'd just as soon be out in the desert working on one of his springs than associating with folks. He works in the mine during the week, but come the weekend he's off in the desert developing one of his water holes. I swear that man cares more about the animals in these parts than he does about people, that is except his son, Billie. He loves that boy. But ever since Charles's wife Lucy died during that flu epidemic six months ago, Billie has become unmanageable. Charles is so lost in his own private grief that he can't see that Billie is out of control most of the time. That child is a holy terror and can think of more mischief than one hundred kids put together."

"You mean I'm going to have to contend with this Billie creature tomorrow?" gasped Lillian.

Mr. Johnson nodded his head, "You'll have that ruffian tomorrow, unless he decides to play hooky. He's not much for schooling. Maybe you'll win out and he'll decide to go fishing, but my guess is that he's going to be just a little bit curious about this new teacher, and he's probably already planning what he can do to make your life pure misery."

Lillian swallowed hard, pushing Billie from her mind. She wanted to know more about this Anderson person.

"Is Mr. Anderson rude and obnoxious with everyone?"

"Almost everyone. Ever since his wife died, he has blamed God and everyone else for her loss. He keeps the schoolhouse supplied with wood and water for Billie's sake, but he'll perform his duties before you get there in the morning, and you won't have to worry about meeting him elsewhere because he's seldom seen at Frisco's social gatherings."

"Well, if he avoids people, maybe I won't have to deal with him again, and that will suit me just fine!" Lillian slammed her hand down on the oak bar for emphasis.

Lillian paced from one end of the bar to the other until she was calm enough to approach another subject that had been on her mind ever since she had entered The Southern last evening, but she knew that she couldn't afford to stay at The Southern forever, so when she felt that she was under control, she took a deep breath, stopped her pacing, and got straight to the point. "Mr. Johnson, I have enjoyed your hospitality, and The Southern is a grand place to stay, but my resources are limited, and I need to find accommodations that are a little easier on my budget. Do you know of anyone who needs help of any kind in exchange for a small amount of money and room and board?"

Mr. Johnson straightened his mustache as he paused to think over the matter. "You know, I was talking to Nettie Harris the other day. She is no stranger to grief. The poor woman lost her eight-year-old son Ed to that flu epidemic about a year ago. As if that wasn't bad enough, her husband Sam was killed two months after that in an accident at the mine.

"Mining around here is a dangerous proposition. The open lifts that they use in the shaft often travel as far as 300 feet per minute. Miners are often close to the edge of the lifts, and Sam Harris was riding on one of those open lifts three weeks ago. As usual the cage was packed to the limit with workers. When the lift jerked on its descending route, Ned was thrown from the lift. As he fell, his head was crushed against some jagged rocks on the side of the shaft. Because he was cut up so bad, they wouldn't even let poor Nettie see him."

"Surely she has some family she can call on for help?" commented Lillian.

Mr. Johnson continued, "She has no family to go to and has just started working at one of the Chinese laundries. She told me just the other day that she wished she had someone to help her with the expenses of that shanty where she lives. It isn't much of a place, but I do believe that she'd have room for you to stay, and she'd welcome whatever financial and other help you could give her. She needs some strong support right now."

"If you have some free time, could you show me where she lives?"

"I can point the way right from my doorway." Walking with Lillian to the front door, he pointed to a small shanty to the north of the school. "You wouldn't have far to walk to the school if she decides to let you stay. Since it's just past noon, she should be home right now."

Lillian thanked him for his time, gathered her bag of belongings from her hotel room, and started a brisk walk to the shanty. On her way she counted at least three saloons, two Chinese wash houses, what appeared to be a dance hall, a mercantile store, the bank, and a post office. On the side of one hill, she saw what appeared to be a racetrack. *What's a racetrack doing in a mining town?* She thought to herself, but her question was left unanswered as she found herself at the door of the shanty.

Lillian's brisk knock was answered by a pretty, young, blonde woman who was dressed in a worn calico dress and full-length work apron.

Lillian held out her hand and said, "I'm Lillian Lewis, the new schoolteacher. I heard that you might need a boarder to help you share expenses."

Lillian's hand was taken by a small hand that was rough and calloused from hours of hard work. Bright blue eyes glistened, setting off a rosy complexion as a sweet, quiet voice answered, "I'm Nettie Harris, and I would welcome some help around this place. Ever since my husband died I've had a struggle trying to make ends meet." She motioned with her hand for Lillian to enter the single-room shanty.

Lillian's spirits fell as she gazed around the 9' x 12' room. At the north end was a fireplace built of rocks and mud. There were two beds in the room, one smaller than the other with rough bedsteads made of pinewood. Both beds were covered with quilts that had once contained bright colored blocks, but were now faded, worn, and tattered. In the middle of the room was a rough table and two boxes which Lillian supposed were used as chairs. An old, square kerosene can sat by the fireplace. *Probably to keep it from freezing,* Lillian thought as she moved closer to the fire, trying to soak in some heat from the fireplace.

Cracks between the boards in the walls and roof made it difficult for the fireplace to chase away the cold. It was mid-September and already the promise of an early winter hung in the frosty air. A small cookstove, which could have been used for warmth and cooking, sat in one corner of the room, useless because the stovepipe had not been connected. Lillian's gaze fell upon a bucket of water, sitting underneath a rough stand, which contained a basin for water and tin cups. *I bet that water cost this poor dear a pretty penny,* Lillian thought.

Nettie wiped her hands on her apron. "I know it doesn't look like much, but it's a sight better than some of the other shanties around here. It could be real cozy if that stove were connected." Tears filled Nettie's beautiful, blue eyes. "My husband Sam was going to get that stove up and working just before the mine accident. I just don't have the know-how to get that stove pipe connected and another chimney constructed to take care of the smoke."

Lillian patted her on the arm. "These are simple problems that can be tackled one at a time. I've done a little bit of construction work myself. My father was an expert carpenter. I'll be glad to help if you decide you'd like to have me stay."

"Stay! My goodness, yes. To have company in this house once again would be a blessing." Her eyes again became misty with tears. "You can sleep in Ed's bed. My darling son has been gone from me this past year. That terrible flu epidemic took so many. I'll only be asking 25 cents a day, and we'll split the cost of the food and water. We can also divide up the chores. Do you think that's fair?"

Lillian's eyes twinkled with excitement. "More than fair. I'm looking forward to us becoming friends."

Hot stew, which had been bubbling in a large kettle suspended over the fireplace, provided a warm beginning for this new friendship. When Nettie left for her job at the Chinese Laundry, Lillian got out her books that she had taken from the school to prepare for that important first day. Tomorrow would be her debut as a teacher, and she wanted it to be a successful beginning.

In the midst of her preparations, a loud "he haw" reverberated through the walls of the shanty. *There's only one animal that sounds like that–Lizzie!* Flinging open the door, Lillian's gaze fell upon two excited mules and a smiling man in buckskin.

Ned hopped down from the loaded freight wagon. "I'm on my way with a load of freight to Beaver. I'll be wishing you luck tomorrow. Those youngins had better beware. I'll bet you're going to make them toe the mark."

Lillian gave Mabel and Lizzy hugs and was rewarded with wet kisses on her cheeks. "I'm going to miss you girls; now don't get into any trouble while you're away." With a hand on each side of Mabel's fuzzy head, she looked into large, brown eyes and said, "Mabel, I don't want to hear that you have mashed someone flat with those two rear feet. You behave, girl."

Lillian turned to find herself crushed in an enormous bear hug. "Good luck, Little Missy. Don't let those ruffians get the best of you. We'll check on you when we bring our next load of freight to Frisco."

Waving to Ned and the furry beasts that she had come to love, Lillian's eyes came to rest on the school and the bearded man whose gaze now met hers. With her braids twisted neatly around the back of her head, she must have looked quite different to him from the long-haired girl he had yelled at in the schoolhouse, but she remembered those piercing, brown eyes and the unpleasantness of their last meeting. As Charles turned to take a bucket of water into the schoolhouse, Lillian didn't miss the firm set of his mouth. If she could have read his thoughts, she would have heard–*Looks like Nettie's taken in a boarder. Apparently she's one of those flibbertigibbet young women who has a man running after her wherever she goes. Spare me from such foolishness!*

"Why does that man constantly infuriate me?" Lillian said aloud as she slammed the door and returned to her books and lesson plans.

Chapter 7

The bottom tip of the sun was just touching the San Francisco Mountains when Nettie returned just as Lillian was finishing her lesson preparations. As she and Nettie prepared for bed that evening, Lillian felt that one chapter of her life had just closed and another was about to begin. *Please, Heavenly Father, help me to succeed tomorrow. Help me to make a difference in this community and in this school,* she prayed as sleep finally came.

Long before the sun ever peeked over the eastern mountains, Lillian and Nettie had the kerosene lamp lit and hot mush cooking over the fireplace. Nettie put apples and buttered bread in two tin pails and handed one to Lillian.

Pausing in the doorway as she headed for work, Nettie gave one last bit of advice–"Good luck, Lilly. You're going to need it. Promise me that when I get home this evening, you'll be here and won't end up being another casualty of that school."

Casualty? Me? Never! Lillian thought as she enjoyed the short walk to school. The air was crisp, and the rosy streaks in the sunrise combined with fluffy, white clouds were breathtaking. Because the colors were so vibrant, it looked like the mountains themselves were on fire.

Warmth hit Lillian the minute she entered the schoolhouse. Someone had been here to start the fire already this morning. *That someone's personality is about as hot and volatile as the coals in this stove,* Lillian thought as she was again reminded of dark, piercing eyes.

She sat at her desk and once again went over the plans for the day. *Time to toll the 30 minute warning bell,* she reminded herself as she gave the bell rope 10 tugs. *My goodness! I was only supposed to ring it three times. It's first day jitters, but that ought to get them up and running.*

And running was the correct word for their entrance. One minute Lillian was alone, and the next minute she was looking into the faces of ten curious children. Some were still eating their breakfast biscuits, and lunch pails clattered as they were thrown under their benches.

She rapped her pointing stick on the desk as a signal for order and stretched to her full height, as she addressed her class for the first time. "I am your new teacher, Miss Lewis. We will begin class each day by singing a patriotic song. This morning let's sing 'America the Beautiful.' Please stand." Everyone stood, and Lillian led them in singing, "Oh Beautiful for spacious skies, for amber waves of grain." Their voices were surprisingly strong, but not as strong as the young man's who rushed into the room, stopped at a seat in the second row, and joined in the singing with tones so loud and resonant that his exuberant voice drowned out all others. The smile on his face seemed to connect itself to the red freckles on his cheeks, and his bright red hair, that stuck out in all directions, swung to and fro as his spirited voice and lanky body propelled him into the very heart of the song. His green eyes sparkled with pure mischief as if to say, "I'm going to be your worst nightmare. What are you going to do about that?"

At the conclusion of the song, Lillian motioned for her students to take their seats. "Since I don't know any of you, I would like to start at the front of the room and have each of you stand, tell your name, age, and something interesting about yourself–maybe what you like to do in your spare time, what subject you enjoy, or you might even tell me about your pet peeve."

A pretty, blonde girl was the first to stand and speak. "I'm Jessica James. I just turned seven, and I love English. I love to dance and sing, and mother's teaching me to be a good cook. All my family thinks my biscuits are as good as mom's."

Another pretty, blonde girl, who had found it difficult to sit ever since she entered the room, spoke up in a loud voice, "I'm Stacy James. Jessica is my sister. Our daddy works at the mine and we have lots of horses. My horse's name is Lightening. I could ride her all day. I'm six years old, and this is my first year of school. I can read already, so I'll probably be the smartest one in this class."

Giggles filled the room, but were silenced when Lillian tried to look stern as she tapped the desk with her pointing stick.

"Clarence Wood here," said a black-haired boy with serious eyes. "I'm eight years old, and I like to play Marbles and Steal the Sticks. I guess math has got to be my favorite subject, but you can take English and throw it down the well and drown it for good!"

At this suggestion, the redheaded rascal and another young man stood up, held their noses as if they were going under water, and then cheered at the top of their lungs, "Hurrah for Clarence. Glub, glub to English!"

Three taps of the stick on the teacher's desk and the sternest looks that Lillian could muster brought order to the room in a matter of seconds.

A younger version of Clarence, with black hair and serious eyes, stood next and timidly said, "I'm Richie. Clarence is my brother. I'm six and I like to play Slap and Pinches cause then I get to kiss the girls."

Oohs and Ahh's erupted from the boys who puckered their lips and made loud smacking sounds as they leaned towards the nearest girl's cheek. The "tap, tap" of Lillian's stick on the desk put an end to the smacking noises as ten eyes once again rested on their new teacher.

A young man with coal black hair, which was glorified by an exaggerated cowlick in back, stood up so abruptly that he caused his bench to rock back and forth, jiggling the other occupants on it until their teeth rattled. The air was filled with more laughter and giggles. "Jamie Parker speaking." A gangly arm pointed to the late, loud-singing redhead. "My best friend's Billie over there, and I'm seven. I am the most important one in the class because me and my cousin LeRoy Parker who lives in Circleville have decided that we're gonna be famous outlaws when we grow up. There won't be a bank that can withstand the two of us once we start our robbing sprees. Billie says he's going to join our gang. We'll be the most fearsome, terrifyingest outlaws in the West." He paused for a minute, and then with a mischievous grin said, "By the way, Teach, I don't like school. The only reason I'm here is because my dad would give me a tanning if I played hooky."

The freckled redhead stood up and pretended to draw revolvers from imaginary holsters as he acted out shooting each young lady in the class as loud gun shots erupted from his smiling lips.

I'm losing it! I'm going to erupt like an angry volcano any minute, Lillian thought as her fists clenched so hard that her fingernails threatened to enter her tender flesh. *Calm down, girl. You've got to show them who's the boss!* With calming, deep breaths and silent prayers, she forced herself to quietly and slowly walk toward Billie, and putting her hands on his shoulders, forced him back into his seat. Billie's eyes widened and he started to say something, but was quieted as he saw the terrifying look on his teacher's face. He'd seen a similar look on the face of a wolverine who had been about to charge him, and he thought he'd best stay in his seat.

When Lillian returned to her desk, a young woman with bright red hair that curled in every direction, and bright red freckles that matched her hair, stood and struck a pose as if she were standing on a New York stage as she dramatically stated, "I'm Laura Johnson, and I'm nine years old. I'm going to be a famous actress some day–even more famous than Lilly Langtry."

"Woooooo" taunted Jamie."

"Tap, tap, tap" once more brought order, but Lillian was beginning to wonder if this slender stick was going to survive the first day.

"I am going to be a nurse when I grow up," piped up a blonde-haired cutie. "I'm Mary Nelson, and I turned ten last Tuesday. I've already helped deliver three babies and will soon be an expert midwife. I play the harmonica and accordion to perfection."

The boys suddenly stood and pretended like they were rocking imaginary babies as they imitated loud cries that might easily have come from hungry infants.

Loud tapping once again from the stick brought order but at the cost of a small piece of the pointer. It broke off and flew across the room like a speeding bullet, hitting the back wall where it stuck between the boards and wobbled to and fro for a minute.

Despite the confusion, Lillian's eyes widened at the thoughts of this blonde ten-year-old being an expert midwife, then saw the mischievousness in Mary's eyes and wondered if she had a fib artist on her hands.

A blonde, young man of about ten stood up, took several bows, then with eyes twinkling said, "I'm Curt Smithson. Mary and I are inseparable and have been ever since my family moved to Frisco. If it's a newspaper article you want written, I'm your man. I hope to be a famous author some day, so you can see that English is my favorite subject. I also believe that I could actually star on the Broadway Stage. I'm that good." Loud laughter accompanied his next move as he bowed again, saying, "Thank you, thank you," then finally took his seat.

A young woman with beautiful, black hair that reached to her waist stood next. In a quiet, timid voice that could hardly be heard she softly stated, "I'm Melissa Cottrell. I'm seven and I love school. I love to play Hopscotch, and I have a pet goat named Samuel." She looked at Billie then continued, "I hate boys who tease."

A soft tittering started up but was silenced when the tardy redhead stood up and yelled, "Anyone who thinks he wants to make fun of Melissa will have me to deal with!" His red freckles sparkled as he jumped up on the bench on which he had been sitting as if he were about to give an important address. Then in a loud voice that needed no megaphone shouted, "Billie here–Billie Anderson. School is stupid and worthless, but if you are forced to go, you go. I enjoy fun, fun, and more fun. My favorite pastime is to get with my friend Jamie Parker and take out the plugs on the water barrels as the freighter brings them into town. We love to make people mad, and that water falling in a stream from the wagon is such a beautiful sight. I do believe that if Frisco had a jail, Jamie and I would have been thrown in it long ago. We're too tough to be contained, so don't try." He jumped down from his bench, took his seat, and sat there with his arms folded, totally pleased with himself.

Loud laughter filled the room, but a strong tap on the desk brought the class to order even though another piece of the stick was lost as it flew so far that it landed on the window sill of the window closest to the teacher's desk.

Lillian breathed deeply. *I've got my work cut out for me, but I will not give in to defeat. I've got to show them who's the boss and make them understand that they have met their match.*

She looked each one of them full in the eyes, giving them her sternest, death-defying stare. The stare was even more terrifying because a sweet smile accompanied it. "You are to call me Miss Lewis," she began. "My methods may not be what you're used to, but if you follow them, you'll gain knowledge, and that's why we're all here. I want you to know right from the beginning that you are all A students. I don't care what has happened in your past school experience; I know that each of you has the capability to succeed. You are the masters of your own ships and the captains of your own souls. You alone will determine whether you succeed or fail. I have faith that every one of you will succeed if you promise yourself that you will always do your best, no matter how hard the task may be."

Lillian saw some expressions of disappointment, particularly on the boys' faces. They had expected her to give them a real Scotch blessing–really let them have it. They found it hard to believe that she had said such nice things to them in the firmest, sternest voice that they had ever heard. Who was this strange creature no bigger than a pint of soap who stood before them to tell them that they were special individuals? Where was the fire and thunder that they had received from their former instructors? The room was suddenly silent. Not even the sound of one shuffling shoe could be heard.

Now is the time to hit them with the idea that I've been toying with over the past few weeks. Lillian tried to quiet her deep breathing as she began, "We will begin the class with my discipline policy."

"Are you going to use that long willow that's hanging on the wall to make us behave?" Billie stood to pull up his pants to expose angry, red welts on his calves. "Just take a gander at what hurtfulness that beast can do."

Lillian looked him straight in the eye, then pulled the willow from the wall and broke it in two as a crisp snap caused her students to sit up at attention in their seats. "We're not going to need the use of that willow in this classroom, Billie."

Melissa, raising her hand to be recognized timidly asked, "I hope you aren't going to spat our hands with a ruler. Our last teacher did that, and it felt perfectly dreadful."

Lillian had to resist the impulse to smile. "I don't believe in striking my students, Melissa, so you won't have to worry about that."

Curt firmly raised his hand. "I've had to take my turn on that dunce stool in the corner. I resent being referred to as stupid. I'm no dunce, so I hope you're not going to be making us feel inferior by having us sit there."

"There will be no dunces in this class, Curt. You've no need to worry about that stool," assured Lillian.

Laura's bright freckles stood out as she said, "Last teacher took hold of my ears and marched me to my seat a number of times. It really hurt. That's why we loosed the frogs on her."

"No ear pulling here," assured Lillian.

"If we're late, do we have to be called a member of the Awkward Squad? The last teacher insisted on calling us that, even if we had a good excuse for being tardy," asked Jamie.

"There'll be no name calling in this class," Lillian firmly stated.

"Then how are you going to keep us from running amuck?" yelled Billie.

Suddenly there was chaos in the classroom as every student turned to their neighbor to discuss the discipline policies of days gone by.

"Attention students," said Lillian in her sternest tone. Ten eyes riveted on her, each student eager to hear how this new teacher was going to make them toe the mark.

Lillian moved in front of her desk so that she was closer to her adversaries. "My discipline policy is simple." Lillian pulled out two jars from beneath her desk. "This jar has REWARD written on it, and this jar has CONSEQUENCE written on it. Each of you is going to write on a slip of paper each month what you consider to be a reward. I will screen all rewards. If I consider the reward to be reasonable, I'll keep it in the jar. If it is something like skipping school for a day, it won't even be considered.

"The consequence jar will contain what you consider to be just punishments for breaking class rules. If I feel the punishment is a good one, we'll keep it in the jar. If I feel it is not just, it will be thrown away. If you are tardy, you will automatically have to draw a slip from the consequence jar. By this method you will govern yourselves, and the consequences for your actions will be just in your own eyes. There's one catch–you must place your name on each slip. That will make you more accountable for choosing good rewards and good consequences. If you agree with this method, please raise your hands." Surprisingly, every hand except Billie and Jamie's went up.

"The majority rules. I have obtained some precious paper from the tops of old newspapers and torn it into strips. I will give each of you two strips. On one strip write a reward, and on the other slip write a consequence. I have a few precious pencils, but since they are hard to come by, you will have to share. When either jar becomes close to being empty, you will write new consequences and new rewards. What you write must be kept a secret so that with the exception of what you have written, you will never know what will be drawn out of the jars. I have placed a few reward and consequence slips in here of my own so that there'll be plenty to last a few weeks. There is one thing to keep in mind regarding the reward and consequence slips. Most of them that you write must either further your learning in some way or benefit someone around you."

Wheels began turning in growing brains, smiles broke out on some faces, and dead seriousness on others as their own personal consequences and rewards were recorded. When they had finished writing, each student walked to the teacher's desk and placed their slips in the jars. *I've got my work cut out for me going over these after school,* Lillian thought.

McGuffey readers were passed out, and the class was divided into age groups. The groups sat at the same table as they read the assigned section quietly. Lillian walked around the room and listened to their reading. It didn't take her long to determine who the strongest readers were. After a few minutes, she assigned the strong readers to be leaders in their group and to help the others as they read.

Tapping her stick on the desk to get their attention she said, "It is important as you read to read with meaning, expression, and enthusiasm. I want you to pick a section of your reading and practice it as a group, reading with as much expression and enthusiasm as you can muster." She then took one of their books and read a section, illustrating to them what she meant. Lillian was a storyteller, and this was her realm of excellence. As she read, the students appeared to be spellbound.

When she stopped, she heard comments of "Don't stop," and "We want to know what happens next."

"Now it's your turn, class. I want you to practice reading in your groups, putting as much expression and enthusiasm into your reading as you can. You can either read the whole section together or take turns reading one at a time. Use your imagination."

"Sweet! Teachers have never let us do anything like this," said Laura. "It's kind of like acting. What a rip!"

The room suddenly sounded like a hive of bees being disturbed by an intruder. When the buzz died down, Lillian determined that they were ready. She then called each group to the front of the room to face the class and give their reading presentation.

Lillian watched in awe as the reading groups began their presentations. Each group tried to outshine the one before them. Words were enunciated properly, expression was given at the right points, and excitement seemed to literally bubble forth from small lips.

When all groups were finished, a smiling teacher faced her class and said, "I have never seen such wonderful performances in all my life. We will continue to do our reading in this manner, and you have convinced me of one thing–you have done this so well, your first reward will be to put on a class play for your parents and anyone else in the community who wants to attend."

"Can I have the main part?" asked Laura.

"All of you will be stars, leading men and ladies," assured Lillian. "I am so proud of all of you."

As Lillian looked into the glowing faces of her students, she knew that she had done something right. Now, if only the rest of the day would go as well.

Slates and chalk were passed out. Lillian wrote the math problems on the board for each group, doing at least two of them with the students. Then each group finished the remainder of the problems on their slates. Answers were checked, slow students were helped, and before she knew it, lunch had arrived. They had been so busy, that the morning recess had been skipped, but when the lunch pails were empty, the students played their favorite games outside until Lillian once again rang the bell for afternoon classes to begin.

History was brought to life as Lillian used her acting ability to talk about George Washington crossing the Delaware. The students were riveted in their seats, all eyes focused on their teacher. Lillian was no longer their instructor. She was George Washington as he and his men crossed the Delaware. Last night before she went to bed, she had practiced making the dialogue between Washington and those with him so interesting and real that while she was talking, her students became mesmerized by the drama that was unfolding before them.

When she finished, Billie piped up, "We've never seen history taught like this. Will you do it again that way?"

Lillian smiled, "That will be one of your rewards. If you all behave, I'll teach history in this manner. If we have some discipline problems, which I know could not possibly come from this special class, history might be pretty boring."

The afternoon seemed to speed along like a fast-flowing river. Before she realized it, Lillian had completed her first day, and it was time to give the students their homework assignments. Pages from their readers were assigned, and class was dismissed. In seconds the room was cleared, and Lillian sat down to go over the slips in the reward and consequence jars.

Surprisingly, she only had to discard two slips. Both of them were consequences. Lillian laughed out loud as she read, "Frozen horse turds are to be dropped on your head from the school roof.–Billie Anderson." The second slip read, "You are to be tied to the dunce chair and tickled by members of the class until you die laughing.–Jamie Parker."

It's obvious who my two challenges are, thought Lillian, *but there's a way to touch these two. I've just got to find it.*

That evening at dinner Lillian related to Nettie the day's events, then spent the rest of the evening getting ready for her second day.

Lillian was so elated about her first day that she had no warning as to the hurricane that was headed her way when she rang the bell to begin day two.

Chapter 8

Day two began with nine children singing "The Star Spangled Banner." Without warning, Jamie came rushing into the room, punching Jessica and Stacy in their arms on his way to his seat, then just sat there, refusing to stand for the National Anthem.

Lillian taped her stick on her desk for the rest of the students to be seated, then looking Jamie directly in the face, withdrew a slip from the consequence jar and read, "Jamie, due to your tardiness and actions, you must stay in at recess this morning and do five extra math problems with the teacher."

Jamie slumped in this seat and his cowlick seemed to stand at attention as if to defend his antics. "Can't make me!" he defiantly stated.

Lillian tried to look stern. "No, I can't make you, but you won't be going home until you have completed this consequence. When your parents come to see why you're late, it will be a good opportunity for us to have a conference."

Jamie was quiet the rest of the morning, but he wasn't too enthusiastic about participating in his reading group. When recess came, he sat there, unmoving, with his mouth set in a firm line and his arms folded.

While the other students were outside playing, Lillian wrote five problems on the board. Jamie sat there a minute, then picked up his slate and began to work. Lillian could see that he was having trouble, so she sat by his side, trying every method she knew to help him solve the problems correctly and praising him when he had the correct answers on all five.

"You are an intelligent student, Jamie. You grasp math concepts quickly. I was so impressed yesterday with the way that you read your reading assignment. I have full confidence that you're not going to be late again." Lillian smiled and patted him on the arm.

Jamie was quiet as the students filed back into class, and Lillian hoped that she had been victorious in the Jamie battle.

Her feeling of victory was only momentary; however, for when she asked Billie to pass out the slates and chalk so that they could begin the math exercises, he lay down on the floor, kicking his legs and throwing his arms as he screamed, "Ahhhhhhhhh! No! No! I ain't gonna do it! It's manual labor!"

Lillian had seen small children throw fits before, but she had never seen an eight-year-old who was as tall as she was throw such a tantrum. Billie's face was bright red, and his screams threatened to burst every ear drum in the room. His heavy work boots were hitting the floor with such force that Lillian expected to see dents in the boards any minute. Gentle Melissa was hit in the legs with his flying hands, causing her to cover her face as tears streamed down her cheeks.

Lillian felt like running out the door, never to return, but she had never run from a problem in her life, so she took deep breaths and stared at Billie intently with her most piercing, disciplinary look as she looked down at him, letting the tantrum run it course. There was no sense in trying to lift him from the floor because she knew his strength far surpassed hers. Finally the screaming and thrashing stopped, and Billie lay quietly for a minute then got up and went to his seat.

Lillian gave him one more of her piercing looks, then quietly, but purposely walked to her desk and faced the consequence jar. Unclenching her fists, she stilled her trembling hands and began to open the lid of the jar. Billie's freckles stood out in pure defiance, and a wide grin covered his face as he watched the lid of the jar come off in his teacher's hands.

Replacing her disciplinary look with a brilliant smile, she read from the slip of paper she had just drawn from the jar, "The person who gets this consequence must stay after school and help Miss Lewis place mud in the cracks of the schoolhouse. They will not be allowed to go home until they have worked for one hour."

"Ain't gonna do it," said Billie. "Dad's expecting me home right after school to do the chores."

"Then you'll sit in that seat until you decide to complete the consequence, and if your father comes to see why you're late, we'll have a conference."

Billie sullenly starred at Lillian throughout the rest of the day, but when the rest of the class was dismissed, he reluctantly followed her outside, a dark scowl covering his face.

"Don't see what the problem is. Can't a feller have a little fun?" he muttered.

"It's not fun when you stop others from learning, Billie. Now let's get started mixing some mud for these cracks. She retrieved two large buckets from the side of the school, and handing one to Billie and gently taking him by the arm, she led him to the two water barrels situated at the front of the school. One was full of rain and snow water for drinking, and the other contained the mineralized water that was used for anything and everything except human or animal consumption.

"This Frisco water will be just fine for mixing the mud, but we'll have to be careful to get just the right consistency," she told him as she lifted the barrel's lid.

They filled the buckets half full of water, and then slowly added the dirt until Lillian nodded her head, signaling that it was okay to start the plastering. Lillian covered herself with a full-length work apron that she had brought to school, and the two of them started to work.

Billie never did anything at a slow pace. He had the crack on the top of one board filled with mud before Lillian could raise her trowel. "I have never seen such an effective mud dabber in my entire days!" laughed Lillian. Let's have a contest to see who can dab the most mud. You start at this end, and I'll start at this end, and we'll see who reaches the middle first. Each time you beat me, the time you spend on your consequence is reduced by five minutes. What do you think about that?"

Billie laughed, "I enjoy a challenge! Let me yell 'ready, set, go,' then let the mud fly."

When the signal was given, mud started splattering in every direction. True to his word, Billie won the first round, but not to be slighted, Lillian won the second. After ten rounds they had the east side of the school completed as high as they could reach. Breathing hard, they stopped to look at each other. Laughter filled the air, for their faces, arms, and hair were incrusted with brown goo. It was impossible to tell where the mud stopped and the person began.

"This was a real hoot, Miss Lewis. Do you think we could do it again sometime?"

"I'd love to do it again, Billie, but that doesn't mean that you can throw another tantrum."

"No more tantrums, Miss Lewis, promise," smiled Billie.

It was then that they realized they were not alone. Standing a few yards from them, glaring with that familiar blazing look was Charles Anderson.

"Billie, boy, what do you think you're doing? Don't you know better than to stay after school and have mud fights with one of your girlfriends when you should be home helping me with the chores?"

Billie giggled, then grabbed his father by the arm and led him to stand in front of his teacher. "Dad, I'd like you to meet my teacher, Lillian Lewis. I kinda threw a fit today in the classroom, and she made me help mud up the cracks in the school for punishment."

Charles looked at Lillian's mud-covered face and had to suppress a smile. Luckily, his thick beard hid the merriment that trickled throughout his body. The face was unrecognizable, but the deep blue eyes told him that it was the same young lady he had confronted sharply in the schoolroom. *My land o' goshen, so I told the teacher to git!* The mirth that this thought brought to his mind was suddenly replaced by the dislike that he had for women in general. *Confounded females! Not one of them has the sense that God gave a turnip!*

Charles pulled down his dusty slouch hat to conceal more of his face and motioned for Billie to come with him. Billie seemed to understand what the motion meant and followed his dad. As he turned to give Lillian a final grin, his freckles shone brightly on the few white spaces that were left on his face.

Lillian realized that her fists were clenched so tightly that her fingernails were digging into the palms of her hands. *The nerve of that man! Why, he didn't say one word to me!* Her anger was calmed somewhat as she paused to remember that the moment she saw Charles Anderson standing in front of her, a strong scent of lavender had replaced the earthy odor of the mud. The minute Charles started to walk away, the scent disappeared. Associating the scent with her mother's carpetbag, she couldn't help but wonder, *what does the scent of the carpetbag have to do with that dusty, filthy beast of a man?*

Chapter 9

"Sounds like your discipline policy is working," praised Nettie that evening following Lillian's recital of what had transpired that day. "I wish we had someone to discipline this town. I don't dare walk home from work. I'm always being stopped by some uncouth ruffian. Today after work two cowboys grabbed me outside of the Western Saloon. They started twirling me around and throwing me back and forth like I was some kind of ball. Each time one of them caught me, they showered slobbery kisses on my cheeks.

"They'd still be throwing me around except Ben Johnson came to my rescue. He yelled in that booming voice of his, 'You let that Little Lady go right now, or you won't be sleeping in my establishment tonight!' It startled them, and they stopped their fun, giving me an opportunity to escape to the safety of this shanty. The silver in this mine has brought in devils of every kind. Gunfighters, gamblers, rustlers, outlaws, and women of the evening frequent the saloons night and day. I've even heard it said that the evilness in Frisco surpasses that of Dodge City and Tombstone."

"If any place needs a jail and a sheriff, this town does!" said Lillian as she cleaned the dishes off the table. Clarence Wood told me this morning that he saw the Death Wagon carrying five bodies when he was walking to school this morning. The children shouldn't have to be subjected to sights like that."

"Maybe there's hope," said Nettie as she began to wash the dishes. I heard some whisperings in the laundry this morning that they're trying to get a lawman from Pioche, Nevada to come in and clean up the town. I hear tell that he's a cold-blooded character, but something has to happen to this sinful city. Why, it's not safe to walk on the streets any more. I'm even afraid to walk to work in the morning."

The pinched look of fear on Nettie's face prompted Lillian to go to her carpetbag and pull out the *Book of Mormon.* "When my insides are in turmoil, I rely on this book," she said softly. "Come sit here at the table with me and let me tell you its marvelous story."

An hour passed quickly, as Lillian explained how the *Book of Mormon* had come forth. Nettie's eyes grew wide with wonder. "We've been taught to hate Mormons here, but there's no hate in my heart for you. You say that this book can bring you peace?"

"I will give you a challenge, Nettie. Let's read this book together every night, and I guarantee that you will find the peace that is needed in your life. Are you willing to give it a try?"

"You are my dear friend, Lillian. You wouldn't suggest anything that would hurt me. Can we start reading, and if I don't like it, we can quit?"

"Certainly! We have a deal," assured Lillian.

Following the reading of Chapters 1 and 2 in 1st Nephi, Nettie said, "That peace you spoke of. It's here. I want to know more. Let's read again tomorrow."

When their chores were finished and they had snuggled into their warm beds, their sleep was amazingly free of the fears that engulfed the other residents of Frisco.

Chapter 10

As Lillian sat at her desk readying herself for the school day, she had a hard time believing that almost two months had passed since she had begun teaching in this schoolroom. The discipline policy had taken a firm hold, and these two months had gone by relatively smoothly with only six consequences being drawn from the consequence jar. *There's been so much improvement in their behavior, that I think it's time for their first reward,* she thought.

Following the beginning song, a large smile covered her face as she informed her class, "You have all done so well since school began, that I am going to give the entire class a reward. Since tomorrow is Halloween, if everyone agrees, two hours before sunset we will take a hike to the Frisco Cemetery. We'll meet here at the school about five. You are to wear a costume of your choice, and we are going to sit among the graves and tell ghost stories followed by other activities of your choosing. You will have to have your parent's permission to participate in this activity, and please assure them that I will see each of you safely home. How many of you would like to participate in this reward?"

Ten enthusiastic hands were instantly raised. "Can we have a costume contest?" asked Stacy.

"Can I play some spooky music on my harmonica?" chimed in Mary.

"Stacy and I want to perform a ghost dance that we made up last night," offered Jessica.

"Please let me read an article that I wrote for the paper on haunted ghost towns," begged Curt.

"All of these ideas sound creative and full of spooky possibilities," said Lillian. "You may participate in any activity as long as it has been cleared with me first and as long as it meets with your parent's approval."

They all deserve this party because all of them, even Billie and Jamie, are sincerely trying, Lillian thought as she gazed into the faces of her excited students.

Just when she was feeling rather pleased with herself, there was one small setback. Ten minutes before dismissal time the students were reading their history assignment when a scream filled the schoolroom. It came from the lips of the most soft-spoken student in Lillian's class, the gentle Melissa. When Lillian went to investigate the matter, she found small holes in Melissa's hand about the size of small pinpricks. "My hair, my hair," Melissa cried hysterically, "Teacher, I went to brush my braid back, and it feels like a porcupine has left its quills there."

Lillian had to restrain herself from laughing out loud when she looked at the back of Melissa's braids. Some little hooligan had placed cockleburs in a creative zig zag pattern down the full length of Melissa's braids. The sharp burrs and the glossy, black hair, which reached to a tiny waist, blended together to make a beautiful but dangerous work of art.

It hadn't taken Lillian long to discover the culprit of the deed. He was sitting on the bench next to Melissa, with his red freckles gleaming, trying not to bust out into full-fledged laughter.

Lillian moved quietly to hover over the offender who by this time had his head bowed as his shoulders shook with unsuppressed glee. "Billie, do you know anything about this?"

The laughter burst from Billie like a gushing fountain. Through his giggles he managed to explain, "I just couldn't help myself, Miss Lewis. On the way to school these cockleburs were so inviting that I put them in my pocket for safekeeping. Knew I'd find a use for them somewhere, somehow. Then when I got here, Melissa's braids were just calling to me to give them an artistic touch. How could I resist? You might say her black, silky braids made me do it! Anyway, tomorrow is Halloween. I was only trying to help Melissa. I saved her from having to find a costume. She can leave those burs in her hair and go to the party as a cocklebur weed! Besides, I thought it was about time that we gave her a new nickname. Instead of calling her Lissa like we usually do, we can now call her Miss Weedy!"

As "Miss Weedy" was spoken, Melissa bowed her head and large tears ran down the sides of her cheeks.

At the sight of Melissa's tears, *That does it!* Passed through Lillian's mind. Without saying a word, she grabbed Billie's arm and marched him to the consequence jar, making him pull out his own punishment slip. The slip read, "Spend one hour cleaning up around the school and town."

As Billie took his seat beside the still sobbing Melissa, Lillian sternly said, "Your cleanup duty will entail gathering up weeds and litter for 45 minutes and then under my supervision, burning them. You must also apologize to Melissa for scaring her half to death."

Billie took out his handkerchief and wiped the tears from Melissa's face as he sweetly said, "I'm sorry, Miss Weedy, for scaring you out of your wits." Unsuppressed giggles reverberated throughout the room.

Lillian rapped her stick on the desk and trying to look as stern as possible said, "Billie, if you don't want another trip to the consequence jar, you will apologize to Melissa in a respectful, polite manner."

Billie pushed aside the bench, got down on his knees in front of Melissa, took her hand in his, and gazing longingly into her eyes began, "My sweet Lady Melissa, I wish to beg your pardon for my rudeness when I called you Miss Weedy. You are the sweetest flower that ever grew in Frisco and could never be a noxious weed. Please forgive my unruliness." He then got up, bowed to Melissa, and gently kissed her hand.

Melissa's eyes grew wide, and Lillian saw a small smile form on her lips before she bowed her head, too embarrassed to look at anyone.

Lillian wondered if she should let this extreme display of politeness pass but decided that further punishment was not needed. Billie had indeed been polite. *Can anyone be too polite?* She asked herself.

Billie was looking at her, expecting another trip to the consequence jar, so he was rather shocked when Lillian sweetly said, "Very well done, Billie. Even Sir Walter Raleigh, who protected Queen Elizabeth's shoes by throwing his cloak in the mud for her to walk on, could not have said it better. You have just given us all a lesson on how a true gentleman should treat a lady."

Billie's eyes widened in disbelief, but he was a perfect angel the rest of the afternoon. *Maybe Billie needs more praise than I have been giving him. I feel like sometimes I'm the student and he's the teacher,* Lillian realized.

When the other students left for home, Billie worked like a Trojan after school gathering up unsightly weeds and litter from the vacant lot next to the school. Lillian joined in the project, and they soon had a mountain of debris. They had decided to burn the rubbish near a water trough that was close to the school in case the fire decided to become unruly. Wind was a frequent visitor to Frisco, but not even a slight breeze was blowing, so Lillian felt that it was safe to light the rubbish on fire; nevertheless, she kept a close watch as the weeds burst into flame.

"What are you two trying to do, burn down the town?" a booming voice rose above the crackle of the blaze.

Lillian didn't have to turn to know who was standing behind them. The scent of lavender and the tone of his voice told her exactly who it was. She turned to face the man she had come to truly dislike. Charles looked even more disgusting today than usual. He had so much dirt on his face that his dark brown eyes blended in perfectly with the grime. *If I had a wash tub and a big bar of lye soap, I'd throw you in it at once, Charles Anderson!* Lillian fumed.

Trying to hold her anger in check, she began, "Billie had more problems in school today, and we had to devise another punishment."

"Well, next time he misbehaves, try giving him a punishment that's not quite so dangerous," yelled Charles above the crackle of the flames.

At this very minute, a slight breeze sent some of the burning tumbleweeds rolling down Main Street. Charles grabbed a shovel from the side of the schoolhouse and ushered them like errant children back into the main blaze.

He stayed until the flames were completely out, and as he stood guard with his trusty shovel, prevented any other disasters from occurring. Through it all he remained silent, but an ever-present surly look rested on his face. When the flames were finally extinguished, Charles motioned to Billie, and Lillian was once again treated to an ear to ear grin from the student who had become not only her greatest challenge, but also her best friend. Watching the retreating figures, Charles's harsh words rang through her mind. She wondered, *Challenge? Is Billie the challenge, or is the challenge that bearded man who's walking beside him?*

Chapter 11

The weather is going to cooperate for the party, Lillian thought as she looked out the window of the shanty Halloween morning. She and Nettie had decided to put mud in the cracks of the shanty that day. They began the task in the early hours of the morning and soon had most of the cracks filled in. Since winter was approaching rapidly, this was a task that they could not put off for another day.

After Lillian had heated some hot water in the fireplace and cleaned up, she made a trip to The Mercantile store to buy ten sticks of candy. She had to spend 10 cents of her money, but she knew the students deserved a special treat.

Since she had asked her students to wear costumes, she knew their teacher must be costumed also. She had found some strong wire which she placed in the center of both her braids. She was then able to stick both braids straight up from her head so that it appeared she had just received a terrible fright. She cut a hole in an old sheet and pulled it over her head. Nettie helped her paint her face with charcoal. Deep, black rings around her eyes added to her startled appearance, and thin, black lines coming from the sides of her mouth added to the illusion that she was a frightening ghoul who had just escaped from the grave.

When Lillian approached the school, eight excited children came running towards her shrieking like banshees, all dressed in their Halloween finery, fully prepared for their walk to the cemetery.

A small fairy princess with wings made from wire and a crown made from sagebrush grabbed her hand and giggled, "Oh, Miss Lewis, your costume is real scary. Did you see the boogeyman? Is that why your braids are going straight up?" giggled Stacy.

As Lillian opened her mouth to answer Stacy's question, she was grabbed from behind and given a hearty hug. Both of her feet left the ground as she literally jumped in the air. A beautiful, blonde Jessica, disguised as a flower with bright petals made from flour sacks, giggled, "Oh, Miss Lewis, I'm so excited. I didn't mean to make you jump, but I've waited all day for this party and the excitement made me do it. I didn't think that tonight would ever come."

Richie and Clarence grinned under their coonskin caps. They were both dressed as trappers. Toy rifles rested on their shoulders, and Richie had a skunk pelt hanging from his belt. As Lillian breathed deeply, she thought, *Luckily that skunk expired some time ago.*

Jamie and Billie galloped along as if they were on horses. Puffs of dust flew up as they slapped their imaginary ponies, and then galloped off at a rapid pace. They were outlaws pretending to rob the next bank. Their bright neckerchiefs signaled that they meant business, and large flour sacks hung from their belts, ready to carry home the loot. They would stop every few steps and yell, "This is a stickup! Give us all your money!"

Melissa came and grabbed Lillian's other hand. She was indeed a weed, but a very beautiful one. The cockleburs still adorned her braids, and leaves from the cocklebur plant adorned her black, glossy hair.

"It's not bad being a weed," she whispered to Lillian.

Then there was Laura. Curls escaped in every direction from beneath her father's mining hat. She even had a small bucket which contained ore that she kept inspecting. Periodically she would yell, "I've stuck the mother lode! Take me to the bank!"

Lillian wondered where Curt and Mary could be, but she couldn't wait for them. The sun would not be in the sky too much longer, and she knew they couldn't be in the graveyard much past dark, even though she had brought a kerosene lantern with her to get the children home safely.

As Lillian worked her way through the tombstones, she thought, *So many children,* as her eyes ran over the inscriptions on the numerous small graves that she passed. She stopped by a small grave surrounded by white stones. A small lamb adorned the top of the stone. The inscription read simply, "Ed Harris, 1870-1878, How much of light how much of joy is buried with our darling boy."

Nettie's son, Ed. Lillian said to herself. *As I look at this small grave, I can feel some of the pain that must be with Nettie every day.*

She was brought back to reality as she felt two small hands tugging on her sheet.

"Let us do our dance first," begged Jessica and Stacy. Lillian sat all the children on the ground among the graves and the dance began. Lillian had never seen such creativity. The girls fluttered around the tombstones, skipping, leaping and sometimes waltzing as they went. They creatively peeped from one stone, then another, then proceeded with their presentation. The dance ended as they sank to the ground in front of two graves that were encircled with white stones.

"Bravo!" said Lillian as she clapped her hands in appreciation, causing the other students to enthusiastically join in the applause. You girls would receive a standing ovation wherever you performed. You're that good." Gazing around the cemetery, and not finding her two lost students, Lillian began, "Well, since Curt isn't here to read his story, and Mary isn't here to play her harmonica, who has a ghost story for us?"

Laura waved her hand enthusiastically back and forth. "I have a real ghost story. It actually happened right here in Frisco a year ago, but you're all going to have to listen carefully. Now, not a peep out of any of you. I need your complete attention."

The atmosphere changed as Laura, a true actress, prepared to tell her story. The approaching sunset created an unearthly light around the metal-spiked and wooden fences that surrounded some of the graves, creating a perfect backdrop for the eerie words that were to follow. Even some old boots placed on top of a deceased person's grave seemed to stand at attention, anticipating a chilling, ghostly treat. Every head was bent towards Laura, and every nerve ending in their bodies was attuned to her words as she began her story in a slow, low, frightening voice.

"It happened about this time last year," Laura began. She drug out each word slowly as if they were all sitting in a haunted ghost town, surrounded by unearthly presences. "One terrible night when the moon was full, six Chinamen were attacked by demented miners who had taken a dislike to them. They were grabbed from behind, and their throats were cut from ear to ear." Laura made a quick motion across her throat, along with a gurgling sound that sent shivers down the spines of all present.

"What happened to the bodies?" whispered Jessica?

Laura continued, "They were found the next day at the bottom of a deep, dark mineshaft."

Then Laura wailed "Oooooooooooooooooooooo" as her hands flew up, fingers curved like claws. "And some nights when the moon is full, they return. You never know when they will appear or what they will say. Ooooooooooooooooooo! Be on the lookout and be careful, because they want revenge!"

Almost as if it were on cue, a cold wind started to blow through the cemetery. Eerie harmonica music began. Goosebumps erupted on tiny necks and even the hair on the children's arms seemed to bristle and stand on end. Suddenly without warning, two Chinamen jumped out from behind two tombstones, yelling, "Ka Cha!" followed by some strange form of eerie Chinese. They started to slowly walk towards the group on the ground, one playing the harmonica as he went, and the other one coming slowly with hands raised in front of him, saying eerily, "Beware the curse of the murdered Chinamen."

Lillian's heart jumped into her throat. The children started to scream and huddled around their teacher, certain that they were being invaded by ghostly presences.

The ghosts kept slowly walking until they stood directly in front of the frightened group. Then without warning, the unearthly Chinamen collapsed to the ground as convulsive giggles shook their bodies. Laura collapsed also into a convulsive fit of glee.

Raising their heads, the Chinamen threw off their Chinese hats and ripped off their thin Foo Man Chu mustaches to reveal the faces of the culprits–Curt and Mary.

"We had you all fooled and scared out of your wits," laughed Mary pointing at the amazed group and wagging her finger at them as if to say, "You didn't see this one coming."

"I'll never forget those horrified looks on your faces," giggled Curt.

"Boy, we really put one over on you this time," giggled Laura, a co-conspirator.

Lillian just sat there for a minute, taking in the events of the past few minutes. Then she rose to stand in front of Curt and Mary. "Yes, you put one over on us all right, but if you ever scare us that badly again, it won't just be the Chinamen who are seeking revenge." Then she put her hands up like claws and said in an eerie voice, "So you beware!"

Excitement quickly won over fright; the candy sticks were enjoyed, and by the aid of the kerosene lantern, each child was seen safely home.

As Lillian sunk into her warm bed, she thought, *Many more outings like that one, and I'll surely lose any wits that I have left!*

Chapter 12

The sun sent vibrant shades of pinks and salmons above the Mineral Mountains to signal the beginning of another school week. It was mid-November, but fall seemed to linger on in the Frisco Valley, like a house guest who is reluctant to leave and so extends his stay. In the beginning rays of the sun, the white granite peaks on the mountains were magnificent monarchs, looking over the valley that they commanded. Lillian had never seen any mountains that could compare with their splendor. As the rising sun spread a pink glow over the white peaks, Lillian wished that she were an artist and could paint the beauty of this sunrise, but she was a teacher, and she had far more important things to think about.

When the final bell rang to begin the school day, Lillian was distressed to find that the room was still in a state of chaos. School seemed to be the farthest thing from her student's minds. They didn't seem to want to stop whispering to their neighbor, so Lillian finally gave up trying to restore order and threw her pointer stick into the air in sheer desperation. It landed on Billie's head and his loud "Ouch" caused the talking to cease as all eyes became riveted on their teacher.

Lillian began speaking as loudly as she could without yelling. "Students, would someone please tell me why you are all so excited this morning?"

Mary waved her hand to be recognized. "Miss Lewis, we're talking about the strike at the mine. They're trying to lower my dad's wages from $3.50 a day to $3.00 a day."

Jamie, waving his hand in the air didn't wait to be recognized. "My dad marched in a group with other miners when I was leaving for school. They were going to the smelter to shut it down. Dad says if they're going to risk their lives every day, they deserve good pay."

Curt stood and pointing to himself pridefully, began, "I helped dad write a set of resolutions last night. Dad and the other miners were going to march to the company's office and present the new superintendent with their grievances and their intentions not to allow operations to continue at the mine until they get their full salary."

"What will we do if all our dads lose their jobs? Who's going to put food on the table?" moaned Laura.

Lillian motioned with her hands for those standing to be seated. "Now, students, I'm sure that your fathers will work this out. They're all strong men. One thing's for sure. We're not going to learn anything worrying about it."

Looking at their animated faces, Lillian knew that she had to take her student's minds off the strike, so she decided to begin something that she had been thinking about for a few days. She faced her worried students and said, "Now, we're going to begin something exciting today. You have been putting so much expression into your reading and learning your history lessons so well, that I promised you that we would put on a special program for our parents, friends, and relatives. I think that we can dramatize certain happenings in history and not only entertain those who come, but also illustrate how well we have learned what has transpired in the past. Starting today, during the time we usually spend on history, we will practice our play. I have spent the weekend working on some of the presentation. I thought we'd begin today with the assassination of President Lincoln."

Each child was assured that each of them would have a major part during some part of the play, so they trusted their teacher to assign the parts. Curt was to be President Lincoln, and Mary would portray his wife Mary. Jamie would act as John Wilkes Booth, and Richie was to be the doctor who helped set his leg. Clarence would have the honor of impersonating a policeman, and everyone else in the class would be part of the presidential funeral entourage.

The students threw themselves enthusiastically into the production. Lillian could see that her instincts in preparing for the special program were good ones. Not only were the children learning how to express themselves, but they were learning a great deal about history and having fun at the same time.

The first practice went well, and the students were assured that they would continue with play practice tomorrow during history time.

A few minutes before afternoon recess, Lillian paused from listening to their reading when a strange man opened the door and entered the room.

He was rather stern-looking in his black suit, and his well-kept, gray beard and black stovepipe hat hinted that he was a person of importance.

Walking toward Lillian, he held out his hand for a firm handshake. "I'm Ralph McNaught, superintendent of schools for this area. May I have a word with you outside, Miss Lewis?"

Lillian assigned the students a section in their reading books and followed the superintendent outside.

Mr. McNaught's eyes crinkled up at the corners, giving away his pleasant personality. "I've heard some impressive things about your teaching methods, Miss Lewis. I've talked to a few parents, and they tell me that their children are enjoying school for the first time."

"I think major obstacles are overcome when you make each student feel that he is important and a person of worth," explained Lillian.

Mr. McNaught was about to speak when the door of the school opened and a strange funeral entourage marched towards them. Curt was lying flat on a board with his hands folded carefully in a death pose. His deathly pallor was due to enormous amounts of precious chalk which had been rubbed onto his face. In his hands he held a bouquet of stink weeds which some stealthy student had crept from the school to pick for the occasion. Mary marched by his side, her hair covered by a black scarf. She was playing the funeral march on her harmonica and periodically stopped to wail, "Oh, my darling husband. Whatever am I and the country going to do without you?"

Jamie hobbled along on a stick which served as a crutch, supported by Richie who assured him, "I'll get you to my office, Mr. Booth, and we'll have that leg set in no time." "If you set that leg, that will be the last act you perform as a doctor," yelled Clarence, his paper star signaling that he was the law, ready to prosecute anyone who aided the assassin.

The rest of the students followed as the strange funeral entourage moved forward. They were all weeping and wailing and practicing theatrics that would have been considered first rate at any theatrical house in the country. The high point of the whole scene was when all the children burst into a loud and melodious, "Amazing Grace, how great thou art." At this point the expired President Lincoln sat up on the board and sang loudly, "who saved a wretch like me!" Then he dropped quickly to his death pose on the board while the class continued with the song.

The superintendent tried to keep his composure, but a broad smile threatened to escape, so he quickly covered his mouth with his handkerchief. Lillian just stood there, eyes wide, filled with pride and humiliation at the same time.

When the song ended, all of the class, including the expired President Lincoln, deeply bowed to Lillian and the superintendent whose look of pure amazement was difficult to read.

"Miss Lewis, this is highly irregular. Can I please have an explanation!" he gasped.

"Come into the schoolroom and I'll let the students explain. This is all the result of a new, innovative method of teaching. I am truly interested in hearing what you think about it."

The students filed into the schoolroom in an orderly manner. The superintendent had never seen faces with such looks of enthusiasm stamped on them. Freckles stood out on rosy cheeks, eyes shone, and the electricity of excitement seemed to crackle in the air.

Lillian proudly faced her class and said a silent prayer before she instructed them, "I want each of you to tell Mr. McNaught something about our project and how you feel about it. We'll begin with Billie!"

Billie brushed his cowlick back and began, "We're going to put on a history play for our parents and friends. We're learning all about history by making it come to life on the stage!"

Melissa stood and quietly said, "History isn't boring since Miss Lewis came to teach! I look forward to school every day."

"Practicing this production has helped me with my dream of being a writer," stated Curt. Miss Lewis has let me write some of the scenes. It's experience that counts in this world, and I'm getting plenty of that every time I write scenes and practice for our history play."

"Miss Lewis is also letting me help with the writing of the production," said Mary. I get to put my medical knowledge to work in some of the scenes that I write. It's a lot more fun than just reading an old, boring history book. I also get to use my musical talent to liven up some of the boring scenes."

"I used to want to skip school every day, but practicing for this play has kept me on the straight and narrow, so to speak. Kinda helped me to realize that being an outlaw maybe isn't for me. I mean, where would we be if President Lincoln had decided to rob banks instead of being president?" added Jamie.

"Before Miss Lewis came, I couldn't learn history for beans, but this play has helped me to learn history and have fun too," proudly stated Richie.

Clarence shuffled his feet and looked at the ground as he humbly stated, "I'm not tempted to get into near as much mischief any more. It's more exciting to come to school than to get involved in mischief that only lands you in trouble."

"Jessica and I love to dance," said Stacy, "and this play gives us an opportunity to show off our talent."

The air fairly crackled with the fire of excitement. The students were clearly proud of what they had done so far on the production.

The smile on the superintendent's face told much about his feelings. "I must admit that I had some negative thoughts about your teacher when that schoolhouse door first opened and that funeral march began, but you have convinced me that her innovative, creative methods are just what this school needs. Miss Lewis gets the highest marks I can give her as an educator, and I want her to be sure and let me know when you're putting on this production. I want a special seat in the front row!"

With that, Mr. McNaught shook Lillian's hand and said, "Keep up the good work, Miss Lewis. I wish we could sprinkle a little of your creativity on the other teachers in my district."

At the conclusion of school, Lillian asked Jamie and Billie to stay for a few minutes. "What are you two doing tomorrow," she asked.

"Well, after we do our chores, we're pretty much free to do what we want," said Billie as Jamie nodded in agreement.

"Would each of you like to earn 25 cents for an afternoon's work and help your teacher at the same time? I need some help installing a wood-burning stove in my shanty. Winter is approaching rapidly, and this project can't wait. Some strong muscle from you two would be a big help. Are you willing?"

"Can we have another contest?" asked Billie.

"Do we get free lunch and 25 cents too?" Jamie followed, always worried about his stomach.

"We can definitely have a contest, and Nettie makes the best biscuits that I have ever tasted. I'm sure that we can talk her into making us some to keep up our energy level. Now, be sure to talk to your parents and see if it's all right with them. If they give you their okay, then I'll see you later in the morning."

Waving goodbye, Billie yelled, "We'll be there about ten. Maybe I can get dad to come and help after he works on his water hole at Antelope Springs."

Lillian wanted to yell back, "Don't bother bringing your dad!" but the boys were already too far down the road to hear her. *That's all I need to make my Saturday complete–that old, crusty crosspatch!*

Chapter 13

As Lillian walked to her shanty Friday after school, Frisco seemed to be in a state of nervous anticipation. The cool breeze that blew the tumbleweeds down Main Street seemed to signal a change that was soon to erupt on this lawless community. The noise from the seven saloons was more raucous than ever. Nobody was speaking in a normal tone of voice, and it appeared that everyone in the community had a bone to pick with someone. Arguments seemed to break out every few minutes as harsh words were spoken and punches were thrown. Two Chinese proprietors were speaking in high, angry voices in front of the Chinese Laundry, and a disgruntled miner was having a major confrontation with the boot maker in front of his shop about some shoes that were just not what he ordered. In front of a worn shanty, a disgruntled wife was swinging a rolling pin at her husband's head. He succeeded in ducking three swings, but the fourth swing knocked him flat, and he just lay on the ground shaking his head for a minute, then lost all consciousness as his head fell to one side, and he passed out altogether.

Maybe it's the strike that's got them all riled up, Lillian thought, but upon entering the shanty, Nettie told her that the strike had been stopped before it actually started. It seems that at 7:30 that morning the miners had marched to the smelter and shut it down. The manager of the smelter agreed to stand by the miners, even though the smelter was not affected by the change in wages.

"What happened next," Lillian questioned.

Nettie set dinner on the table and continued, "The miners then marched to the company office and presented the new superintendent with a letter stating their grievances. The letter stated that they intended to hold up the operation of the mine until their wages were restored to the $3.50 rate. They would make sure that no man went into the mine to work until the question of wages was settled."

Lillian stopped eating long enough to ask, "That took a lot of courage on their part. They could have lost their jobs altogether."

"Well, I guess about then the new superintendent saw lost dollar signs in front of his eyes as he realized all of the money that he was going to lose. After only a few minutes of deliberation on his part, he told the irate miners that they could go to work at the old wages."

"That had to be one of the shortest strikes in history," laughed Lillian. "Praises be that everyone in Frisco can sleep peacefully tonight, especially my students and their families."

As they were cleaning up after dinner, Lillian warned Nettie about the work party that was scheduled to descend upon them tomorrow. "Are you sure you're up to making biscuits for two hungry boys?"

"I love nothing better than cooking. If they're willing to do the work, I'm willing to feed their bellies."

As Lillian and Nettie read from the *Book of Mormon* that evening, peace once again filled their souls, but Lillian couldn't help but wonder, *if the strike's not causing all this unrest, what is?*

Chapter 14

Lillian and Nettie were up bright and early making preparations for installing the stove. There was a chill in the air, but the sun shone brightly, promising welcome warmth in a few hours. They began hauling rocks from a mountainside near the shanty to be used to construct the chimney and gathered the materials to make the adobe mud to cement the rocks together. A hole was carefully cut in the ceiling, and the stovepipe was pushed through it. Rocks and adobe mud were placed around the hole to seal it.

Lillian had borrowed a pair of old flannel pants, fastened with a string around the waist, and an old flannel shirt that had belonged to Nettie's husband. An old slouch hat that had also belonged to Nettie's husband covered her black braids. It was so big that she could pull it down over her ears to keep them warm while she was on the roof constructing the chimney. Nettie had let her wear an old pair of her boots that she often wore to do chores. They were scuffed and worn, but would not prove hazardous on the sharply-slanted roof. Unless a person looked closely at the bright blue eyes shining under the hat, Lillian appeared to be a thin youngster, too small for the clothes that he was wearing.

When she opened the door to Billie and Jamie's knock, their wide eyes and open mouths told Lillian that they had no idea who was standing in the doorway.

"It's your old teacher, boys. A dress on the roof would be a bit hazardous on a windy day like this," chuckled Lillian as she motioned for them to enter the shanty.

They began the project with some of Nettie's hot biscuits fresh from the Dutch oven hanging over the fireplace. They smothered them with fresh butter and plenty of molasses, and the biscuit's fluffy, sweet goodness gave them the energy they needed to tackle the difficult project that lay ahead.

More rocks were hauled, adobe mud was mixed in a large bucket, and Billie and Lillian climbed on the roof by standing on a saw horse and pulling themselves up. Jamie stood on the saw horse and handed them the adobe bucket and the rocks so they could begin constructing the chimney.

They had been working for about an hour when a loud, strident voice yelled, "Billie, you renegade, you and your friend are going to break your darn, fool necks. Both of you get down at once and let me up there. Where's that crazy teacher of yours? Hasn't she got more sense than to leave you up on a shanty roof unsupervised?"

Lillian didn't have to look to know who was yelling. If the smell of lavender hadn't warned her, the anger in the words did.

She knew she must look a sight. Not only were mud splotches all over her clothes, but she had a nagging suspicion that her face must be powdered heavily with dirt and mud too. *Why do I always have to look a mess whenever that man comes around?* She groaned.

In a matter of minutes, Charles had pulled himself onto the roof. He gave Billie a soft spat on his rear end and lowered him to the saw horse. He grabbed Lillian by the shoulders with both hands and gruffly said, "Young man, don't you have more sense than to climb up on a steep roof with nobody to supervise you? Who do you belong to? Whoever it is, they must not have much sense, letting you put yourself in danger like...." Charles stopped in mid-sentence when his dark brown eyes met up with two dark blue ones. "Miss Lewis?"

"Unhand me, Sir," yelled Lillian, pulling away from his grasp. She was so angry that she wanted to stamp both her feet and throw an actual fit, but her quick action in pulling away, combined with the force of the wind, caused her to lose her balance, and she waved her arms wildly to steady herself.

Two strong arms reached out to prevent the fall, and she found herself in the arms of her dreaded adversary. However, it wasn't a feeling of revulsion that ran through her body, but something akin to the flow of a warm current that started at the tip of her toes and traveled swiftly to her head. The wind was cold on the roof, but Lillian felt like she had just begun to wade in a hot spring.

I'm not really feeling this way, she reasoned, but one glance into two brown eyes gazing down at her told her that she was not the only one affected. They stood suspended in time for only a matter of seconds, but the feeling persisted until Charles released her. He wasn't any too stable on his feet either, and for some reason, he quickly lowered his gaze, avoiding any further eye contact.

"Let me stay on the roof and help with the chimney," said Lillian in a soft voice. "I've helped my father many times to construct similar chimneys. He taught me when I was just a young girl."

"Well, if you sit on the roof and let me hand you the rocks, I guess we can work together."

And work together they did. They seemed to make a perfect team. The boys handed up the rocks and kept the adobe bucket filled, and Charles and Lillian became expert architects of a near-perfect chimney. Charles did not say another word, but motioned with his hands when he wanted Lillian to do something. After an hour of silent work, they stopped to lean back and survey their masterpiece.

An excited voice broke the silence. "Miss Lewis, Miss Lewis!"

Turning in the direction of the voice, Lillian and Charles saw a red-faced Curt running at full speed towards the shanty, yelling as loudly as his overtaxed lungs would allow him, "Come quick! He's here! He's here!"

Charles carefully walked to the edge of the shanty roof so he could be sure to get a full view of the agitated Curt. "Wait a minute, boy. Slow down and tell us who's here!"

"The new sheriff! He's at The Southern, and he's ready to give a speech to the whole town. Come quick, or you're going to miss it!" yelled Curt as he turned and raced away in the direction of The Southern.

Curt's excitement was so contagious that washing the mud off their splattered bodies was the furthest thing from their minds. Jamie and Billie raced off without so much as a backward glance. Charles hopped down from the roof, stood on the saw horse, held out his arms, and motioned with his open hands as if to say, "You better jump now, or you're going to be on that roof for a mighty long time."

When Lillian jumped and landed in his arms, he dropped her quicker than a hot branding iron, then jumping down from the saw horse, he grabbed her hand and forced her to run with him at a full gallop. Her short legs found it almost impossible to keep up with Charles's lanky ones, but she was in good physical condition and by taking two steps to his one, she managed to match his stride. *Thank heavens I don't have to drop his hand and resort to running alone and eating his dust. That would be too embarrassing to bear,* she thought as they approached a large crowd that was gathered in front of The Southern.

Chapter 15

By the time they reached The Southern, a huge crowd had assembled, and excited townsfolk covered the front of the building and spilled out into the street, making it impossible for wagons or horses to pass.

Charles and Lillian stopped at the edge of the crowd, and when Lillian had taken a few seconds to catch her breath, her attention was drawn to the imposing figure who was standing on the porch of The Southern. His blazing, green eyes seemed to make it impossible for any of the spectators to divert their attention from his face.

Every man in the crowd seemed to shrink in comparison to the stranger. *He's got to be at least 6 feet 3* Lillian thought as she scrutinized the black-clad figure. And dressed in black he was. There wasn't any article of his clothing that wasn't as dark as the infernal depths of the dark regions where demons dwell. His ash blonde hair, which cascaded to his shoulders, handlebar mustache, and bushy eyebrows were in stark contrast to his dark attire. He was a commanding presence that demanded the attention of all onlookers. All eyes were riveted on him as he began to speak.

Because his voice was loud, abrasive, and forceful, his first words elicited fear in the hearts of all who were present. "W.P. Phillips of Pioche, Nevada here. I was hired to clean up this lawless community and clean it up I will. The first thing I was asked when I entered town was when your new jail would be built. I will only say this once, so listen closely. I will have no need of a jail and no use for a judge. If anyone breaks the law, they will be shot on the spot. I alone will serve as judge and jury. There will be no appeals."

Never one to hide her emotions, Lillian's face betrayed the fear and surprise that Sheriff Phillips's words invoked in her.

Suddenly green eyes riveted on hers as an imposing hand pointed in her direction. "Don't question my words, boy, or you'll be the first one to end up in the cemetery!"

Lillian lowered her head and moved a little closer to Charles. She had never before been drawn to someone and repulsed by them at the same time.

Just then two men rushed from a saloon swinging fists and throwing punch for punch. They had been so involved in a card game and were so inebriated that they had missed Phillips's speech.

"You sidewinder!" bellowed one of the enraged miners as the sun glinted on his drawn gun, but the shot was never fired because without warning, gunshots from the direction of The Southern's porch broke the stillness of the air. The confrontation between the two miners ended immediately when both men fell lifeless to the street.

Frisco's new sheriff replaced the smoking guns in his holsters as quickly as he had drawn them. Having made his point, he turned and entered The Southern which would serve as his office. The dead men were pulled from the center of the street and left in front of the saloon for the Death Wagon when it made its rounds.

The stillness in the air was so heavy that it weighed down on all present, creating a unpleasant atmosphere. Everyone just stood in their places for a few minutes, then quietly turned and went to their homes or back to work. If there was any talking at all, it was in muted whispers.

Charles gently grasped Lillian's shoulder and headed her quietly in the direction of her shanty. After walking in silence for a few minutes, Charles almost whispered, "I've never seen anyone faster with a gun. When he drew, it was like a flash of lightning, a blur. I didn't even see his guns until after the shots rang out."

"He is indeed a man to be feared," whispered Lillian. "I know everyone was looking forward to his coming, but I'm afraid most of Frisco is now wishing that he had never come."

They stopped in front of the shanty and surveyed the new chimney that they had created together.

"You're living in one of the few shanties in Frisco that has two chimneys on its roof. I have to make a confession to you. A few weeks ago, I didn't know you lived in this shanty. I saw you hugging an old freighter and convinced myself that whoever had moved in here was a piece of worthless fluff. Now, as I look at that chimney, I can see that you're not made of fluff. You're definitely made of steel. When it comes to work, you can hold your own with any man, Miss Lewis."

Lillian's eyes softened as she looked into two, deep brown eyes. "Coming from you, that's quite a compliment, Mr. Anderson. And that old freighter you saw me hugging was the dear person who is responsible for getting me here to Frisco. I don't know who is dearer to me, Ned Druthers or his two mules. Since I recently lost both of my parents, Ned has become a second father to me."

Father to her, Charles tried to stifle a smile that threatened to break through his stern lips. He avoided looking directly at her as he softly said, "A Bow Dance is gonna be held next Saturday at the dance hall. Ladies bring their own ribbons, and the men who are present bid on the bows, not knowing who fashioned them. When all the bidding is done, the man who bought the bow and the woman who created it get to dance. I vow it's just plain foolishness, and I'm not much for dancing, but I do enjoy listening to the music. Just thought you might like to know about it." With his head still down, Charles turned to go.

"Thanks for your help with the chimney, Mr. Anderson, and I'll certainly give the Bow Dance some thought." Lillian was rewarded as Charles turned and gave her one of his rare smiles.

Then he had to put a damper on that smile and spoil everything as he said, "If you come, you might want to get gussied up some and bury that outfit you're wearing."

As she opened the door to the shanty, Lillian felt like stamping both feet. *That infernal man! Just when I think he's sweetening up some, he has to ruin it all!*

Lillian and Nettie spent the evening talking about Sheriff Phillips and worked their way around to the Bow Dance.

"It's been so long since I went to a dance that I've probably forgotten all the steps, but listening to the music and watching the other couples would be nice. I think I've got some old ribbon that I can take off two of my bonnets. I should have enough for you, too," offered Nettie.

Lillian thought a moment then said, "My big problem is that I don't have anything nice enough to wear. I only have the three dresses I brought with me to Frisco, and they're getting faded and worn-looking. Does The Mercantile sell ready-made dresses?"

"They just hired a new seamstress. I hear she's been sewing up a storm. I saw a beautiful one in the window that looks like it's just your size. I think maybe that's why it hasn't sold yet. I'll bet you're the only woman in Frisco with an 18-inch waist."

"I get my monthly paycheck Monday, and I just might spend some of that hard-earned money on something that I've never really had–a nice dress."

That night as they settled down to study the *Book of Mormon*, they read about the Gadianton Robbers. Lillian softly closed the book and gently placed it in her carpetbag as she quietly said, "I think someone like Sheriff Phillips was needed when the Gadianton Robbers came on the scene. I'll bet he could have struck a cord of fear even in the hearts of that dreadful bunch!"

Chapter 16

Wind and snow blew in Lillian's face and pierced her coat like unwelcome guests as she walked to school on a blustery Monday morning, just two days after Sheriff Phillips began his reign of terror. *I'm glad we got that chimney installed Saturday, because winter has descended on us with a vengeance,* Lillian thought. The warm scarf she had wrapped around her hair and neck made walking only bearable. It was the week of Thanksgiving, and fall had departed, making way for winter to descend on Frisco without so much as a warning.

The wind had picked up velocity Saturday night, bringing with it the first snowstorm of the winter season. Everything was now covered in a beautiful blanket of white, and icicles dropped from rooftops, reaching halfway to the ground. The sagebrush looked like large, cotton balls, concealing the bushes that lay under the white, pristine snow. The water troughs had frozen solid, and those who were brave enough to venture out in the freezing weather were bundled and wrapped in so many layers of clothing that their walking was more of a waddle than a quick, easy stride. Upon opening the door to the schoolhouse, a blast of warm air enveloped her, letting her know that Charles had been here early to stoke the fire. It was evident that he had been here some time ago because the potbellied stove had a deep red glow.

Thank heavens for plenty of wood and large, black stoves she thought. She tried not to think of the warm, brown eyes and strong arms that were responsible for the warmth. Just thinking about being in his arms for a few minutes on the roof sent a flood of warmth throughout her body. *How can I have feelings like this toward that infernal man?* she wondered.

Her thoughts were interrupted as children flowed into the school without warning. She hadn't even had to ring the bell today. They were all so anxious to get in out of the cold that being late had been driven right out of their minds by the icy blasts of the wind.

After they sang "My Country, 'Tis of Thee," Lillian decided to institute something new into the classroom. She sensed by the actions of all her students that they were just busting at the seams to let something out.

She rapped softly on her desk for all of them to be seated. "Starting today, following our song, we are going to take 15 minutes and talk about our community–Frisco. During these 15 minutes, we are going to talk about things that are happening right here in our own town. They may be problems, interesting happenings, or just plain questions that you may have about what's going on in our community. If there are problems involved, we are going to talk about what we can do to help solve them. Now, who wants to be first?"

Mary waved her hands frantically back and forth and almost bolted from her seat to be the first to speak. "Miss Lewis, did you know that Sheriff Phillips killed six men his first day on the job?"

Curt, not waiting to be recognized, blurted out, "And he fired the driver of the Death Wagon and took over the job himself. Dad said by the looks of the number of dead people, the sheriff must have been up all night."

"And, Miss Lewis," yelled Clarence, "he wants to change the name of the Death Wagon to Meat Wagon. Don't you think that sounds yucky?"

Jessica, unusually loud, crowded in with, "Don't you think he's worse than having no sheriff at all? Mom says that she's afraid to walk the streets now. You never know when that sheriff is going to explode and shoot someone."

Lillian rapidly tapped her stick on the table to get some semblance of order in the classroom.

"Now, children, let's talk about this. Why was it necessary that Frisco have a sheriff in the first place?"

Jesse blurted, "Cause we were afraid to walk the streets. You never knew when a gunfight was going to happen. Mom said she was afraid to let us out on the streets alone."

"Gunfighters, and really bad people come to Frisco because they know they can do anything they want and nobody will punish them for it," said Melissa.

"Do you think we'll have less shootings with the sheriff here?" Lillian asked.

"Well, I'm going to do a lot of thinkin' before I pull a plug out of another water wagon," said Jamie.

"I think there will be a lot of lawbreakers who will do some thinking from now on," stated Lillian quietly.

"Our time is up. Now I want all of you to divide into your class groups and discuss why it is necessary to have a law of some kind in a community. Also discuss whether Sheriff Phillips will be good for Frisco or bad and why you think that way. I will give you 10 minutes, then each group will send a spokesman to the front, and that person will summarize the decisions made by your group."

The students moved to their usual group tables, and the room suddenly sounded like a chicken coop that was undergoing a wolf invasion.

When the groups reported, all of them had concluded that some type of law was necessary in Frisco. They also unanimously decided that Sheriff Phillips was better than no sheriff at all, even if his methods were a bit extreme. The lesson that all of the children seemed to have learned was that they would be less likely to break the law with Sheriff Phillips around.

Everything ran smoothly the rest of the day. When it came time for reading, the reading groups came forward and read with such feeling and expression that Lillian was sure that if the Territorial Governor of Utah had been present, he would have been impressed. *All this success goes back to our play. Each day the students seem to gain more enthusiasm for the project,* Lillian thought.

A crackle of anticipation filled the air until that awaited time when play practice would begin. Lillian rapped softly on the desk to signal that it was time to change routine and begin rehearsal for the play. "Class, today we are going to practice the woman's suffrage movement and the life of Susan B. Anthony. Miss Anthony was a teacher whose zeal and efforts helped to launch the Woman's State Temperance Society of New York. She felt that opposition to women in public affairs was unjust and spent her life trying to convince the leaders of our country that women were important and that they did have rights. She also campaigned to get the vote for women by having the Fourteenth Amendment passed, but her efforts failed. She also led the temperance movement to abolish alcohol."

"Curt, you will read a short excerpt on Miss Anthony, similar to what I just related to you, and then you girls will circle the room singing a women's suffrage song, and waving signs that have sayings on them like, 'Give Women the Vote,' and 'Down with Whiskey and Beer.'"

Soon the practice was in full swing. The girls were marching around the room waving imaginary signs chanting, "Stand up, stand up for women. They all need the vote. Take all that rotten whiskey and feed it to your goats." This chant was an original cheer written by the girls, and they took great pride in shouting it so loudly and with such exhilaration that Lillian felt sure that the walls would fall down at any minute from the vibrations. The boys, on the other hand, just sat on their benches, looking like bored toads that couldn't even be excited by a passing fly.

When recess time rolled around, Lillian breathed a sigh of relief as the children threw on their coats and rushed outside in the frosty air to get rid of some of that energy that was threatening to break loose at any minute. The snow had stopped, but there was at least 4 inches of white powder lying on the ground. Because of preparations that she had to complete for the next class session, Lillian just glanced through the window intermittently as she worked steadily at her desk.

Suddenly shrill shrieks got her full attention. She flung open the door and froze in her tracks at the scene that lay before her. The girls formed a ring around the outhouse, held hostage by a strong rope. When they saw her standing in the doorway, the real hysterics began. With eyes wide and wrists writhing, the girls tried to escape the rope that held them securely to the odorous edifice as shrill cries for help issued from their indignant lips. Laura's red curls were flying in every direction as high-pitched cries of "Miss Lewis, let us loose!" and "When I get out of here, you boys are going to die!" issued from her lips. Melissa's head was bowed as soft cries of "Help me, help me," could just barely be heard. Stacy, Jessica, and Mary were screaming "Rascals! Heathens!" as they kicked snow in the direction of the boys, hoping to hit their assailants' shins in retaliation for this outrage. Meanwhile, the boys were marching around the circle of girls chanting, "No votes for women! Women have no brains! If they ever get the vote, the men will go insane!"

Reaching the scene in a matter of seconds, Lillian grabbed the ringleaders of the riot, Billie and Jamie, by their ears, bringing the march to a standstill. Raising her voice louder than any dynamite blast, she yelled, "Just what is going on here, boys?"

Jamie's cowlick stood up in defiance, and his large, blue eyes put on an innocent look. "Miss Lewis, we're just enforcing the law our way. We all decided in class that there had to be laws. These girls were getting out of control. We had to take desperate measures!"

"Ya, everyone knows that girls are too stupid to make important decisions like voting. Dad always says if you let a woman take charge, everything goes to h---." Billie stopped before that forbidden word was uttered.

"Well, my dad says that the only place for a woman is in the kitchen, filling the men's tummies with good food!" explained Clarence.

Lillian struggled to look stern as she marched the students back into the classroom. The boys hung their heads, and the girls glared at them in righteous indignation.

"For the rest of the day we are going to have a much-needed lesson on the Constitution of the United States," said Lillian.

She didn't need to open a book because she knew the Preamble of the Constitution by heart. She looked into the eyes of each of her students and began, "We the People of the United States, in Order to form a more perfect Union, establish Justice, insure domestic Tranquility, provide for the common defense, promote the general Welfare, and secure the Blessings of Liberty to ourselves and our Posterity, do ordain and establish this Constitution for the United States of America."

"That, students, is the powerful beginning to the most important document in the United States–the Preamble to the Constitution of the United States. Now let's use this Preamble to analyze what has just occurred."

"Billie, the Preamble says one of the purposes of the Constitution is to establish justice. Do you think it was just to burn innocent classmate's wrists with a harsh rope? Would you have liked that same type of justice measured on you?"

Billie raised his head, "No, Miss Lewis, I've had rope burns before. I don't want them again. One time last summer I was swinging from a rope hangin' from a tree, trying to land in a pond of water. The rope burned me somethin' terrible. The girls were just practicing for the play. It really wasn't their fault that they were acting uppity. I guess what we did weren't justice at all."

"And Curt, part of the purpose of the Constitution is to insure domestic tranquility. Do you know what that means?"

Curt's large, blue eyes had suddenly lost their mischievous sparkle. "Tranquility means peace."

"Well, do you think you established peace and tranquility in this classroom when you held these girls hostage around the outhouse?"

"No, Ma'am. They're going to want revenge something fierce. I don't even want to see in my worst nightmares what they're going to cook up for us!"

"And, Jamie, the Constitution tells us that we need to provide for the general welfare. Did you have the welfare of these girls in mind when you tightened the rope to hold them prisoner?"

"Well, I don't think it did the general welfare of them girls any good to stand out in the cold against a smelly privy and have us yell and scream at them," admitted Jamie.

"And Richie and Clarence, the Constitution states that we need to secure the blessings of liberty to ourselves and our posterity. Did you abide by this part of the Preamble just a few minutes ago?"

"No, Miss Lewis," said Richie. We didn't have the right to tie them so tight that they had no freedom at all to move about."

"They weren't at liberty to do nothing after we secured them to the privy," admitted Clarence, suppressing a large grin by ducking his head as he covered his mouth with his hand.

"Were any of you boys thinking about what the beginning of the Constitution says when you began your rash action?" Dead silence filled the schoolroom as five heads were hung in shame.

Then Lillian's eyes caught the self-righteous look on the faces of the girls.

"And are you girls going to seek revenge for this incident?"

Laura's red curls framed a freckled face, "Well, don't you think we are entitled to some kind of revenge?"

Lillian looked Laura in the eyes and said, "If you do seek revenge, are you obeying the Constitution? Are you creating peace and tranquility in this classroom? Are you securing the boys' liberty or taking it away from them?"

Laura's red freckles stood out a little brighter as she blurted, "Ah, Miss Lewis, I had such a dandy plan. I was going to smear the top of their lunch pails with lard, then laugh when they couldn't get them open, but....well, I guess, if you put it that way, we wouldn't be living by the Constitution if we decided on getting back at them."

Lillian let silence reign in the classroom following Laura's words. "I hope we have all learned a valuable lesson today, students. If we believe in our Constitution, and we must in order to survive, we must start to think about the feelings of others, the Constitution that our country was built on, and the purpose of this important document."

"Boys, I don't even have to reach into the consequence jar to get your punishment. By tomorrow, I want each one of you to have the Preamble to the Constitution memorized and be able to recite it in front of the class, followed by your personal explanation of what this Preamble means to you and how it is going to change your life. I suggest that you complete this assignment, or you won't want to know what the consequences will be. Girls, your assignment is to think good thoughts about the boys and be prepared tomorrow to stand and say something good about each one of them."

All of the students nodded in agreement and gave Lillian no more trouble the rest of the day. When it came time to dismiss school, silence reigned as the students bundled up in their coats and quietly headed for home.

Lillian herself had learned her own lessons. From now on she would look for the good in each of her students and respect their rights, keeping in mind that each one of them was a special individual protected by the Constitution.

Chapter 17

Lillian breathed a sigh of relief when she rang the closing bell two days later to signal the beginning of the Thanksgiving vacation. The boys had indeed memorized the Preamble and had done some serious thinking about what it meant to them. The girls had also cooperated and said some unusually good things about the boys. Lillian felt that they had been taught a lesson and said a silent thanks for the inspiration she had received to pick the two forms of punishment. As she walked home to the shanty, the display in the window of The Mercantile drew her.

There was indeed a beautiful dress in the store window. Ben Johnson had delivered her pay for the month after school, and the money was literally burning a hole in her dress pocket. A force more powerful than any she had felt before propelled her through the door of the store, and she found herself staring at the beautiful creation.

Suzie Littlefield, the proprietor's wife, couldn't help but notice how intently Lillian was gazing at the dress. "Isn't it beautiful, Miss Lewis? There's only one problem, that dressmaker we hired is so inexperienced that she made it for a fairy queen of dainty proportions. There have been several ladies who were interested in purchasing it, but none of them were petite enough to even get it over their heads. You know what? I'll bet you're the only female in Frisco who has the petite figure that this dress requires. Why, I dare say that a man could circle your small waist with his two hands and make his fingers meet. How about trying it on just for fun?"

Lillian couldn't resist. She was led to a dressing room in the back of The Mercantile where she carefully tried on the dress. Suzie was indeed right. Every line and seam fit her body perfectly as if it had been fashioned just for her. When she faced the mirror in the dressing room, she saw a stranger gazing back at her. The starched petticoats, which were part of the underskirt of the dress, gave it a fullness that made it sway back and forth like a beautiful bell on a Christmas tree. The deep blue color of the dress was a perfect match for her own blue eyes, making them more full and luminous.

The neck of the dress was designed to rest under the wearer's chin and was accentuated with a band of silk of a slightly darker color which encircled the throat. The sleeves were long, fitting tightly at Lillian's wrists, while the bodice of the dress was form fitting and buttoned all the way down the front with small, round covered buttons.

The flounce on the bottom of the skirt moved gracefully as Lillian pretended to dance a stately waltz. As she admired herself in the mirror, she felt somewhat like a princess who was about to be presented at her first ball. Startled by the rustle of the curtain, she turned to catch a glimpse of a pair of eyes peering through the curtains which rapidly opened to reveal a smiling Suzie.

"Miss Lewis, you're a sight to behold in that dress! I didn't think I would find anyone who could wear it, and here you are, showing it off to perfection. If you decide to buy it, there won't be a man in Frisco who will be able to take his eyes off of you."

"That depends on the price. How much do you want for it?"

"Well, since you're the only one who can get into it, I think I ought to sell it to you at a discount. How does $5 sound to you? We've spent that much just for the material."

"What a bargain!" said Lillian. "I know I shouldn't buy it, but at that price I can't resist."

"And we just happen to have a pair of women's dress shoes that we haven't been able to sell because no woman's foot in Frisco's is that small and narrow, but something tells me that they might be a perfect fit for you, and they certainly would match the dress."

The shoes were beautiful, black leather slippers with small heels and three straps across the instep of the foot. They did indeed fit and were a perfect compliment for the dress. When Lillian learned they were only $2, it wasn't long until she found herself leaving The Mercantile with two packages tucked securely under her arms.

Nettie was so excited when Lillian showed her the dress and shoes that supper had to be postponed while they talked about their plans for the upcoming dance. Their conversation was interrupted by a loud knocking that set the hinges to rattling on the shanty door.

A familiar boy with unruly red hair and freckles stood in the doorway, proudly holding two, large sage hens.

Billie placed the hens on the table. They had been cleaned and plucked and were ready to cook. "Dad went hunting today and got these hens. He wants you to have them for your Thanksgiving dinner."

"Oh, Billie! What a great gift!" said Nettie. "We really hadn't anything special to have tomorrow, and these sage hens will be wonderful. What are you and your dad going to do for dinner?"

"Well, dad shot a rabbit today. I guess we'll have some rabbit stew."

"Rabbit stew on Thanksgiving? That's not a feast. Why don't you and your dad come over here tomorrow and have dinner with us? After all, you've supplied the main course."

A large grin burst over Billie's face. "Oh, Mrs. Harris, could we really? Nobody makes biscuits like you do! It's awfully lonely with just dad and me and our old hound dog, Duster."

Nettie patted the red hair. "You and your dad be here about three tomorrow, and we'll feed you a feast that will tickle your innards and keep you full for a week!"

"Golly whiz!" Billie yelled as he ran through the door. "Wait till dad hears that he won't have to cook tomorrow!"

Lillian was silent the rest of the evening, wanting to be alone with her own thoughts. She wasn't sure that sitting next to Charles Anderson at her Thanksgiving table was something she was looking forward to, but then her thoughts returned to Billie's bright eyes and the excitement in his voice. How could she begrudge one of her class favorites a happy Thanksgiving?

When she said her prayers that evening, she gave special thanks for all of her students and thanked Heavenly Father for entrusting them to her care. There was a strong bond forming between her and all of her students, but a far stronger bond had formed between her and Billie.

Chapter 18

Lillian and Nettie rose early to begin preparations for the feast. Nettie got out some apples that she had purchased when the Dixie peddler stopped by last summer. She had stored them in the cool cellar of the shanty, and before long, the tantalizing smell of apple pies seasoned with cinnamon and cloves filled the air. Lillian set to work making the rolls that had been a Thanksgiving tradition in her family for as long as she could remember. Memories of her mother teaching her step by step how to make them filled her mind. *I hope they turn out as light and fluffy as mom's* she thought.

Nettie's best tablecloth, given to her as a wedding gift, covered the table, and a bouquet of dried flowers served as the centerpiece. Beautiful dishes given to Nettie as an inheritance from her great grandmother signaled that this was indeed a special occasion. The sage hens filled with dressing were browning nicely on a spit in the fireplace, and a large pan of potatoes and a saucepan full of carrots were ready to be placed on the top of the new stove when the proper moment arrived. Lillian had just finished placing the rolls in a pan to rise when a loud knock followed by familiar "Hee Haws" broke the silence of the busy morning.

Lillian literally flew to the door as she yelled, "It's Mabel and Lizzy and where you find them, there's got to be Ned!" As she swung the door open, she was greeted by the sight of a jolly man in buckskin and his precious mules. Then the commotion began. Mabel and Lizzy set up such a fuss when they saw Lillian that she had to give each bristley head a hug and kiss before she could hug her old friend.

"Ned Druthers, you old rascal. The sight of you outside my house is more welcome than the sight of Santa at a Christmas gathering. What a Thanksgiving surprise!"

Lillian ushered Ned into the warmth of the shanty and introduced him to Nettie.

Without warning, Nettie found herself engulfed in an exuberant hug.

When she was released and had a few seconds to catch her breath, she smiled at the old freighter and said, "Mr. Druthers, finally I get to meet the colorful man who Lillian can't seem to stop talking about."

"I hope what you heard ain't all been bad," chuckled Ned.

"On the contrary, I have learned that even though you are somewhat of an unconventional character, you're an old softy underneath that rough exterior. Let us give you a real Frisco welcome. We will sit down to Thanksgiving dinner in just two hours. Please say you'll grace our table with your friendship and humor. A friend of Lillian's is always welcome in this shanty."

"That's a special kindness, Mam. Since I'm usually traveling here or there, I don't know when I've been able to sit down to a real Thanksgiving dinner. Two hours is just enough time to unload my wagon and get Lizzie and Mabel settled down in my friend Ned's barn. I wouldn't miss this dinner if someone offered me double price for a freight haul. Lillian and Nettie were once again treated to bone-crushing hugs, and as Ned turned to leave he yelled, "Won't be late– promise."

At his leaving, preparations for the dinner took a serious turn. Another box, which would serve as a chair, had to be found and another place set at the table. Lillian and Nettie bustled around the shanty and had everything cooked to perfection when a knock sounded on the door. All three guests stood smiling in the doorway. It was evident that each of them had taken special pains to look their best. Ned's hair was still wet from a recent washing, and Billie's cowlick didn't make an appearance because his hair was slicked down so firmly that not a hair escaped. When Lillian's glance fell upon Charles, her eyes widened in disbelief. Was this the same dusty, didn't-give-a-darn-about-his-appearance man with whom she was familiar? His face was so clean that it actually shone, and his rough, unmanageable beard had been trimmed and washed. The blue shirt that he wore had seen much wear, but it was clean and free of wrinkles.

The three stepped into the shanty as Charles managed a low, gruff, "Thanks for inviting us, ladies."

Lillian, motioning them inside, took their coats and seated them at the festive table, except for Billie who insisted on helping dish up the food.

When all were seated, Lillian said, "I would like to keep one of my family traditions by everyone holding hands as we say grace."

Lillian suddenly found herself holding Charles's hand with her right hand and Billie's hand with her left. The contact made her feel whole and complete and gave her a feeling of complete peace that she had not felt since the death of her parents.

Heads were bowed and Lillian began in a soft voice, "Thank you, Lord, for all our blessings, and for the friends who grace our table. Thank you for the abundant food we are about to eat, and bless it that it will nourish our bodies and make them strong. Bless all those in this circle that thy spirit will be with them throughout the coming year, and bless us that we will remember and aid those around us who are less fortunate than ourselves and who are in need of our help. Thanking thee once again for our blessings, we say this in the name of Jesus Christ, amen." Heads were raised and everyone released hands except for Charles who continued to grasp Lillian's hand as if his very life depended on the warmth that was coming from that dainty appendage. Silence filled the room as everyone seemed to focus on those two hands—one large, work-worn hand clasping a small, capable one. It was Ned who seemed to bring everyone back to the present.

"Can we start passin' the food, Miss Nettie. I'm pert neigh starved out of my senses," and it was then that two hands were quietly unclasped and Thanksgiving dinner got underway.

Dinner conversation centered around Squaw Springs which was about 2 miles southwest of Frisco. Here a large farmhouse, barn, and a small spring beckoned weary travelers who were looking for a place to rest for the night and water their horses. Ned had stopped there last night to appease his thirsty mules. When Si and Mary Rollins, the owners of the property, didn't come out to welcome him, he sensed that something was wrong. Upon receiving no answer to his loud knock, he swung open the door of the farmhouse to find it empty. He knew that something was amiss because food had not been cleared from the table, and Mary was a meticulous housekeeper. Under normal conditions, she never would have left her kitchen in this state of disarray.

Ned's whiskers moved gently as he related, "I wondered about these strange happenings, and when I got to Frisco, Nelson told me that Mary was found dead two days ago by some travelers who stopped by. They found her lying stone dead right in the middle of her kitchen floor. Si was nowhere to be found. When Sheriff Phillips did the investigating, he found Si at his still, which is hidden in the foothills near the spring. Passed out he was, and out of his senses by his own brew."

"Did the sheriff shoot him on the spot?" burst out Billie.

"No, little feller. You see, Sheriff Phillips knew all about Mary. It appears she had to keep the ranch running all by herself cause Si was a little on the lazy side. Every night they got a little groggy, drinkin' their own moonshine, and this often caused a real ruckus, which usually ended in a knock down, punch-throwing fight. Since Mary was three times bigger than Si, he suffered something fierce from her beatings. I'm a thinkin' that Sheriff Phillips kinda thought in Si's case, it was a matter of self-defense. He let the little feller go when he sobered up some. I understand the sheriff's still trying to get to the bottom of what happened. When he got to questioning Si, the sheriff learned that Si didn't have any recollection of anything the night of Mary's death after he finished off his nightly jug of joy juice."

A loud knocking at the door put an abrupt end to the Squaw Springs saga. When Nettie swung open the shanty door, she stepped back to allow Sheriff Phillips into the room. Ducking to prevent his head from hitting the low door, his grim presence brought an end to any festive thoughts. He was even more imposing and fearsome at close range. Silence reigned as the sheriff stared down each guest seated at the table. He seemed to glare at each member of the group, but his glance paused and softened somewhat as it fell on Lillian, then changed to pure ruthlessness as it fell on Ned.

"Are you the freighter who just came into town today?" he boomed. His firm, commanding voice jarred the nerves of everyone in the room.

"I am indeed," answered Ned.

"Heard you stopped by Squaw Springs on your way here."

"You heard right. I stopped there to water my mules early this morning, but found the house all messed up and not a soul in sight. Only the critters in the corral signaled that it was a place that was lived in. Looked like Mary and Si had hightailed it out of there real fast! Then I got to Frisco a few hours later to find out about Mary's death. Musta happened way before I went through."

Sheriff Phillips placed his hands on his hips as he continued to glare at Ned. "Do you have anyone to vouch for the fact that you got into town around ten o'clock this morning and when you left your destination to get here?"

Lillian decided to put her fears aside and face the sheriff head on. "That would be me, Sheriff Phillips. Ned is a good friend of mine, and he stopped by the shanty today about ten o'clock to tell me he was in town. I can also vouch for Ned's character.

There isn't a more honest, upright man in all of Southern Utah. If you're insinuating that he might have had something to do with Mary's death, you had better look elsewhere!"

Unafraid, deep blue eyes met the sheriff's blazing, green ones. There was a stand off of sorts for a few seconds, then much to everyone's surprise, it was Sheriff Phillips who seemed to back down and gentle up a bit.

"And just who is this pretty miss who is standing up for this old freighter?" he asked in a somewhat lower tone than he had used when he first entered the shanty.

"Lillian Lewis, the new teacher at the Frisco School, Sheriff."

"Well, Miss Lewis, I guess I'll just have to take your word on that. Can't go disbelieving the teacher of our children, now can I? I won't travel down that road, cause I'd be liable to get myself into one mess of trouble."

Ned spoke up, "And, Sheriff, Mack Peterson at the Caliente Feed Store in Caliente, Nevada can tell you the day and exact time that I left Nevada. If Mary was killed three days ago, the information that you get from him will prove me innocent. I'd have to have been flying faster than a chased squirrel to reach Squaw Springs that fast."

Sheriff Phillips backed towards the door, never once losing eye contact with the blue eyes that seemed to hold his interest. Before he turned to leave, he addressed Lillian with a gentlemanly tip of his hat, "Hope to see you at the dance tomorrow night, Miss Lewis. And, Mr. Druthers, if your story doesn't check out, you'll have my revolvers to answer to."

The festiveness of the occasion seemed to be smothered even after the unwelcome visitor made his departure. The apple pie was delicious, but the dinner conversation had come to a literal standstill. Lillian noticed that frequently two, deep brown eyes looked in her direction even though Charles had said very little all evening. She was very much aware that he used a form of sign language to tell Billie what he wanted. Billie seemed to understand what his father wanted by the signal given. At times the sign language got so intricate that it was all Lillian could do to keep from bursting out into full-fledged laughter. Watching the exchanges between father and son, Lillian realized how much the tragedy of losing his wife had cost Charles. No wonder Billie was a problem at times. There appeared to be very little verbal communication between father and son. When the dishes were cleared and placed in the sink and the dish water was heating on the new stove, Billie courageously offered to help with the dishes.

"That's women's work, Billie," said Nettie. "You and your father can run along now. I'm sure that there are chores needing to be done."

As Charles and Billie turned to leave, Billie ran to Lillian and Nettie to give them exuberant hugs. "Thanks, Miss Lewis and Nettie. This has got to be the best Thanksgiving ever!"

Lillian was once more drawn to two brown eyes that had examined her carefully all evening. A voice that was usually loud and booming was suddenly lowered to almost a whisper so that she barely heard, "Miss Lewis, I hope the ribbon you choose for the dance tomorrow night is the same color as your eyes," as the door closed on Billie and his father.

"Well I'll be," muttered Ned on his way out the door, "It's plain to see that young feller is a bit twitterpated!"

Chapter 19

Nettie and Lillian were ready for the Bow Dance a good thirty minutes before it was time to leave. Lillian had washed her hair with melted snow water and let it dry naturally. Since her hair was naturally curly, when she brushed it out, it fell in soft waves to her waist.

She had decided to let it fall freely instead of go to the dance in the braids that she usually secured to the back of her head each day. The sides of her hair were pulled away from her face and arranged in an attractive mass of curls at the top of her head, while the back fell freely.

The deep blue of the new dress made Lillian's eyes seem larger and brighter, and its tight bodice sent forth the vista of a beautiful hourglass in human form. The new slippers peeked from beneath the flounce of the dress and seemed to invite all callers to come and dance if they dared.

When Nettie saw Lillian for the first time, she held her breath for a few seconds before she softly said, "You'll be the belle of the ball, Lillian. When you enter the dance hall, all eyes will be on you. You're a sight to behold!"

Lillian's eyes widened as she suddenly realized that there was a vision speaking to her. Nettie's blonde hair was pulled up and arranged in curls at the top of her head. The dress she was wearing was fashioned of pink cotton lawn and white lace, giving her the appearance of an elegant Cinderella all dressed up for the ball.

Lillian gave her friend a warm hug. "I'm not too sure who they'll be staring at, Nettie–you or me. I've never seen you look lovelier. You seem to literally sparkle. Wherever did you get that lovely pink creation?"

"It's my wedding dress," said Nettie softly. This is the first time I have worn it since my wedding day. Do you think my late husband Sam would object to my wearing it?"

"Nettie, it's too lovely to be packed away and not worn. If Sam's looking down from heaven, I'm sure he has a smile on his face. You have a glow about you that will draw men to you like fireflies are drawn to a lantern."

"You don't think it's too soon after my husband's death for me to be dancing about?"

"Nonsense," said Lillian. "It's been over a year. You need to get on with your life. Tonight's a good time to begin."

For their contribution to the refreshments, they carefully wrapped an apple cake in a clean cloth and placed it in a basket. After a final inspection of their attire in the mirror that hung above the washbasin on the left wall, they put on their coats and wrapped mufflers around their necks. Since a cold wind was blowing, they needed to dress warmly for their walk to the dance hall which was located in the middle of Main Street.

As they stepped out the door, the cold wind was forgotten when they heard the music coming from the dance hall, just three blocks away. It was so lively and inviting that Lillian and Nettie found themselves wanting to stop and tap their feet in the newly-fallen snow that had visited Frisco about noon. An hour ago, the snow had stopped, and looking up at the sky, they could see the beautiful stars peeking through the heavens, leading them on to the warmth and excitement of the dance hall.

As they entered the dance hall, an attendant took their coats and mufflers and hung them on nails that had been carefully placed on the wall behind him. The sea of coats was an indication that the dance was already in full swing. Exhilarating–that was the word for the sight that lay before them. At the top of the dance floor a picturesque band was playing with every ounce of energy that they could muster.

A middle-aged lady was sitting on a chair, ringing delightful music from an accordion. The bows on four fiddlers' fiddles were gliding so fast across the strings that they were blurs to the sight of the onlookers. The fiddlers wore colorful kerchiefs around their necks, and their western hats were tilted at an angle, giving them a jaunty, devil-may-care appearance. A portly lady sat at a pump organ and seemed to tie the whole strange ensemble together. They were playing "Turkey in the Straw," and numerous dancers were engaged in a lively polka as they twirled around the floor, smiles wide and eyes sparkling.

Lillian and Nettie sat on the benches that were lined up against two of the walls, and as their feet began to tap, they were immediately caught up in the excitement.

Sensing that someone was gazing at her intently, she looked across the hall to see two brown eyes fastened to her blue ones. Charles and Billie were seated next to some other men who had not yet joined the others on the dance floor. Charles was again well-groomed, a new pair of denim pants accentuating his tall lankiness. It was clear that just as he had for Thanksgiving, he had taken great pains with his appearance. Billie, not satisfied with just tapping his feet in time with the music was also clapping his hands and moving his head back and forth to the irresistible rhythm that vibrated throughout the dance hall.

When the fiddling stopped, the dancers stopped dancing and continued to talk in excited tones, waiting for the next dance to begin. Suddenly a hush fell over the once exuberant assembly. All eyes turned to the doorway where Sheriff Phillips stood in full majesty. His six- foot-three body and the revolvers strapped to his black pants signaled that he was the Lord over all he surveyed. Time stood still as fear engulfed the once festive room.

The sheriff's eyes roamed the room and rested on Lillian. A large smile spread over his face, and he motioned for the band to resume their playing. He seated himself on the wall opposite Nettie and Lillian, but his eyes never left the petite lady in blue. Being the object of this man's attention was definitely not a pleasure–it was pure torture. Lillian was considering leaving and returning home when the next dance ended, and the floor manager stood in front of the band, raising his hands to get everyone's attention.

"It's now time for the Bow Dance. Gentlemen, lower your heads and close your eyes, while the ladies come up and place their bows in this basket. Any gentleman caught peeking will immediately be expelled from the dance hall, so shut your peepers tight!"

The ladies filed up to the front and placed their bows in the basket. Even if the men had opened their eyes, the mass of women in front of the basket would have prevented them from seeing which bow belonged to which young lady. Lillian and Nettie placed their bows in the basket. Lillian pushed aside the top bows to place hers near the bottom. Her bow was a deep blue color, darker than the new dress, but an exact match for the blue of her eyes.

When the ladies had taken their seats on the benches, the floor manager instructed, "Gentlemen, you may now open your eyes and the bidding for the bows will begin. The men who wish to bid on a particular bow come to the area in front of the basket, and the bidding will begin. When you have reached a price that you can afford and wish to bid no more, you are to quietly return to your seat, and the bidding will resume until there is only one bidder left. The young lady who fashioned the bow will then come forward and take the arm of the young man who purchased her bow. The winners of the auction will get to dance three dances with the young lady who created the bow and be in her company for the eating of the refreshments, which will follow the third dance. After refreshments have been eaten, it's every man for himself."

The smile disappeared from the lips of the floor master as he got down to serious business. "May I remind you of the rules of the dance floor. Daylight must be seen between the two dancers at all times. Since I am the floor manager, anyone who does not abide by the daylight rule will be expelled from the dance floor and have to sit out the next three dances. If they break the daylight rule a second time, they will be expelled from the dance hall."

"Remember, Ladies and Gents, that it is rude to laugh too loudly or to fail to thank your partner after each dance, so observe these rules and everyone will enjoy the occasion. Let the bidding begin!"

The bidding was fast and furious. Some miners smiled when they saw whose bow they had purchased, while other seemed disappointed when they realized that they had spent hard-earned money for a sour-faced damsel, not the beauty they had hoped was the bow's owner.

When Nettie's bow was withdrawn from the basket, five miners joined in the bidding. When the last bid shouted was $2.25, four of the miners sat down, leaving Ben Johnson, proprietor of The Southern, standing. Nettie quietly walked up to Ben, and as was the custom, he placed the pink bow she had fashioned in her hair, then led her off the floor to stand with the other couples.

Lillian's bow was the next one drawn from the basket. Her intention in placing it near the bottom of the basket was to make it difficult for the bidders to determine which bow was hers. It suddenly dawned on her that by placing it at the bottom, the remaining men knew that it was hers because she was one of the few women remaining without a partner.

Much to her dismay, Charles and Sheriff Phillips stepped into the bidder's semicircle. The sheriff towered over Charles by a good 3 inches, but Charles didn't even flinch when the sheriff came to stand by him. Ned Druthers joined the semicircle and the bidding began.

When Sheriff Phillips yelled "$10," A gasp ran through the crowd because it was the highest bid of the evening.

"That's too steep for me," said Ned as he walked to the sidelines.

A forceful "$20" rang out as Charles was recognized.

"One hundred dollars!" firmly stated Sheriff Phillips, causing everyone's mouths to open in astonishment and a look of disappointment to form on Charles's face.

There was silence in the hall for a few seconds. Everyone knew the rules. You didn't bid for the bow unless you had the money on your person. Charles walked to the sidelines and left Sheriff Phillips grinning like a hyena who had just caught his prey.

Lillian swallowed twice, then slowly walked to Sheriff Phillips and allowed him to fix the bow in her hair and lead her off the dance floor.

She stood by the side of this black specter while the last two bows were auctioned. Every nerve in her body was fine tuned for what she knew was going to happen next–she would soon be in the arms of the man who never ceased to cause her heart to pound in her chest and fear to engulf her entire body.

There was no running away from the situation. When the music began, she found herself wrapped in a vice-like grip from which there was no escape. It was clear from the beginning that Sheriff Phillips had no intention of abiding by the daylight rule. The band was playing "The Tennessee Waltz," and Lillian found herself pressed firmly to the black-clad body of this fearsome lawman.

The sheriff held her away from him long enough to say, "Miss Lewis, you are a sight to behold. Why, I do believe that you would put Lilly Langtree to shame tonight." Without giving her a chance to reply, she was again grasped in that vice-like grip and whirled around the floor so fast that she found it difficult to catch her breath.

She did manage to get out, "Sheriff, do you mind not holding me so tightly. Here comes the floor manager, and you'll surely be asked to leave."

The floor manager tapped the sheriff on the shoulder and was about to speak when he looked into those piercing, green eyes. He kind of backed away a few steps and stammered, "Just wanted to know if you were having a good time, Sheriff." It was apparent that nobody was going to expel Sheriff Phillips from the floor, even if he was flagrantly breaking the daylight rule.

Lillian breathed a sigh of relief as the waltz ended, and it was announced that the next dance would be the Virginia Reel. This meant that the ladies and gents would form two rows facing each other, and each couple would take a turn going down the middle of the rows, taking turns swinging each lady or gent on the row, then returning to the middle to grab their partner's arm and precede in this manner until they reached the end of the rows. When it came time for Lillian to take Charles's arm and swing around, she was conscious of his nearness and wasn't surprised when the familiar scent of lavender filled her senses. *What is there about this man that produces this scent?* But before she could have too much time to think, she was linking arms with the sheriff in the middle of the rows again.

The dance was so heart-stirring that everyone clapped, stamped their feet, and shouted a loud "Ya Hoo!" when the music stopped.

Lillian was bracing herself to endure a third dance with the sheriff when the door to the dance hall flew open and the sheriff's deputy raced into the hall.

"Sheriff, you've got to come quick. There's a fight in the Rockn' K Saloon and there's not a window left in the place. Ten men have already been knocked out and are lying in the street like drowned squirrels. If you don't come now, there won't be anything left of the Rockn' K, and that's the best saloon in town."

The sheriff released his grip on Lillian and with a tip of his hat said, "Thanks for the dances, Miss Lewis. Keep those cheeks rosy, girl, cause I have more plans as far as you're concerned!"

Minutes later gunshots were heard, then silence. "The sheriff will be out late with the Death Wagon tonight," said Ben Johnson under his breath.

Lillian raised her head to find Charles by her side.

"Since I'm the second highest bidder, I claim the next dance, Miss Lewis."

And dance they did to a stately waltz. At first Charles seemed unsure of his dancing ability, but Lillian followed his steps closely and above all, didn't try to lead. Soon, the music took over, and Lillian found that for a man with many sharp edges, Charles was a surprisingly good dancer. He followed the daylight rule, but instead of holding her right hand out to the side like the other dancers, he gathered it to his body and held it softly on his chest. His simple act of placing her hand close to his heart sent a warm glow radiating throughout her whole body.

Her head was just below Charles's chin and intermittently she felt that chin finding a resting place in her hair. Most of the dance was passed in silence until she barely heard a soft, "I'm glad you buried that chimney-building outfit. The dress you're wearing is quite an improvement." She couldn't resist a smile and realized that sometimes Charles's crusty exterior cracked just a little.

Following the third dance, everyone rushed to the refreshment table which had been set up at the top of the hall. Cakes, pies, bread, and confections of every kind were arranged in beautiful array. The ladies of Frisco had truly outdone themselves for the occasion. Billie followed Lillian and Charles to the refreshment table and started to fill his plate to the brim. Before he got too carried away, Charles moved his right arm from left to right, a signal to Billie that he had enough on his plate.

Seated on one of the side benches, Charles and Lillian ate in silence, but Billie talked non-stop. Wound up like a tight spring, he seemed compelled to relate every detail of the evening. "I danced with Laura and stepped on her toes. She boxed my ears and then stomped off, leaving me standing in the middle of the floor. Then I gave Melissa some dried apples and she gave me the sweetest smile. Did you know that her hair is so curly tonight because she put some old rags in it last night and left them there until just before the dance. Don't understand girls and what they do. Who would ever think that rags could make someone look like that? That Lissa, she's a pip!" Then looking for an okay from his father, he was off to the refreshment table for a second helping.

A soft voice managed, "The dance will be over in a few minutes. Let's find our coats before the last dance ends and avoid the rush that always follows."

Silently they walked towards where the coats were hung. Charles helped Lillian into her coat, then put on his own heavy one. A sense of aloneness filled them as dark brown eyes met deep blue ones. Without warning the strong sent of lavender, seeming to come from the ceiling, almost overwhelmed Lillian, who immediately glanced upward, trying to determine the source of the scent. Charles stopped and also looked upward, trying to see what had caught Lillian's attention. Their eyes came to rest on a sprig of mistletoe placed there by some early wisher of Christmas cheer.

It was at this very moment that they were pushed into each other's arms by an invisible gentle breeze, as a lavender scent swirled around them. Lillian found herself looking into Charles's eyes, as he slowly put his arms around her and lowered his head to gently touch her lips with his. Lillian's arms naturally found themselves around Charles's neck and both of them were lost in the wonder of the moment.

After only a few seconds, they both backed away slowly, embarrassed by the strong emotions which had taken hold of them and which they now chose to cloak with silence. It was at this moment that a rush of people, anxious to get their wraps and return to their homes, joined them.

Lillian and Charles, separated by the crowd, were rushed out the door. An excited Nettie grabbed Lillian's arm and couldn't stop talking about what a good time she'd had and what a nice, gentle man Ben Johnson was.

As they walked home, Nettie's words seemed to blur as Lillian's mind was filled with thoughts of her hand being held against a warm heart, the scent of lavender, hanging mistletoe, and the gentle kiss that had shaken her very being.

Chapter 20

Monday morning arrived all too soon. Lillian pulled back the calico curtains of the shanty to see the snow softly falling. She saw Charles enter the schoolhouse with a fresh load of wood, and once more emotions, new to her, filled her mind. She could feel the heat flowing to her cheeks and knew that they must be bright red as she remembered the gentle touch of his lips on hers. She didn't want to feel this way towards this infuriating man.

Ever since they had met, he had seemed to feel that it was his main purpose in life to set her on her ear, and now thoughts of the gentleness that he had shown her at Thanksgiving and during the dance Friday night merely confused and somewhat terrified her.

Shaking her head, trying to get rid of thoughts she refused to dwell on, she hurried about the business of getting ready for school. The history play was only three weeks away, and she had to get serious about practicing for it.

As she walked to school, she came to the conclusion that she would have to put thoughts of Charles away on a shelf while she prepared her students for their big event. *I think today we'll work on the Indian and Calvary portion of the play–in particular, Custer and Sitting Bull.*

Because Custer's defeat at Little Big Horn had occurred just a few years ago, the event was fresh in the minds of the children, so it should be easy to get them interested and involved in this portion of the play. Her thoughts were interrupted as she noticed Charles leaving the schoolhouse. Since she was just a few feet from Charles, she looked for him to glance her way, but he ducked his head and trudged through the snow without so much as one wave of recognition.

Hurt feelings threatened to overwhelm her, but were rapidly erased when after the ringing of the morning bell, eight students rushed upon her all chattering about their Thanksgiving vacation. *Put Charles on the shelf for a while,* she reminded herself as she proceeded with the routine of getting her students regimented for Monday morning.

The students were literally bouncing off the walls after their long vacation, and it was almost impossible to get them settled into their daily routine. During the singing of "God Bless America," Jamie hurried in, his hands holding his coat over a distended belly. *He must have really enjoyed Thanksgiving,* Lillian thought. Immediately after his entrance, giggles erupted, which the offenders attempted to conceal by placing their hands over their twittering mouths. Then the unthinkable happened. Shrill squealing sounds reverberated throughout the room. It was then that the children burst into loud, raucous laughter which they could no longer hold in check.

Lillian stopped singing and tapped her stick on her desk, her signal that the class needed to come to order at once. The stern look on her face and the loud rapping of the stick stopped the laughter, but the shrill high-pitched sounds continued. Lillian's acute hearing helped her trace the commotion to Jamie's seat. In a matter of seconds, she was towering over the culprit whose bright red cheeks witnessed his guilt.

Her eyes traveled to Jamie's coat from which the sounds were resounding. The coat acted as if it had a life of it's own as it rose up and down and wiggled in every direction. Two small, pink feet had forced their way through Jamie's coat and were kicking up a storm.

As Lillian raised Jamie's coat, her eyes widened as they fell upon a wiggling object that was securely wrapped in a blanket except for the escaped kicking feet and a face that not even a mother could love. A pink mouth directly below a large flat nose was sending forth sounds so shrill that Lillian was afraid that all the ear drums in the room would soon be broken.

"Jamie, remove the blanket from whatever it is that you are holding," sternly demanded Lillian, as she clasped her hands together to help maintain her composure.

"Ah, don't make me do that, Miss Lewis. It's my baby sister Jane, and she gets mighty upset if I wake her up. Mom said I had to tend her today because she had so many chores to do."

Lillian looked Jamie straight in his eyes and for the second time demanded, "Jamie, take that blanket off now!"

Jamie knew when he had pushed the issue too far. He removed the blanket to reveal a baby pig dressed in a baby's nightgown and bonnet, wiggling and squealing like she was on death row and was going to end up on tomorrow's breakfast table as the morning sausage.

"Jamie, I think you owe me an explanation," managed Lillian as she placed her hand over her mouth to hide the smile that would be a sign of weakness if she let it shine forth.

"Ah, Miss Lewis, I just wanted to show the class one of my new baby pigs. They were born on Thanksgiving Day. The mother had nine babies. Shucks, I didn't mean no harm. Just wanted to liven' things up a bit. School is always boring after the holidays, specially in the winter when it's so cold, and we can't go outside to play Steal the Sticks and Mud Daubs."

Lillian was about ready to suggest that Jamie take the pig home when laughter combined with high-pitched screams brought uncontrolled pandemonium into the schoolroom. Melissa climbed up on her desk and pointed towards the window. Her screams were soft but terrifying. Stacy and Jessica were hugging each other for comfort as they screamed, fixing their large, fear-filled eyes on the window. Mary and Melissa stood behind Curt, staring over his shoulders as if his small body could protect them from the evil something that was now the center of attention.

Richie and Curt's reaction was in strong contrast to the girl's hysteria as they laughed hysterically, almost doubling over with glee. Looking in the direction of the offending window, Lillian shook her head in disbelief. She couldn't be seeing the furry object that was dangling from a rope and swinging back and forth like the pendulum in a grandfather clock.

Surely it was an apparition. It couldn't be real. Maybe it was a large gopher that had found its way on top of the roof and got tangled in some vines, then fallen, but gophers don't have enormous red eyes protruding from their small heads, and they don't have stringy foot-long tails which are so light that they can be carried every which way as the fuzzy mass kept it rhythmic swing.

Amid the laughter and screams, Lillian hurried to the window to find that it was not a gopher, but what appeared to be an oversized rat with fluffy fur. It indeed was not an apparition, but thank goodness, it was not a real rat either. Someone had cleverly constructed a fake rat out of some kind of animal fur and used large red buttons for eyes and an orange button for a nose. The tail looked like an old shoelace that Lillian had often seen on miners' boots. It even had little rat ears that were flying in the breeze, and its pink tongue dangling from the side of its mouth was a sure signal that this rat was indeed stone dead. On the rat was pinned a note which read, "Help me, please!"

That did it! Lillian had reached her boiling point. She raced out the door and sprinted to the side of the schoolhouse, her eyes focused on the roof. A familiar redhead was standing close to the end of the roof, dangling the offending rat as he giggled and then burst into raucous laughter as he slapped his leg in unsuppressed glee, keeping the dead rat swinging all the while.

Lillian's eyes flashed as she clapped her hands together loudly, stamping her right foot on the ground at the same time. "Billie Anderson, you get down from there this minute!" Billie knew from the tone of Lillian's voice that the jig was up. He had been caught and must now pay the piper or in this case, Miss Lewis.

The rope and the disgusting rat fell to the ground, and Billie descended from the roof by placing his hands and feet in the cracks of the schoolhouse logs, exiting from the roof as gracefully as a skilled mountain climber.

There was silence for a few seconds. As Billie gazed into the blazing eyes of his teacher, he realized that he had never seen Miss Lewis in this state of agitation before. Her mouth was set in a firm line; her arms were folded; and wild wisps of hair had escaped from her usually immaculately-groomed braids. She tapped her foot on the ground as if she were keeping time to some kind of wild music. Billie would have been terrified if he could have read his teacher's thoughts.

What I want to do, Mr. Billie Anderson, is grab both of your ears and twist them until those freckles pop right off your face! Lillian's arms unfolded to attempt to do just that when she was brought to reality by the sight of eight curious faces gazing at her from the schoolhouse window. *You are a teacher of young people, and as their teacher you must control your temper at all costs, now calm yourself, Lillian.*

Lillian breathed deeply, and then addressed the transgressor in a quiet, controlled voice. "Billie Anderson, you will quietly enter the schoolhouse, not make a peep unless I call on you, and I will deal with you after school."

Billie turned and with head hung low, walked slowly into the schoolhouse. The rest of Lillian's students could see that their teacher had been tried to her limit. They stood quietly as she strode to the front of the room. Thankfully, the pig had apparently gone to sleep during all of the pandemonium because its little eyes were closed, and it was now emitting soft, snoring sounds as it lay peacefully in Jamie's arms.

"Jamie, please put the pig in the wood box and be careful not to wake it. I will allow you to take it home at noon, and we will settle on your punishment after school," said Lillian in a firm, controlled voice.

The pig, tired out from it's ordeal, didn't move when Jamie placed it in the empty side of the box. The culprit quietly returned to his seat, careful not to do anything further to rile up his teacher. He could clearly sense that judgment day was approaching, and he wished there was some way that he could avoid it.

Before Lillian addressed the class, she gave herself a quiet lecture. *Calm down, Lillian. Raising your voice in anger accomplishes nothing, and the students can sense when anger is your master, signaling them to act up again.*

Once again in control of her emotions, Lillian was able to proceed with the day's routine. During the history period, she directed her students as they practiced the part of the play which concerned the Indians and the Calvary, particularly Custer and Sitting Bull. Mary read a narrative about Custer being called to Dakota Territory to put down unrest by the Sioux and Cheyenne due to a large influx of miners searching for gold in the Black Hills. Following her narrative, Lillian taught Billie, Curt, Jamie, Richie and Clarence a military routine and song during which they positioned their rifles creatively and showed their muscles and military powers to the audience as their song gave them courage for the campaign.

Now Curt stepped forward and presented a narrative about Sitting Bull, the Sioux leader, and how he gathered a force of about 4,000 Indians on the Little Bighorn River in Southern Montana. Following the narrative on Sitting Bull and the Indians, Lillian taught Melissa, Mary, Laura, Stacy, and Jessica an Indian dance which the maidens performed to prepare their men for battle.

Clarence closed this segment of the play with a narrative on the battle itself. He explained that Custer, in ignorance of the strength of Sitting Bull's force, arrived at the Indian encampment on the morning of June 25 and without thinking, decided to attack at once. Clarence related how Custer rode for the center of the Indian line and how a rise of land hid a large group of Indians. As Custer swept down upon the Indians, he was surrounded by them and the hidden mass. The narrative dramatically ended with Clarence giving a narration on how Custer fought his way back up the ridge and finally how he and his immediate command of 264 men were all killed. Clarence ended the narrative with the thought that Custer had been blamed for foolhardiness in attacking so large a force of Indians and for launching the attack before the agreed time.

He then defended Custer as he explained that the size of the Indian force was not known when Custer set out, and the disaster might not have occurred if Reno, one of Custer's generals had not retreated and if Benteen, another of Custer's generals, had come to Custer's aid.

Both the Indians and soldiers were quick learners, and sensing the agitated state of their teacher, they followed instructions perfectly. Before the end of the history lesson, both boys and girls performed their routines to near perfection.

When the school day came to an end, Lillian dismissed everyone except Jamie and Billie. She sat Billie down in his desk and ordered him to complete his math homework while she talked to Jamie. She then directed Jamie towards the consequence jar and unscrewed the lid for him so that he could draw out his punishment.

"Read it aloud, Jamie," she instructed.

Jamie unfolded the piece of paper and read, "You decide how to make things right."

Jamie, squinted his brown eyes, and his lips turned down in a decisive frown. "Miss, Lewis, this ain't a fair consequence," he complained. "How am I supposed to know what to do for dressing a pig up like a baby? Who did I hurt anyways?"

"Who did you hurt, Jamie? Now think about it for a minute."

"Ah, Miss Lewis, I can't rightly say that I hurt nobody. Give me a clue."

"Who suffered because a small riot almost broke out in the classroom?"

"Nobody that I could see. Everyone was having fun. I thought Mary and Laura were going to bust a gusset cause they were laughing so hard."

"Think about it a minute, Jamie. Did we cover as many pages in our math books as we usually do?"

"Well, come to think about it, we only covered three today and we usually cover four."

"So who was wronged?"

"I guess we was, Miss Lewis, on account of we didn't learn near as much."

"So, how can you right this wrong of not enough learning, Jamie?"

"Ah, Miss Lewis, give a guy a break. I don't know any way to do that. Come on. How about giving a guy a hint!"

"Well, what do you think about staying after school an extra half hour for two weeks? One week you will tutor Richie on his math assignments–he's really struggling–and the next week you will help me tutor Stacy on her spelling skills. She has a hard time even spelling cat and dog correctly. If the tutoring doesn't take quite a half hour, you can help me write math problems on the board, giving me bonus time to teach more effectively. That way, you will be helping with the learning of all your classmates, and that will go a long way towards righting your wrong. We might even be able to help you with your English skills. I don't think you realize how badly you're murdering the King's English. What do you think?"

"By golly! I'm no murderer, Miss Lewis, but maybe I could use some help on how I talk. Maybe it'd help me impress the girls! It just might work, and maybe I'll get to figuring better and can spell some of those big words in that there dictionary at the same time. Do we start tomorrow?"

"Restitution starts immediately after school tomorrow, Jamie. Now go home and get your chores done."

As Jamie raced for the door, Lillian's attention was drawn to Billie. He had completed all of his math homework on his slate and was waiting for judgment day to fall upon him.

She could see that somehow Billie was hurting inside, so she placed her hand on his shoulder and began in a soft voice, "Billie, you have been doing so well lately. Every day I have seen consistent improvement in all of your studies. Why did you decide to disrupt the entire class today with that dreadful rat?"

Billie hung his head as he quietly said, "I don't rightly know, Miss Lewis. Things haven't been exactly peachy at home lately. Ever since the dance Pa has hardly said one word to me. He has talked a lot in sign language ever since Ma died, but ever since the dance it's been worse than ever. He just drags around the place and acts a lot like when we lost Ma and the time that our old hound Duster died. I don't know what's bothering him, but it must be something bad. I've never seen him have the blues so fierce. I guess I thought bringing the rat would liven things up for the class and for me too. It's as if happiness drowned itself in our old well and has gone to the great beyond."

"Your father hasn't told you what's bothering him, Billie?"

"No, like I said, I haven't been able to get him to say anything. Ever since the dance, he just sits and stares out the window, but I can tell by his eyes that he's really not seeing anything out there. This morning I caught him with his head in his hands, and he hadn't even bothered to fix us breakfast."

"Do you think your problems with your father entitle you to disrupt the schooling of the whole class?"

"Well, if you put it that way, no."

"Can you see why you need to draw from the consequence jar?"

"Well, like you told Jamie, I did let the learning run amuck when I swung that rat across the window."

Lillian brought the consequence jar to Billie and had him pull out a strip.

Billie unfolded the paper and read aloud, "Find someone in town who is in need of your help. Help this person for six hours."

A smile spread over Billie's face. "That's easy! Old Marty Smith at the livery broke his leg two days ago. I could go and help him with the horses and stuff. I saw him hobbling around on crutches trying to feed the horses before I came to school. That all right with you, Miss Lewis?"

"Marty does need some help. Can you put in an hour tonight before you go home?"

"Sure can, Miss Lewis."

"Have Marty sign a paper each day telling me when you came and when you left. When the six hours are completed, bring the paper to me, and you are released from this punishment. And, Billie, keep me posted on your Dad. See if you can determine what's bothering him."

As Billie raced for the door, he had to rush past a black-clad figure. When Lillian's blue eyes met the visitor's smoldering green ones, her heart began to pound in her chest. Taking up almost the entire doorway and staring at her intensely stood the sheriff of Frisco in all his black glory, complete with a pistol on each hip.

Today his blonde hair was tied back in a neat ponytail, and his trimmed mustache and clean clothes made it clear that he had paid special attention to his physical appearance.

A large smile broke out on a usually stern face to show two rows of perfect, white teeth. "Afternoon, Miss Lewis. Thought I'd stop by to see if you'd like an escort home. Lots of disturbance in the streets today. I'm thinking you might feel safer walking home if you had the law for company."

How am I going to get out of this? fretted Lillian. The last thing she wanted to do right now was walk home with this fearsome man and have all the eyes of Frisco looking in her direction. His flaming green eyes told her that he wasn't going to take no for an answer.

Then a loud "hee haw" resounded through the chilly December air. *Ned, Mabel, Lizzy! Thank you, dear Lord, for sending the troops to my aid!* "If you'll excuse me, Sheriff, it appears that I have company outside. Pardon me for just a moment."

Throwing on her coat, Lillian rushed past the sheriff to greet her rescuers. Lizzy and Mabel would not shut up their caterwauling until she had given each furry head a kiss and a hug. Ned had to wait for his hug until the mules quieted, satisfied that their dear friend still loved them.

"I'm headed to Milford, then Beaver, Little Missy. I've got to pick up some supplies for The Mercantile. Just wanted to say goodbye and let you know that I'll only be gone a little over a week."

From the corner of her eye, Lillian could see Sheriff Phillips leave the schoolhouse and come to stand by the wagon. Mabel started a ruckus again, and Lillian and Ned were startled to see that the sheriff was standing by Mabel's tail. Mabel's hind foot was pawing the earth, and her eyes were beginning to glass over with something akin to rage! It was clear that Sheriff Phillips was not only in the wrong place, but also that Mabel seemed to detest his very presence.

Ned took quick action. First he rubbed Mabel's ears, then he talked to her in soothing tones. When Mabel stopped pawing the ground, he addressed the sheriff. "As long as you're here, Sheriff, I'd like you to check this load of ore that I'm taking to the assayer in Beaver. I'd like your opinion on whether it's loaded properly."

As Sheriff Phillips followed Ned to the back of the wagon, Mabel kicked so high that she almost flicked her right ear with her hoof.

Lillian breathed a sigh of relief. The sheriff had no idea how close he had come to becoming flat as a fritter. She knew he would never have forgiven being slammed into the schoolhouse wall by a pair of flying hooves.

"Woah, Mabel!" Ned softly cautioned his precious critter.

"That mule is a lethal weapon. Better keep her away from me," barked the sheriff.

"Can't imagine what got her all riled up," apologized Ned, placing his hand over his mouth, pretending to cough, but really hiding a smile that was aching for a chance to escape.

"Your freight's loaded just fine. But maybe you need an extra rope around the end here. I'd hate to have all of this ore spilling out onto the street. It'd be a real mess to clean up."

Thoughts of escape entered Lillian's mind when the rope was mentioned. Jumping up on the wagon seat she explained, "The extra rope is a good idea, Ned. Why don't you take me home, and Nettie and I will lend you an old one that we have. I need to talk to you about some things on the way." As Ned jumped up on the seat beside her, she whispered under her breath, "Get me out of here quick."

The sheriff of Frisco was left to close the schoolhouse door as he watched the retreating wagon carrying his prize further away from him. He kicked at the snow and clenched his fists as a rough word escaped from his tightened lips.

At the shanty, Lillian asked Ned to come in for a few minutes. "You going to be all right, Little Missy? Looks like that black demon has a hankering to get to know you better."

"I'm going to be fine, Ned. Maybe if I don't give him any encouragement, he'll just give up."

"And hell isn't murky! You've got to start watching your step around that one cause givin' up just ain't part of his nature."

They said their goodbyes. When Ned left, Lillian sat down with her *Book of Mormon* and tried to find some comfort and peace in its pages. As she read, pictures of Charles kept entering her mind–Charles holding her on the dance floor, her hand held tightly to his heart; pictures of a work-worn hand that had refused to release her small one at the Thanksgiving table;

and pictures of Christmas mistletoe and a soft kiss that had sent her senses reeling.

She knew that events over the past month had changed her feelings for Charles. As much as she didn't want to care for this exasperating man, she found herself very concerned about his well-being and what was bothering him.

She bowed her head as she prayed, "Heavenly Father, please show me the way to help Charles and Billie. Charles appears to be hurting badly, and his pain is affecting his son. Give them peace, and Heavenly Father, please help me to deal with Sheriff Phillips."

Chapter 21

The Saturday before the Christmas program, Lillian found herself on the way to The Mercantile. She needed to purchase decorations for the Christmas tree that Ben Johnson had dropped by last night. He seemed to be finding excuses to drop by almost daily, and it wasn't unusual for him to enjoy supper with her and Nettie at least twice a week. Anyone who had any sense could tell that Nettie and Ben were becoming very attached to each other. Lillian was happy for her dear friend, but she couldn't help but wonder where she would be staying if they really got serious about one another.

The sun shone brightly on the pristine white snow that had blanketed Frisco the night before. The Mormon tea bushes and the sagebrush looked like large balls of cotton as they glistened in the bright sunshine. Somehow the snow's whiteness seemed to have washed away the lawlessness of the community–with the help of Sheriff Phillips.

Business had become so lucrative for the Death Wagon ever since the sheriff's arrival, that he had assigned one of his deputies the task of driving it each night so that he could get some sleep. The saloons were even quiet this afternoon. The music issuing from their doors seemed to be muted and less lively.

As Lillian looked at the mine entrance, located a short distance above the town beneath a hill, she could see that shifts for the mine were changing. The men changing shifts were quieter than usual. Those who had finished their shift appeared to be headed home for some much-needed rest. Before Sheriff Phillips came, these same men would have headed for the saloons to celebrate the end of a work day with cards and whiskey. *That sheriff has definitely made a difference; then why do I wish Frisco had never seen him,* Lillian thought. *Thank heavens he's been too busy with that rough Reno bunch that rolled in last week to bother me. They were definitely incorrigible characters.*

As she opened the door of The Mercantile, she saw that it was full of customers who were happily engaged in their Christmas shopping. Her pulse quickened when she saw Charles in the west corner of the store, looking intently at something in the jewelry case. The old slouch hat was pulled down over his face, but she would have known that hat and the man underneath it anywhere. He looked even more thin and lanky this morning. *Are you eating properly?* she asked herself.

She began gathering up the decorations for the tree, but kept Charles in sight through the corner of her eye. He asked the proprietor to take something out of the jewelry case, then a few seconds later paid for it and shoved the small package in his coat pocket. When he turned to leave, his eyes met hers, and a pained look came over his face. He lowered his head and hurriedly left the store without saying a word or giving her another glance.

The pain on Charles's face seemed to transfer itself to Lillian's chest. As she watched his retreating figure, her thoughts ran wild. *What have I done to you to make you act this way? Why haven't you spoken to me since the dance? I got upset with you when you spoke roughly to me, but this indifference is much worse!*

Thoughts like these just seemed to worsen the pain, so Lillian tried to clear her head of thoughts of Charles as she paid for the decorations and headed home to the shanty.

The hot stew and warm cornbread that Nettie had made them for lunch did little to cheer Lillian's spirits. When Ben Johnson came to help them decorate the tree, Lillian just couldn't get in a festive mood. She decided to leave them alone with the excuse that she needed to get to the dance hall to get ready for her play's dress rehearsal. The play was scheduled to be performed this coming Monday, the day that school would let out for the holidays. She had decided to hold the play in the dance hall because the school was too small to accommodate all the relatives and townspeople who would want to attend. Plus, the pump organ in the hall could be used to accompany the songs and dances in the production.

As she opened the door, her gaze fell upon the stage, ordinarily used by the orchestra at the dances. It extended the full length of the front of the dance hall and was raised two feet, the perfect height to enable parents and relatives to comfortably see the production. When the children came, she would instruct them to move the benches from the sides of the hall to form even rows in the center with plenty of walking room on the sides and an aisle down the middle.

Lillian gathered wood from the pile outside and started a fire in the potbellied stove. She startled herself by saying out loud, "Charles, why didn't you think about starting a fire before the dress rehearsal began," but then rationalized that the dance hall wasn't Charles's responsibility, and maybe Billie hadn't told him about the Saturday practice. *Enough thoughts about Charles,* she cautioned herself as she moved props around the stage to get ready for the dress rehearsal.

She straightened the calico curtains, which hung on ropes at the back of the stage and also its sides. The curtains, which had been added to the dance hall stage by Lillian and the children, were designed to hide the actors when they were not performing. The area to the left of the stage, nicknamed "the pit" by her students, was framed with hay bales, making a makeshift music pit for the organist and the fiddlers. The front bales proudly displayed the United States and Utah Territorrial State flags.

Just as Lillian finished straightening the curtains, Mrs. Reese, the dance hall organist and piano player for the Silver Dollar Saloon, entered the room and seated herself at the organ.

Tim and Keith Summerville followed her, carrying their prized fiddles, taking their places in the hay-enclosed music pit.

This cheerful threesome had volunteered to provide the music for the play, and as Lillian looked at them in their western attire, she thought that they provided a vivid splash of color in this often drab and colorless mining town. It was clear that Mrs. Reese was taking time off from her job at the saloon. She had a bright pink, feather boa around her neck, and her plump body was stuffed into a silk dress, which was adorned with sequins. A colorful feather headpiece matched the boa on the dress and jiggled, along with her sizeable belly, as she swayed her head in time with the music.

I must remind myself to mention to her that she has got to dress sensibly for the real performance, Lillian thought. Tim and Keith sported white ten gallon hats, chaps, bright blue neckerchiefs, and bright red, homespun shirts. *They will do just fine. No need to talk to them,* Lillian reasoned.

The play would begin with Laura reading a narrative about the Pilgrims and that first Thanksgiving. The narrative would include the love story of Priscilla and John Alden, and this first segment would conclude with a lively dance from the two lovers. Mary and Curt, who portrayed Priscilla and John, had been practicing long hours on this particular dance. They had natural rhythm, and since they had a special friendship, they moved in perfect unity to create a lively, attention-getting beginning for the play.

Lillian had barely finished setting up the Thanksgiving table and the dried sheaves of wheat and corn when the children descended on her. Enthusiasm seemed to ooze from every pore in their bodies, and Clarence, Richie, Jamie, and Billie, who had come dressed in full headdresses and bright war paint, acted like they were on the warpath. They ran around the room in a circle with their hands moving back and forth over their mouths, simulating blood-curdling cries of Indians gearing up for a battle.

"Calm down, boys! You're supposed to be peaceful Indians.. I don't want to see war paint on you Monday night!"

"Ah, Miss Lewis, can't we have just a little fun?" begged Jamie.

"This is the final rehearsal, Jamie. It's got to be dead serious. Now, students, take your places behind the curtain and ..."

Suddenly all attention was drawn to the doorway as loud crying and sobs reverberated throughout the room. In the doorway stood Mary, a pitiful sight to behold. Tears ran down the sides of both cheeks, and her blond hair hung limply about her ravaged face. It was apparent that she had been crying for some time because her eyes were red and swollen. She was moving towards her teacher on crutches, using only her left leg. Her right leg was strapped with splints and hung limply, apparently not capable of holding her weight.

Mary's lips quivered as she managed to sob out, "Miss Lewis, I'm so sorry, but I've broken my right leg. I was throwing hay down from the top of the barn this morning for the horses when I got this idea to use my umbrella to sail from the top of the barn to the corral. I was sure that the umbrella and the strong wind that was blowing would glide me down gracefully, just like a feather, and land me safely on the ground. Well, I ran and got the umbrella and without a second thought, I opened it and jumped. Ahhhhh, Miss Lewis, I didn't glide at all! I fell faster than a dead albatross and landed like a brick on the hard dirt of the corral. When I looked at my right leg, I really started to bawl because it hurt like the holy dickens, and it was twisted at a weird angle. Dad heard me a bawling and came a runnin'. He just shook his head, took me in his arms, and told me it was broke for sure. He set it and put these splints and bandages on it, but there's no way I'm going to be better by Monday night. I won't be able to dance with Curt. You've got a lame Priscilla on your hands, and I'm so sorry. I wanted to do that dance more than anything in the world." A new flood of tears began, and Lillian felt tears starting to form in her own eyes.

As she looked at the faces of the other children, she could see that they were also close to tears. *Oh, Heavenly Father, they've worked so hard. Why does this have to happen now?* Lillian put her arm around Mary and sat her down carefully in a front row seat. "It's all right, Mary, I'll figure something out. Maybe Melissa can be Priscilla, and you can be a crippled Pilgrim."

Mary pulled Lillian's head down and whispered in her ear, "But, Miss Lewis, you know Melissa is too shy to be the center of attention. She's liable to just stand there like a frozen statue and stare at the audience."

Lillian placed her arm around Mary. "Its okay, Mary. We may have to cut the dance out altogether if Melissa gets too scared."

And so the rehearsal began with Mary sobbing and crying throughout the entire Pilgrim presentation. When it came to Priscilla and John Alden's dance, Melissa just stood in the middle of the stage with tears rolling down her eyes saying softly, "I can't. I can't!"

Lillian glanced at Laura, Stacy, and Jessica. She walked to where they were sitting and knelt in front of them so that she could look them directly in the eyes. "Do one of you three think you can handle the part of Priscilla?" All three girls shook their heads vigorously.

The room was filled with long faces and silence. Billie hung his head and said, "Ah, Miss Lewis, this is terrible. The dance was a swell way to start the program."

As gloom and doom descended on the small acting troop, the unthinkable happened.

Mary yelled "Whoopie" as she threw her crutches in the air, hurriedly unwrapped the bandages, and threw away the splints. Gathering up the bandages, she encircled her head with them so that they resembled an Indian turban, then sprinted to the stage. Her tear-ravaged eyes were now twinkling and full of pure delight. She was giggling so hard that every inch of her body was literally shaking. She grabbed Curt by the hands and said, "Let's show them how to dance, Curt baby. After all, the performance is Monday night. Wouldn't want to disappoint the audience now, would we?"

Lillian's eyes widened in disbelief, then she found herself screaming, "Mary, you rascal! You hoodwinked all of us! I could shake you till your teeth rattle." Then the entire room was filled with laughter, and total chaos reigned for a few minutes. Curt was laughing so hard that he was doubled over, then he sank to the stage and just lay there, convulsed with merriment, letting the hilarity of the moment take over.

Lillian was shaking with laughter, but she controlled herself long enough to get up on the stage, kneel by Mary, and take her by both shoulders. She got her complete attention by getting within inches of her face as dark blue eyes met light blue ones.

"Mary, you gave all of us the scare of our lives. Don't you ever do that again or I swear I'll make you draw every consequence out of the jar and make good every single punishment. Do you know how much pain and suffering you have caused all of us by your little prank?"

"Ah, Miss Lewis, I really didn't think it would get this far. You're all pretty gullible, ya know. You just sat there and drunk in the part about the umbrella and jumping from the barn. Do you really think I would have done something that foolish?"

"Well, Mary, I've seen you stage President Lincoln's funeral in front of the superintendent of schools with not so much as a glimmer of a smile on your face. That wasn't necessarily a sane action."

"I know, Miss Lewis. I've done wrong, but sometimes these ideas come into my brain and there's nothin' I can do to shake them out. I tried to tell them to go away and leave me be, but the thoughts had me in their grasp, and then I saw grandpa's crutches in the barn and there was no help for what happened next. Sorry, I promise to dance extra special Monday night."

"Well, I guess there's no real harm done, but if you ever pull another stunt like that, I won't be able to control my anger.

Who knows, I might take you up on top of your barn with that umbrella and see if you really can fly." Lillian pulled one of her most fearsome faces, and Mary pretended to be terribly frightened.

The rest of the rehearsal went smoothly, and after giving her students final instructions, the dance hall door was thrown open and was quickly filled with a line of excited children, wildly racing for home. Lillian stepped to the door to watch their retreating figures and was surprised to see Charles approaching in a wagon. When he reached the door of the dance hall, he ducked his head, causing the large brim of his hat to hide his face, and motioned for Billie to get up on the seat.

He lifted his head for just a second, giving Lillian a view of two tortured eyes, and then without a word, he shook the reins to signal the team that it was time for them to go. Lillian could have just imagined it, but before he turned his head, she could have sworn that his lips trembled slightly.

Billie looked back and waved as the team started down Main Street, "Goodbye, Miss Lewis! I can't wait until Monday! We're going to wow em!"

The way it looks, you might just as well give up on Charles Anderson and wipe all thoughts of him out of your mind, thought Lillian as she locked the dance hall door and started towards the shanty. The strong scent of lavender caused her to stop in her tracks as a familiar soft, gentle voice flowed sweetly through her brain. *Lillian, you've never given up on anything in your life. Don't give up on Charles. It is now that he needs you the most.*

Shaken to her very core by the familiar voice and the prompting, Lillian said out loud, "No, I won't give up, but please, Heavenly Father, show me the way to help Billie and Charles."

She stopped by the shanty window and smiled at the picture that met her gaze. Nettie and Ben were dancing around the Christmas tree, gazing into each other's eyes. Their eyes told Lillian that as far as Nettie and Ben were concerned, at this moment, they were the only two people in Frisco. She took care to make a lot of noise when she opened the door to warn them of her coming. Looking into their excited faces, she knew that not only was Christmas coming, but that the holiday spirit had brought love with it.

Chapter 22

The sun seemed to shine just a little brighter Monday morning, signaling that it was indeed a momentous day for Lillian and the students of the Frisco School. They met at the dance hall and spent most of the day going over their parts one last time and getting last minute instructions from Lillian on how to polish up their masterpiece.

A minor disaster occurred when Stacy and Jessica disagreed on a segment of the Indian dance. Both girls felt that they had a right to direct the dance since they both performed solos in it. Stacy insisted that they were to turn three times in a circle while stomping their feet to the rhythm of the drums, and Jessica insisted that they were only to turn twice. The argument got so heated that Stacy pulled Jessica's braids, causing her sister to scream hysterically and large tears to run like rivers down her pink cheeks. Then Jessica totally lost it, as she grabbed the feather out of Stacy's headband and threw it in the air. When it landed on the stage, she stomped on it, destroying some of its fluffiness as she glared defiantly at her sister. Through her tears, Stacy screamed, "You always have to be right, don't you? Last night you said it was my turn to churn the butter, and it was really yours!"

"Was not, Miss Perfect!" sobbed Jessica.

The girls were moving towards each other with clenched fists when Lillian stepped in between them and quietly said, "You are the two most important members of this dance. You can't argue and do your best job. Besides, those tears running down your face ruin your good looks, and we can't have you looking ugly tonight. Now give each other a hug and let's finish your dance. And, for your information, it's two turns."

Stacy and Jessica reluctantly gave each other a hug, then performed their dance so exuberantly that following the last step the boys yelled, cheered, and clapped as they stood, treating all the girls to a standing ovation. Wide smiles covered the girl's faces as they ran to hug their teacher. "What a marvelous performance!" Lillian praised. "I'm glad that you didn't let opening night jitters spoil one of the best parts of the program."

When every segment of the play had been practiced over and over so that it ran like a well-oiled machine, Lillian sat her students down and reminded them of their refreshment assignments. A large table had been set up in the back of the room for punch and all sorts of cookies and cakes.

"Mom's sending her special fruit cake," said Richie, but if you eat it, plan on rolling out of here because it's loaded with butter."

"Mom's coming with her homemade eggnog. She only makes it at Christmas, but dad says that she has to leave out the secret ingredient because children will be drinking it," bragged Curt.

"I'm sure that everything you bring will be delicious. Now don't forget to be here by 6:30 at the latest so that we can start the program promptly at seven," reminded Lillian.

After the students left, she spent the remaining time straightening up the room and arranging the chairs for the audience. She was too nervous and too busy to leave, so shortly before anyone arrived, she straightened her hair in the mirror that hung in the foyer and washed her face and hands in the basin at the front of the room. She pinched her cheeks to give them added color, and as she was drawing some deep breaths, the students started to arrive, and she busied herself with last minute makeup and costume alterations.

She was pricked with curiosity when she saw Laura intently talking to each member of the cast individually. Laura shook hands with each cast member as if she were sealing a pact. If Lillian hadn't been so busy getting everyone ready, she would have taken time to get close enough to Laura to eavesdrop and find out just what the mischievous redhead was up to now, but there wasn't a minute to spare.

Ten minutes before the performance, she made her students stand in back of the calico curtain until they were ready to start the play. She threatened them with their lives if they didn't behave. The ten-minute wait was difficult for some hooligans; however, and she saw a boot she recognized as Jamie's kicking at a boot that she had often seen Billie wear. Muffled cuss words resulted, and she had to step in back of the curtain to enforce the peace.

Since it wouldn't do to yell in front of the audience, she grabbed Jamie and Billie each by an ear, made them face her and look her in the eyes, then made a fearsome face that would have sent a mountain lion running. The boys settled some, but quieted immediately when Lillian placed Laura and Mary in between them.

Removing her pocket watch from her skirt pocket, Lillian faced her students and pointed at the watch, signaling that it was two minutes before seven and almost time to start the performance.

When Lillian stepped through the curtains, she saw a deluge of people streaming through the doors, filling up the seats rapidly. On the front row, sat Superintendent McNaught, dressed in a somber black suit. Seated beside him was a sour-faced lady who must certainly be his wife. *Boy I'm glad I saved him two seats. I hope there's something in this play to make that old persimmon wife of his smile,* Lillian told herself.

Lillian spotted Sheriff Phillips standing at the back door, making sure that there were no disturbances at this gathering. When he caught her glace, his face broke out in a wide grin, and as if he were the only gentleman in the room, he tipped his hat in her direction. A dirty slouch hat and brown beard drew Lillian's attention. Charles was sitting on the second from the last row by Ben Johnson and Nettie. Lillian hoped for a glance or some sign of recognition, but he quietly stared straight forward, and his lips were set in a firm line, making it impossible for a smile to intrude.

When Lillian made her way to the center of the stage, the crowd hushed in respect for the Frisco teacher who had made such an impact on their children's lives.

Lillian stood a mere 5 feet 2 inches, but there was nothing small about the voice that announced, "The Frisco School is now proud to present 'Glimpses from History.' Please help us begin our play by standing and singing 'My Country 'Tis of Thee.'"

Mrs. Reese, who had dressed in somber clothes for the occasion, gave a powerful introduction on the organ, and Tim and Keith joined in with their fiddles as the audience began to sing. The sound that resulted was so full of patriotism that it brought tears to Lillian's eyes. Everyone in the audience seemed to feel the spirit, for the longer the song continued the more resonate and powerful it became. More than one eye blinked back moisture as Lillian motioned for them to take their seats at the song's conclusion.

When the crowd was seated, Lillian announced, "The Frisco School now presents 'Glimpses from History.'" She then took her seat on a chair below the left side of the stage where she could direct her students.

The calico curtains parted, and Laura Johnson in all her Pilgrim splendor entered center stage. There was confidence in her green eyes, brought about by hours of practice when she had carefully memorized and polished her role. She was one of the writers of the production, and the narration she was about to read was her own creation.

"I would like to have been there on that day– December 21, 1620. When the Pilgrims landed at Plymouth Rock to begin our mighty nation.

"Faith, morality, education and law, and let's not forget freedom were a vital part of their Pilgrim creed, giving strength to this new country.

"John Alden, hired to repair the Mayflower, was the first to step ashore. And the last of those original Pilgrims to return to his Heavenly home.

"He courted Priscilla Mullens and though he spoke for Miles Standish, Priscilla urged him to speak for himself and soon they both were married.

"Let's share in the joy of these newlyweds on their first day of wedded bliss. They'll dance for us, show their happiness, and end it all with a kiss."

Laura's eyes glistened as she left the stage and Mary and Curt entered from center stage and took the beginning pose that signaled the beginning of their dance.

Tim and Keith struck up a lively tune unlike anything ever heard in Frisco. Mrs. Reese joined in on the organ. The bows were streaks of motion moving across the fiddles, and Mrs. Reese was pushing the two pedals of the organ so fast that it was a wonder smoke didn't erupt from the tops of her high top boots. It was an original piece composed by the three musicians that set feet to tapping, hands to clapping, and pure joy resonating from every face in the audience.

The audience had expected a courtly minuet or maybe even a cotillion, but what they were witnessing was so innovative and creative that it produced pure wonderment and excitement throughout their very beings.

Mary and Curt were dancing a jig–a dance that they had choreographed themselves. The dance contained many complex steps and improvisations that wowed the crowd and flushed more than one cheek in the audience. They were kicking, jumping, twirling, and circling so fast that their faces were often just blurs. But when their faces did become visible, they were a pure delight to behold. Curt and Mary's faces weren't just smiling; they were showing excitement, wonderment, surprise, and pure unadulterated joy. At one point Mary pulled away from Curt and dancing all the time, shook her finger at him, giving him a piece of her mind as she set her mouth in a pout. Curt grabbed Mary, knelt and pulling her down on his knee, gave her a sound paddling, all in rhythm with the music.

The men in the audience went wild. They simply loved it. One loud voice screamed, "Show her who's boss, Curt." Another yelled, "Way to put her in her place."

Then Curt pulled Mary to her feet, took her head in his hands, and gave her a kiss that resounded throughout the entire hall. Suddenly they were off again, doing even more intricate steps than before, and when the music ended, they bowed to the audience and then danced off stage.

Suddenly everyone was on their feet for a standing ovation. Lillian was overwhelmed. She had witnessed performances before when the crowd had booed and hissed at the performers. She had even been in one audience where a full scale riot had erupted, but a standing ovation–this was something that she had not expected.

The music continued for a few minutes while the students dressed back stage for the spotlight on Davy Crocket.

After two minutes of the best toe-tapping music in the West, five buckskin clad frontiersmen, with coonskin caps atop their heads, appeared on stage. Chuckles filtered from the audience as they realized that the tails on the caps were black and white skunk pelts that had been fashioned into tails. Eyes shining, each young man took their turn saying something about the legendary Crockett.

Such phrases as "Davy Crockett stands for the spirit of the American Frontier," and "He left home at a young age to escape a licking from his dad" were part of the narrative. Then the narrative became filled with familiar quotes from Davy such as "That bear was a rip snorter!" and "That would be like singing psalms to a dead horse." At the end of the segment, each student told some tall tale about the frontiersman that was passed around following his death. "Davy could wrestle tornadoes," and "It wasn't unusual to see Davy riding lightning bolts" brought loud chuckles from the audience.

As the young frontiersman exited right stage, the ladies marched on the stage, holding their women's suffrage signs. Curt read the short narrative on Susan B. Anthony, then the girls left the stage and circled the room waving their "Give Women the Vote," and "Down with Whiskey and Beer" signs. The vibrations from the girls' chants filled the room. Lillian had never heard them chant before with such feeling and vocal strength. Suddenly the men in the audience were on their feet, yelling at the marchers. "Put them darned women in their place," one screamed, and another yelled, "A woman's place is in the kitchen making my supper!" Still another screamed, "I'd rather let my mule Tilly vote than my wife!"

The girls kept marching, but their chant softened just a little. It was then that the women in the audience came to life. Wives jumped to their feet and pulled, pushed, and shoved their husbands down in their chairs and forcibly held them there. When one man did succeed in getting up, his wife grabbed him and twisted his nose until he sat down, then she plopped on his lap. Since the wife weighed well over 200 pounds, it was for certain that this particular husband wasn't going to rise again.

The girls quickly marched to the stage and hid themselves behind the curtain. Since utter pandemonium seemed to rule, Lillian rushed to the center of the stage and held her two hands up, a gesture that she wanted the crowd's attention.

When a hush fell over the crowd, Lillian announced, "Keep in mind that we are merely presenting glimpses in history. This is no place to voice your dislike of any historic event that we depict. If the crowd cannot watch respectfully from now on, this production is over, and if you men don't behave, I can promise you that you won't be eating supper for at least a week!"

A large yell of jubilation from the women filled the air. Then a black-clad lawman circled the audience with his hands on his two revolvers. No one wanted to question this Frisco demon, so silence descended immediately, a signal to Lillian that the law was on her side. She hoped that it wasn't just fear that had restored order and that part of the reason for the silence was that the audience really was enjoying the production and didn't want to see it end.

President Lincoln's assassination and funeral was a huge success. When the funeral entourage circled the audience singing "Amazing Grace" and Curt sat up in the coffin to belt out "Who saved a wretch like me," the laughter which resulted was so ear-shattering that it threatened to blow out the walls in the dance hall. When the funeral entourage lined up on the stage to give their final bows, new laughter erupted as Curt stepped from the coffin to bow with his fellow actors.

Custer, Sitting Bull, and the intricate dances by the soldiers and Indians also drew thunderous applause from the audience. Jessica and Stacy literally beamed, and their faces became flushed when they received a standing ovation at the end of the Indian dance that they had choreographed.

Where has the time gone? Lillian thought. It's time for our last glimpse into history. She had chosen the founding of Frisco on purpose, knowing that this history glimpse would be the most appreciated segment of the program.

Billie and Jamie portrayed James Ryan and Samuel Hawkes as they entered stage left and stopped by a large rock that had been moved from the back of the curtain to the center of the stage to represent the limestone outcropping where the silver was first discovered. Jamie started chipping away at the rock when the unthinkable happened. Billie was standing close to the rock, and on the third swing of the pick, the pick missed the rock and somehow found itself hooked to Billie's pants. Billie wasn't aware that he had been snagged and attempted to move away from the rock at the same time that Jamie tried to remove the pick. A loud ripping sound signaled the fact that the pick had ripped Billy's pants down the middle, leaving his red flannel underwear exposed for the entire audience to see. The roar of laughter from the audience caused a sea of red to move from the boys' necks to their foreheads.

Lillian wanted to crawl in a hole and stay there until this was all over and forgotten, but Jamie and Billie went on with the sketch as if nothing had happened.

"Whoopie! Look at this silver!" Screamed Jamie. "Why it's so soft I can cut it with my knife!"

"Whoopie is right!" yelled Billie as he went on to ad lib, "This is my last pair of trousers, and now that we're going to be rich, I need you to ride into Milford and get me another pair right now, cause I got a date with Maybell tonight, and her pa won't take kindly to me going to her house in my red undies!"

More laughter from the audience showed that this was the audience's type of humor, and the boys finished the sketch in grand style, red underwear and all.

When Jamie and Billie exited center stage to yet another standing ovation from the crowd, Lillian found that she could quit holding her breath and breathe freely. Then suddenly her eyes flew open and once again her breathing stopped.

A blur suddenly streaked from behind the curtain at center stage. It couldn't be–but it certainly was–Laura was riding an imaginary steed and using an invisible whip to get her horse up to maximum speed. Sitting on top of her red curls was a strange headpiece that could have passed for a Colonial hat if the onlooker used his imagination. Drawing from every ounce of power that she had stored in her young body she bellowed, "The British are coming! The British are coming!" She jumped from the stage and began to circle the audience, sounding the warning over and over. The audience became convinced that Paul Revere was alive and well as Laura circled the audience twice, sounding the famous warning.

Why would she do something like this? Lillian anguished. *This isn't part of our program!* At the end of Laura's second revolution, she abruptly stopped in front of the superintendent and his wife, grabbed Mr. McNaught by both cheeks and gave him a kiss on his forehead that resounded throughout the entire hall. Laura didn't stop to gaze into the superintendent's amazed face but turned and raced though the curtains at the back of the stage.

Lillian sat there with her mouth wide open, wondering if she would have a job come Monday morning, when the superintendent rose to his feet and began clapping enthusiastically. His wife joined him, followed by a standing ovation from the entire audience.

Lillian couldn't contain her joy. She, too, began clapping enthusiastically. She suddenly realized that everyone in the hall thought that Paul Revere was a planned part of the program. As she wiped the moisture from her forehead, she thought, *Thank heavens I still have a job and don't have to wring Laura's neck.*

As the clapping continued, all the children were suddenly on the stage, giving their final bows. When cries of "teacher" filled the hall, Lillian joined her students as they all held hands for one final bow. Suddenly, laughter mixed in with the clapping. Lillian looked at the line of bowing students to see what had once again tickled everyone's funny bone. What she saw made her join the audience in hearty laughter. Billie had removed his ripped pants, leaving him in his red altogethers. Instead of bowing with his front to the audience, he was bowing to the backstage curtain so that his backside was facing the audience, showing off the button panel of his red flannel underwear to its best advantage. He swung his backside from side to side as he bowed, adding to the comic effect.

The applause and laughter seemed to go on forever, but when Lillian motioned for the crowd to take their seats, they eventually obeyed and gave her their attention. "Thank you all for coming," she announced. "Please feel free to enjoy the refreshments on the tables at the back of the hall. Some of the best cooks in Frisco have outdone themselves this evening, supplying delectable treats just for your enjoyment."

While the audience busied themselves with the refreshments, Lillian turned to see Laura gathering something from each member of the cast. Laura was grinning broadly, and her classmates seemed to be reluctant to part with whatever it was they were slipping in her hand.

"Laura, whatever are you doing?" asked Lillian.

"I won the bet, Miss Lewis. They didn't believe that I would do the Paul Revere bit and kiss the superintendent. They said they'd each pay me a nickel if I finished the dare. As you can see, I am now a wealthy woman." She opened her hand to let Lillian see nine nickels, proof that Laura had indeed won her wager.

"One thing you probably don't know about me, Miss Lewis, is that when someone dares me to do something, I just can't resist the challenge."

Lillian put on one of her stern teacher looks and grabbed Laura by both shoulders. "Well, young lady, if the audience hadn't loved it, you'd be on your way to the consequence jar right now, but I'll have to admit that it was the final touch that made this evening a very special one, and besides, I refuse to give consequences at Christmas time."

As her students gathered around her, she looked each one directly in the eye and said softly, "I am so proud of all of you. Tonight you could have performed on the Broadway Stage and brought the audience to their feet to show their appreciation. Now, go and enjoy the treats and have a Merry Christmas." Each student in turn came to give her a hug and a Christmas present that they had made just for her. Billie was the last one to present his gift. Unlike the other gifts, his was not wrapped. He had carved a beautiful antelope. The intricacy of the animal spoke of the many hours that it had taken to fashion.

"Have a Merry Christmas, Miss Lewis," he quietly said.

"Why, you have a Merry Christmas, too, Billie."

Billie looked at the floor, hung his head, and shuffled his feet. "Won't be too happy this year, Miss Lewis. Dad and I are going away early tomorrow morning to work on one of his springs, and we'll be gone until dark. He's been so mean and ornery that he won't even let us have a Christmas tree. Things are so bad at our house that Santa won't even want to stop by

Christmas Eve. Don't know the last time that Pa fixed a decent meal. When Ma was alive, Christmas was special. We used to pull taffy and have all sorts of treats. Dad says I can't even hang up my sock–that it's time I stopped believing in Santa Claus, but you have a Merry Christmas, Miss Lewis. Being in this program has meant a lot to me. Sorry if my red underwear scared the 'Billy be darn' out of you."

Billie left the stage and joined Charles who grabbed his hand and led him to the door, not even giving his son a chance to pick up something from the refreshment table.

Charles Anderson, it's one thing when you are sharp with me, but it's quite another when you spoil your son's Christmas, thought Lillian as a swirl of lavender flooded her senses, reminding her that giving up on Charles was not the answer.

Lillian was taken back to the present as her gaze fell upon a black-clad lawman, who was moving the benches to their proper place at the sides of the room. With the benches back in place, he grabbed a broom and began sweeping up the debris on the floor. He became so exuberant around the refreshment table that his janitorial efforts had the effect of hurrying everyone out the door before a friendly visit with friends and neighbors could take place. The flying broom became more deadly than the revolvers that the sheriff wore on his hips, and many a gentle lady could be seen grabbing her leftover treats, holding her hand over her heart, and rushing her husband out the door while he was still consuming a delectable goodie.

In a matter of just a few minutes, Lillian found herself alone with the dark specter of justice. *Nettie, why did you have to go home with Ben and leave me to fend for myself?* she anguished. The sheriff tipped his hat, smiled, and in a soft, gentle voice that she had never before heard him use he said, "Miss Lewis, this was a delightful evening. I don't know when I have been better entertained. It's cold and blustery outside. Could I please have the pleasure of driving you home in my wagon?"

His gentleness took her by surprise. She couldn't even think of one excuse, even a weak one.

Knowing that she was trapped more securely than a bobcat in a steel vise, she faced two twinkling, green eyes and somewhere in the back of her consciousness heard herself say, "It would be nice to have a ride home, Sheriff."

He helped her turn off the lanterns, then gently helped her on with her coat and carefully wrapped her wool scarf around her neck to ward off the winter chill. When she had locked the door, he lifted her into the wagon and carefully secured a warm blanket around her. He could have entered a manners contest with any first-rate gentleman in the surrounding area and emerged as the winner.

It wasn't until the horses broke into their rhythmic trot that Lillian realized she was riding in the dreaded, "Death Wagon." *How many poor souls that have gone to their eternal reward have made their final journey in this wagon? There's probably dried blood in the back,* she thought, but all thoughts of the dead were wiped from her mind as she realized that her left hand was firmly held in the grasp of Frisco's sheriff. A sideward glance told her that he was driving the team with one hand.

She was about to attempt to take her hand from his when she realized that they had stopped and that he had turned to face her on the seat. The gentle voice so uncharacteristic of him said, "Miss Lewis, I get more enjoyment out of holding your hand than I do out of kissing and dancing with the ladies at the Last Chance Saloon."

Lillian could feel the warm color entering her cheeks. She was finding that Sheriff Phillips had every bit as much charisma as Rudolph Valentino. Before she had time to even consider his startling words, he had pulled her toward him on the wagon seat and kissed her politely on the cheek. Then in just a few seconds, she found her hand released as he leapt from the wagon, encircled her waist with his two large hands, and lifted her to the ground.

At the door of the shanty, he again tipped his hat, gave her that earth-shattering smile, and in that strange, gentle voice said, "Miss Lewis, thanks again for a wonderful evening."

She didn't want to admit it, but there was a strong force that seemed to draw her to this fearsome lawman. As she watched him drive away to begin yet another evening of keeping the peace, Lillian couldn't help but wonder, *how could I be even slightly attracted to that frightful person who stands for everything that I abhor?*

But as Lillian softly opened the door to the shanty, there was no answer to that puzzling question. The lantern was turned down low and Nettie lay fast asleep in her bed, fatigued by the excitement of the evening. Lillian sat on her bed trying to find peace as she read a chapter from the *Book of Mormon*, but long after she had turned off the lantern, sleep eluded her. Every time she started to doze off, laughing green eyes and flashing white teeth would make sleep impossible. Then her thoughts would turn in another direction to a red-haired, freckle-faced boy and the words that remained branded in her brain, "We won't have much Christmas this year, Miss Lewis. Dad won't even let us have a Christmas tree." The scent of lavender filled her senses, telling her exactly what she must do. *Well, Mr. Scrooge Anderson, just you wait! Christmas is coming to your house whether you want it or not!*

Chapter 23

Lillian was awakened from a fitful sleep by the warmth of the sun shining through the shanty window. Nettie was standing at the new stove stirring the breakfast cereal as she quietly hummed a Christmas carol under her breath. When she turned to find Lillian's eyes open and looking in her direction, she jokingly said, "Well, it's about time, sleepyhead. It's eight o'clock, and with just one day before Christmas, there's no time to be a lazy bones. I don't remember you ever sleeping this late since you moved into the shanty. I was asleep last night when you got home. Ben had to get right back to The Southern, and I was so tired that I didn't wait up for you. You must have spent hours cleaning up the dance hall after that program. When I got home, I felt sorry that I didn't stay to help you clean up, but sometimes when I'm around Ben, I lose my senses."

"It's all right, Nettie. I had plenty of help last night, but I'd rather not talk about the source of that help this morning. What I would like to discuss with you is something that I have been thinking about all night long. It's part of the reason why I spent a sleepless night and the reason for my sleeping in this morning."

The spoon stirring the cereal got a rest as Nettie turned to ask, "It can't be last night's program. It was the most entertaining event in Frisco's short history."

"No, it wasn't the program. I'm so proud of all the children."

Nettie put her hands on her hips and wrinkled her brow as she impatiently said, "Well, don't keep me in suspense. Just what is it that has kept you from your sleep?"

Lillian walked to the stove and took the pot of hot cereal and divided it equally between two bowls. Seeing that the perplexed look was still on Nettie's face, she got straight to the point. "For some reason that I can't understand, Charles has decided that there will be no Christmas for Billie and himself this year. Billie told me last night that they weren't even going to have a Christmas tree, and that presents and stockings filled with goodies were out of the question. Charles has taken Billie off for a few days to work on Antelope Springs just west of here. With your help, I want to give them a special Christmas. Are you willing to be a silent partner in Operation Secret Santa?"

Nettie grabbed Lillian's arm. "Oh Lillian, you know how much I love Billie. I'd do anything for him, but we haven't much time, so what do you need me to do?"

"Well, I noticed that Ben had some extra Christmas trees for sale outside of The Southern. Do you think he'll let us have one?"

"Oh, I know he will, and I have some extra ornaments and candles to make it come to life."

Lillian's eyes glowed as she continued, "And you've been baking goodies and making candy all week long. We have much more than we can consume ourselves. Would you like to share? We can just put it on their table, and when they open the door, their eyes will fall on the most glorious Christmas feast that ever tickled their taste buds and warmed their hearts."

Nettie's eyebrows drew together and her eyes began to twinkle. "I have two Christmas stockings that belonged to my husband and son. I haven't wanted to give them away before now, but if they'll make Charles and Billie happy, I think now is the time to give them a new home. We can fill them with homemade candy, and there are some dried apples left from when the Dixie peddler visited me this summer. I think I even kept my son's whistle. I'll never forget how he drove us all crazy the Christmas that he found it in his stocking. It's a wonder that our ear drums were still in tact when bedtime rolled around."

"Charles needs some warm socks," said Lillian, "and I noticed that The Mercantile has some in the front window. I'll get some first thing this morning and place them in his Christmas stocking, along with the candy. And you remember that old slouch hat that Charles always wears? Well, The Mercantile has some brand-spanking new ones that could be the beginning of a whole new Charles Anderson. I've been wanting to rip his old one off and either give it a good washing, or set fire to it. At one point I was so disgusted with its grimy condition that if a stick of dynamite had been available, I'd have blown it to smithereens!"

Laughter filled the shanty's kitchen at the mere thought of pieces of Charles's hat flying in all directions. When the merriment ceased, Lillian continued, " I'd like to sit the new one under the tree in a prominent place, but I wish we had something to put under the tree for Billie."

"Oh, I know just the thing," gushed Nettie–my son's old sled. I haven't had the heart to throw it away or give it to anyone. It's just sitting down in the cellar with the fruit and other food supplies. With a little bit of cleaning up, it'll look good as new."

From that point on, their morning was filled with bustling activity. They both hummed Christmas carols as they went about their work. "There's nothing like making others happy to get that old Christmas spirit burning," said Lillian between humming strains of "Deck the Halls With Boughs of Holly."

It was two hours later before they had everything ready to take to the Anderson shanty. Lillian had made a trip to The Mercantile, and returned with the new hat and socks and a few other items which would be carried to their Christmas destination.

Nettie had dropped off the sled at the Anderson shanty when she went to The Southern to get a Christmas tree from Ben. On her way home, she sat the tree by the sled. The tree stood there straight as a soldier with a jaunty air about it as if to say, "Look at me and this sled! We're the beginning of a Christmas miracle!"

With the tree and sled taken care of, it wasn't a burden for Lillian and Nettie to throw the two large sacks that remained over their shoulders and start off on what they both termed, "Destination Christmas." With the sacks slung over their shoulders, they felt somewhat like the jolly old man himself starting out on his Christmas Eve journey.

When they first swung the door of the shanty open, they were tempted to quickly close it and return home. Never had they seen such disorder and clutter. Dirty dishes were unevenly stacked by the wash bowl, threatening to spill off on the floor at any minute. More dirty dishes filled the makeshift table, and there were dirty clothes lying all over the floor, which from the looks of things hadn't been swept for months. Someone had spilled flour by the cookstove and then stepped in it, tracking white footprints throughout the shanty. The mixture of flour and dirt on the floor would have turned the stomach of the most iron-willed lady.

As Lillian looked at Nettie, she saw that her friend had the look of a deer who is taken by surprise when it is blinded by the light of a lantern.

She saw Nettie swallow hard as she grabbed a bucket of soapy water and made a quick exit as she hurriedly yelled, "You start in here. I'll go outside and work on the sled."

"Coward," Lillian shouted to the closing door.

Softly she gave herself a real pep talk. "Now, this is your idea, Lillian Lewis. If it's going to work, you've got to get bustling!" She drew in deep breaths as she hung up her coat on a nail, rolled up the sleeves of her dress, and faced the mucky mess head on. Without flinching or giving the slightest shudder, she organized the dishes while water was heating on the cookstove. Even though her stomach rebelled when she saw the green water covering the dishes in the wash pan, she removed the dishes, marched to the door, and threw the disgusting contents of the pan onto the white snow. Warm water from the cookstove and strong soap helped her to attack the slimy objects with courage and gusto. In no time at all, the dishes were winking back at her from the cupboards, sparkling and stacked neatly.

I'll take a breather and check on Nettie's progress with the sled, she thought as she donned her coat and exited the shanty, breathing in the fresh, winter air.

When Lillian got to the side of the shanty, Nettie was standing back, admiring her work. The runners of the sled had been washed thoroughly and shined until they sparked and glistened in the winter sun. She had sanded the boards of the sled so that not a spare splinter remained, giving them a smooth, perfected finish. Lillian gave her friend a hug as she praised her efforts. "Nettie, not even a practiced eye could tell this from a brand new one. Why you've even got creative with that red paint I brought from the school. When Billie sees, 'Billie's Lighting Rod' running down the center of the sled, he's liable to have a complete come apart!"

Pleased with themselves, they walked arm in arm into the shanty where more hot water for the general cleaning was starting to steam. While the water heated, Nettie gathered the clothes off the floor and took them to the Chinese Laundry. They didn't have time to do the laundry themselves, and Nettie was sure that the proprietor of the laundry, who was her boss, would be more than willing to wash them at no cost to them if she promised to put in some extra hours.

While Nettie was away at the laundry, Lillian tackled the floor with an old broom that she found in the corner. After 30 minutes of constant sweeping, she smiled and said out loud, "Well, well, there appears to be a wood floor in this shanty. I never would have guessed that when we opened the door."

When Nettie returned, they scrubbed the floor on their hands and knees, then wiped down everything in the entire shanty. After two hours of hard work, there wasn't a speck of dirt to be found in the small room. The sparkle of the windows matched the sparkling eyes of the two good-deed doers.

"I don't believe that this is the same house we entered just a few hours ago," said Nettie.

"Now, for the real fun," said Lillian. "Let's bring in the tree."

The tree was placed in front of the window, and Nettie's extra ornaments and candles soon made it a creation of shimmering beauty. The sled was placed to the side of the tree, and Charles's new hat found a distinguished place beneath the bottom branches, seeming to say to all onlookers, "I'm the latest fashion. Wear me if you dare!"

The stockings, which had been filled with the whistle, socks, and candy, were hung to the sides of the beds at jaunty angles, suspended from nails normally used for coats and mufflers.

In minutes the table became a vision of beauty. Lillian and Nettie placed a beautiful Christmas candle in the middle, surrounded by holly bought at The Mercantile. An apple pie, cookies, bread, roast pheasant and dressing were carefully wrapped and placed around the candle and holly, creating a festive masterpiece. Nettie took a few minutes to return to the laundry and retrieve Billie and Charles's clothes. The dry ones were carefully folded and placed on the bottom of their beds for their owners to put away, and those that were still damp were hung to dry on the makeshift clothesline on the west wall of the shanty.

As they stood back to survey their work, the tiredness that had threatened to overcome them just a few moments before was soon forgotten as the Christmas glow of what they had just accomplished filled them with happiness.

"We've got to get home," said Lillian. "Charles and Billie could come home any time now. We don't want them to find us here when they open that door, no matter how much I'd like to see the looks on their faces."

It was dusk when they started for home. Christmas Eve and the glory of the season shone all around them. The snow-covered peaks of the San Francisco Mountains seemed to take on a special glow all their own as the light pink and salmon sunset flared across the Frisco sky. As they opened the door to their shanty, they paused to look in the direction of the Anderson's home. Charles's wagon was now parked to the side of the shanty, and he was leading his horses to the stable where he lodged them just a few feet away.

"Now that was a close call," sighed Nettie.

Just then a wild "Wahoo!" filled the night. Billie came screaming from the shanty yelling, "Dad, you've got to come and take a look at this. Santa has been here for sure. He left me a real zip zinger of a present! I knew he wouldn't forget."

Tears formed in the eyes of the two young women as they watched father and son enter their shanty. This Christmas had taken on a special meaning for them–one that would remain a warm glow in their memories for many years to come.

Chapter 24

Christmas morning! Nettie and Lillian's eyes opened slowly, and aching muscles kept them from moving at their usual lightning pace. They had worked so fast and furiously yesterday that their muscles were crying out in protest. But soon the air was filled with the delectable smell of Lillian's Christmas muffins, her mother's recipe.

Christmas memories filled her thoughts of past Christmas breakfasts with these very same muffins. She remembered how her mother had often baked Christmas surprises in the muffins. A bright recollection came to mind of biting into a delicious muffin to find a beautiful ring with a red stone which she still wore on her little finger. Her mother's carpetbag and the ring were the only material things that she had to bring those memories to life. Oh, how she missed them. She remembered mother always singing and Pa sitting by the Christmas tree playing his fiddle and tapping his foot as Lillian and her brother Jesse danced around the room. When little Jesse's legs couldn't move as fast as hers, she remembered lifting him in her arms and finishing the dance with his tiny body held close to hers.

But those days were gone, and she must return to the present and her first Christmas in Frisco. After breakfast, Nettie and Lillian turned their attention to opening their presents. Lillian's eyes filled with tears as she opened the gifts from her students. Stacy and Jessica had given her a lovely pillowcase with beautiful flowers of every shade embroidered on it. Each girl had carefully stitched her name underneath the flowers that she had created. Jamie had given her a beautiful charcoal sketch of a wild horse running free on the prairie. The detail of the sketch was so breathtaking that looking at it, Lillian could imagine almost being able to touch the flying mane and feel the breath of the wild mustang on her cheeks.

The other students had taken great care to give their teacher something special that spoke of them and their talents, but Lillian's eyes came back again and again to the antelope that Billie had given her the night of the program. Her love for the boy was becoming ingrained in every part of her mind and body.

Nettie's eyes held a special glow as she unwrapped Ben's gift. It was a beautiful light pink shawl, softer than a baby lamb's wool. She gasped in delight as she placed it over her shoulders, then twirled around the room to show off her new possession.

"Oh, I just love it. Won't it look beautiful over my pink dress that I'm going to wear to the Swat Dance tonight? Ben said he'd pick us both up about eight and be our escort to the dance. You were planning on going, weren't you?"

"Why, in all the excitement of the program and getting Christmas for Billie and Charles, I'd forgotten all about the dance. Why do they call it a Swat Dance? It seems like such a strange name for a Christmas get together."

"You've never been to a Swat Dance? It's the most exciting dance of the year. Christmas stockings are stuffed with Christmas surprises and trinkets, then sewn up. I've learned that it doesn't pay to put anything in the sock that might break or crumble because the swats given in this dance can be full of energy and force. The socks are spread across the stage where the orchestra sits. If a gentleman sees some young lady who takes his eye, and she is dancing with someone else, he grabs a sock from the stage and uses it to swat the fellow she is dancing with. The lady's dancing partner now has to relinquish her to the swatter, so to speak, and must run off with the sock to swat yet another unsuspecting gentleman. The rules of the dance make it impossible to seek revenge on the man who just swatted you.

Proper etiquette for this occasion demands that you cannot turn around and hit the gentlemen who has just swatted you. If this swatee rule wasn't instituted, there would be all-out war on the dance floor."

"I went with my late husband to a Swat Dance before we were married," chuckled Nettie. "I declare, one gentleman was swatted so hard on the back of his head that he was knocked clean out and lay sprawled in the middle of the dance floor a good five minutes before they could revive him. I think that was the first time that I ever had a fight with my husband. Rufus Smith was determined that he was going to dance with me, and a real war ensued. Ed told me that night that if he ever saw me with Rufus again, he wouldn't come calling any more. Since I'd pretty much fallen for Ed by then, I decided that I wouldn't go to another Swat Dance, but now that Ed's gone, I guess it's all right for me to join in the fun."

"This has to be seen to be believed," said Lillian. "If I didn't know you for an honest soul, I'd think you were pulling my leg. For curiosity's sake, I'll go just to take in how this unique western custom really works."

Nettie and Lillian were dressed in their finery shortly before the sun set behind the San Francisco Mountains. Lillian's new blue dress and Nettie's pink wedding dress took on a special holiday glow as the two young ladies took turns dressing each other's hair and pinching each other's cheeks to give their faces some added color.

True to his word, Ben Johnson drove them to the dance in his wagon. Lillian noticed that his eyes were solely for Nettie, especially when she thanked him for the shawl which she wore proudly beneath her warm coat.

As they entered the dance hall, the warmth from the potbellied stove at the front of the room was a welcome relief from the 8 degree December weather. After Nettie and Lillian had hung their coats and mufflers in the hallway, their eyes were treated to a sight which stirred their blood and caused their eyes to sparkle.

Mrs. Amanda Smith, the buxom accordion player, wore a sprig of Mormon tea bush in her hair. Even though it didn't look much like holly, it gave her appearance a festive air. The sprig and Amanda's frame jiggled as she swang the accordion with real fervor.

Tim and Keith had adorned their fiddles with red and green ribbon and had tied bright green and red scarves around their necks for the occasion. Sprigs of the Mormon tea bush adorned their hats, and they seemed to be having a contest with the organist, Mrs. Reese, who seemed determined to set the pace for the jolly foursome. A bright red feather boa swayed back and forth on Mrs. Reese's chest, keeping time with the bright red feather on her hat that swayed from side to side as her head, like the pendulum of a clock, kept time with the music. Pieces of the red boa had been attached up and down her high top shoes, and as they swayed when she pushed the pedals, they looked like tiny birds fluttering in the breeze as her feet brought about a multitude of loud, rambunctious music. The smiling faces and red cheeks of the orchestra members, along with the pace they were setting, indicated that they had all been dipping into the large bowl of Christmas eggnog.

Lillian's eyes opened wide as she witnessed a young man grab a sock from the stage, then race to the floor and swat a portly gentleman soundly on his backside. The startled gentleman yelped, rubbed his backside, and raced off to smack an unsuspecting miner so hard on the back of his knees, that the young miner's legs buckled, and he almost toppled over. There was a good deal of raucous laughter, loud oaths of vengeance, and bubbling enthusiasm spreading around the dance floor.

Lillian didn't have much time to enjoy the scene as she suddenly found herself in the vise-like grip of Sheriff Phillips. It was clear that he wasn't going to observe the daylight rule again tonight as she found her entire body crushed against his steel frame.

"I was hoping that you'd come tonight. I would have offered to bring you, but Christmas brings out the bad in some people. I've been pretty busy all..."

"Smack!" Sheriff Phillips found himself hit to the side of the head so hard that he reached for his revolvers before he realized that at this dance, no swat could be disputed. Ned Druthers handed the sock to an irate sheriff and waltzed off with Lillian before the sheriff could retaliate with a disgruntled word.

"Ned, you're home. It's so good to see..."

"Wham!" Ned received a hard hit to his right arm that almost doubled him over, but he merely grabbed the sock, chuckled, and ran to smack yet another unsuspecting dancer.

Lillian found herself looking down at the tousled head of Jamie whose bright-colored cheeks and mischievous eyes showed that he was having the time of his life. "This is more fun than pulling the corks out of water barrels, Miss Lewis. This is the only time of year when you don't get punished for knocking somebody out," he chuckled. Out of the corner of her eye, Lillian noticed that Charles and Billie had just entered the hall. Charles had his new hat on, and the change was dramatic. *I do believe Charles can be quite handsome when he pays a little attention to his appearance,* Lillian thought.

"Whop!" Jamie's head swung to one side as Sheriff Phillips scored a direct hit on his right ear, but Jamie took it all in his stride, as he ran off to give Billie a good hit so that he could dance with Melissa. Billie's bellow resembled the wail of a wounded water buffalo as he stood in the middle of the floor, stomping his feet in a full-blown fit.

Sheriff Phillips was now circling the floor at record speed, as he dodged flying socks which were coming from every direction. His mouth was set in a firm line, and when one sock actually connected with his waist, he refused to relinquish Lillian and just danced a little faster.

It was then that Lillian saw Charles grab the new hat off his head and throw it on the floor, kind of like throwing down a white glove, which signaled a duel.

Lillian's breath caught as she saw Charles grab the Christmas sock from Billie who was still throwing his fit, and head in her direction on the dead run. But catching up with Sheriff Phillips was impossible because her partner was now dancing so fast that he could have outrun the wildest mustang.

Having finally caught up with the sheriff and Lillian, Charles swung the sock. "Ohh!" moaned Lillian as the sock, which had been aimed at Sheriff Phillips hit her on her neck. Because the sheriff turned Lillian at the same time that the sock was swung, the sock had hit the wrong target.

The sheriff released Lillian as they both stood to face Charles. Lillian's eyes were filled with tears, and her hand clutched her neck where a bright bruise was beginning to form.

"Lilly, I didn't mean to hit you," said Charles with concern in his eyes.

Sheriff Phillip's eyes glared as he shouted, "You, no good desert rat! You're lucky I don't drill you right here and now!"

It was then that Herbert Blakely, the floor manager, stepped between Charles and the sheriff and stretched out his arms to keep them away from each other. This was Herbert's first night as the new floor manager. He had been appointed to the job because he was built like a steam locomotive with muscles that rippled as he walked. A disturbance at the last dance had convinced the Frisco citizens a new floor manager needed to be hired—one who would scare the living daylights out of all the toughies.

"There will be order on this dance floor, or you'll answer to me," Herbert barked. The sheriff opened his mouth to protest, but Herbert grabbed him by his arm, handed him the sock, and yelled, "Now obey the rules of this dance hall, or I'll evict you both."

Sheriff Phillips could see that he was dwarfed by this giant by about 3 inches, and he didn't like the sight of those rippling muscles. He had met his match, and even though he wasn't used to backing down to any man, his inner sense told him that he could impress Miss Lewis more as a gentleman than as a barroom fighter, so he took the sock and used it to get possession of Maybell Riggs, the most beautiful dance hall lady in Frisco.

"Is your neck all right?" a gentle voice said as she was swung into Charles's gentle embrace.

"It will mend," whispered Lillian as the couple gave themselves up to the wonder of the beautiful waltz and the deep feelings of once again being in each other's arms. It was not necessary for words to be spoken. Charles gently placed her right hand over his heart and Lillian found herself softly drawn to his body. The top of her head barely reached his chin, and after a few minutes, she felt a soft kiss implanted in the curls at the top of her head.

Charles released Lillian as a sock hit him squarely on his back. "My turn, dad," a familiar voice yelled.

Billie handed the sock to Charles, and hardly missing a step, guided Lillian around the floor.

Lillian saw Charles place the sock on the stage and walk to the sidelines where he retrieved his hat, folded his arms, and directed his burning gaze in her direction.

"Had a jim dandy Christmas. You've got to come and see my sled. Dad said Santa wouldn't come, but he showed up and brought socks and everything. Even got a whistle in my sock. Bout drove dad near crazy Christmas Day, and he had to hide it for a while, but I get to have it back at the end of the day if I do all my chores," gushed Billie. "Don't know when I've had such a Christmas!"

The waltz ended and Charles motioned for Billie to come with a "let's go" wave of his hand. Billie's freckles caught the glimmer of the lanterns as he yelled, "Got to go, Miss Lewis. See you back at school in a few days."

As Lillian watched Charles and Billie leave the hall, she wondered, *Why has Charles avoided me for so long, then treated me with such tenderness tonight?* Thoughts of his gentle kiss in her hair filled her senses.

Sheriff Phillips approached and led her to a darkened corner of the hall. His eyes never left hers as he retrieved a box from his pocket. "Merry Christmas, Miss Lewis," he said softly. Lillian opened the box to find a delicate bracelet made of intertwining flowers.

"It's made from silver taken from the Horn Silver," said a soft voice close to her ear. "I hope you like it." There wasn't even a second for Lillian to thank the sheriff for the gift. His main deputy raced in, grabbed him by the arm, yelling something about a disturbance at the Chinese Laundry. Lillian was left alone to gaze at the beautiful bracelet as conflicting feelings filled her head. *Thank heavens for disturbances,* Lillian thought. *I am mysteriously drawn to that man, but everything he stands for repels me.*

Lillian didn't have a chance to rest her tired feet all evening. She seemed to be the center of attention as dancer after dancer swung that sock to get the opportunity to dance with her.

Finally, Ben and Nettie motioned to her that they were ready to go. When the wagon stopped at the shanty door, Lillian went into the house first, giving the lovers a chance to say their Christmas goodbyes.

As she took off her coat, she noticed a bulge in the right pocket. Reaching inside, she pulled out a dark blue, velvet jewelry box. As her trembling fingers opened the lid, a beautiful object winked back at her. Nestled inside was an exquisite pin with three pearls, mounted on three circles of narrow silver threads.

Now how did this get here? she wondered. Then a picture of Charles at The Mercantile, buying something from the jewelry case filled her mind, and as if on cue, the scent of lavender told her that her suspicions were true.

Her eyes gazed at the pin and then were drawn to the new silver bracelet, and for the second time this evening her eyes again filled with tears as she realized what a wonderful, magical Christmas this had been.

Chapter 25

Nettie and Lillian spent a quiet New Years alone. Ben was traveling to Beaver to bring back some material that he was going to use to refurbish the chairs in the lobby of The Southern. Ned and the mules had stopped to say goodbye before they took off on yet another freighting trip to Milford, but the rest of New Year's Day had been uneventful. They had seen the Death Wagon pass the shanty window at least three times, a signal that even though it was a holiday, there was no rest for Frisco's sheriff.

Lillian spent the afternoon making lesson plans. She knew that the children would be especially rambunctious after the holidays and that she would have to have plenty to keep them busy.

As she watched them race through the schoolroom door the next day in a rather rip-roaring fashion, she wondered if she was going to be able to calm them down long enough to resume the regiment of an organized school day.

But to her relief, the tap of her ruler on the desk brought them all to order in a few seconds, and she was able to proceed with her daily routine.

Halfway through the reading classes, Superintendent McNaught entered the school. Shaking the snow from his winter coat, he walked to the front of the room where he addressed them in a strong, firm voice. "First of all, I want to tell you how much I enjoyed your history play. The dancing and singing were wonderful. Your creativity and knowledge of history was worthy of the highest merit." Gazing at Laura's red curls, which seemed to spring out like coiled wires from both sides of her head, he grinned as he said, "Young lady, your rendition of Paul Revere and the kiss that you bestowed on me will be one of the most memorable experiences of my life."

Laura beamed as she gave Superintendent McNaught one of her brightest smiles.

"Secondly, I have come to inform you and Miss Lewis about a contest that is going to be held this spring right here in Frisco. Your history play gave me the idea for the contest. May 1st, the top history students from the Milford, Newhouse, Minersville, and Beaver schools will be transported here to participate in a history contest.

"Myself and a panel of other educators from Southern Utah will ask students from these schools various history questions. If a question is missed, that student will be declared out of the contest. The last school standing will be awarded a large trophy, $100 to spend for school materials, and be treated to a scrumptious picnic at the place of your choosing. How many of you are in favor of participating in the contest?"

All hands immediately waved in the air as a loud "Yippee!" broke the silence.

"I take it that those waving hands and that shout of joy mean the decision is unanimous," said Superintendent McNaught, "so I'll leave so you can begin today to prepare for the contest."

There was a chorus of cheery goodbyes as the superintendent waved on his way out the door.

The rest of the day was spent talking about the contest and how they would prepare for it. As Lillian watched their animated faces, she thought, *this contest will provide the needed motivation to get these students invigorated and excited about learning again.*

Since it was the regular time for the history lesson, training for the contest began immediately. She began the review by having the students take turns filling in the blanks to sentences she spoke aloud that described moments in history. She was amazed at how much they remembered. Even events from the very beginning of the year seemed to be ingrained in their minds. When she asked Billie who the seventh president of the United States was and he yelled out, "Andrew Jackson," Lillian smiled with pride, but when she asked Mary how President Jackson was different from the Presidents before him and Mary replied, "He was the President who didn't win a majority in the Electoral College, so the House of Represents had to choose him as President." Lillian corrected "Representatives," then praised Mary as she realized just how much knowledge her students had retained.

Excitement could be smelled in the air as the review continued. The students were so engrossed in trying to outdo one another that they seemed reluctant to leave when three o'clock rolled around. Instead of fidgeting and wiggling in their seats the last ten minutes of school, they sat quietly with their eyes focused on their teacher, ready for more questions.

Lillian, caught up in the animation she saw on her students' faces, gave them her biggest smile. She was so full of their spirit of learning that she could have hugged them all, but convention called for closing the class in the conventional way.

"I am proud of all of you today. Your retention of the material that we studied earlier in the year amazes and delights me. I am convinced that with hard work and vigorous study, we can defeat the other schools. With victory in mind, the assignment for tonight is to review the first ten pages in your history books and come prepared tomorrow for further review. I want you to read the page, then close your books and say back to yourself what you have read. In this way, the material will be retained and ingrained in your minds for the review tomorrow. Will we be victorious?"

A loud "Yes" reverberated throughout the room as the students grabbed their books and lunch pails and raced out the door, eager to finish their chores and get to their studies.

Lillian sat at her desk to prepare the review for tomorrow, but the sound of the schoolroom door opening caused her to raise her head from her work.

There in the doorway in all his fierce glory stood the sheriff of Frisco, wearing a smile that showed his white teeth off to perfection. It was evident that he had taken great care with his appearance as not a hair escaped from his blonde ponytail that shone from a recent washing.

"Good afternoon, Ma'am," he drawled. "Got something to ask you today."

"I hope I'm not in trouble with the law," Lillian smiled.

"Not at all, Ma'am. You are the epitome of perfection in every way."

Where does a man of his character get such big words, Lillian thought, but raised her eyebrows to give him the go ahead to say his piece.

Sheriff Phillips crossed the room and sat himself on a bench in the first row as he began, "I have talked to the mine superintendent and got his okay to take a group of four ladies, and the mine superintendent and myself on a tour of the Horn Silver Mine. It seems the ladies of the community have a terrible curiosity concerning what the mine is like down below. I figured if we let some of them go down in the mine, they might stop pestering their husbands and driving them out of the house and into the saloons where they exhibit rowdiness that often breaks out into fights and such. Wondered if you would like to be one of the ladies to take the tour? I chose you because you could report your findings to your students and give them first-hand knowledge about what the mine is like. How about it? Would you like to be one of the honored females to first enter the mine?"

Lillian was suddenly at a loss for words. Did she really want to enter a mine shaft that went as far down as 300 feet? She had heard disturbing stories about the mine and the dangers that it held. Extremely cold or hot temperatures, foul air, and the danger of cave-ins raced through her mind as she sat silent for a few minutes, gazing into the face of the black specter before her.

Then she thought of her students and their inquisitive minds. She could gain first-hand knowledge about the mine by taking the tour. As her students' excited faces flashed in vivid pictures before her, she found herself saying "Yes, Sheriff. I'd very much like to learn more about this silver mine."

The sheriff's smile deepened, showing his pleasure. "Well, that's that. I'll pick you up at your shanty at nine o'clock Saturday morning. The mine superintendent is going to let us go down for an hour between shifts. Dress warm, because the temperatures in the mine this time of year are below freezing."

"See you Saturday," he said as he tipped his hat, gave her a wink, and strode through the door.

What have I gotten myself into now? Lillian agonized, but all disturbing thoughts were blotted from her mind as she returned to the task of preparing for tomorrow's history review.

Chapter 26

As she prepared for her Friday's lessons, one thing was uppermost in Lillian's mind–she needed to tell her students about tomorrow's excursion into the mine. Finally, following the history review for the contest, Lillian could no longer hold the information to herself.

Getting directly to the point, she began, "Students, I want you to know that tomorrow I am going to be taking a tour of the Horn Silver Mine. I decided to accept the sheriff's invitation to be lowered into the mine so that I will be better prepared to answer your questions about what takes place there. Do you have any suggestions about what I should look for in the mine? What are some of your fathers' experiences that will help me know what to expect when I go underground?" Ten hands suddenly went up, most of them waving frantically in the air, hoping to be the first one to get their teacher's attention.

Lillian called on the quiet Melissa, who usually was too shy to express her opinion.

"Miss Lewis," she softly began. "Please don't go into the mine. There's Tommyknockers there." Melissa's lips started to quiver, and Lillian could see that she wasn't going to get anything more from her. It was clear that the sweet Melissa was scared out of her wits.

Billie didn't wait to be recognized. He just blurted out, "Ya, watch out for the Tommyknockers. They know where the silver is, and they'll knock on the mine wall to get your attention.

Beware, Miss Lewis! That knock could mean that silver lies in that spot, but it could also mean to beware of a cave-in. You never know about them mischievous little fellers."

"Dad says if he hears the knocking, he won't drill in that spot cause it might be a Tommyknocker, tryin' to fool him," added Curt.

When Lillian recognized Clarence, he excitedly added, "Dad says the Tommyknockers aren't all bad. They can be a miner's friend, cause they warn of cave-ins and such. That's why he refuses to enter any mine unless the man in charge tells him that the Tommyknockers are on duty. They can also be your companion when you're workin' hard. Dad says that he knows many a Tommyknocker has worked alongside him, and even though he's never seen one, he has felt their breath on his arms and neck many times. Their presence has brought him comfort when he's under stress, but they can be real mischievous. One time dad's hammer came up missing, and he looked all over but never did find it. Another time he was walking in the mine and rocks appeared in the path. They came out of nowhere, making him stumble and fall. Told me those pranks were for sure pulled by the Tommyknockers. Seems they get their jollies out of having fun with the miners. But he says he can put up with a few pranks cause their presence more times than not saves lives."

"Miss Lewis, my Uncle Casey was saved by them Tommyknockers," yelled Richie. "He was mining in California when he heard some of them little critters knocking with their tiny picks on a wall next to him. First, he just backed away and tried to get the sound out of his head, but the picking sound only got louder, so he backed up further, and the further he backed, the louder the knocking sound became. He had a clear thought that the picking was a warning and that he and the rest of the men had to get out of the tunnel, so he yelled, 'cave-in!' and they all scurried to the top. It wasn't but 10 seconds after they reached the top that their ears were nearly blown out by a large boom, and they were covered with flying dust coming from the mine shaft. My uncle knew for sure that they all would have been dead fellers if he hadn't listened to the Tommyknockers."

Lillian's eyes widened as she said, "I'll be sure to look for these little guys, but what do they look like, so that I can recognize them?"

"Oh, nobody's seen them, Miss Lewis," said Jamie. "But if you could see one, he'd be about 4 feet tall, dressed like a miner, and be so full of energy that you wouldn't be able to calm him down. Them Tommyknockers are expert miners and work right 'longside the men."

"I'll keep an eye out for them," said Lillian. "Now since it's time to dismiss school, we'll have to leave discussion of the Tommyknockers until another day. Please study the next ten pages of your history books for Monday's contest review."

Tommyknockers, Lillian chuckled to herself. *That's the most ridiculous superstition I've ever heard.*

She was laughing as she entered the shanty and had to explain to Nettie what had put her in this mood.

After hearing the students' comments about the Tommyknockers, Nettie added some information of her own about them.

"My husband told me all about the Tommyknocker legend. The Cornish miners started it when they came from Cornwall, England. These Cornish miners were some of the best mining men in the business. They had years of experience at tunneling and mining and were respected as mining authorities in many mines. The Tommyknockers were part of their Cornish legend and lore. According to legend, the Tommyknockers were the undergound cousins of the Piskies and Vogs who lived in the Cornish moors. As your students have told you, many Cornish miners won't go into the mines unless they know the Tommyknockers are on duty. Ed told me that following the closing of one mine, the men lobbied the general manager to release the Tommyknockers from employment so that they could be transferred to other working mines. It's interesting to know that the mining company agreed to release them. There are many

Cornish miners who work at the Horn Silver. It's no wonder that their children know so much about this legend."

"I promised the students that I'd listen carefully for those picking sounds," chuckled Lillian. "If they really do exist, it will be comforting to have friendly spirits to get me through this tour."

"Maybe with little, green men picking about, you'd better think seriously about cancelling the tour," cautioned Nettie as she dished up dinner.

"I can't go back on my word, Nettie. There's too much knowledge to be gained from it, and I won't disappoint my students. They were all so excited about listening to my report about what I found there."

Following dinner, Lillian tried to put the Tommyknockers from her mind as she helped with the dishes and sat at the table to prepare for Monday's review.

But when she climbed in bed and attempted to sleep, pictures of small, smiling imps, laughing and jumping around, filled her mind. When sleep finally did come, she dreamt of a little impish miner, wearing a ridiculous green hat, beckoning her to enter the shaft of the mine. When she got into the lift to descend into the depths of the mine, the little prankster jumped on her back and playfully pinched her neck.

Chapter 27

Lillian was up long before the sun. The light from the full moon had become a deterrent to sleep as it illuminated the small shanty. She had not spent a restful night, being plagued by visions of her journey into the black pit of the mine. During one dream, as she was lowered into the mine, leaping flames flickered upwards to scorch her bare skin as though she were being lowered into the infernal pit where demons surely dwelt.

Calm down, Lillian. Everything is going to be fine. You always did have an active imagination, now reach up and turn that imagination button off! Lillian chided herself as she pulled on a pair of red flannel underwear and warm flannel pants and shirt, courtesy of Nettie's dead husband. She found herself feeling pretty toasty even before she put on her heavy winter coat and muffler. A warm wool hat that Ned Druthers had given her for Christmas pulled down over her ears and forehead, leaving two large, blue eyes peeking from beneath the brim, wide and startled, as if they had just seen their first ghostly apparition.

"Surely, you're not leaving the house looking like that!" chided Nettie. "In that getup, nobody would even guess that you had a drop of femininity running through your veins."

"Nettie, can you imagine what an encumbrance a dress would be in that mine? It could get caught on a number of things and cost me my life. This getup may look ridiculous, but it's practical, and it will certainly provide the warmth I need in the dampness of the mine. I'm so warm right now that I feel like running outside and rolling in the snow."

Nettie parted the shanty curtains as she said, "Well, don't do something that ridiculous right now. Sheriff Phillips just pulled up outside in the Death Wagon. I wish he were taking you to the mine in something else," laughed Nettie. "The sight of that wagon just gives me the willies."

When Lillian answered the door, she found herself face to face with a new Sheriff Phillips. He, too, had dressed for the weather. Warm wool pants and coat hid his usual black attire. His wide-brim Stetson was replaced with a warm wool cap that covered his head, ears, and much of his face.

His green eyes twinkled, giving away his true identity. "Looks like you're dressed plenty warm, Little Lady. If I didn't know I was at the right shanty, I'd think I had knocked on the wrong door by mistake; however, no matter what getup you choose to wear, you still manage to be the most attractive female in these parts!"

Sheriff Phillips held out his arm as a gentlemanly invitation and escorted her to the Death Wagon where he lifted her as if she were a mere feather, then carefully wrapped a warm blanket around her. Lillian stretched her legs under the blanket to become more comfortable. As she did so, she pulled them back quickly when her feet encountered a hot object on the floor of the wagon.

"I see you found my bricks, Little Lady. Warmed them in my fireplace just this morning and wrapped them in heavy cloths. Nothing like hot bricks to chase away the chill of winter."

"They're wonderful, Sheriff. They feel heavenly on my cold feet. Thanks for your thoughtfulness," murmured Lillian in a soft voice.

The sheriff seemed reluctant to begin the trip. He seemed to be perfectly content to just sit in the wagon and stare into a pair of large, blue eyes that seemed to hold his interest.

Feeling uncomfortable under his penetrating gaze, Lillian lowered her eyes and said, "Sheriff, when are they expecting us at the mine?"

The sheriff moved his gaze to the road ahead and shook the reins, setting the mules into a fast trot. "We're expected at 9:30 sharp–just in time for the shift change," he said. "The mine's management agreed to let us go down the shaft for a short time before the next shift takes over. Maybe after this tour, the women of Frisco will give up their pestering and give us all the peace and rest that we need," he chuckled.

The road up to the mine was rough, at times just two deep ruts that made it difficult for the mules to progress through the snow and mud. It was a clear day, but about one foot of snow lay on the ground, covering the sagebrush and giving a pristine whiteness to the landscape.

The sheriff stopped the mules at the hosting works, which signaled the entrance to the mine shaft. The shaft itself was about 30 feet wide, and as Lillian watched, one miner's cage came to the surface of the shaft, carrying a load of men who were just finishing their shift. They exited the cage as one man yelled, "Last one to the saloon is a drowned skunk!" and they were packed into the large wagon for their return trip to town before anyone could snap their fingers.

Lillian knew why the saloon was their destination. Many of her students had confided that conditions in the mine were so rough that their fathers often drowned their weariness after work at their favorite saloon before they ventured home.

Waiting for them at the shaft was Molly Smithson, the mayor's wife; Sally Reynolds, the most upstanding lady in Frisco society; and Beatrice Small who ran the local boardinghouse. All three women's cups ran over with warm gossip that seemed to slip through their lips and spew forth every second of the day. They frequently caused their husbands' nerves to crack and split with their nagging tongues and sassy personalities. As Lillian looked at the three, she realized that she was the only partially-sweet thing who would be entering the mine this day.

Standing by the three women was Emit McGrady, the assistant mine superintendent. "Superintendent Jensen sends his regrets, ladies," he stammered. "He came down just this morning with an attack of the influenza and asked me to take his place."

Lillian covered her lips to suppress the smile that threatened to reveal her true thoughts, but Sheriff Phillips made no attempt to hide his wide grin.

Influenza indeed inwardly chuckled Lillian. *It's more like a case of cowarditis. I don't know one man who would volunteer to go underground with these three snipping pine hens!*

Sheriff Phillips, sensing Lillian's constrained mirth, grabbed her arm and squeezed it, just to let her know that his thoughts were merging with hers.

Unlike Lillian, the three rumormongers were not sensibly dressed. They wore large hats and full dresses and looked more like they were dressed for a fine dinner at a restaurant rather than a trip down a mine shaft.

They all looked at Lillian as though she were a disgusting, filthy bug. As their piercing gazes threatened to squash her for good, Mr. McGrady broke the silence.

"Molly, Sally, and Beatrice, I'll have to ask you to remove your hats and place them in the wagon before you enter the cage. This cage proceeds down the shaft at a high speed. Harvey, the hoist man, is often in his cups and not responsible for how fast he drops the cage down the shaft. I'd hate to see those hats flying into thin air like lost birds, and no way to retrieve them. Besides, there's no way all of us and those hats will fit in the same cage."

"Well, I never!" mumbled Molly as she removed her hat and started for the wagon.

"How can you be properly dressed without a hat?" shrieked Sally, and Beatrice pursed her mouth into a pucker, making her look like a dried-up persimmon as she stomped off with the other two to deposit their headpieces.

When they returned, Mr. McGrady gave them warm wool scarves to wrap around their heads and throats and then made them place mining hats on top of the scarves.

"If anybody's looking, I'll be the laughing stock of Frisco," whined Molly, but she and the others soon calmed down when the hoist man signaled them to enter the cage.

The inside of the hoisting works was powdered with snow as they approached the cage which was now at ground level to the right of the shaft.

"Watch you step, ladies, as you get into the cage," cautioned Mr. McGrady. "As you can see, it has no sides, just four posts in the corners, so stand as close to the middle as you can to ensure your own safety."

Sheriff Phillips grabbed Lillian's arm and escorted her to the center of the cage. The sounds coming from the tunnel boilers and the furnace which operated the hoist and stood just a few yards from the shaft, only seemed to add to the women's anxiety.

The sheriff and Mr. McGrady carried kerosene lanterns to light the way in the dark shaft, but one of the lanterns was quickly extinguished as the cage began to drop down the shaft at a rapid rate. Gasps were heard from all four of the ladies as their hearts rose into their throats and their breaths were almost stopped by the lightning speed that the cage was traveling. During this rapid descent, the cage passed blurs of light that Lillian could just barely recognize as large lanterns held upright in metal holders which were attached to the walls of the shaft.

"I'm going to faint–please somebody help..." whispered Molly, but her cries were silenced as the cage abruptly stopped, along with all of the faint hearts in the cage.

"Oh, thank goodness! Now I think I might live," murmured Beatrice. Looking at the other ladies, Lillian could see relief mixed with fear in their pale faces.

"Sorry, ladies, I forgot to tell Harvey to take it easy. He gets in the habit of doing things a certain way, and then there's no changing him. Look to your right and you'll see that we're at the end of the shaft and at the mouth of the strope that we're going to enter, but first we must wait for the ore cage on the left of us to reach the surface." He had no sooner said this than "whoosh!" the ore cage, located in the center of the shaft, passed them so rapidly that it created a strong breeze which rushed through the cage in which they were standing.

"We should be safe to enter the strope now," said Mr. McGrady. "Look up at the top of the shaft, and you can see light showing around the sides of the ore cage. That indicates that it's at the surface and won't be coming down for a few minutes while they're unloading the ore."

Holding the lantern in front of him and shining it on the floor of the strope, Mr. McGrady began the task of leading the excursion party out of the cage.

Since Lillian and the sheriff were on the far side of the cage, they had to wait until Mr. McGrady led the other three ladies into the strope. Getting the three ladies out of the cage turned out to be a Herculean task.

"Don't force me to go faster!" screamed the illustrious Mrs. Reynolds. "I just know I'm going to step on some creepy, crawly thing! Heavens to Betsy, I can't even see the ground, let alone what's on it!"

"Tell me there's no rats! Please tell me there's no rats!" begged Beatrice. "I can stand a room full of drunken miners in my boardinghouse, but just let me see a rat and I can't stop screaming!"

"Don't worry about rats, Beatrice." Mr. McGrady's voice softly sounded through the stillness. "They're probably more scared of you than you are of them."

"That's the truth," the sheriff whispered to Lillian. "I'd hate to meet that woman in a dark alley." Laughter was mixed in with the whisper, and Lillian couldn't keep herself from smiling. After all, who was going to see her in this near darkness. It seemed like forever before Mr. McGrady finally got the last of the three ladies out of the cage and onto the floor of the strope.

Sheriff Phillips wrapped a strong arm around Lillian's waist and started to lead her into the dark cavern. Just then, a rush of air to the side of them, followed by a loud whooshing sound caused Lillian to literally jump from the floor of the cage. The force of the air was so strong that Lillian felt like her face had been scorched. In seconds strong arms were wrapped around her, as the sheriff's gruff voice said, "I bet you jumped a good 6 inches. It's just the ore cage returning so it will be ready for another load of ore when the next shift begins."

Without warning the ore car quickly rose to the top of the shaft. "Must have forgotten to repair the car's railings," chuckled Mr. McGrady from inside the strope. "We'll have to watch out for speeding cars when we return. Nothing to worry about, Miss Lewis. You and the Sherrif can get out of that cage now. There's only one ore car, and it will take them an hour to repair that one."

The dark cavern beckoned ominously as Sheriff Phillips led Lillian onto the dirt floor of the strope.

They were 300 feet underground, and the cold penetrated into their very bones. Lanterns attached to the walls of the strope did little to show the appearance of the dark cavern made by the miners, but Lillian could see that it was immense. There were large pillars in the center of the strope, left there, Mr. McGrady told them, as a support to prevent cave-ins. In the center of the strope was an ore car sitting on a tressel and a donkey near the car, quietly chewing on his feed.

"What's a donkey doing in a black pit like this?" questioned Sally. "If I'd known there was going to be a dirty, filthy beast like this one, I'd not have come."

"This donkey is a very important part of the mining operation," explained Mr. McGrady. "He was hoisted down here to pull the ore cars and is a valuable piece of mining equipment, so don't you complain about this dirty, filthy beast."

Sally pursed her lips in annoyance, but blessedly for the rest of the party, her lips stopped their murmuring.

"How big is the strope where we're standing?" asked Lillian as she tried to see through the blackness.

"I've been told that it's big enough to hold the entire town of Frisco. There's no way in this light that you can see just how large it really is," commented Mr. McGrady.

"Oh my!" exclaimed Molly. "What's that shiny stuff in the pillars?"

"It's silver, Mrs. Smithson. The amount of glitter in those pillars gives you some idea as to how rich this mine really is. Some experts say that this is one of the richest silver mines in the West."

"Well, isn't it a waste to leave all that silver in those pillars?" questioned Sally.

"Those pillars prevent cave-ins, Mrs. Reynolds. If we started taking the silver out of them, that support that they're giving the ceiling would be gone, and we'd have a cave-in that could destroy much of this immense strope."

Beatrice wrinkled her brow and held her handkerchief in front of her mouth. "What's that terrible stench?" she whined.

"It's just the smell of gunpowder, mixed with stale air. There are air pipes in this strope that come from up above. You saw them in the manway that makes up the third compartment in the shaft. The manway's full of ladders, pump columns, air pipes, and other equipment, but even though there are air pipes leading into this strope, there's no such thing as really fresh air down here. That's why so many miners wind up with consumption and die at an early age. Mining isn't for the faint of heart."

"Gunpowder! Did I hear you say gunpowder? I didn't realize that you used such a dangerous substance in this mine. What in heaven's name do you use that for?" questioned Sally.

"Let me do a little explaining, ladies." Mr. McGrady picked up a piece of steel with a wedge-shaped chisel point and a large sledge hammer from the dirt floor. He walked to the wall of the strope and motioned for everyone to follow. He placed the chisel on the wall and motioned for the sheriff to come. Handing the sledge hammer to the sheriff, he explained, "I'm going to have Sheriff Phillips hit this chisel with his sledge hammer as I turn it. This is called 'double jacking,'" Mr. McGrady explained. "Two men working together can make holes for the dynamite in just a few minutes." The excursion party watched in fascination as true to his word, Mr. McGrady, with the sheriff's help, created a large hole in the wall of the strope in less than five minutes.

McGrady then placed a large steel plate underneath the hole. "This is a muck plate, ladies. When the explosives break up the wall, the ore will fall on this plate and make it easy to load the ore car for its return trip to the top."

"But don't the explosives pose a real danger to the miners?" inquired Molly.

"Since the dynamite is mostly nitro, there's always a danger to the miners, but every safety precaution is taken. After the explosives are placed in the holes, the men are evacuated to a safe location. Then, and only then, are the explosives detonated. When the dust clears, the men enter the strope once again, deposit the ore from the muck plate into the ore car, then load it on the ore cage which transports it to the surface."

"But don't the explosives still pose an extreme danger even with the best of precautions?" asked Beatrice.

"There's always a danger when you work with explosives, but since the timing device is always 100 feet from the working place..."

Mr. Grady stopped in mid-sentence. The lantern light that fell on his face showed something akin to fright as he turned to face the mouth of the strope.

Then the rest of the party heard it. A light tapping noise was coming from the entrance of the strope. "Tap, tap, tap." Each tap seemed to become just a little louder than the tap before it. In the dead silence that followed the tapping, the timbers which shored up the entrance, ceiling, and sides of the strope started creaking and groaning just as the timbers in a ship must creak and groan when the sea is rough and a real storm is on the way.

Dead silence descended on the group, heavy and thicker than any silence in a neglected tomb. Suddenly, the floor of the strope came alive. In the dim light, rats, mice, and bugs of every sort started to scurry to the mouth of the strope.

The silence was broken by Beatrice's shrill scream "Rats! Rats!" followed by what seemed to be the end of the world itself. Massive groans sounded throughout the strope as cracking timbers burst into pieces and began to give way. Lillian watched in horror as the sheriff raced to the mouth of the strope, attempting to shore up the opening by placing a spare timber in the strope's entrance, hopelessly trying to prevent the entryway from collapsing and trapping them inside. An unearthly cry of pain sounded as he disappeared beneath falling timbers, rocks, and dirt. Then all thought stopped as Lillian found herself thrown to the ground, as rocks and debris descended without warning upon herself and the rest of the unwary party.

She awakened to the sound of soft crying. Her lungs burned as they struggled for that life-giving substance that she had always taken for granted. She needed air, and she needed it immediately. She knew that she had to somehow get her face uncovered if she were to live.

Luckily, she found that she was covered by only a thin layer of debris, and after a few long seconds, she was able to brace herself on her hands and sit up, causing dirt and rocks to fall from her face. She struggled to gulp in air, but started to cough as the air she breathed choked her lungs with the dust that it contained.

Strong arms helped her to her feet and brushed the dirt from her face. As she gazed at her rescuer, she noticed that Mr. McGrady's body was totally encrusted with dirt. Only his bright eyes shone through the grime on his face.

"Are you all right, Miss Lewis?" he asked between coughing spasms. He appeared to be mobile and not physically hurt.

"I just need to get some air," whispered Lillian.

"As soon as you're able, we need to check the other ladies and then attempt to uncover the sheriff. He seems to have received the full force of the cave-in."

Molly was a few feet away from where they stood. She was sitting on the floor of the strope with her head in her hands, crying softly.

"Mitch didn't want me to do this. Oh why didn't I listen?" she sobbed.

Lillian and Mr. McGrady helped her to her feet, and Lillian put her arms around her as she comforted, "Now, Molly, everything's going to be all right, but we need your help. We've got to uncover the sheriff right now."

A few feet away they saw Sally and Beatrice sitting on the floor of the strope, holding each other, their bodies convulsed in sobs.

They appeared to be unhurt, but it was clear that no amount of laundering was going to bring those designer outfits back to life. Fortunately, they had been standing in a fairly safe place when the cave-in occurred because there was a minimal amount of debris around them.

"Come, ladies," said Mr. McGrady. "We've all got to work together to help the sheriff. It's going to take all of us working as a team if there is any chance of saving his life. We may already be too late."

"Let's start with this timber. I saw him fall, and I think it's lying over his face and the major part of his body. It's lying across a rock. If we're lucky, and there's a space between the timber and his body, that space might just have saved his life." The party began frantically to remove the rocks that covered the sheriff.

A great deal of rocks and debris had to be cleared before they reached the timber. When the timber was exposed, McGrady positioned the ladies along various parts of it, and on the count of three told them to lift. Adrenalin filled their blood stream, and after only a few seconds, the timber was lifted and thrown into the darkness of the strope.

With the timber removed, an outline of the sheriff's face could be seen. In just a few seconds, Mr. McGrady had whipped the red bandana from the sheriff's neck and wiped away the dirt and grime from the injured face.

When he placed his trembling fingers to the sheriff's neck, a half smile crossed his weathered features. "Someone's watchin' over him. He's alive, but his pulse is very weak. That timber may have saved his life. Must have been just enough air underneath it to keep him breathing, but it's not going to be an easy task to get the rest of him uncovered."

Without a word, rocks, dirt, and pieces of timber started flying in all directions. There was no question in their minds. They knew that they had to work fast. Dainty hands that had never known such labor did not hesitate. Jagged rocks cut into white skin, and blood flowed, but they did not cease their efforts until a clear outline of the sheriff's body was visible.

"Oh look at his poor leg," groaned Molly.

"It's at such a funny angle," said Beatrice. "My brother's leg looked just like that when he was thrown from his horse and landed on the hard dirt of the corral."

"It's broken all right," affirmed Mr. McGrady. "I can see the bone trying to poke through his pants. It's a bad break for sure."

Mr. McGrady knelt by the sheriff, then carefully felt the injured leg. "We've got to try and set it now. If we don't, he might lose it altogether. Won't be the first time I've had to attend to a broken limb. Since Frisco's never had a real doctor, I've had to learn to do terrible tasks that aren't fit for ladies' ears. You ladies have got to find me some wood to use for splints. Surely there's something around here that will serve the purpose."

Lillian grabbed Sally's hand. "Surely, the two of us can find some kind of wood to brace the leg," she said. She clasped Sally's hand in hers and headed her into the north part of the strope, but searching in the dim light was an experience in terror. Lillian jumped at every little sound.

The lanterns attached to the walls of the strope threw eerie shadows on the honeycombed surface of the strope's walls as the two women moved about hunting for wood. Then a distinct "Tap, tap, tap" sounded once again through the cold silence.

Tommyknockers! Lillian couldn't stop the name from entering her mind. She felt with a certainty that the little men had tapped to warn of the cave-in. *Now, what are they signaling?* She wondered. She was so certain of their presence that she expected to see little men dressed in green any minute.

"It's the Tommyknockers!" whispered Sally. "Walt talks about them all the time. He says that he's comforted by their presence, but the thought of them scares the living daylights out of me. Walt didn't want me to come down here, especially after one of the men broke a board on a ladder, leaving it with 13 rungs. 'That's bad luck, for sure,' he told me. He said he'd not let me out of the house for a week if I went today, but I snuck away when he left the house this morning. He's not a forgiving man. I don't know how I'll ever explain..." her voice stopped, then shook as she continued–"if I ever get the chance to explain."

Sally's arm was shaking as Lillian gently took it. "If your husband trusts these green miners, then I suggest we walk in the direction of the tapping."

Stepping cautiously towards the tapping took every ounce of courage that Sally and Lillian had, but an inner voice told Lillian that she was headed in the right direction.

Following the tapping sound, Lillian almost stumbled when her feet hit a hidden object on the strope's floor.

Both ladies stooped to feel what had impeded their search. "It's a wooden box!" cried Sally. "That's why they were tapping. They wanted us to find it."

As they felt the box in the dim light, their fingers encountered a crate made of thin strips of wood. At a closer glance, they could barely make out the word "explosives" on one strip.

"If we pry them off, I think these strips are about the right width for splints," said Lillian.

Carefully, the weary twosome headed back to the front of the strope where they found Mr. McGrady kneeling by the sheriff.

When he saw the crate, his eyes lit up. "Wherever did you find just what we needed?"

"Well, it all had to do with tapping, but we'll leave that story for another day when we can breathe fresh air and see the bright sun overhead," said Sally.

"Come and hold this crate, ladies, while I try to pry some of these strips loose; then we can try to set the leg."

Lillian and Sally held tightly to the crate while Mr. McGrady used a mine chisel to pry some strips loose.

"These should be just about the right length," McGrady said as they knelt by the sheriff's quiet body.

Positioning himself on his knees by the sheriff's feet, Mr. McGrady instructed, "Miss Lewis, you hold his head in your lap, and Sally and Molly, each of you hold one of his arms. Beatrice, you come down here by me and hold on tight to his other leg. He's really out of it and probably won't move, but the pain might cause him to come to his senses and undo all our efforts if he starts thrashing about."

Lillian gently took the sheriff's head and placed it in her lap. She had a strong urge to smooth his hair back from his face and say some words to comfort him, but his pale, drawn face and closed eyelids told her that he wasn't aware of anything.

His beautiful long eyelashes don't match his stern disposition, thought Lillian. She lightly shook her head to clear such thoughts and fixed her gaze on Mr. McGrady and Beatrice who had firm holds on the sheriff's legs.

Molly and Sally had a firm grip on the sheriff's arms. Their faces were strained and pale, and their lips were drawn in firm lines, preparing them for the ordeal.

Mr. MrGrady looked sternly at his assistants as he said, "On the count of three, ladies, hold fast, and let's hope that I can set this leg on the first try."

"One, two, three!"

A light snapping noise sounded throughout the dark strope as all three strained to do their part.

The sheriff's eyes remained closed, but a small cry came from his lips, and his body shuddered when the bones snapped together.

Mr. McGrady leaned forward to feel the leg. "I believe we did it! Yes sir, I believe that leg is set right and proper. Good thing he was out, or it'd been pretty tough on him. I've seen strong men pass out from the pain. It's that bad! Now, Miss Lewis, hand me those boards."

Lillian passed the boards to Mr. McGrady, and silence fell on the party for a few seconds as Mr. McGrady appeared to be analyzing Sally, Beatrice, and Molly.

"I hate to ask this question, ladies, but there's no getting away from it. Which one of you is wearing an old petticoat that you wouldn't mind ripping up a bit? I need something to hold these splints on his leg."

Lillian was positive that if there had been sufficient light, all three ladies would have had cheeks the color of the Indian paintbrush that she had seen in the mountain meadows on her way to Frisco.

Beatrice did not hesitate. "I put on my old work petticoat this morning. I didn't want to get my Sunday best one ripped in the mine. How many strips do you need?"

"Three about a foot longer than the width of his leg so that I can tie these splints on tight."

Beatrice turned her back, lifted her skirt, and ripping sounds rang throughout the strope. In just a few seconds, she handed Mr. McGrady three strips which he used to securely fasten the splints onto the injured leg.

As they looked at the pale face of the sheriff, the enormity of their situation hit them full force.

"Oh, what are we going to do now? The cold and dampness down here is seeping into my very bones," whined Sally.

"I'm terribly hungry," complained Beatrice. "What I wouldn't give for one of my hot biscuits and an extra helping of rabbit stew. It seems like an eternity since I ate breakfast."

Molly turned to Mr. McGrady and placing her hand on his arm said, "Do you think there's any chance that we'll ever get out of here? Do you think they know about the cave-in up above?"

"I'm sure they are aware that we're in trouble, ladies. Depending on how bad the slide is, they're probably down here already–as far as they can come, that is. If the car that carries passengers is lodged in by the cave-in, they can hoist down help by using the ore car. If luck is with us, the ore car was up above when the cave-in happened."

Lillian stilled her trembling lips long enough to get out, "How will they know we're still alive? For all they know, we're underneath that pile of rubble that's now clogging the entrance portal."

Mr. McGrady's face showed the strain of their situation. He was probably in his late 50's by Lillian's determination, but men who spend a great deal of time in the mines always look older than they actually are.

"I might as well lay it out like I see it, ladies. You see that broken pipe over there? Well, it's the air pipe. The part of the pipe coming from the outside which delivers fresh air is covered up in the slide. It's likely crushed and closed shut. What that means is no fresh air can get to us. If they don't rescue us within the next 24 hours, the bad air that we breathe out will replace the good air, and we'll not have a chance of making it. We have a little water in that barrel over there, but no food. Then, too, the cold and dampness could get us if we're not careful.

"Our only chance is to huddle together, giving each other our body warmth. I suggest that you sit on the floor of the strope, hold the sheriff on your laps, and cover him with your skirts.

Hug each other real tight. I'm going to go over here by these pipes and tap on them ever so often. That will tell the rescuers that we're still alive and let them know that they can't give up."

Sitting on the ground with the sheriff on their laps, Lillian finally had time to bow her head and silently talk to the one person that she knew could help her.

Heavenly Father, we really need your help. If it is your will that we survive this cave-in, please direct the rescue efforts so that we can go on living our lives on this earth.

Please bless the sheriff, if it is your will that he will survive and be able to go back to his duties. Give us peace, Heavenly Father, and the strength to withstand this conflict.

Our lives are in your hands, dear Lord, she thought as she grabbed on tightly to her companions, hoping body heat would indeed be their savior.

Chapter 28

The quiet group who sat in the dim light below was in stark contrast with the scene above ground.

When the next shift of miners arrived, they found Harvey, the hoist man, sitting on the ground, his bottle tipped to his lips as he sobbed and rambled on in almost unintelligible sentences.

"They're gone for sure. Poor souls and Old McGrady too...There's no hope. Nothin' I could do. Sheriff crushed too. No peace now! Wanted to say, 'Don't go!' Wouldn't listen. Nobody listens to Harvey. Now they're gone. Crushed for sure!"

Charles Anderson stepped from the group of miners and knelt by the old man. He took Harvey's sobbing face in his hands and forced him to look directly at him.

"Harvey, who's gone for sure? Who's crushed?"

"Sally, Beatrice, Molly and Miss Lewis–crushed for sure!"

At the mention of Lillian's name, Charles's face paled and his hands trembled. "Women in the mine? There's never been women in the mine? Are you sure Miss Lewis is down there? Tell me it's the whiskey talking," he pleaded as he grabbed Harvey by his shoulders and shook him so hard that a painful moan came from Harvey's lips.

"Sheriff and McGrady gone too! I told 'em women in the mine was unlucky. Wouldn't listen," sobbed the old man as he covered his face with his gnarled hands.

Not wanting to believe what he had just heard, Charles stumbled to the shaft where the rest of the men were gazing down into the dark abyss, looks of horror on their faces.

"It's a bad cave-in," gasped Mitch Smithson. "Did I hear Harvey say Molly? I told her not to go. Threatened her with her life, but she was determined to be one of the first ladies in Frisco to enter the mine. Surely she obeyed me! Surely she's home!" He put his hands over his face as tears flowed freely down his cheeks.

Charles shook Harvey gently, "Harvey, can you stop blubbering long enough to see if you can bring up the crew cage?"

"Tried...stuck fast," sobbed the old man.

"We're lucky," said Charles. "The ore car is on top and free to carry us down to see just how bad the situation is."

Charles motioned to Red and Jude to follow him into the cage. "Lower us down, Harvey," he yelled.

Any breath that the men had in their lungs was expelled quickly as the cage descended like a speeding bullet down the shaft, landing with a thud on a large pile of rubble.

"Heaven help us now," moaned Charles. "The entire portal to the strope has collapsed, along with some of the wall on the inside of the shaft. Who knows how much on the other side of the portal has collapsed too. It'll take us hours–probably days–to get all this cleared away so that we can get to them. I don't know if our efforts will be in time. If only we knew they were still..."

A muffled "tap, tap, tap" sounded from behind the mound of rubble.

Deep breaths were expelled from fatigued lungs as the three men sighed in relief.

"Yes!" Yelled Charles. "We have survivors!"

"Red, yank on the rope so that Harvey will pull us up. We've got to get picks, shovels, and buckets. We can't waste one minute of precious time."

When they reached the top, they gathered up the needed materials, and Charles divided the men into teams of eight. Each team would stay down in the shaft and work for an hour, then the next team would be ready to take over.

When the first team was lowered into the shaft, Charles gave three men picks and shovels and told them to hack away at the dirt and rocks. Two men behind them were to fill buckets with the loose material and pass the buckets on to the three other men in back of them. The eight men formed a brigade, leading to the ore cage. The last man was to dump the bucket into the ore cage. With everyone doing their job, it didn't take long for the cage to be filled. The rope was then yanked, the cage pulled to the top, then emptied by another team above ground.

Ned Druthers had heard of the cave-in when he pulled into town. When he learned that his beloved Missy was in the mine, he frantically drove his beloved mules to the site of the tragedy. His old, weathered face showed the stress that flowed through his body. Mabel and Lizzy seemed to sense the seriousness of the moment as they emitted loud neighs every few seconds and wildly flicked their ears and tails.

"Quiet, girls," commanded Ned. "We'll get her out if we have to hoist Mabel down and have her kick her way in!"

All through the afternoon, the shifts of men hacked away at the mound that separated them from the trapped party. Then it happened. There was total quiet, then the walls of the shaft took on a life of their own as timbers started groaning and cracking as the shaft walls eerily began to close in on the rescue party.

"Into the cage!" Screamed Charles, frantically pulling on the hoist, followed by shouts of, "Pull us up!" and "Cave-in!" After what seemed like hours, but was really seconds, the cage began moving at the very instant that the shaft began to collapse below them.

They felt like they were living a nightmare as they gazed below at the dirt, wood, and pipes which were filling in the shaft, chasing them with a vengeance to the surface. Dust and dirt flew around them in every direction, so that when they reached the top, they had to wipe their eyes and wait for the dust to settle before they realized that they were above ground, safe and sound.

Stumbling from the cage, Charles fell to his knees on the snowy ground. *No chance of getting to her now,* he thought as tears made bright furrows down his dirty cheeks. *We tried, Lilly, oh how we tried! Please someone tell me this isn't real. I've been so stupid. Now she'll never know..."*

It was then that a worn hat was removed and a dusty head bowed to do something that Charles hadn't done since his boyhood visits to his grandmother's. There the day always ended as grandmother knelt beside him and they visited with God as if He were their dearest friend. Silently, Charles began his prayer. *Heavenly Father, I know I haven't talked to you lately, and you certainly have no reason to help me, but if anyone ever needed you, it's me. I want to make a deal with you. If you will just help me find a way to help these poor, trapped souls, I promise to be a better man—one who is closer to you in every way. If you'll just help me with this one thing, I promise to change my ways and do your will for the rest of my days. I know you can hear me. Please send your help.*

A gentle hand and a familiar voice awakened Charles from his grief. "Dad, what's wrong?"

Charles lifted his tear-stained face to look into the concerned eyes of his son.

He couldn't keep his voice from cracking as he explained, "It's Miss Lewis, Billie. There's been a bad cave-in. Miss Lewis and five others are trapped, and there's no way to get them out. We were almost to them when the whole shaft gave way. No way I know of to reach them in time now unless a miracle alternative route can be found."

Silence reigned for a few seconds while Charles bowed his head and once more gave way to his grief.

A small hand gently shook his shoulder once again. "But, Pa, I might just know another way."

Afraid to even hope or smile, Charles lifted his head to gaze into his son's excited face. "What do you mean another way?"

"Well, last summer, Jamie and me were doing our wanderings, like we usually do when we're looking for excitement." Billie hesitated as he gazed into his father's tear-stained eyes.

"Are you sure you're not going to get mad at me, Pa? If you are, I'll just stop right here."

"There'll be no punishment, if there's a way to save lives. Hurry, Billie, we're wasting precious time!"

"Well, during our wanderings, we saw the strangest thing. A mother mountain lion and her cubs were walking along the ridge. Before we knew it, they had disappeared into the brush on the mountain. Course we had to check this out, so we ran up there and by golly, we found a pretty good cave behind that brush. We weren't foolish enough to follow that mother lion in right then, but we decided that we'd wait until another day. When we saw her leave, we'd investigate this cave right and proper. It seemed to draw us with its black arms, and that's all we could talk about for the next week.

"Finally, Saturday rolled around. We hid in the brush facing the mouth of the cave early in the morning, and it wasn't long until that old mamma and her two little ones came out to hunt. After we were sure she was gone, we lit our kerosene lantern and started our cave explorin'. It was pretty dark inside, but the lantern gave us enough light. The floor of the cave soon dropped off, taking us down into the mountain side. Good thing we had the lantern, cause we were stopped short by a deep drop off that seemed to go down forever. Jamie and me threw rocks down it. It was so deep that we hardly heard a sound when they landed."

"What has this got to do with saving Miss Lewis? Let's have it, son!"

"Well, Pa, when we looked down, we saw a little light shining from down below. Jamie and I figured that the end of that drop off more than likely was close to the ceiling of the main strope in the mine. The light from some lanterns in the strope was shining through to us cause the floor of the cave had somehow broke through into the strope ceiling. We were convinced of this when we heard a booming sound coming from below the light. We both figured that boom was more than likely the muffled sound of dynamite like they use in the mine. Maybe there's a way into the strope at the bottom of that drop-off."

A gnarled hand on his shoulder caused Charles to turn around. Ned's eyes were wet and his withered hand was shaking. "My Little Missy's down there for sure?"

"She's down there for sure along with five others. Billie thinks he knows of an alternate route to reach them. Can we depend on you and your mules to help?"

"There's nothing I wouldn't do for that Little Missy. Just tell me what to do and I'll do it."

Charles motioned in the direction of the mules. "Just pull your wagon over here and help us get things loaded. Billie, you've got to give us a hand. There can't be one wasted minute. Lives are depending on us."

Charles gathered up ten men, quickly explained the situation to them, and then directed them to load the necessary supplies needed for the rescue. A great deal of rope was quickly thrown into an empty ore wagon, which was complete with two mules, waiting for the next ore shipment. An old, empty ore cage was also loaded under Charles's direction as well as picks, shovels, and buckets. Warm blankets and five kerosene lanterns were quickly placed inside the old ore cage. With the ore wagon full, all but two of the rescue team would travel in Ned's wagon which was at this minute positioned in front of the ore wagon which was driven by the remaining two men.

Charles motioned for the rescue team to jump in as he lost no time hoisting himself onto the wagon seat beside Billie.

"Little Missy will be fine, Charles. Molly and Lizzie won't let nothing harm that little gal," comforted Ned as he shook the reins and made clucking sounds, a signal to the mules that they needed to proceed at lightning speed.

As Charles motioned to the driver of the ore wagon to follow behind, Billie blurted out directions on how to reach the mountain trail, and within 15 minutes, Molly and Lizzy were moving along the mountainside, running as they had never run before, somehow sensing that lives did indeed depend on their speed and agility. Excited brays filled the frosty air as the mules pulled deeply from their reservoirs of energy.

When Billie yelled, "Stop, Pa! We're here!" Charles and Billie scrambled from the wagon.

"Stay here until we get back," Charles yelled to Ned and the rest of the rescue team.

The mouth of the cave was hidden from view by brush, but lion tracks could be seen emerging from the corner of the brush, giving away the location of the cave's mouth. When Billie pulled aside some of the thicket, Charles looked into the blackness of a small cave. The mouth of the cave was about 6 feet high and wide enough to accommodate their wagons, making it possible for Charles and Billie to easily step inside. The light from the lantern illuminated a cavern about the size of a large shanty. Through the middle of the cavern ran a streambed where spring water flowed from the mountain runoff. When the rays of the lantern fell upon white bones lying in the corner of the cave, Billie gave a started cry and jumped. Charles shuddered, then calmed himself and his son as he placed his arm around Billie's shaking body.

"It's all right, son. They're just left overs from momma lion's dinners. We're in luck. Her absence means she's probably out hunting right now."

Their calm was shattered as eerie high-pitched squeals pierced through the black silence of the cavern and got louder and stronger each minute.

A small furry object flew by Billie's face, causing him to scream and hold tightly to his dad's arm.

"Dad! What's that?" screamed Billie as he moved closer to his father.

Charles held the lantern so that the light fell on the ceiling of the cavern. The high-pitched sound appeared to be coming from hundreds of furry creatures hanging upside down on the rocks that made up the cavern's ceiling.

"Bats, son. If we're real quiet and don't rile them up, they'll likely stay put. It's their time to hibernate and sleep some, but their high-pitched squeals mean that we've disturbed them. They're shy creatures, and if we don't bother them, they won't bother us."

Billie inched closer to his father as he whispered, "I think you're right, Dad. They seem to be quieting down." Grabbing his father's arm, Billie led him to the end of the cavern where through the lantern's light they could see a passage about 10 feet wide.

"We have to go down this passage, Dad, but you'll have to duck your head a bit or you might get cold cocked!"

Being careful to shine the light before them, they stopped when they encountered a large boulder that was hanging from the ceiling. Most of the boulder was showing and seemed to be barely attached to the top of the passageway.

As Charles ducked to avoid the huge rock he said, "I hope that rock doesn't decide to give way while we're gone and block the passage. If that happens, we'll be trapped in here with no escape route."

Billie's shaking hand grabbed his father's steadier one. "We've got to go slow now, Dad. The drop-off is just a few feet from here. I didn't tell you before, but Jamie and me almost fell down the hole. If Jamie hadn't stumbled on a rock and fell flat in front of the drop-off, we'd both have been goners for sure."

Carefully shining the lantern in front of them, Charles saw the trail disappear into blackness as the drop-off loomed a few inches ahead of them. As they stood on the rim of the black abyss, they could faintly see another light shining from the floor below.

Excitement filled Charles's voice as he said, "I think you may be right, son. That main strope in the mine is a big one, and that light might just lead us into the strope's north end where they're trapped. Pray to God that we're not too late."

In just a matter of a few minutes, they were back outside the cave, organizing the men and getting the materials that they would need.

The rescue party entered the cave with the ore cage, rope, picks and shovels, and a reluctant Lizzy. Because they were full of adrenaline, which flowed through their veins like liquid excitement, not even the squeaks emitting from the cave's ceiling slowed them down. Only Lizzy seemed reluctant to move forward at a rapid pace. When the mule heard the high-pitched bat squeals, she dug her feet in and refused to go any further. Ned took some pieces of dried apples out of his pockets and walked just far enough ahead of her so that she couldn't reach her favorite treats. When they reached the hanging rock, they left Ned and an apple-munching Lizzy on the other side of the boulder. Before they continued on down the passage, the long rope that was attached to the ore cage was tied around Lizzy's middle.

When the men reached the drop-off, Charles looked into the worry-worn faces of the party as his own eyes issued a challenge. "Who wants to get in the cage with me and be lowered down to that faint light that you see below?"

"I'll go. My Molly's down there," said Mitch Smithson.

"Count me in," said Walt Reynolds. "If somebody got to my Sally before me, I'd never forgive myself."

Billie shook his dad's arm and begged, "Let me go, dad. I'm the one who led you here. Please let a feller follow through till the end. It's my Miss Lewis that's down there. Please, Dad."

"All right, if you promise to be careful and stay close to me," Charles said as he led Billie into the cage.

"The rest of you men stay up above to lower us down. Don't worry if you drop the rope. Remember, it's attached to

Lizzy, and she's solid as a boulder," said Charles as he stepped into the cage with Walt and Mitch.

Three men pushed the cage over the side while the other men held tightly to the rope. Slowly the men holding the rope began to lower the ore cage into the blackness. It was deathly cold inside the cave, and even though their hands were covered with gloves, they were frigid and stiff. It was no easy task to slowly lower the cage in the frosty air. At one point the rope slipped through all their fingers, and the cage descended rapidly before the men above once again gained control of the rope and brought the cage to an abrupt halt.

"Holy jeepers, Dad! My heart almost jumped outta my throat. I thought we were goners for sure. But look, we're almost to the bottom–just another foot, and we're near that spot of light." Billie pointed to the light shining in the darkness.

When the cage hit solid ground, the rescue party stepped outside the cage to survey the spot where the light shone through.

Charles now whipped the rescue team into action. "This has got to be close to the ceiling of the strope, and that light must be coming from a strope lantern. Get the picks and shovels and see if we can make a hole big enough to fit the ore cage through. We've got to be careful so that the whole ceiling doesn't collapse, and speed has to be our goal. Those poor souls have been trapped for almost 24 hours. If we don't get to them soon, we may be too late. From the looks of the cave-in, the air hose is broken, and there hasn't been any fresh air other than what's coming through this hole for all that time." Charles filled the first shovel with dirt and the work began.

As they enlarged the hole, great care had to be taken so that the actual dirt under their feet didn't give way and send them crashing to the floor of the strope which lay in the near blackness below. After only a few minutes of shoveling, their theory about where this hole led became fact. They could see the honeycombed walls of the strope, illuminated by the strope lanterns which were attached to the walls.

"Hallelujah! I believe we've found that alternate route," yelled Walt.

"Hang on, Miss, Lewis. The rescue party's on the way!" gushed Billie.

In 30 minutes time, the hole was a little larger than the ore cage. The men pushed the cage to the edge of the hole and then entered it.

Charles looked up and yelled, "Hey you up there, pull up a little on the cage and move it to the right until it has completely blocked out the light from below. When you can't see the light below any more, you'll know that we're over the hole. Then hold tight to the rope and lower us down. We're certain that we've found a way into the strope. When you feel us hit the bottom, pray that we find everyone alive and safe. When we need you to raise the cage, we'll give three tugs on the rope and give you a loud holler."

The men inside the cage held their breaths as they felt themselves being raised and slowly moved slightly to the right. Prickles of excitement caused goose bumps to form on their arms as they felt themselves being lowered into what they hoped was the strope where the cave-in had occurred. Looking out of the cage into the near darkness, it seemed as if they were being lowered into the depths of an infernal pit.

When the cage hit the floor of the strope, Charles threw the door of the cage open, and the rescue party lost no time exiting.

Billie hugged his father as he yelled, "Gee Whilikers! We've found it, Dad! Now what?" Charles had to squelch his joy long enough to think clearly. "I'm guessing that they're trapped to the south of us, but in case I'm turned around, Mitch and Walt, you go north, and I'll take Billie and head south. Whoever finds them first will let out a loud yell. Good luck!" Charles gave Walt and Mitch a pat on their arms as he grabbed Billie, and they began to run in a southerly direction as fast as the dim light would allow.

Billie slowed down as he started coughing and sputtered, "Dad, this air in here is terrible. My lungs are hurting somethin' fearful, and there's a sick feeling in my stomach."

Charles, still holding Billie's hand, slowed the pace down to a fast walk. "I know, son. There hasn't been fresh air in here for 24 hours. That hole we just dug will help some, but we're just going to have to forget about how our lungs and stomachs feel. There's no time to waste."

Luckily, the air from the new opening was enough to keep their lantern burning because the further they went into the strope, they found that most of the lanterns which hung on the walls had been extinguished when the oxygen level diminished. After about 50 more feet and still nothing in sight but a dim, empty strope, Charles began to fear that they were headed in the wrong direction.

Taking hold of Billie's arm, he brought them to a halt. "I'm starting to think that we won't find them going this direction, son. Maybe we'd better turn around and join the others." Just then a strong scent of lavender filled Charles's nostrils. It was the same scent that had been present when he kissed Lillian under the mistletoe the night of the dance. The scent seemed to be coming from in front of them, beckoning them to follow it into the southernmost part of the strope.

"Do you smell it, Billie?"

"You mean that sweet flower-like scent? Sure do. It's a sign for sure. I've often smelled that same smell when Miss Lewis bent to help me with my schoolwork. Let's keep going, Pa."

Two sets of boots threw rocks in every direction as father and son ran alongside the ore car trestle.

A faint sound some distance ahead of them prompted Charles to bring Billie to a halt so that they could listen intently.

"You heard that, Billie?"

"Ya. It sounded like somebody was coughing."

"God be praised! They've got to be close by!" Charles said as he grabbed Billie's arm and started them once again into a full run.

The coughing sounds got louder the further south they went. Now, low moans of pain could also be heard intermingled with the coughs. Then the light from the lantern revealed forms, arranged in a semicircle, lying prostrate on the ground. Some forms were perfectly still, while others moved slightly in the dim light.

Charles quickly scanned the circle for the one dear face that had led him on throughout this entire ordeal. Starting at one end of the circle, he illuminated each face. When he found Lillian's dust-covered face and saw the jagged, bloody scar running down her right cheek and the dusty, closed eyelids, he seemed to lose all sense of reason. He quickly knelt and took the unconscious body into his arms, showering soft kisses onto the dusty hair and cheeks.

Softly, he murmured, "Lilly, oh my sweet Lilly. Don't leave me now. I've been such a fool. I can't go on another minute without you." The tears ran freely down his cheeks, leaving glistening spots on his unkempt beard. She felt so small and still in his arms, but as he held her tightly to him, a rush of joy gave strength to his tired muscles as he felt her chest slowly rising and falling in stark contrast to the beating of his own racing heart.

Out of the corner of his eye, he thought he saw a shaking hand move up to rest on his shoulder as eyelids fluttered and a weak voice whispered, "Charles, Charles..." Then long, dusty eyelashes became still once more, and the tiny hand slid down his arm to rest upon her chest.

Billie's eyes widened and his mouth flew open at the sight of his father holding and showering kisses on his teacher. *You've lost your senses, Pa. I've never seen you carry on like this–not even with Ma!*

His confusion was only momentary, however, as coughing and moaning to the right and left of Lillian brought both Charles and Billie back to reality.

Gently placing Lillian back on the ground, Charles yelled, "Hey! They're here!" Then he lost no time in checking the dusty form next to Lillian.

Even a thick layer of dust couldn't hide the fine features of Molly Smithson. Her small hand raised to her mouth as spasms of coughing convulsed her body.

Charles took her face in his hands, as half-shut eyes met his. "Charles Anderson? Can't move–so dizzy." Then dusty eyelashes fell on dust-powdered cheeks once more, but her labored breathing signaled that she was still among the living.

"Mrs. Reynolds is out cold, Pa, but she's breathing regular," said Billie, his small head resting on Sally's chest.

They could see or feel no movement in the body of Beatrice Small, but when Charles held his fingers to her wrist, he could feel the flutter of a faint pulse.

"If we get her out of here soon, Billie, she might yet be saved," said Charles.

It was then that Walt Reynolds and Mitch Smithson joined them. Each man found his wife, took her in his arms, as tears ran freely down their faces with the realization that they were not too late.

Kneeling beside the sheriff, Charles gave him a quick examination. "Phillips is in bad shape. He's still breathing, but it looks like he's crushed up pretty bad. The splint on his leg tells us they had the presence of mind to set the bone, but his head appears to be badly crushed on the right side."

Billie yelled from the caved-in strope opening, "Mr. McGrady's breathing, too. He's here by the cave-in. His arm's hanging kind of funny like, but he's coughing somethin' fierce. That has to be a good sign."

"We've got to get them out of here quick!" said Charles. Trying to reason clearly, he knew that as much as he was concerned about Lillian, she was not the most critical member of the group. "Beatrice has got to be the first one out if she's going to make it," he told the others.

Charles started gathering pieces of broken timbers as he continued, "We've got to get them all down by the new opening we just made in the ceiling. The air that's coming in from that hole might just make the difference between life and death."

Broken timbers were fashioned into a makeshift stretcher, and Beatrice was placed on it. Charles motioned for Billie to go to the bottom of the stretcher as he turned to the other two men. "Billie and I will carry Beatrice on the stretcher. Mitch and Walt, do you think you can carry your wives? That way we can get three of them to the cage all at once."

Two men's cold hands gathered precious bundles into weak arms that seemed to be given strength of their own as the husbands realized the priceless load that they carried.

Charles took one last glance at the dear face that he knew he must leave behind if only for a few minutes. He then signaled to Billie, and the stretcher which held Beatrice was lifted as the four rescuers began to move as rapidly as their tired muscles would allow them in the direction of the ore cage.

After what seemed an eternity, they reached the cage. Mitch and Walt wanted to go up to the surface with their wives, but Charles convinced them that Billie could go up in the cage with the women. "It's vital that we get back to the other three so that we can have them back here when the cage comes down again."

The unconscious women were laid carefully in the center of the ore cage, and Billie positioned himself in the center of them, ready to shout directions to those above should there be any problem.

"Hey, you up there!"

"We hear you!" was the muted reply from above.

Charles cupped his hands over his mouth as he yelled, "We've found them. They're alive. Three of them are in the ore car with Billie. Pull them up slowly when you hear me yell, 'pull!'" Looking at his son, his heart swelled with pride as he realized that the boy's courage and bravery over the past 24 hours could have matched that of a much older man.

"Billie, we're going back for the other three. You've got to help them get these three loaded into the wagon and then be sure that they cover them with those blankets we brought. It's up to you to see that the ore cage is sent back down as soon as possible so that it's here when we get Miss Lewis, the sheriff, and Emit back. I'm depending on you, son."

"Don't worry about me, Dad. I can do it. You just worry about saving Miss Lewis and the others."

"Pull!" Charles yelled. The minute the ore car started to move upward, the three men began their return trip to the site of the cave-in. The further they moved from the ceiling hole, the more difficult it became to continue. Muscle weakness and fatigue threatened to defeat them at every footstep.

They became dizzy and disoriented and had to stop every few feet to lower their heads and get their bearings. The cold air seemed to reach into their bones with its icy fingers and take every last bit of energy that they had stored like a thief who steals the last pennies from a dying woman.

Charles knew that the nausea he was feeling was a result of the bad air. He couldn't remember a time in his life when he had felt worse. With every breath he took, his body became weaker. *If we don't get out of here soon, none of us will make it to the top alive*, he thought as he shook his head to try to drive away the searing headache that had plagued him ever since he had entered the strope.

When they stopped to catch their breath, Charles saw an ore car attached to the tracks in the middle of the strope and a donkey lying beside it, another victim of the cave-in. A lover of animals, Charles quickly checked the hairy frame to find that there was yet another survivor. The donkey was unconscious, but its heart was beating strongly.

"When we get everyone out and back home, we'll send someone back for him. I won't leave him down here as long as he's alive."

"Get behind this ore car," he said as he motioned to the other men. "I don't know why we didn't think of it before, but this car may be the very vehicle that will help us get the remaining three out of here."

Grabbing onto the car to push it seemed to give them stability and support, making the way easier and helping to conserve what strength they had left. Empty, it was fairly light and moved rapidly down the trestle.

When they reached the three unconscious forms, they loaded the sheriff into the car first. There was plenty of room for Mr. McGrady next to him.

Charles lifted Lillian and shook his head when Mitch and Walt tried to take her from him and place her in the car with the other two. *I don't want to let you go ever again,* he thought as he tried to memorize every line in her face. She was unconscious, but gave a slight groan when he hugged her to him. *Hang in there, Lilly. You can't leave me now.*

"You've got to put her in the car, man. You're not strong enough to carry her all by yourself," said Mitch. "She'll be easier to push than carry."

Charles resisted for a few minutes, then nodded and reluctantly let them help him put Lillian in the car, opposite the other two.

All three men positioned themselves at the end of the car and pushed with every ounce of their remaining energy.

The empty cage was a welcome sight when they reached their destination. They laid the sheriff and Mr. Grady on the floor of the cage. Charles picked up Lillian, and when Mitch and Walt offered their assistance, he shook his head and held tightly to her still form, refusing to relinquish her. When all three men were inside the car, Charles yelled, "Hey, up there! Pull away!" and the cage began its upward climb.

What seemed like hours was in reality only a few minutes until the cage rested on the solid ground of the cave. Strength from waiting hands and arms took the burdens from two weary men whose strength had been exhausted hours ago, but still Charles held tightly to Lillian, refusing to release her. It appeared that her tiny body was frozen solid in his grip.

Only Ned Druthers was able to assist him with her as he helped load his precious "Little Missy" into his wagon. Ned led his beloved Lizzy from the cave. He stroked her ears lovingly and whispered in her ear, "That ore cage would never have made it to the surface without some superior mule power. Thanks, old girl." He then hitched her carefully to his freight wagon.

The victims were divided equally into the two wagons where they were covered with warm blankets.

The early morning sun shone brightly on the newly-fallen snow as the wagons headed for town. Mabel and Lizzy seemed to sense the seriousness of the situation as they drew on hidden reservoirs of energy, enabling the party to quickly bridge the gap between the rescue scene and Frisco. It had been a full 30 hours since the cave-in, and the rescuers were as much in need of medical attention and food as those who had been trapped in the mine. No one in the party had eaten or slept since this ordeal began.

"Take them to The Southern," said Charles. "I know Ben won't mind if we make some kind of a temporary hospital there for them. If only we had a doctor nearby. As soon as we get to Frisco and get them into The Southern, we'll send the fastest rider we've got in town to Milford to bring the Milford doctor here. Billie, we go past Mrs. Nelson's house on the way to The Southern. We'll stop the wagon there, and you run in and tell Mrs. Nelson we need her at The Southern. Almost every baby brought into the world in Frisco has been welcomed by her friendly face. She's the best help that we've got right now. Get her daughter Mary to come too. I understand that she's almost as good as her mother. Tell Mrs. Nelson to enlist anyone else that she can think of who might be of help. Tell her that you'll be a messenger and get them to The Southern. The important thing is that we need her right now."

Molly and Lizzy never broke their stride as Ned conveyed to them the importance of speed through the pressure he put on the reins. It was early afternoon in Frisco, but Main Street was lined with curious citizens, anxious to know about the survivors. Many of them ran after the wagons, yelling questions about their fears and concerns.

"Did they make it? Are there survivors?"

When the wagons stopped in front of The Southern, Charles yelled to the crowd, "They're all alive, but please step back so that we can get them out of the cold, or they won't have a chance."

The crowd retreated, leaving a clear path to the front door of The Southern. Charles gently lifted Lillian into his arms. Her face was pale as death, but as he hugged her to him, he could feel the gentle rise and fall of her chest, and as he lowered his face to her lips, a gentle flow of air gave him hope. Helping hands from the rescue group and bystanders gently lifted the other survivors from the wagon. Charles felt someone grab his arm and turned to see Nettie with tears glistening in her eyes.

"Please let me help, Charles."

Charles nodded his head, and Nettie followed him into the warmth of The Southern's lobby where Ben approached them.

"Have you enough rooms on the bottom floor to take care of six critically injured people?" The stress in Charles's voice signaled the precariousness of the situation.

Ben motioned for Charles to follow him. Doors were quickly thrown open as Ben motioned for the rescuers to deposit their precious cargos on waiting beds.

"We need lots of hot water and clean cloths," Nettie told Ben.

"Yes, and keep that water and cloths coming," joined in Mrs. Nelson as she came running into the first bedroom. Mary was right behind her, and tears began to flow freely when she caught her first sight of her dear Miss Lewis.

Mrs. Nelson was all business as she organized the Frisco ladies and sent them with specific orders into their designated sick rooms. "While one of you is taking off their outer clothing, the others warm their beds with hot bricks taken from the fire and wrapped in cloths. When the hot water and cloths get here, sponge them down, then dress the ladies in these flannel nightgowns that I brought from home and the men in my husband's long johns–he'll never miss them. Get them into the heated beds as soon as you can and throw four or five blankets over them. Ben has been kind enough to supply us with extra ones from The Southern."

When Charles refused to place Lillian on the bed and leave the room, Mrs. Nelson placed her hands on her hips and in a forceful, demanding tone that showed she was authority personified said, "Charles, you've got to lay her on the bed and get out of here so that we can do our work. When she's washed down and safely underneath a pile of covers, we might let you back in, if you promise to behave yourself and not get in our way." Charles reluctantly placed Lillian on the bed, but did not leave her side until he had taken her face in his hands and ran his fingers over her cheeks in a gentle goodbye gesture. It was then that Mrs. Nelson focused on the pale, haggard faces of Charles and the others who were responsible for the rescue.

"Ben, please take these poor men into the kitchen and get them something warm to eat so we can get on with the task of bringing these poor unfortunates back into the world of the healthy living!"

Charles would have preferred to wait in the hall outside Lillian's door, but one look at the face of his son told him to use some common sense.

"I'm awfully hungry, dad. We've got to leave Miss Lewis and let Mrs. Nelson do her work. I'm kind of dizzy, and my stomach hurts somethin' fierce!"

At this point, Charles let himself be led with the others into the warm, cozy kitchen of The Southern. A large pot of hot stew was bubbling on the cast iron stove, and the fresh biscuits that had just come from the oven smelled like a bit of heaven.

Sixty minutes later not one drop of the savory stew remained in the iron pot. Every drop of it had disappeared into hungry stomachs or been sopped up by the fluffy biscuits, making the plates as clean as if they had just undergone a thorough washing. Everything seemed to look better through the eyes of a full stomach, and warmth and contentment settled like a warm blanket around the men sitting at the large table.

The kitchen door swung open to reveal the work-worn faces of Mrs. Nelson and Mary. Some of Mrs. Nelson's brown hair, which was streaked with gray, had escaped the tight bun secured to the top of her head to stand out in wisps around her pleasant face. The front of her work apron was damp from sponging down her patients, and it was clear that she was exhausted, but as she hugged Mary, a wide smile brought out the dimples in each cheek, causing beauty to shine forth through the fine lines that were just beginning to form at the corners of her eyes.

"Just thought you'd like to know–you got them here just in time. All of them seem to be showing some improvement, even the sheriff and Beatrice. I thought Beatrice was a goner for sure when I first saw her, but just minutes ago she opened her eyes and asked for some water. It'd take a major disaster to keep that one down. The sheriff is still in a coma, and only time will tell whether or not he'll mend. We've been able to get some liquid down him by squeezing a wet rag into his mouth. His head injury is a bad one, but he's young and strong and a real fighter. If I were a betting woman, I'd put money down that he'll survive. We've got McGrady in the room next to the sheriff. We've been able to get some liquid down him, too, and his broken arm has been set right and proper. I hope we can handle things here because a relative of the Milford doctor told me that he's been called to St. George. By the time we reached him, it would be too late for the critical ones."

"How's my Molly?" asked Mitch Smithson.

"She and Sally have both come to long enough to drink some liquid and sip a little bit of broth. The effort has tired them out, and they're now sleeping peacefully. Mitch and Walt, you may sit in their rooms, but don't keep them from their sleep. I won't have you disturbing my patients. What they need now is lots of rest."

Mrs. Nelson's eyes fell upon Charles and Billie. She had noticed the care and attention that they had given Miss Lewis, and she sensed their deep feelings for her. "Miss Lewis is going to be all right, too. She has a nasty gash on her face, but I'm going to get my sewing needle and get it stitched up as soon as Mary and I have a bite to eat. Billie, your teacher came to long enough for us to get a drink of water and some broth down her. Charles, if you and Billie go in to see her, be careful that you don't disturb her sleep."

Charles ran his hand through his dusty hair and turned to the owner of The Southern. "Ben, do you have an extra bed for Billie here? He's dead on his feet, and I'd like to spend some more time here if you don't mind."

"Sure, Charles, put him in Room 3 on the bottom floor. There are plenty of rooms for any of you men if you need a few hours rest, and you know where the bathroom is. From the looks of you, a warm soak in a hot tub might feel pretty good right now," Ben offered.

Mitch and Walt headed for the bathroom to clean themselves up while Charles took Billie to Room 3. He took advantage of the hot water left for them as he washed away the dust from his son's face and removed his outer clothing, then helped him into a warm bed.

Billie heaved a contented sigh as he snuggled under the covers. "Feels like a feather mattress, dad....so soft...don't forget to check on Miss Lewis...school wouldn't be the same..." then all was quiet as sandy lashes fell upon freckled cheeks as Billie fell into a deep slumber.

Charles kissed his son's forehead, then, careful not to wake him, crossed the room slowly, carefully opened and closed the door, and headed for the next room. There was only one person on his mind, and he could think of nothing else until he made sure for himself the nature of her condition.

When he opened the door to Lillian's room and gazed at her lying so still in the bed, he was struck by how small and fragile she was. Her face, now free from dust, was still pale, but a small amount of color was beginning to return to her cheeks, and her breathing was not labored.

Mrs. Nelson had been in and carefully stitched up the wound on her face and dressed her in a warm, flannel nightgown. Lillian's long hair had been brushed and arranged attractively around her face; its deep blackness was in stark contrast to her pallid complexion.

Charles dropped to his knees, and reaching for a small hand, kissed it tenderly. After a few minutes of staring into the dear face that had held him captive ever since he first beheld it, he gave way to exhaustion as his head slowly lowered to the bed, and he became lost in a world of dreams, still tightly clasping Lillian's hand.

Chapter 29

Lillian awakened just as the rosy rays of the early morning sun began streaking through the window. As her eyes took in the unfamiliar surroundings, a sea of panic swept over her. *What am I doing in this strange room? One of the last things I remember was being trapped in the strope and the desperation I felt when we heard the shaft outside the strope collapsing. The terrified cries of the rescue party as they struggled to reach the surface will remain with me forever.*

Her throat felt like rough sandpaper as she tried to swallow, and there was a fierce throbbing in her head. She tried to move her left hand to touch her forehead and find the source of the pain but found that someone was holding it in a firm grasp. It was then that she became aware of a dusty head lying next to her arm.

The unkempt beard and the long, narrow fingers which held her hand prisoner could only belong to one person–*Charles, what are you doing here?* Then memories of that same dusty head bent over hers as she lay on the hard ground of the strope and strong arms giving her comfort when she most needed it filled her muddled thoughts. *Thank God you escaped the shaft cave-in, but why after ignoring me for weeks were you holding me in the mine, and why are you here now?*

Lillian's eyes caught a slight movement of the door as it slowly opened. Mary's face was the first to be seen. Mary turned to look behind her and placed her finger to her lips–the signal for silence. But as it is impossible to quiet a wild stampede of cattle, so it is impossible to control a class of concerned children who are determined to see their teacher. Lillian opened her eyes to find all ten of her students encircling her bed.

Their entrance awakened Charles who quickly released Lillian's hand as he rose from his kneeling position. Billie, awake and once more dressed in his dirty clothes, ran to his father and hugged him as he blurted out, "Told them she was all right, Pa, but they wouldn't believe me. Had to see for themselves."

"You can't get through to some people," said Mary. "Told them I'd been checking on her all night and she was fine, but there was no convincing them."

Melissa gently took her teacher's hand and softly stooped to kiss her forehead. Tears were falling freely down her cheeks, but she only managed a weak, "Miss Lewis," then she was pushed aside by Curt who felt Lillian's forehead, then checked her pulse as he jokingly said, "The only good thing about today is that we don't have to go to school, but what's fun about that when I did all my homework? I was so prepared for that history review."

At this point, all the children started talking at once, and Lillian had to raise her hands and bring them down to weakly rap on the bed, her signal for order.

Her voice was lacking the strength and firmness that it had in the classroom as she said, "Children, it's so good to see all of you. I've had quite an adventure, but I'm just fine. Just a little weak, but I'm sure that I'll recover nicely. Just give me a couple of days and I'll be my old self again. Then it will be work as usual."

At this point, Mrs. Nelson appeared in the doorway and started to shoo all the children out of the room. "Children, your teacher is just fine, but she needs her rest. Now that you've seen that she's on the mend, go home and enjoy your free day."

Jamie refused to be pushed through the door. "Hold on, Mrs. Nelson. We've talked it out and decided that one of us will be with Miss Lewis at all times. That way we'll feel like we're doing somethin' to help her and not just leaving her care to someone else. Whoever stays with her will report to the others when his turn is over. Is that okay with you?"

"Well, I suppose it's fine if whoever is on duty doesn't get in my way. Agreed?"

"Agreed," said Jamie. "I'm on duty first."

Jamie pulled up a chair by the side of the bed, and after he was sure that he had Lillian's full attention, he began, "Anything you want, Miss Lewis, anything at all, I'm here to see that you get it. Besides, I intend to keep you entertained by telling you how Cousin LeRoy and me robbed The Mercantile last summer and got away with two pairs of bib overalls. Can't have you getting bored just lying there, can we? I'll be sure to put in lots of expression like you taught us. Well, my cousin's last name is Parker. We're full cousins, and last summer he come across the mountain from Circleville to visit me. One night when we was roamin', we just happened to come upon an open window in the back of The Mercantile that started to beckon to us. There was no help for it, and before we knew it, we was inside slicker than snot running down a pig's snout. We almost spilled the beans when we knocked over the rakes in the corner, but we hid real clever like under the counter...."

Jamie's words settled into the background as Mrs. Nelson started pushing the remaining children out the door. Her task accomplished, she interrupted the animated ragamuffin in mid-sentence. "Miss Lewis, if his chatter gets too much for you, just let me know. Jamie, keep in mind that your teacher has got to rest once in a while. I'm off to the kitchen to bring her some broth."

She turned to Charles who was standing in the shadows. "Charles, you better come and have some breakfast. Looks like you could use a good bath. Let's leave Miss Lewis in Jamie's capable hands until I can get back with her breakfast."

With one last lingering glace at Lillian, Charles reluctantly followed Mrs. Nelson. He paused a few seconds before he shut the door to let his brown eyes give the patient on the bed a final, silent message. *There will come a time, Lilly, when I'll tell you what lies in my heart. Have patience, my love.*

As he entered the lobby, he found Billie curled up asleep on a velvet love seat. When he saw the condition of his son, all thoughts of the promised breakfast left his mind. He gathered him in his arms before he realized that there was no way in his weakened state that he would be able to carry him all the way to their shanty.

"Let me drive you home, Charles," came a gruff voice from behind him. He turned to find the weathered face of Ned Druthers. "You can tell me how my Little Missy is faring as we drive."

After carefully wrapping Billie's coat around him and jumping into the freight wagon, Charles told the old freighter the good news that he was hoping to hear. "She's going to be all right, Ned. She might have a rough go of it for a while, but she's got lots of spunk and a real determined spirit. We're lucky that we got to her when we did. If it'd been a few more hours, I don't know if any of them would have made it."

When they stopped at the door of the Anderson shanty, Ned reached underneath the driver's seat to retrieve a crumpled envelope. "This letter's for you. I was passing the Milford Jail when I saw a hand waving out of the metal bars and a voice yelled, 'Hey, mister, please stop.'

"Looking at the man through the bars near tore my heart out. He was so pitiful looking, and his chest was all bandaged up. Appeared to me that he didn't have any will to continue livin'. What really brought me amazement was that he started asking about you. He wanted to know if I knew a Charles Anderson, and when I told him I did, he wanted to know where you were. When I told him you was in Frisco and that I knew you well, he got tears in his eyes. Then, when I mentioned Billie, he got so choked up and lost it so bad that he had to duck his head because of his pridefulness. Didn't want me to see him cry. When he learned I was haulin' freight to Frisco, he made me wait while he wrote this letter. Looked like he's been saving the paper it's on for a long time. It was pretty crumbled and dirty. Seemed like he'd saved that paper for just this purpose. The envelope it's in has seen better days too–it's near worn through in places. He asked me for a pencil and wrote the message quickly, then made me promise to give it to you. The way he handled it and the look in his eyes told me that he considered it to be pretty important. By the looks of him, what's in this here envelope is probably a dying man's last wish. I was on my way to give it to you when I pulled up and heard about the cave-in. When I heard about my Little Missy being trapped, all thoughts of this letter left this old noggin."

Charles took the letter, and his heart leaped as he saw the name in the corner and realized that he had seen this handwriting before. Pulling his slouch hat down over his eyes to cover his emotions, he placed the letter carefully in his coat pocket for safekeeping. "Thanks, Ned. Couldn't have gotten Billie home on my own. Looks like it's going to snow, so I better get Billie inside. He's all tuckered out, poor little feller. The last few hours he's done a man's work. He's earned a good rest."

Ned jumped from the wagon to open the door to the shanty, so Billie wouldn't have to be awakened as his father carried him through the door, placed him in bed, and covered him with quilts.

After Charles said goodbye to Ned, he sat down at the table and retrieved the letter from his coat pocket. In the upper left-hand corner, the name William Anderson became a hot brand that instantly seared his brain with unwelcome memories.

An endless line of mining camps swirled like muddy water through his troubled thoughts. He was beside his father on top of a bar where they had found a few pieces of shiny stuff scattered on the surface. He could remember the excited look on his father's face, then how it had turned to dejection when the surface of the bar was panned out and no more shiny rocks could be found.

Names like Coloma and Hangtown became a part of his thoughts. He found himself in the 1850's when the California gold rush was at its peak. His thoughts traveled to the banks of numerous creeks where as a child he had played away his time. His mind reflected pictures of miners dressed in ragged clothes, slouch hats, and big boots as they wielded picks and shovels to find the illusive, shiny, yellow rocks. He remembered the noise and clatter and the mud, dirt, stones, and water that were continually being thrown in all directions.

Then his mind took him to a day that would be ingrained in his memory forever. His mother was crying as she stirred the breakfast oatmeal. A fierce wind was blowing outside, and the canvas which hung down from a wooden frame to form the walls of their house was little protection against the harsh elements.

His father clutched his mother's shoulders as he pleaded, "Don't cry, Ruthie. I'm doing this for us. Virginia City is becoming one of the largest boom towns in the West. They've not only found gold, but they've found a rich kind of silver, a heavy blue stuff that clings to the gold. They call it the Comstock Lode. I can go there and earn enough in a short time to pay all our bills and put us on easy street. I've got to go.

"You know I want to take you and Charles, but there's no decent place to stay in Virginia City right now, just tents not near as good as this one, and the elements are pretty harsh there, especially in February when there's still snow on the ground–foot after foot of it. Being built on the foothills makes for harsh winter conditions. You and Charles will be fine until I get back. There's enough money in our savings bottle to keep you for a few weeks. Hopefully, I'll be back in June, and Charles can get odd jobs working in the livery stable. He's good with horses. I can't give up this opportunity, Ruthie. It's the chance of a lifetime. Tell me you understand."

But his mother had been too overcome with emotion to give an answer. With tears flowing down her cheeks, she watched her husband pack his saddlebags.

When his father gave him that last hug, the pain in his chest had cut like a sharp knife, and the smile that was on his father's face as he waved goodbye to them and headed for the silver fields of Virginia City had remained ingrained in his memory as if it had happened yesterday, not twenty years ago.

That was the last time that he had seen his father. There had been no word all these years—until now.

As he looked at the letter, the anger in Charles's heart made him consider ripping it up into tiny pieces and then forgetting the traitor who had sent his mother to an early grave and left him to fend for himself at the age of twelve.

But reason stopped him from completing such a rash action. The envelope was destroyed as he ripped it open with little care for what lay inside.

The message was short but penetrated his heart like a cold gust of icy wind. His fingers shook as he read the message. *Dear Charles,*

Found you after a year of searching. Got to make my peace with you. Come to Milford Jail quickly. Haven't much time left. Dad

Troubled thoughts raced through Charles's mind. *Why should I give him the satisfaction of making his peace? There was no peace for mother and me after he deserted us.*

But then his softer side that he had buried ever since his wife's death seven years ago took over. He heard a quiet voice in his mind softly say, *He is your father. You owe him that much.*

His mind began to race with things to be done before his departure. Missing work was not a problem because the mine would be shut down until the old shaft could be cleaned out and shored up, but there were two things that had to be taken care of before he even considered the trip to Milford–Billie and Lillian. He quietly packed a small bag, kissed his sleeping son, and quickly rode toward Nettie Harris's shanty. He was ready to dismount when he saw her coming out of The Southern's front door.

Losing no time in covering the distance between her shanty and The Southern, he dismounted quickly and approached her in a hurried manner.

"Nettie, there is a pressing need for me to travel to Milford. Would you go and sit with Billie until he wakes up, then take him to your shanty and watch over him until I return. I don't imagine school will be starting for a few days, but you can take him to the laundry if you have to work. He's helped out there before. I can't leave him with just anybody, but I know you'll take good care of him."

"I'd be glad to take care of Billie for you, Charles. You know Lillian and I always enjoy having him in our home. Do you know how long you'll be gone?"

"No way of knowing that, but I'm hoping not more than a week. How's Li —Miss Lewis?"

"She was sleeping soundly when I checked on her a few minutes ago. Mrs. Nelson said that all of them are steadily improving, all except the sheriff who is still in a coma. He's the one to be worried about now. Since today's my day off, I'll go right now and check on Billie."

"When you see Miss Lewis, tell her where I've gone and that I'll explain everything when I get back."

"I'll surely tell her. When she's well enough to return home, Billie will cheer her up. She does love that boy. I'll go and check on him now. Have a safe trip."

When Nettie headed for the Anderson shanty, Charles lost no time entering The Southern and finding Lillian's room. She was indeed fast asleep. It was Laura's watch because part of her was on a chair by Lillian's bedside, but because fatigue had overcome her, too, her red curls now spread over Lillian's bedspread as soft snores indicated the deepness of her sleep.

Charles approached the bedside, stooped to place a soft kiss on Lillian's forehead and whispered, "I'll be back soon, my Lilly."

The added color in her cheeks and the gentle rise and fall of her chest signaled him that he need not worry about leaving her for a few days.

He quietly left The Southern, and as he quickly mounted his horse, his gaze fell on the Mineral Mountains, the eastern border for the town of Milford. Their white granite peaks seemed to be suspended in the light blue of the sky, just as his thoughts were now suspended on a letter and his approaching meeting with his lost father.

Chapter 30

Charles reached Milford just as the rays of the setting sun sent streaks of muted pinks and salmons above the San Francisco Mountains. Milford had been settled in 1873, just four years before the birth of Frisco, so it was a child which had just begun to grow. Different mining camps around the surrounding area had increased its population. Because of its geographical location, it had become a trading post for freighters and miners. Since water could be found readily by merely sinking a hole down 12 feet, farmers and livestock men were attracted to the area.

Charles passed such prominent buildings as the Milford Mercantile store and the Stoddard House, the only structure with visitor accommodations for miles around. Attached to the lobby of the Stoddard House was a saloon where even now miners could be seen through the windows kicking up their heels with brightly-dressed saloon girls or bellied up to the bar for a cool sip of brew. Charles remembered the controversy that had swirled around the door which the owners had put between the lobby of the hotel and the saloon. The lobby of the hotel contained a picture of Brigham Young, and one Mormon bishop had almost had a nervous breakdown when he claimed he saw Brigham's eyes in the picture open wide as they looked through the door at the antics going on in the saloon. Charles chuckled to himself as he thought about the uproar this door had caused.

It didn't take him long to locate the jail which was at the south end of Milford's Main Street. Milford's place of incarceration was a square, cement building with metal bars running halfway along the top of its south side. Charles was surprised to see that it wasn't much larger than his own shanty in Frisco. He tied his horse to the hitching post and lost no time in entering the jail through the metal-spiked oak door that was the jail's only entrance.

In a chair with his feet on his desk lounged a sleeping lawman. The star on his shirt hinted that he could possibly be the sheriff. Charles cleared his throat loudly, and the man jumped from his sleeping position, now fully alert.

"I'm Charles Anderson. I understand you have a prisoner by the name of William Anderson in your jail."

"Yes, we do," answered the lawman.

"Could I see him?"

The sheriff stood and offered his hand to Charles for a proper welcome. "Sheriff Washburn here. Be glad to let you see the prisoner, but I don't know how much talkin' you'll get out of him. He's in a pretty bad way. If he wasn't a fugitive from the law, we'd have put him in some place more comfortable–cause of the shape he's in, but I've had a poster hanging on my wall for at least a month that said he was wanted in Nevada for escaping from the Nevada State Prison.

"We probably wouldn't have caught him, but he got in a fight four nights ago over a card game, and the feller he was playing with carved him up pretty bad. When they called me to settle the ruckus, I recognized him as the man on the poster, but he won't have to worry about being transported back to Nevada for trial–he won't live that long. He hasn't eaten for two days, but he's refused to give in. Says he's waiting for a visitor. I hope it's you. I don't care what he's done. I just hate to see anyone suffer like this."

Taking the keys from the nail on the wall, the sheriff opened up the only cell that the jail contained. The eyes of the man lying on the cot were glazed with pain, but when he saw Charles, the pain disappeared somewhat to make way for a glimmer of hope.

"Charles, is it you? Have you really come?"

"It's me, Dad," Charles whispered.

The prisoner weakly motioned to a stool by the bed. "Sit here, son. I've much to tell you, and not much time to do it. Come closer so that I can see you."

Charles sat on the stool and looked into the face of his father for the first time in twenty years. The dim light from the kerosene lantern revealed that the years had not been kind to William Anderson. Charles figured his father was in his early fifties, but the way his steel-gray hair fell in a tangled mass past his shoulders, and the appearance of his unkempt beard, untouched by any razor, made him appear to be a much older man. Even the dim light of the lantern could not hide the sickly white pallor of his father's skin. The only recognizable feature that shone through the dimness was his father's large, brown eyes, which Charles remembered always being full of excitement and adventure. Now these same eyes told of pain, suffering, and regret.

"Charles, promise you'll hear me out. I can't leave this earth until I have explained to you why I didn't come back for you and your mother. What I'm about to tell you doesn't mean that what I did was right, but it will explain why I couldn't come back as I promised."

Charles bent his head, obscuring his face from his father's view as he whispered, "I'm listening."

William Anderson began telling his story as fast as his labored breathing would enable him to relate it.

His eyes never left his son as he began. "I did make it to Virginia City, and I did mine for silver for a few months..." then a spasm of coughing shook his thin frame, and he had to take deep breaths before he could continue. "There's no excuse for what happened next, only my own weakness for taking the easy way out. It was the end of winter and the going was tough. Foot after foot of snow covered the city, and it was difficult to do any mining at all. Spring was late in coming, and the pickins were getting mighty slim. I was about starved to death, and I didn't have a warm place to stay. Didn't have money for any decent accommodations."

Another spasm of coughing prevented the injured man from continuing. He raised a worn handkerchief to his mouth, and when the coughing had subsided, he rested the handkerchief, which was now covered with spots of red, on his chest. William Anderson had to rest for a few minutes and breathe deeply to get up the strength to continue.

With half-closed eyes, William seemed determined to finish his story. "Then I ran into a real rough bunch. Maybe if I hadn't taken up with them, things would have been different. The Wells Fargo Express and Banking Company had just started up. They delivered mail, gold, silver, and valuables to various points all over the area and frequently carried large shipments of gold and silver to San Francisco banks. This wild bunch I took up with convinced me that it would be easy to rob these stages and make some easy money."

"You became a stage robber?" whispered Charles.

"Yes, and a pretty rich one for a time. We robbed five stages and got away with a lot of loot before they caught us on our sixth holdup. Someone had tipped them off what stage we were going to hit, and the sheriff and his deputies were hidden in the forest near the stage route when we attempted our last job."

"They caught you red-handed?" asked Charles quietly.

"They were upon us, and we were in handcuffs before we even realized what was happening. Then we were given a trial and sentenced to thirty years in the Nevada State Prison. That's where I've been for the past twenty years, and I do not need to burden you with the horrors that I experienced there. It was a rough place.

"I knew that I'd never make it through another ten years alive, so me and a couple of my buddies planned a break. We dug a tunnel that came out on the outside of the prison fence.

We made it, and I've been searching for you ever since. Knew I had to make it right with you."

At this point, William Anderson reached out to take his son's hand and placed it on his chest. "Couldn't go to my grave without telling you how sorry I am for not being there for you and your mother when you needed me. I checked all around Virginia City. Asked about your whereabouts everywhere. Finally I run up against a man who you used to work for. He remembered that you were headed for Frisco, Utah. It's taken me a while to get here, and if it wasn't for my weakness for gamblin' I'd have made it to Frisco instead of lying on my death bed in this cold cell."

Another spasm of coughing racked his frail body. When it stopped, there was silence in the cell for a few minutes. Charles could see moisture in his father's eyes as the dying man whispered, "And your mother? What became of my Ruthie?"

Charles gave his answer in a soft, subdued voice. "Life was pretty tough for us after you left. Mom had to wash clothes on the board to make ends meet, and I worked some in the livery stable. She'd scrub those clothes until her fingers cracked and started to bleed, and the water would turn red from her own blood. When I was twelve, she caught cold because of all that washing in cold streams, and it penetrated into her lungs. Took her real fast."

Deep brown eyes never left Charles's face as he asked, "You were all alone with her when she died? Did she say anything about me?"

"Yes, we were alone together when she took her last breath. But just before she passed on, she grabbed my hand and asked me to grant her one favor. 'If you ever meet up with your dad, again, promise me that you'll forgive him, no matter what he's done. Hate will canker your soul, son. Please promise.' It was a hard promise to give, but I gave it, and then held her in my arms until she left this life."

"And her resting place? Where is she buried?"

"I buried her in that meadow where we used to like to picnic–the one with the gentle stream running through it. I dug her grave myself. Didn't have the money for a proper casket, but I did wrap her in a nice blanket and tried to say a decent prayer over her."

As Charles glanced at his father's face, he noticed that the grizzled beard had become wet with the stream of tears that flowed like gentle streams down his pale cheeks. Another coughing spell racked his father's body, but when he was able to talk, he managed to ask, "And you, Charles, how did you survive without father or mother?"

"It wasn't easy, but the owner of the livery let me continue working for him. He even let me stay in the livery with the horses. Things could have been a lot worse."

"And I understand you have a son, Billie? What about his mother? Is he like you?"

I met and married Lucy Henderson in 1869. Billie was born a year later. She was a gentle woman but always frail in health and strength. I worked at the livery and gold fields for a time. Then in 1877 I learned of the silver strike in Frisco at the Horn Silver Mine. I should never have moved her there. The Utah winters are harsh, and she didn't have the constitution to stand up under them. The flu epidemic came when we had been in Frisco only a few months, and in a few days she was gone. I've been trying to raise Billie on my own ever since, which hasn't been an easy task, cause he's a willful, rambunctious youngin."

"I wish I could see him. Promise me you'll try to raise him right. Try to put all that energy to good use. Don't let him make the mistakes that I did."

William Anderson released his son's hand, as he grasped his bandaged chest and uttered a tortured cry. With pain-sharpened features he began, "Like Billie, I had a lot of restless energy in my early twenties. I could have channeled that energy in the right direction, but it seems that I was determined to travel the wrong road. The sad thing was that I didn't have to make those wrong choices. Back in Illinois where I was raised, I had a chance at another life–one that could have brought out the good in me. I was madly in love with a young woman by the name of Marian Page. She was special, and I think she loved me too, but it was 1846, and Joe Smith and his followers were preaching the Mormon religion to anyone who would listen. Marian got all wrapped up in that Mormon mumbo jumbo. She wanted to be baptized and tried to pull me over to her side. She even went so far as to try to read the *Book of Mormon* to me. As far as I could see, it was all a bunch of hogwash, and I told her so.

"One night things came to a head. I told her it was me or the Mormons. Told her to let me know when she had given up on them and then we'd be married. When I left her at her door, I told her that I would be waiting to hear from her soon. Looking back, I can see that I was a hot-headed fool. A few weeks after that I heard that she had married a Mormon, and later I heard that they had left to be with the so-called 'Saints' in Salt Lake City.

"I realized my mistake, but it was too late. I think every bit of goodness in me died when I lost her. Hurt and confused, I married your mother a few weeks later and took her to the gold fields in Coloma, California. From there, we moved to Placerville where you were born a year later."

Breathing deeply, William Anderson continued. "Don't get me wrong–I loved your mother. She was a good woman, but I know that the road I would have traveled would have been a different one had I married Marian."

"Did you ever hear about her again?"

"Never saw nor heard of her again, but sometimes I feel her near, and something deep inside me tells me that the goodness that surrounded her is not lost. It's as if her influence cannot be destroyed."

Huge, racking coughs silenced the withered man on the cot. When they subsided, he raised watery eyes to his son's deep brown ones and whispered, "Can you ever forgive me, son? I don't want to meet my maker without your forgiveness."

Empty silence descended on the cold cell for a few minutes, then a weak hand squeezed a strong one, and the silence was broken as an unsteady voice whispered, "Please." Charles swallowed hard, then a soft "I forgive you, Dad" gave the dying man the answer he had been waiting for. Immediately the body that had been in agony just a few minutes before was stilled. The breathing, though raspy, became more regular, and as the tortured eyes closed, peace seemed to settle on the face of the dying man.

Charles covered his father with another blanket that had been lying at the foot of the bed. The sheriff brought in a tray of food, but when Charles gently shook his father, he was unable to rouse him.

"He's not eaten these past two days, young man. No sense trying. There's no sense in letting it go to waste. You've had a long journey, so you enjoy it."

The well-seasoned stew was hot, and it went a long way towards removing the cold that had penetrated Charles's bones.

When the sheriff was relieved by his deputy, he handed Charles a warm blanket and told him that he could sleep on one of the extra cots in the cell if he wanted to stay. "Deputy Russell will stay here for the night shift. I'll be here in the morning. There's wood for the stove if the fire gets low. I'm leaving this cell door open. Don't think the prisoner is going anywhere. See you in the morning."

Deputy Russell put his feet on the desk and settled down for the night while Charles pulled the extra cot close to his father. He rested his arm against his father's arm, so that the dying man could sense his nearness. When sleep did come, his dreams were full of stagecoach robberies, prisons, and a beautiful lady who looked like an angel. Her face was blurred, but the warmth and goodness that came from her angelic being penetrated into the far reaches of his heart, bringing him a restful sleep.

Chapter 31

Lillian knew that if she didn't get out of bed soon, a doctor would come into the room and declare her certifiably insane. For the past two days she had been subjected to a special brand of loving kindness from her pupils as they had each taken their turns sitting by her bed and watching over her.

During these hours with her students, she had been instructed on the art of how to play the games that monopolized their recess period at school. After two days she knew every rule involved when playing Fox and Geese, and how to come out victorious in Mud Daubs, Slap and Pinches, and Indian Ball. She even learned that there were certain forfeit games that you never played unless you wanted to be subjected to kissing.

Right now her brain was ringing with the non-stop chatter that had been going on for the last eight hours. Thankfully, Richie was helping with chores at home and had missed his shift. At last there was quiet–blessed quiet.

But when she thought back on the conversations with her students, she realized that the time spent with them included much more than just idle chatter. Valuable information had been mixed in with their young thoughts. Jessica, the animal lover in her class, had informed her that the mule had been rescued from the mine and that it was now being attended to at the livery stable where it was improving daily.

Mary told her that all the cave-in survivors were mending so nicely that all of them had been sent home except her and the sheriff, who had just regained consciousness a few hours ago. Beatrice had been told to stay in bed for another two days, but she had insisted on rising and going home. As she dressed hurriedly, she had told those who would keep her in bed, "It'll take more than an old mine cave-in to keep me down!"

"Now you've done it, Miss Lewis!" Jamie had exclaimed on his shift. "Because of you they'll be no more women allowed in the mine. You're bad luck, they say, so don't plan on another trip down there. Hey! They've started cleaning out the old shaft already. Right now everyone, except those working on the shaft are out of work, so lots of miners are leaving here to work in the Old Hickory and Grampion mines. Dad says we're going to stick it out here. We're going to shoot our own meat. I'm a dead shot, so we won't go hungry. Turkey hunts are a blast! Did you know that, Miss Lewis?"

During his shift, Billie had excitedly reported that he was going to be staying with Nettie and her because his dad had gone on a trip to Milford on some mysterious adventure. Then he got such a look of seriousness on his face that Lillian wondered if it was really Billie in her room.

After a few minutes of silence, during which he swung his legs back and forth on his chair and ducked his head, his eyes finally met hers, and he let her know what had brought about this change in his usual devil-may-care personality.

"I hope when dad gets back from Milford, he's all right in the head. He kind of lost it in the mine."

"Lost it? What do you mean, Billie?"

"Well, when we found you, he started acting real weird. It scares me to even think about it. He wouldn't want me to tell you how he carried on. I will say that he just wasn't Pa. He was crying and blubbering on something fierce, but I really couldn't understand what he was saying. When he saw me looking at him kind of strange, he sort of came to his senses."

Lillian's heart raced into an erratic beat, and she had to digest the information she had just heard before she could speak. *I didn't just imagine those strong arms and words of endearment. It was Charles.*

"And we couldn't get him to let go of you. They had to almost pry you out of his arms, and Mrs. Nelson told me that he wouldn't leave your room all night and that he slept with his head on your bed."

A feeling of warmth filled Lillian as she thought of what Billie had just said. *So I didn't dream all those things. Charles, when you get back from Milford, there's much that you need to explain.*

The opening of her room door brought her back to the present. Mrs. Nelson and Nettie crossed to the bed where Mrs. Nelson felt Lillian's head and checked her pulse.

"You'll be glad to know that I've told Nettie here she can take you back to your shanty in just a few minutes if you promise to be a good patient and take it easy for the rest of the week. Those youngins can do without you that long. Now, mind you, I've given her instructions for your care. Mind your p's and q's, and if you feel like it, you can start teaching school Monday morning. By the way, the first thing Sheriff Phillips said when he came to was that he wanted to see you when you felt up to it."

When Mrs. Nelson left the room, Nettie helped her take off her nightgown and get into some clean clothes that she had brought from the shanty.

Lillian found that even the minor exertion of getting dressed proved to be a major chore. She had been out of bed only for short periods of time during the past two days, and her unused muscles refused to cooperate when she attempted to make any kind of movement. Because she was still suffering from the bad air in the mine, the simple act of getting dressed only added to the overall feeling of fatigue and muscle weakness.

Nettie, noticing how difficult it was for Lillian to make the most simple of movements suggested, "Maybe you ought to wait and see the sheriff some other day when you're feeling just a bit stronger."

"I'm fine, Nettie. It'll only take a minute, and if I don't find out what the sheriff wants, I'll never get any sleep tonight. Mary told me that he had been at the very point of death when they brought him in, but you know how Mary exaggerates."

"Well, if I can't talk you out of it, he's in the room right next door. Now promise me that you'll only stay for a few minutes, and that if he starts to say anything that upsets you, you'll leave immediately."

"I'll be fine, Nettie," Lillian assured her friend as she held onto Nettie's arm as they walked the short distance to the room next to hers. Neither Nettie nor Lillian was prepared for what they saw when the door to the sheriff's room swung open. The strong, vibrant man, who had kept a rigid peace in Frisco ever since his arrival, lay pale and lifeless in the bed. His head was tightly bandaged with a clean, white cloth, and his still body now posed no threat to lawbreakers. Nettie helped an unsteady Lillian approach the bedside where Lillian reached down and gently shook the sheriff's arm.

"Sheriff, it's Miss Lewis," she spoke softly.

Golden eyelashes fluttered and eyelids slowly opened to reveal green eyes that were laced with pain. Then pale lips smiled as a weak voice said, "Miss Lewis, you came?"

"Of course I came. I got the message that you wanted to speak to me, but I also came to make sure that you were indeed conscious and on the way to a recovery." Lillian sat down in a chair that Nettie had placed by the side of the bed. Coming to the sheriff's room, though a short distance, had been an exertion for her, leaving her legs shaky and weak.

The sheriff now directed his attention to Nettie. "Miss Harris, could I ask you to leave the room for just a few minutes? What I have to say is between Miss Lewis and me."

Nettie nodded and quickly departed. When the door had closed, Sheriff Phillips took Lillian's hand in his, and green eyes that had lost their old fire when she first entered the room, suddenly took on a glow that Lillian had seen many times before when his gaze had met hers.

"First of all, I want your permission to stop calling you Miss Lewis. For some time now, you have been 'Lil' to me. Is it all right with you if I use that name when we're alone? I don't want to embarrass you by using it when others are present."

"I like 'Lil.' My father used to call me that when I was a little girl. And you, Sheriff, what do you want to be called in private?"

"The W in my name stands for William. My parents always called me Will, and I would like it if you would do the same."

"Well, as long as we don't say those names together. They rhyme, and there are a few people who would get a chuckle out of that one."

Lillian found the gentle clasp of the sheriff's hand tighten as he began, "Lil, I never have been good at hiding my feelings, so you must know how I feel about you. I have been with a great many women in my lifetime, and with the exception of one who was lost to me when I was young, not one of those women gave me cause to think about mending my ways and settling down–until I met you. When I look at you, I start to think about buying a ranch, raising children, turning in my badge, and hanging up my guns for good. I love you, Lil, and I promise to do anything you ask if you'll consider being my wife."

Lillian now found her hand raised as a gentle kiss was placed upon it. The sheriff's question lingered in the air, waiting to be answered as Lillian struggled with words to express her feelings.

After a few minutes, she began, "Sheriff–Will–I will admit that there has been a strange force that has seemed to pull me to you ever since we met, but you must know how I abhor everything that you stand for–violence and bloodshed–they are very frightening to me. I realized from the moment that I first saw you that the attraction existed, but I have kept pushing you out of my thoughts because it's almost as if we come from two different worlds. Ranching and raising children could be pretty boring compared to being the sheriff of one of the wildest towns in the West. I think you had better think this proposition over. Right now your heart is speaking, but the man inside of you would hate making the changes that you are suggesting."

"It is the man inside who longs for you and the changes that our marriage would bring into my life. Please say you'll consider my offer."

Silence reigned for a few moments, then a soft voice said, "I will give it consideration."

As a wide smile broke out on the sheriff's lips he said, "Consideration is more than I deserve, but it gives me hope. Promise me that you'll come and visit often. I feel stronger already just having you this close."

"I promise to visit when I can. Right now, you need your rest." She picked up a clean cloth on the stand by the bed and began wiping his forehead which was covered with beads of sweat. "I'm afraid that this meeting has taken away what little strength you had."

"I'll rest, but grant me just one favor before you leave–one kiss."

Lillian hesitated only a moment, then rose from the chair and gently kissed the sheriff's lips. When she tried to raise her head, she found it once again lowered by a shaky hand, so that two cheeks met.

After a few moments, that same hand gently moved her head so that two lips were once more joined in a kiss that lingered just a few seconds longer than the first. It was not a kiss of passion, but one so gentle and affectionate that Lillian was touched to the very core of her being with the fact that Sheriff Phillips did indeed love her.

When Lillian raised her head and forced her trembling hands to give her the strength to rise from her chair, she heard a soft, breathless voice say, "Til we meet again, my sweet."

Her hand was once again raised to those same lips as blazing green eyes conveyed strong emotions, reminding her of what she had promised. She crossed the room, opened the door, then turned to find that golden eyelashes once again fanned pale cheeks as fatigue brought the welcome visitor of sleep to the sheriff of Frisco.

Chapter 32

Throughout the remainder of the week, Lillian's mind was a turmoil of swirling emotions. She was continually being pulled between two forces. Her attraction to the sheriff was strong, but she questioned that love alone could change the years of violence that were a part of his nature. Could she be strong enough to bring about that change? Did a rancher and loving father lie somewhere within this violent man, or would he in time learn to hate her because he had changed into someone who was foreign to his inner nature in order to obtain her love?

Then there was Charles. He was infuriating, exasperating, and could cause her anger to surface at every turn, yet she realized that inside of her lay deep feelings for this man in his soiled slouch hat and heavy miner's boots. She seemed to be drawn to him with a force much stronger than her attraction to the sheriff. Yet, the sheriff had spoken what was in his heart, and Charles refused to say anything about his true feelings. Instead, he had gone out of his way to avoid her before the mine accident and hadn't even told her goodbye before he left for Milford. *If only I knew what Billie meant when he talked about his dad totally losing it in the mine. Charles, if you won't be truthful to me about your feelings, how am I to know what's in your heart?* She thought of the many times that Charles had conveyed his emotions through actions, but never words. *Charles, why can't you express your feelings aloud?*

But Charles was still in Milford on that mysterious errand, and there had been no word from him. Billie pestered her and Nettie every day about when they thought he would return, and they had to reassure him that his pa had a good reason for leaving and that he would come home in his own good time; however, the weekend came, and there was still no word from Charles.

Lillian was getting stronger each day. She had even walked to the schoolhouse Saturday morning to be sure that everything was ready for class on Monday. Billie had accompanied her and helped her straighten the room and prepare questions for the history review. He was so eager to help her with the questions that he had no idea that he was the recipient of a comprehensive review as the preparation progressed. They both knew that urgency was in the air, for the history contest was only three months away, and there was much to be done if the Frisco School was to emerge victorious.

On Sunday Lillian walked to The Southern to visit the sheriff. Before she entered his room, Mrs. Nelson approached her. "Miss Lewis, thank heavens you came. In all my born days, I have never dealt with a more difficult patient. Hour after hour he'd look for you, and when you didn't show up, he'd get more cantankerous than an old she bear who was trying to protect her cubs. He got so mad yesterday when I told him there had been no sign of you, that he threw his coffee cup at the wall and shattered it to pieces. I'm afraid that big dent in the wall isn't likely to recover from the force of that throw. I think getting better for him isn't necessarily a good thing unless you happen to be with him."

Lillian chuckled under her breath at the thought of the broken coffee mug, then opened the door ever so slowly so that she could peek in.

"Lil, that better be you, or I swear, something is going to break loose in me, and I'm going to do some real damage to someone or something!"

"Sounds like you're mending rather nicely, Will. Tell me, how are the coffee cups holding up today?" she said as she moved to his bedside.

"Who told you about that blasted cup? Has Mrs. Nelson taken up tattling?"

Lillian gave him her best smile, then appearing to be concerned about his welfare, she felt his forehead and cheeks. "I see that despite your bad temperament there has been considerable improvement since I last saw you.

"You've got color again in those cheeks, and your lips that were white and strained during our last visit are now stretched into a wide, welcome grin that's a pleasant contrast to your usual starchy nature."

Green eyes twinkled with pure joy as he smilingly said, "Lil, you finally came. What in tarnation kept you so long?"

"Will, I've been slowly getting my strength back. I didn't really feel like walking over here to see you before today. That doesn't mean that I'm not concerned about how you've been feeling. I understand that at least one temper tantrum has erupted since we last visited."

It was evident that the sheriff was recovering his strength when Lillian suddenly found her hand enclosed in an iron grip. Then a second hand, stronger then the first, joined the other to securely hold her small hand captive.

"The more I thought about your not coming, the more I became convinced that you had decided against my offer and were afraid to face me with your decision. When those thoughts entered my mind, I had to take my anger out on the nearest thing–goodbye coffee cup!"

Lillian stared into green eyes that seemed to have gained strength and gathered smoldering emotion since their last meeting. "I have thought about your proposal, Will, but something that important cannot be decided in just a few days. I need some time. Until I have made that decision, please be kind to the dishes and silverware."

"Don't wait days to come back, or I can't be responsible for my actions," he chuckled.

The sheriff's voice now took on a more serious tone. "Lil, sit here beside me. I don't want any secrets between us. There's something that I have to tell you about my early years. I hinted that there was another young woman in my life that I loved dearly. I grew up in Caliente, Nevada with a little girl named Mandy Caldwell. She was more than my friend. She was my confident, my shelter from the storms of life, and my true soul mate. We did everything together, and we spent hours fishing or hunting rabbits and squirrels.

"Each of us had our crosses to bear. Both of our fathers were drunks and often took their anger out on us. Mandy and I would sit for hours at our favorite fishing hole and talk away the problems of the day. It just happened kind of natural like that as we grew up, that friendship turned into deep love."

"If you loved her so much, why didn't you marry?" Lillian asked, never taking her eyes from his face.

"That was all my fault. You see, as I said, my old man used to beat me regular. I still have scars on my back from the many times that he struck me with the strap. Instead of those beatings making me obedient, they only served to bring out the violent side in me. He got pleasure from giving me pain, and I, in turn, turned to violence, trying in some way to retaliate for the wrongs that he had heaped on me."

Lillian found her hand enclosed in a firmer grip as the sheriff continued. "I got in with the wrong bunch. We started drinking and began pushing around the weaker folks in the town. When I was hurting others, I felt a kind of satisfaction that I was somehow getting back at my dad. One night my friends and I got liquored up and stole some horses from an old man's barn. When he came out to stop us, we made him dance as we shot bullets at his feet. Oh, how we laughed! I still get sick when I think about it. Then one of the bullets went astray and before we knew it, the old man was lying on the ground dead. I'll never know if that was the first man that I killed or if that fatal bullet came from one of my friend's guns."

There was silence for a few minutes as Lillian digested what she had just heard. "How did Mandy react to your violent nature?"

"She hated it. She said I was becoming just like her dad, and that if I continued down this road, she didn't want anything more to do with me. I thought sweet words and soft kisses would win her over to my side, but I couldn't seem to stop the violence. It seemed to become a part of my blood, flowing through my body like molten lava. I started being obsessed with being the fastest gun in the West, and I practiced hours each day. It paid off in a lightning-fast draw, but when Mandy learned that I had picked a fight with a poor, defenseless rancher, forced him to draw, then shot him dead in the street, she gave me an ultimatum. She told me that either I stopped my violent ways, or she didn't want to see me again."

"Did you try to change?"

"For a short time I did. I loved her more than anything that had ever entered my life, but the violence kept erupting inside me again and again. One night my friends and I got liquored up and shot out the windows of about every place in town. The sheriff put us in jail for a week and gave us a big fine.

"The minute I got out of jail I headed for her place. When her ma answered the door, she had this look of pure suffering on her face, and I knew something was dreadfully wrong. Through her tears, she told me that Mandy had packed what few things she had and left in the night without so much as a goodbye. Her mother handed me a letter addressed to me. The note simply said, 'I love you too much to stay and see you destroy yourself. Love always, Mandy.'

"I tried to track her down, but her trail had gone cold. After two years of searching, I gave up, fearing that she had died. But I determined to make some changes in my life in case she ever decided to return. I channeled my violent nature in a better direction–enforcing the law. Pioche took a chance on me when they hired me as sheriff, and I've been enforcing the law ever since.

"What's important about all this, Lil, is that I'm determined not to make the same mistake twice. I lost one woman I loved dearly. I'll not lose another. Lil, when I tell you I'll change, I mean it."

Lillian removed her hand from his grasp and gently placed it on his arm. "Will, be sure that the changes you are suggesting are changes that will make you happy in the end. If they aren't and we married, you'd learn to hate me."

"Please say yes," was his soft reply.

"You must give me more time. There are things that I must weigh in my mind before I give you that final answer."

"It's Anderson, isn't it? Surely you can't be considering that hermit. I've never met a more disagreeable man."

Lillian squeezed his arm in a parting gesture. "We'll not speak of Charles right now. You just concentrate on getting better, or I won't come to see you again."

"You stay away, and they'll have no dishes left to eat on," he chuckled.

Lillian stooped to place a kiss on his forehead, then placed her hands on either side of his face and left him with one parting word–"time."

As she walked back to the shanty, feelings of remorse filled her thoughts. Will had been honest with her about his early years, but she had left unsaid something that was more important to her than life itself–she was a Mormon. How would he feel if he knew that she was a member of the Mormon Church and just how much this membership meant to her? She then began to rationalize why she had been silent about something so important. *If I decide to spend my life with him, then I must be honest about my beliefs, but until I make my decision, the fact that I am a Mormon can stay hidden.*

Chapter 33

As Billie and Lillian walked to school Monday morning, the sun shone so brightly on the newly fallen snow that at times they were blinded by the strong rays. When they opened the schoolhouse door, a loud "Welcome back, Miss Lewis," resounded throughout the school, and without warning Frisco's teacher was bombarded with small bodies flying from every direction, each eager to give their teacher a hug and tell her how glad they were to have her back.

When she finally succeeded in getting them back into their seats, she spent the morning telling them about the cave-in and what she had learned from the excursion. When she talked about the mysterious tapping, Richie yelled, "I told you there'd be Tommyknockers!"

The children sat spellbound as she told them of her thoughts when it appeared the entire mine had collapsed on their heads. Lillian ended her remarks by saying, "I don't think that I would have made it out of there alive if it hadn't been for you children. Every time I was tempted to give up, one by one, each of your faces would flash into my mind, giving me added strength to hold on so that I could get back to you."

There was more than one tear that emerged from watery eyes as the children realized how close they had come to losing the teacher who had come to mean so much to them.

During lunch she organized herself to begin the review for the history contest. As she was placing the review questions in order and deciding just how she was going to conduct this review, Laura ran in the door to stand by her teacher's desk, but not a word escaped her lips until her teacher looked up from her work and asked, "What is it, Laura?"

"Miss Lewis, remember when we set aside 15 minutes when we needed it to talk about Frisco?"

"I do indeed, Laura."

Laura's red curls stuck out in every direction as she excitedly continued, "You've got to give us some time today, Miss Lewis. You've just got to. There's something been going on the last few days that is absolutely petrifying! It is of the utmost importance that we talk about it!"

"Well, Laura, if it is of the utmost importance, then by all means we must talk about it. That's the first thing we'll do when the bell rings to end lunch."

Laura ran from the room to shout the news to the rest of the students, and true to her word, Lillian began the afternoon by saying, "Let's take a few minutes to discuss what's happening in Frisco."

Lillian's eyes opened wide as all ten hands went up and started frantically waving to be recognized. It was almost as if there was a contest to see who could speak first.

Since Laura had asked for this time period, Lillian pointed her pointing stick at her, giving her permission to speak first.

Laura's eyes grew wide, and she talked in a soft, shaky voice as if she were telling the spookiest of Halloween stories. "Attention! The Lady in Black has invaded Frisco! My dad saw her two nights ago walking down the alley in back of the Chinese Laundry."

Laura, the actress of the group, now demonstrated how this black specter walked with her head held high and her arms out in front of her, fingers turned down, forming terrifying claws. Now, slowly, Laura stopped and continued in the same slow, spooky voice.

"Dad said she was dressed all in black and even though

a black veil covered her face, he knew that she was looking at him cause her gaze was like a lightning bolt that left the black veil and nearly knocked him clean out of his senses!"

At this point Laura demonstrated how the Lady in Black could zap unsuspecting people by extending her fingers towards the class and hissing forth a terrible sound like a lighting bolt would make as it connected with a tree. Jessica and Stacy cowered down in their seats, and Melissa covered her expressive eyes with her visibly shaking hands. Having succeeded in frightening the entire class out of their wits, Laura slowly returned to her seat with a large smile on her face, proud of how her performance had affected her classmates.

Running up to Lillian's desk and tugging insistently on her arm, Curt demanded to be recognized next. When Lillian raised her hand towards him, a signal that he could begin, he faced the class and began in the most serious of tones, "And I was talking to Mr. Groover, the newspaper editor. He claims a lady dressed in black walked past his window Saturday night and stopped to look at him through her black veil. He said her gaze was like a hot branding iron that entered his brain, almost sizzling him silly, and totally paralyzing him for a full five minutes after she left. He swears that she's a demon from the darkest depths of the infernal pit cause he hasn't been able to write another thing since he saw her!"

It was then that things got out of control, and the spirit of pandemonium entered the classroom. Everyone started talking at once as they turned to their neighbor to relate their own personal story about the Lady in Black.

Lillian rapped her stick on the desk as she firmly said, "Students, order! One at a time! Wait until I have given you permission to speak." The class quieted, raised their hands, and looked to their teacher to be recognized.

"I've heard that her gaze is piercing enough to shatter glass," said Clarence.

Stacy chimed in with "We heard that if she touches a horse or one of your cows, they drop dead on the spot and if the cows do survive, all you'll get from them is curdled milk! Dad's got all of our animals locked in the barn!"

"My aunt told me that the grass that she walks on turns black like it's burnt, and if you walk in her footsteps, you're most likely going to disappear and never be found again," whispered Melissa who now dropped her head to hide the tears that were beginning to flow.

Mary stood and waved her hands to be recognized. "Ma made a special cake yesterday. It looked absolutely beautiful when she placed it on the window sill to cool, but when she looked at it ten minutes later, the middle had sunk, and it looked perfectly dreadful. Pa swore that just before the cake fell he saw a black shadow stop at the window, point at the cake, and then move on."

At this point, everyone was talking excitedly to one another, and Lillian could see that she must once again take measures to bring control back to the class.

After she rapped her stick on her desk four times and said in her firmest voice, "Students!" a cloak of blissful silence fell over the room, and she found ten eyes focused on her as they awaited her comments.

"Students, this Lady in Black has to have a good reason for visiting Frisco. I don't believe she is a ghost because the same ghost doesn't ordinarily appear to this many people. She has to have a reason for being here, and I promise you that I will investigate thoroughly. Please don't believe everything that you hear about her until I can get to the bottom of this matter."

The rest of the afternoon Lillian used the questions she had organized to drill her students for the upcoming contest. Her spirits fell as they missed question after question.

When it was time to go home, Clarence came to stand by her desk. "Don't blame yourself for the review, Miss Lewis. The Lady in Black has blown out the smart pockets in our minds and left them all empty!" He then made a beeline for the door, running as if the dreaded Black Lady herself was in pursuit of him.

Chapter 34

Lillian sent Billie home to help Nettie with the chores while she stayed at the school to prepare the lessons for the next day. She was so engrossed in her preparations that she was unaware that she was not alone until she felt a prickling sensation in the hairs on the back of her neck, causing her to raise her eyes from her work and look at the doorway.

A figure in a dirty slouch hat, muddy boots, and bulky wool coat blocked out the light from the small window in the entry way. The brown eyes were filled with weariness, but the emotion that they expressed as they gazed at her could have set the wood ablaze in any fireplace. Lillian's heart began to race as she rose from her desk and whispered, "Charles?"

In a matter of seconds the familiar figure was by her side, and she was enclosed in strong arms as a well-remembered voice whispered, "Lilly, my Lilly."

No words were necessary as they clung together, not two separate beings, but one complete unit, one not complete without the other.

Then she felt soft kisses being showered on her hair and cheeks followed by a whispered, "My dear love, how I've missed you."

Lillian's mind was now open to the truth–*Billie, this is what you meant when you said your pa lost it in the mine. This same scene has been played before.*

Then two rough hands which had ridden long, hard miles to reach her, positioned her head so that she could now read the depth of his emotions.

Charles paused a moment to gain some composure, then he began, "Lillian Lewis, I can't live one more day without you in my life. I have loved you since I first set eyes on you in this very room and treated you so rudely. I have tried to fight my love for you at every turn and in every way, but all in vain. When I finally reached you in the mine, I knew that I could no longer hide my feelings–you had become my world and my reason for living."

There was a brief pause as Charles struggled to get control of his emotions. His hands were visibly shaking as he continued, "Would you consider spending the rest of your life with an old, crusty desert rat?"

Lillian was so choked with emotion that she could not utter one word. Her eyes brimmed with tears that flowed softly down her cheeks.

Shaking hands wiped away the tears as expressive brown eyes asked for an answer.

Finally, when she was able to gain some composure, she said, "But Charles, if you felt this way, why did you avoid me all these weeks and refuse to even speak? Why didn't you tell me your true feelings?"

Charles held her head to his chest to rest quietly while he explained, "When I lost Billie's mother, I swore I'd never love again. The pain was too deep. I thought if I avoided love, I would also avoid the hurt and turmoil it would bring if it were ever lost again. My father deserted me and my mother when I was just twelve, teaching me that love could only end in unhappiness, and so I decided that I would run the other direction if love ever did threaten to enter my world again."

Lillian raised her head to question, "What changed your mind? Why are you now declaring your love?"

"When I realized how close I had come to losing you in the mine, I knew that life wasn't worth living if I couldn't live it with you," stated Charles as he lowered his head to touch his lips to hers in a fiery kiss.

They were both breathless when he raised his head and said softly, "And your answer? Can you possibly bear spending the rest of your life with a cantankerous ruffian like me?"

Lillian put her arms around his neck and her head once more rested on his chest as she answered, "Charles, right now I can't imagine spending my life with anyone else."

Lillian raised her head and standing on her tip toes once again touched Charles's lips to hers, sealing the promise that she hoped to honor for the rest of their lives.

Since they were both a little unsteady on their feet, Charles guided Lillian to a bench under one of the windows where they could sit quietly and talk about these new emotions that had just emerged.

Turning her towards him and holding both of her hands, Charles explained why he had traveled to Milford, his meeting with his father, and what had transpired between them.

"Regardless of how much he hurt me, I could not leave him during his final hours. I seldom left his side, and the day after I arrived, he slipped into a coma and died quietly two days later. It took a few days to arrange for his burial in the Milford Cemetery. I would have liked to have buried him by Ma, but there was no practical way I could have done that."

Lillian nodded in agreement, then still holding tightly to Charles's hand, changed the conversation to another subject. "Billie has been so worried about you. Did you stop to see him before you came here?"

"I love my son, but I had to settle things between us before I talked to anybody. We'll go and tell him the good news together. Something tells me that he's going to be as happy as his father is."

Lillian released her hands from Charles's grasp and placed them on his shoulders as her eyes now conveyed seriousness. "Charles, there must never be anything left unsaid between us.

After you hear what I am about to tell you, you may change your mind about spending the rest of your life with me."

"Nothing could ever change the way I feel about you, Lilly. Whatever could you tell me that would cause me to change my mind?"

"You know how the majority of Frisco citizens feel about those dreaded Mormons?"

"I know Mormons aren't exactly made welcome in Frisco, but why do we need to talk about them now?"

"We need to talk about them, Charles, because it seems you've fallen in love with one of them. I was baptized into the Mormon Church when I was eight years of age."

Charles stared at her for a few minutes, but the glow of love did not leave his eyes. "If Mormonism means so much to you, there's got to be some good in it. I promised God before I entered that mine that if he would let me save you somehow, I'd devote my life to him. If this religion that you belong to can help me keep that promise, I'll gladly embrace it."

Lillian's eyes once more grew wet with tears. "Then I'll have the pleasure of teaching you all about it. I promise you won't be sorry. It's a way of life that leads to true happiness. We can start some study sessions right away."

"Not right away, Lilly. I'm afraid I'm going to have to leave you and Billie for about five months. When I return the last of June, we'll be married–that is, if you'll still have me."

"But, Charles, you just got back. Where are you going, and why must you leave so soon?"

"There's no work here, Lilly. After the cave-in, things pretty much shut down for a while until they can clear the old shaft. Clearing the old shaft will employ a limited amount of men. I'm sure I wouldn't be hired to help. If I'm going to be a married man, I've got to make some money to support you and Billie. I refuse to marry you and ask you to live in that weather-beaten shanty of mine, and I know that you want to finish out this school year–the students mean so much to you."

The fading light from the windows hid most of the emotion in Charles's face as he continued. "While I was in Milford with my father, an old friend of mine who used to work here in Frisco came into the jail. We got to talking, and he told me that when he left Frisco, he went to work out at Hay Springs, about eight or nine miles southwest of Milford. He said they were just crying for good ranch hands. He'd heard about the Frisco cave-in and suggested that I ride out to Hay Springs and apply for a job. After I buried my father, I took the time to ride out to the ranch. John Ryan, the owner, hired me on the spot."

"Hay Springs–I've heard it's a beautiful place."

"Lilly, at first glance it's like a piece of heaven. The natural springs there provide an abundance of water which accumulates in a number of ponds. Water lilies float on the pools, and the gentle wind, which is blowing most of the time, causes the tall grasses and cattails to sway gracefully. It is a beautiful sight even in the winter with patches of ice on the water. I can imagine how spectacular it will become when everything greens up with the spring. Ryan told me that during migration periods there are thousands of ducks and geese that gather on the surface of the ponds, making it a popular hunting spot."

Lillian's eyes widened as she tried to take all this in. "What would you be doing, Charles?"

"Well, when Ryan learned that I had experience working with water holes and springs, he told me that I would be responsible for maintaining the quality of the ponds and diverting the springs into them so that no water would be lost. Then there's the care of the horses–hundreds of them. The ranch raises and sells horses for personal use, pulling freight, and a few of them are sold for racing competition. There's even a racetrack there where horses are trained and races are held."

"Would you enjoy this type of work more than what you've been doing here in Frisco?"

Charles squeezed Lillian's hands, showing how excited he was by this prospect of a new job.

"Lilly, I know I'd love it. Wildlife and working outdoors have always been my true love. I've never enjoyed working underground in a mine. After the cave-in, I'm not so sure that I could go back to being a miner. Besides, Ryan is going to be paying me one-third more than I've been making here. There's a small house on the ranch that he'll sell me. A small portion of my salary will be withheld each month until the house is ours. I have a small nest egg put away, and I plan to use it to add rooms and do some remodeling in my spare time so that we can have a proper home. Being away from you and Billie for a few months won't be so bad if I know that I can bring you to a respectable house following the wedding. Do I have your go ahead to start work at Hay Springs?"

"Billie and I will miss you for all those months, but if working there will make you happy, my answer is yes."

Charles stood, bringing them both to their feet. "Now, my intended, we have a young man to talk to, and I need to take a much needed bath. I was so eager to find you that I didn't stop to clean up. I'm afraid I must smell like a dead polecat."

Lillian sniffed the air and was not surprised by the familiar fragrance that always seemed to be present when they were together. "You don't smell like a dead polecat, Charles. That is, unless a dead polecat smells like lavender."

Charles's eyes grew wide with wonder. "Lavender? But, Lilly, that's the scent that you always wear. You can't associate it with me."

"I've never used the scent of lavender in my life," said Lillian as they locked up the schoolhouse and headed for the shanty to tell Billie the good news.

Chapter 35

Events of the day kept swirling through Lillian's mind long after she had climbed in her bed and the lamps had been extinguished. Images of an excited Billie squeezing her so tightly that it was almost impossible to breathe, and the excitement on Nettie's face when she had asked her to be her maid of honor filled her with the type of static excitement that made sleep impossible.

Then green eyes asking an unanswered question entered her thoughts, lingered there, and refused to leave. *Will–I've forgotten all about Will. How will I explain tonight's decision to him?* Before her eyes finally closed in sleep, she promised herself that the sheriff of Frisco would get an answer to his question before the sun set tomorrow.

It seemed like her eyelids had been closed only a few minutes when she felt Nettie shaking her gently to rise and greet the day.

Lillian opened one eye to see a large smile on her friend's face. "I know you had a big day yesterday, but if you don't get out of that bed, you're going to be late for school. You don't want Billie to be the one to tell all of your students that their teacher is soon to be a married woman."

Billie had gone home with Charles last night to their shanty, and Lillian knew that the state of exuberance he was in when they told him the news would cause him to blurt the whole thing out unless she arrived at school before him.

Even though she got ready in record time, and Charles came to drive her to school, she was too late. When Charles lifted her from the wagon and kissed her soundly, mirthful giggles and laughter caused them to look at the schoolhouse. There they were–all ten of them–noses pressed to the windows, eyes wide, and mouths bubbling over with unsuppressed jubilation.

Suddenly, the faces disappeared from the windows, the schoolhouse door flew open, and ten excited children attacked their teacher and Charles with hugs and kisses for ammunition.

Billie, who had led the charge by placing a sound kiss on his teacher's cheek, then giving his father a breath-stopping hug, stood back with his hands on his suspenders, watching the wild commotion and sharing the happiness with the two most important people in his world.

When each child had expressed their joy in their own way, they backed away with silly grins on their faces, too shy to say a word.

Lillian, overcome with their greetings, waved her hands toward the schoolhouse as she gently said, "Children, go in and sit at your desks. I'll be there in a few minutes."

When they were sure that the schoolhouse door was shut and that there were no curious eyes peeking through the windows, Charles took hold of Lillian's two hands, and without saying a word, expressed his deep feelings through the affection that shone throughout his entire countenance.

Holding her hands a little too tightly he began, "Lilly, I'm going to go home and clean out my shanty. I've promised it to a mining engineer who has come to help with the cleaning out and shoring up of the old shaft. I'll drop Billie's stuff off at Nellie's. I hate to leave his entire care to you, but as of yet there's no school at Hay Springs, and I don't want his learning to be disturbed. I'll stop by about noon before I leave to say goodbye."

After a hurried kiss, Lillian found herself standing in the middle of the street. She found it difficult to return to the school until Charles turned and waved, giving her permission to break the bonds that held them and return to her everyday activities.

When she entered the school, she was bombarded with a barrage of questions. She had heard that curiosity often killed the cat, but she was positive at the present moment that curiosity was going to kill the teacher.

Finally, she tapped her pointer stick on the desk, then put her hand on the consequence jar and shook it to restore order.

When bedlam gave way to silence, she began, "I am going to make one statement that I think will answer most of your questions. Billie's father and I are getting married July Fourth as part of the Independence Day celebration. The wedding will be held in the field south of the racetrack. Girls, I would like each of you to serve as my flower girls, and boys, each of you will serve as attendants to the groom and will have the important duty of escorting the flower girls in the wedding procession. I couldn't get married without all of you. If each of your mothers will furnish refreshments, then the wedding will be complete. Are there any questions?"

"Does that mean you won't be our teacher next year?" asked Mary.

Lillian paused for a moment, uncertain how to answer them, then slowly said, "Let's worry about that when the time comes."

Tapping her pointer stick on the desk, she continued, "Now we must get down to business. We have a contest to win."

She then divided the class into two groups. She was going to make a contest of the review today, and the girls would compete against the boys.

The class took the competition seriously, thinking carefully before answering the questions. After 60 questions, the score was boys 29, girls 30. You could almost smell tenseness in the air when Lillian said, "Boys, you have the last question of today's review. The score is boys 29 and girls 30. If the boys can give the correct answer, today's review will end in a tie."

At this moment, more than one face was moistened by drops of sweat.

"Billie, it's your question. What was the name of the famous address President Lincoln gave as he spoke at a famous Civil War battlefield?"

Billie appeared to be concentrating so hard that his red freckles threatened to pop off at any second. He paused for a few moments, then slowly and forcefully answered, "That would have to be the Shilo Message."

Groans bounced off the walls and came to reside in Billie's ears as he realized that he had truly blown it for his team.

Billie raised his arms in the air to be recognized as he shouted, "It was the Lady in Black. I swear I saw her peeking in the window. She put a hex on me."

At the mention of the Lady in Black, a ruckus erupted, and the students were off and running with more wild stories about the black specter.

Rapping her desk to restore order, Lillian did not mention the Lady in Black, but praised the entire class for the number of questions they had gotten correct and tried to make Billie feel better by saying, "Billie, that mistake showed that you had indeed been studying. Shilo is another famous Civil War battlefield, which shows me that you have been doing some intensive study for the review. All of you keep up the good work and study the next ten pages in your history book for tomorrow's review. Now sit at your desks and relax while you eat your lunch. Then you can put on your warm coats and go outside for a game of Indian Ball."

Out of the corner of her eye, Lillian had noticed through the window that Charles was sitting in his wagon, waiting to have a word with her.

When she reached him, he took her left hand in his, reached in his pocket for something that shone brightly as it caught the rays of the winter sun, and placed it on her finger.

"Since you have already given me your promise, this

ring says to all young men, 'Go elsewhere. This young lady is spoken for.'"

Lillian's breath caught in her throat. The ring was composed of one pearl set in a beautiful setting of silver threads. "Charles, this matches the Christmas pin someone gave me in secret." Her eyes glistened with unshed tears as she threw her arms around his neck and gave him a proper thank you. With her lips against his neck, she whispered, "Oh, I knew it was you all the time!"

When she leaned back in his arms to look into his eyes, he said, "It's a match for the pin. I hoped but never dreamed that I would be purchasing it for you. Will you wear it while I'm gone, or have the thoughts of being tied for the rest of your life to a crusty, old ruffian driven all thoughts of marriage from your mind?"

"I've taken quite a liking to a certain crusty, old ruffian. My life is now set on a new course with you by my side. I'll wear it with pride and not remove it until the wedding band is placed beside it. I do have something that I want to send with you. It has gotten me through the toughest times in my life." She reached inside her coat pocket to retrieve her personal copy of the *Book of Mormon*. As she handed it to him she asked, "Promise me that you'll read it in your spare time. Praying often about what you've read will give you a testimony as to its truthfulness."

Charles carefully placed the book in his saddlebag, then gave her a hug as he softly said, "I promise to read it carefully and have an open mind about its message."

As they stood gazing into each other's eyes, Lillian knew that the moment of parting, no matter how painful it might be, had to take place now. "Now, I have students to teach, and if you're going to make it to Hay Springs before nightfall, you'd better get started."

She hooked her arm in his and started to walk him to his wagon when their final goodbyes were interrupted by ten exuberant children who seemed to be everywhere, attempting to hit anyone and everyone they could with their famous Indian Ball.

Charles gave Lillian a hurried hug, then jumped in the wagon and drove off in haste, afraid that the stray ball would spook the horses and set them running. From that moment on, Lillian had to play the part of teacher and try to swallow the emotions that threatened to overcome her as she watched Charles drive off into the distance.

The afternoon ran smoothly, and the busy routine of the day left Lillian little time to think about Charles's leaving. Long after she had released her students to go to their homes, she sat at her desk, working on tomorrow's review questions and lesson plans. Before she realized how late it was, the pink glow from the sunset was shining through the west windows, and she knew she had better get back to the shanty.

After she locked up the school and started down Main Street, the fine hair on her arms prickled and stood on end, sending chills throughout her entire body, for going into The Southern was a woman, dressed in a long, black dress. On her head was a black hat and attached to it was a black veil that covered her face. As the figure turned to look in her direction, Lillian felt as if fiery darts, which were coming from the woman's eyes, were bombarding her.

Chapter 36

Lillian had never been one to be frightened easily, but the sight of that black figure entering The Southern caused her heart to beat wildly in her chest and her legs to become unsteady.

After a few minutes, she calmed herself down, and her sense of reason took over. *Lady in Black, I saw you put your hand on the door and open it just like any ordinary person. You're not a ghost, but what or who are you?* She decided that after her visit with Will she would talk to Ben Johnson about his mysterious guest. What concerned her more than the Lady in Black right now was how she was going to tell Will that she could not marry him because she was engaged to another.

Trying to delay the difficult task that lay before her, she shortened her steps and took her time walking down the hall to Will's room. She gently turned the knob on the door and opened it slowly so that it would not creak. *Maybe he'll be asleep and I won't have to go through this today–there's always tomorrow,* she thought.

When she stepped into the room, it was difficult for Lillian to fully take in the scene that lay before her. Will was fully awake, and sitting by his bedside with her hand tightly clasped in the sheriff's hand was the very Lady in Black that Lillian had just seen entering The Southern. The black veil was lifted, and with the left side of her face visible, it was easy to see that she was a strikingly beautiful woman. Long, blonde hair cascaded under the veil and long eyelashes framed deep blue eyes. What was even more earth shattering than seeing the Woman in Black sitting by the sheriff's bedside was the adoration and love that Lillian saw shining in both of their faces.

Without warning, the lady, who had struck fear into the hearts of all of Frisco for about a week, leaned over and gently kissed the bedridden man. It was evident that the kiss was returned when the sheriff's arm encircled the black veil, pulling the black-clad lady to his chest, inviting her to lengthen the kiss.

Lillian's first thought was of retreat. *I've got to get out of here. This is no place for me.* She probably would have made it out of the room without them noticing her except her high-button shoe hit the water pail which was standing close to the door, making a high-pitched clang.

The kiss was abruptly ended as two startled lovers turned their attention to the sound. A gasp escaped Lillian's lips as she caught her first glimpse of the woman's entire face. The left side of the woman's face was smooth and youthful with roses breaking though to color the cheek. The right side of her face could only be described as grotesque. Ugly pink scars covered skin that should have been pale and smooth. The scars were raised somewhat, causing the skin to look swollen and lumpy.

When she saw Lillian, a gasp escaped the woman's lips as she gathered the black veil around her damaged face, once more hiding her disfigurement. Her head automatically bowed as if she were embarrassed to be seen by anyone even with her scars now covered.

Will sat up in bed, but retained a tight grip on the small hand that he held. He motioned for Lillian to approach the empty side of the bed as he softy said, "Lil, I can't begin to comprehend how you must feel at this moment, but come and sit beside me, and I'll try to explain everything."

Lillian would much rather have turned and left the room, but she hesitantly walked to the bedside where Will immediately took her hand with his free one and gently squeezed it. If anyone had entered the room at this moment, the sight of the sheriff of Frisco lying in bed as he grasped the hands of two women would have sent the most fainthearted to their beds for weeks and would have given the rumormongers enough to talk about for the next year. Had word of this unusual sight gotten to the newspaper editor, it most certainly would have made the front page of the *Frisco Times,* sending shock waves throughout the entire Frisco community.

Lillian sat in a chair by the sheriff's bedside as he began, "Lil, I would like you to meet Mandy Caldwell. Mandy, there's no need to be afraid of your scars. Remove your veil so that we can both tell Lil your story."

The veil was thrown back to reveal deep blue eyes whose beauty were in no way diminished by the unsightly scars.

A gentle, melodic voice began, "Miss Lewis, Will has told me about you. I feel a bit overwhelmed coming face to face with such a beautiful rival."

"Rival?" Lillian paused for a moment as she came to realize just who this young lady was. "Mandy? Why you're Will's first love–the one he spent months trying to find when you ran away from him."

Long, blonde eyelashes fell on pale cheeks for a few seconds, and a blonde head was bowed, then raised as Mandy looked directly at Lillian and began, "Yes, I'm Mandy Caldwell. I guess I've been in love with Will ever since he caught that monster fish in our favorite fishing pond, then just to make me feel better, told everybody that I had made the catch. As I remember, my father had given me a particularly brutal beating the night before, and Will knew that I needed something to take my mind off that terrible scene.

"He was always doing things like that–trying to make me forget the terrible things that happened to me at home, but then without warning his violent nature would erupt. He couldn't seem to stop it, and every time it did emerge in violence of some sort, he reminded me of my father. When he was involved in the killing of that defenseless rancher, leaving his family without a provider, I couldn't forgive him. I tried to give him a second chance, thinking that he would change, but after the shooting spree when he and his friends broke all the windows, I knew that I had to leave. I couldn't stand to see the only man I had ever loved destroy himself, so when they put him in jail, I packed up what few things I had and caught a late stage which was leaving for the Utah mining town of Shauntie."

Lillian interrupted, "But that's just a few miles from here."

"Yes, just nine miles southeast of here," Mandy continued. "Little did I realize that a few years later Will would travel to the same area to enforce the law in Frisco."

"And little did I realize that Mandy was only a few miles away," said Will.

Without thinking, Lillian approached a delicate subject, "But how did your face get burned? I know those scars are the result of burns because my parents were killed in a fire and one of the men who tried to save them had scars similar to yours."

"These scars are a result of a terrible fire which nearly destroyed the mining camp of Shauntie," explained Mandy.

Lillian broke in, "Yes, some of my students told me about that fire. It was just two years ago in 1875. How did it start?"

To give Mandy a rest, Will continued, "Mandy told me that there are many stories about how the fire began. Some say that it was caused by a spark from a blacksmith shop which landed in a rubbish pile nearby. Another story is that the saloon, which was next to the blacksmith shop was the scene of its beginning. The proprietor of the saloon often washed his saloon floors down with kerosene, a common practice often used to disinfect them. It was well-known how he loved his cigars, and the story circulated that one of those cigars might have dropped on the newly kerosened floor, causing an immediate inferno which engulfed his saloon and set him instantly ablaze. Since the proprietor and blacksmith both died in the fire, the true cause of the blaze will never be known."

Lillian's eyes grew wide with curiosity as she asked, "Mandy, where were you when the fire began?"

"I was working in the telegraph office when I noticed the smoke and flames billowing from the saloon across the street. It was unfortunate that the wind was sending great gusts from the south, which was scattering the fire rapidly. I got on the telegraph and just had time to send the message, 'Shauntie is burning!' before my own building caught fire. The wind was carrying burning shingles everywhere, and the roof of the telegraph office was ablaze before I even had time to think. I made the mistake of trying to salvage what I could. I ran to my room, which was located in the telegraph office, and grabbed some clothes. Then I rushed back and snatched a new relay and headed for the door, but by then the entire roof of the office was engulfed in flames. Without warning, a burning timber from the roof fell, hitting me on the right side of my face and right arm on its way to the floor. I was stunned and thrown to the floor for a few minutes but managed to get up and rush from the building, unharmed except for a scorched face and blistered right arm."

"Was there nothing that could have been done to contain the blaze?" asked Will.

"There was only one well in the town," continued Mandy, "but the rope and curbing were burned at the beginning of the fire, so there was not even one drop of water to extinguish the inferno."

Will continued the story with, "Mandy told me that everyone had to flee for their lives and that almost every article of food and clothing was burned. One story I heard said that there was a great deal of wood and coal at the smelter which caught fire and continued to burn for hours, and that the smoke from the coal and wood was so immense that it could be seen from nearby Milford."

"It was a terrible site of destruction," continued Mandy. "But some horses and wagons were saved, and we managed to get to Minersville where kindly people took us in when they realized that we were all literally destitute."

"Have you been in Minersville since the fire?" asked Lillian.

Beautiful, blue eyes glistened with unshed tears as Mandy continued, "I will always be grateful to a sweet boardinghouse woman who did what she could for my burns and took me in. She found out I could cook and gave me a job in the boardinghouse kitchen. The kitchen was the perfect place to hide my scarred face, and when I did go out in public, I started wearing a black veil to cover my scars. After a while I purchased a black dress to match the hat and veil and instantly became a legend. I didn't need to worry about anybody approaching me because I soon became a mysterious apparition that engendered fear in the hearts of anyone who saw me."

"So how did the mysterious Lady in Black come to visit Frisco?" inquired Lillian.

Will seemed eager to relate this part of the story as he continued, "The owner of the boardinghouse where Mandy worked told her of a conversation that she had overheard while she was serving some hungry miners. A Frisco miner, who had come to Minersville to seek work, explained that he was here because of the Frisco cave-in which had left numerous miners unemployed. As the conversation continued, he talked about W. P. Phillips, the sheriff of Frisco. He explained that Frisco was getting pretty unruly again because the sheriff had been in the cave-in and was seriously injured, leaving Frisco without law enforcement of any kind. The real kicker came when the miner said that the sheriff's injuries were so critical that it was not certain whether he would live or die."

Mandy's face became animated as she continued, "When my boss relayed the information about the sheriff, I asked her to go back to the dining room and question the miner further as to what this W. P. Phillips looked like. When she came back to tell me that Frisco's sheriff had long, blonde hair and green eyes, there was no doubt in my mind. I had found Will, and what's more, I knew that I had to see him before he died. I had never lost my love for him, and I felt that if I could comfort him in some way in his last hours, I owed him that much."

"So you traveled to Frisco and began walking around at night, scaring all of its citizens clean out of their wits," chuckled Lillian.

"Yes, I've been here a few days. When I found that Will's condition wasn't critical, it took me a couple of days to get up the nerve to see him. I tried to remain unseen by only walking around at night, but it seemed that there was always someone up and about, peering through the shadows; hence the legend of the Lady in Black began. This morning I could wait no longer. I entered this very room, made my appearance known, and I've been here ever since except for taking a short walk just a few minutes ago."

Lillian was struggling to take all of this in as she asked, "Will, you must have been frightened out of your wits when you saw her for the first time."

"It was quite a shock to wake up and find a woman with a black veil standing by my bedside, but when a quiet voice managed to say 'Will, it's Mandy,' I felt a wonderful rush of happiness—I knew the lost had at last been found."

Lillian noticed that Will's grasp on Mandy's hand tightened, and that tears were beginning to flow freely down her face.

Mandy now struggled to control her emotions as she softly said, "When Will asked me to lift the veil, I will never forget that he did not cringe or turn away at the sight of my scars. The love and devotion that he felt for me never left his face for one minute, and when he pulled my face down to kiss the very scars that I thought would repulse him, I knew that he still loved me deeply."

It was now Lillian's turn to have her hand squeezed as Will's gaze remained on her for what seemed like endless moments. "Lil, I'm forgetting you and your feelings. If I remember right, I did ask you to spend the rest of your life with me. I promised myself after the cave-in that I would be a man of my word. If you came here to accept my proposal, then Mandy and I have decided that we will part and never see one another again."

Lillian's eyes twinkled and a soft laugh rippled from down deep inside of her. When she finally restrained her merriment, her gaze met two questioning faces that were waiting for an immediate answer.

"Do you two want to know what's tickled me so? The explanation is simple. Coming here today was one of the hardest things that I have ever done. You see, Will, I came here to tell you that I couldn't marry you because I had just become engaged to Charles Anderson."

Laughter filled the room as the three realized that all problems had just been solved by Lillian's simple explanation.

When the merriment ceased, Will looked at Lillian and asked, "Now that you have spurned me for another man, I am going to ask that you keep a secret. No matter how tempted you may be, will you please promise me right here and now that what I am about to tell you will never be revealed to another living soul?"

"You have my solemn promise," agreed Lillian.

"Mandy and I have decided that if you refused me, we would sneak away in the dead of night and leave Frisco and all its violence behind. I think if I have some help, I'll be able to sit in a stagecoach. I've heard tell that there's land for the taking up north in Cache Valley. I've a little saved and so has Mandy. When we find the type of spread that suits us, we'll buy it and settle down. Besides, Mandy heard that there's a doctor in Salt Lake City who has done wonderful work with burns similar to hers. Maybe with the right kind of medical treatment, she won't have to wear that black veil forever."

Lillian squeezed Will's hand and gave Mandy one of her brightest smiles. "I'm so happy for you. Let me be the first to offer you congratulations, but you'll have to promise me that you'll send me a letter every once in a while–under disguise, of course–and let me know how you're doing. I promise not to disclose your whereabouts, even though it's going to be hard keeping a secret of that magnitude."

A note of seriousness entered the sheriff's voice as he said, "Lil, I give you credit for making me see that I had to make a big change in my life. The genuine goodness that lies within you convinced me that I couldn't continue on the course that I was going. I did some serious soul searching and realized that despite my violent nature, I did have a softer side that I could nurture. If it wasn't for you, I doubt that I would have reacted as I did when Mandy removed her veil. You and Mandy are the two best things that have ever happened to me. Thanks for being the type of young lady who inspires even the most incorrigible of men like myself to rise to the goodness that is lying hidden within them."

Lillian's eyes clouded up as she said softly, "And you, my dear Sheriff, will never know how close I came to saying yes to your proposal, but you and Mandy are destined to spend your lives together just as Charles and I are fated to travel the road of life side by side. Please don't tell me the day or hour that you are going to leave. That way, I can't possibly disclose the secret. Now, no more words; when it comes to goodbyes, my emotions are too close to the surface."

Lillian bent to kiss Will on the forehead, then walked to the other side of the bed to give Mandy a hug. As she turned, crossed the room, and quickly opened the door, she refused to look back. Tears should have filled her eyes, but as she shut the door, she felt herself smiling. How could she be sad when she realized that she and the two people she had just said goodbye to were at this moment three of the happiest people in Frisco, if not the entire world.

Chapter 37

When Lillian had watched Charles drive away, a sad heaviness had weighed on her heart because at that time, six months had seemed like an eternity. But time, like a runner in a race, had sprinted on, and today as she looked at her plan book, she had a hard time believing that it was May 22, 1880, just one day before the big history contest.

She let her mind slip back in time as she reminisced over events that seemed like only yesterday. She could see the bright, excited faces of her students three days after her final meeting with Will and Mandy. At the beginning of their "What's Happening in Frisco" portion of the day, Mary could not stay in her seat because of her agitated state. She rose without permission from her teacher and in a dramatic fashion related, "Sheriff Phillips disappeared last night like a puff of smoke drifting upward, quickly vanishing in the vast expanse of the sky." She dramatically raised both arms to the ceiling before sitting in her seat.

Curt said his father has seen the Lady in Black in the sheriff's recovery room at The Southern. "I know for a fact," Curt began in his most dramatic voice, "that the Black Lady has cast a spell on the sheriff. He is at this very minute held prisoner in her secret cave. As I speak to you, she is training him to be her apprentice, instructing him in the arts of mystery and the powers of darkness." All of the eyes of the class were riveted on Curt as he took his seat.

Keeping a straight face had been almost impossible for Lillian, but she had kept her promise and had not revealed the truth. Then the talk had centered around how the town had elected a new sheriff, one of the out-of-work miners, and how he was a real softy compared to Sheriff Phillips. "But we don't really want Sheriff Phillips back," said Jamie, as he shivered and stuck out his tongue at the very thought of such a terrible occurrence.

When the children left to play outdoor games at recess, Lillian's thoughts left her schoolroom for a moment, and her attention was drawn to her carpetbag which held the precious letters that she had received from Charles. Retrieving them from the bag, she noticed that they were worn from frequent reading, but the message that they held sent a flood of happiness straight to her heart. Without fail, one of these letters had arrived each week, and she had answered each of them, always closing with the phrase, "God bless you till we meet again, my love."

Charles wrote of his work on the house and how it was progressing. He had added another bedroom for Billie and designed new cupboards for the kitchen. He was enjoying his work on the ponds and wrote of the beautiful birds that often found a home there. Lillian could plainly tell from the tone of his letters that Charles had found a special happiness in his new work.

The most tender and dearest parts of his letters concerned his reading of the *Book of Mormon*. He wrote of reading it faithfully every night, and how he had knelt the night he finished it to take the prayer challenge. The part of the letter which said, "That night as I prayed, a warmness filled my heart and my entire body, an answer to its truthfulness," was now difficult to read because the writing was blurred from Lillian's tears.

It was hard for her to believe that the wedding, scheduled for the Fourth of July, was just a few weeks away. She smiled as she realized that her wedding day would be a special one for Nettie as well. Shortly after Charles had left for Hay Springs, Nettie had become engaged to Ben Johnson, and the two dear friends had decided that they would be married together in a double wedding ceremony. When she wrote Charles about these plans, he wrote back that he was delighted with such an idea.

Back to the present, Lillian, she chided herself. *There is no time to dwell in the past or Charles. The big day is tomorrow!*

When recess was over, Lillian and the class started to prepare in earnest for the big events that would take place tomorrow. The students from Milford and Minersville had arrived today by wagon teams and were at this very minute setting up their camps near the competition field. Beaver and Newhouse had pulled out of the competition, so only three towns would be competing. She and the children spent the rest of the day in the dance hall setting up for the contest.

On the raised stage in the room, they had set up three tables with seats for ten students on each table. Each school had created their own poster, using their own personal art work. Minersville had chosen a mining theme, adorning their sign with elaborate, artistic picks and shovels. Milford's sign showed a picture of the old mill from which Milford had received its name. Lillian's students had drawn an ore car on their sign with dynamite sticks on each corner with the saying, "Frisco will blow the lid off of this competition!"

The benches in the dance hall had been carefully arranged below the stage so that the spectators could enjoy the contest. The pump organ proudly sat to the right of the tables on the platform to supply lively music to signal the beginning of the contest.

As news of the competition had circulated around the communities of Milford and Minersville, the events of the day had escalated into something entirely different from what Lillian had envisioned. The mayors of the three towns had gotten together and decided that this should be a day of celebration and competition for not only the school children, but also for the adults in the three communities. The mayors decided among themselves that before the history contest, adults as well as children in the three communities were going to compete in various contests of their own making. The entire morning was going to be devoted to these contests, leaving the afternoon for the history competition, which would culminate the events of the day. The Minersville and Milford camps were bustling with activity as the contestants and their families finished setting up their camps, getting some much-needed rest, and preparing for the big day.

Who would have thought that a simple history contest would have developed into such an extravaganza of competitiveness, thought Lillian as she closed and locked the schoolhouse door. *There's no sense in worrying about tomorrow,* she thought. *Tomorrow will come whether we're ready or not. I only hope that after all those carefully-planned reviews, the Frisco School is ready!*

Chapter 38

Lillian rose long before the sunrise. She had tossed and turned all night, sleep eluding her, as the upcoming events of the day refused to let her mind retire into the silken world of dreams.

She took special care with her appearance. She wanted to look like the type of professional who had complete control over her students. Her high-button shoes were shined to a high gloss, and she wore a new white blouse with a high-neck collar that she had just purchased at The Mercantile the day before. She made sure that not a hair escaped from the braids which were carefully wound in a circle at the back of her head. As she looked at her image in the mirror over the washbowl, she thought, *You may look young, Lillian, but you also look like you have the confidence of Sarah Bernhardt and the tenacity of Daniel Boone. You'll do, girl.*

Billie hadn't been able to get much sleep either. He was wound up tighter than a drum and was filled with nonstop chatter all morning long. Lillian was ready to totally lose every ounce of wits that she had, but she knew that with Billie, patience was the key. She took special care to slick his cowlick down and to see that his face was washed until his freckles shone. It was difficult to get him to settle down long enough to eat some breakfast, and after he literally gulped his oatmeal, he rushed out the door screaming, "You guys are too slow. See ya there!"

After she and Nettie finished their breakfast, they both walked to the large field north of town and adjacent to the racetrack where the games would begin. When they arrived at the designated contest field, the glory of the sunrise was painting the sky with a pink glow. The white peaks of the Mineral Mountains were transformed into brilliant shades of pinks and light reds as the rays of the sun filled the eastern sky with a profusion of vibrant colors.

Even though Lillian and Nettie were at least an hour early, they were not the first to arrive. The shaft of the mine had been cleared and shored up one month ago, and the mine was once again in full operation. Frisco was busting at the seams with miners who had returned to resume their jobs as well as new folks who had moved here for employment. Because of this deluge of people into the city, an enormous crowd was expected; therefore, many contestants and observers had risen before the sun, picked out prime seats to view the events, and thrown their blankets on the ground, thus claiming an excellent seat to view the festivities. It was clear that some of them had been there all night, for they were wrapped in their blankets, sound asleep, holding down their special observation positions.

Nettie and Lillian spread their blankets and watched as members of the contest committee went about setting up for the competitions. On one end of the field, a clothesline was being raised, and cow ponies were being tied to a hitching post at the north end of the field, their saddles nearby. At the west side of the field a large pole was pounded into the ground, and Lillian smiled when she saw her own Billie hoisted on the shoulders of the tallest man in Frisco so that he could grease the pole liberally with lard. Lillian had brought him some clean clothes because she knew that the ones he was wearing now would not be fit for anything after he finished. His old gloves would also have to be discarded, but what did that matter when fun and excitement were the order of the day.

Billie finished his job and joined them to change into clean clothes as Nettie and Lillian held a blanket in front of him. "Nobody's going to get up that pole today," he gushed. "It's slicker than snot on a hot griddle."

"Billie! Mind your tongue," warned Lillian. "Remember, you must act like you're a member of a winning team!"

"Yes, Ma'am! Oh, there's Melissa and Jamie! Do you think they remembered that we're going to sit together?"

"Well, go and remind them and gather the others up. We've got to be the best cheering squad on the field if we're going to pump up the spirit."

Within minutes the Frisco School members had joined their teacher, and after spreading their blankets, stood in their practice formation, ready to cheer their favorites on to victory.

After a formal welcome from Frisco's mayor, the competition began. The first contest was the cow pony race. Ben Johnson, who proudly represented Frisco, wore Nettie's scarf for good luck.

Lillian stood with her students as they chanted, "Who's the man to win the race? Who's the man to set the pace? Ben! Ben! Ben!"

When a gunshot broke the silence of the morning, saddles were flung over three ponies and saddle straps were frantically fastened as the contestants tried to gain some sort of advantage. The Minersville contestant was the first to mount his pony, but the Frisco and Milford contestants were only seconds behind him. Then manes flew and hooves flicked up dirt as the contestants raced the required 100 yards before they turned to return back to their starting position. The Minersville contestant lost his advantage when his horse reared as he attempted to turn him, costing him precious seconds. Neck to neck, the remaining two raced for their starting position where they had to dismount, then unsaddle their mounts. The thud of the saddle hitting the ground was the signal that the contestant had finished his race. Ben Johnson was poetry in motion as he dismounted, removed his saddle, and then threw it on the ground just seconds before his competitors. As he raised his arms to signal victory, a huge smile covered his face.

The Frisco crowd went wild. Lillian found herself jumping and screaming with Nettie and the rest of her students.

For a change, it was the students who had to bring their teacher to order.

"Throw those clothes upon the line. Pin them up in record time!" was chanted three times in succession by the Frisco cheering squad, signaling the beginning of the next contest.

At the sounding of the gun, three lady contestants frantically began attaching shirts to three clotheslines. After about three minutes, the gun was once again sounded, shirts were counted on each line, and now it was Minersville's turn to scream and shout. When time was called, Minersville's competitor had pinned one more shirt to her line than the Frisco and Milford contestants. Beatrice Small, who represented Frisco, stamped her feet and marched off with a stormy look on her face.

Next, grown men wiggled into burlap bags, then jumped like kangaroos to the finish line in the potato sack race. Milford's contestant must have been practicing for this event, because each time he hopped, he covered twice as much ground as the other two competitors. As he raised his arms in a victory signal, Ronald Gillins, the Minersville competitor, flopped on the ground, lowered his head, and refused all attempts to get him up for at least three minutes.

Husbands and wives now stepped forward for the wheelbarrow race. It was clear that great care had been taken to choose just the right couple–the three men were bulky specimens with bulging muscles, while their wives were as petite and dainty as the most delicate flowers. With the wives carefully positioned in the wheelbarrows, at the sound of the gun, three wheelbarrows surged forward like strong arrows shot from a tight bow.

Calamity struck when the front tire of the Minersville wheelbarrow struck an invisible rock, turning the wheelbarrow on its side and flinging the Minersville lady face down in the dirt. As she raised her dirt-powered face, she saw her husband flying like a speeding bullet over the wheelbarrow, creating a dust cloud that rose as he hit the loose dirt. Undaunted, the courageous couple limped back to their wheelbarrow and finished the race. Showing good sportsmanship, the Milford competitors congratulated the Frisco contestants who had defeated the Milford couple by mere inches.

The Frisco crowd went wild. There was a great deal of screaming, shouting, and exuberant jumping which continued until the gentlemen in charge of the races shot his gun in the air to bring them to order.

Lillian's cheering section knew exactly what competition was next. Taking deep breaths to give them added lung power, they chanted, "Roll that pig over; squash him flat; Frisco will win despite all that fat! Yaaaaah Frisco!"

Squeals filled the air as the cage which contained the greased pig was brought forward. One man from each community positioned themselves in a running stance, ready to catch that greasy varmint the minute the cage was opened. The cage door opened just one second before the shot, and that pig was a mere greasy streak, emitting squeals that were shrill enough to be heard in the Frisco Cemetery. The Frisco contestant lunged forward, hitting the ground with a loud thud, as he literally tackled the pig, who promptly slipped from his fingers as the race continued. With the pig in his arms, the Minersville contestant thought that he had the race won until the pig wiggled his snout against his lips, causing him to gag and loosen his hold, giving the pig the opportunity to slip away once again. The Milford contestant was victorious when he finally tackled the greasy critter and just lay on top of him, giving the pig no opportunity for escape. The score now stood at Frisco, 2; Milford, 2; and Minersville, 1.

Lillian and her cheering section knew that they had to pump up the spirit, so with all the enthusiasm they could muster, they yelled, "Climb up the greased pole; take a firm hold; who can? We can! Brave Frisco can! Go Frisco!"

But victory was not in store for the Frisco pole climber. He got no further than a couple of feet in the allotted three minutes. Lady Luck chose not to be with the Milford contestant as he could not even manage to climb a foot. Then the Minersville contestant shocked all observers as he somehow managed to climb to the top of the pole before the three minutes were up. When complaints were logged following the contest that someone had seen him liberally cover his hands with dirt shortly before he began to climb, the contest referee still awarded him first place because there were no rules against dirt dusting. Pandemonium broke out when the Milford and Frisco contestants had to be pulled off the field and restrained from using fisticuffs to demonstrate their displeasure at the unfairness of the referee's decision.

Three contestants now positioned themselves at a table which contained one large pitcher of lemonade and three pint jars. Each jar was filled to exactly the same height, the signal that the lemonade guzzling contest was about to begin. "Guzzle that lemonade; drink it all down. Who's the quickest guzzler around? – Frisco! Frisco! Frisco!" yelled the Frisco cheering section. The gun sounded and the contest was on. What the contestants didn't know was that this particular lemonade was made with lemons, water, and no sugar. It was sour!

The contestants took a big gulp of the lemonade, and then removed the jar from their lips as their lips puckered and their eyes bugged out like frogs. Forcing themselves to continue was difficult, but continue they did, pausing in their guzzling at times to gag, pucker some more, then drink again. They all finished and held their jars in front of them at exactly the same second, but the judge disqualified the Frisco contestant for spilling too much lemonade on his beard; therefore, the lemonade guzzle ended in a tie between the Minersville and Milford contestants who forced a smile through their puckered lips. The Frisco contestant would have shook his wet beard in the judge's face, but his friends restrained him by grabbing his arms and forcing him away from the table. The score now stood at Frisco 2; Minersville 3; and Milford 3.

Pressure settled like a heavy cloud over the Frisco community. If Frisco could win this last competition, the events of the morning would end in a tie. Many a finger was crossed as the time rapidly approached for the final showdown between the three communities. This contest was the only competition for children only. Called the pony trot, the contest required four children to ride bareback on ponies of the same size. When the gun sounded, the ponies were to head for the finish line which was 100 yards away. If at any time any young person fell from the pony, the whole team was automatically disqualified. Billie, Jamie, Melissa, and Mary were representing Frisco. Jamie positioned himself first, then Melissa, and Mary, followed by Billie who sat in the rear.

" Bang!" They were off! The shot frightened the ponies, and they surged forward like pellets from a shotgun. Lillian sensed trouble when she saw that Billie had on his stressed-out face. Then she saw the reason. He was slowly slipping backwards, about to slip off the pony's bottom at any minute. Lillian feared for the worst, but smiled when she realized that her Billie didn't know the meaning of the word quit. Billie took command as he yelled, "Mary, hold on tight to Melissa, and Melissa, you grab Jamie and don't let go." He then grabbed hold of Mary with his left hand and with his right hand took a firm hold on the pony's tail. To those watching, it looked like he was going to hit the ground at any minute, but with Jamie holding tightly to the pony's neck and all of them securely chained together with firm holds, somehow Billie stayed on, even though his body was halfway down the pony's rear.

Halfway to the finish line, Minersville was disqualified when the pony they were riding kicked up its back legs, throwing two riders to the ground. It was now up to Milford and Frisco. They were neck to neck until seconds before they hit the finish line. At this point the Frisco pony surged forward to win by a nose. Four ecstatic children jumped from the pony, gave several victory screams, kissed their pony, then joined hands and formed a circle. Four heads lowered as butts stuck out and a loud chant filled the air, "Frisco's number one! Frisco's number one! Frisco's number one!"

Lillian couldn't have been more proud. Her team had just tied up the competition. Each town had been victorious in three events. Now, she realized everything hinged on the history contest that would take place following lunch. The winner of that contest would take home the large trophy which would be given to the overall winner.

Lunch was a smorgasbord of pure delight. Large tables had been set up at the west end of the field. Everyone placed their own special dish or dishes on the tables. The Minersville and Milford citizens proudly added their special treats to complement the feast. It was a time of rest, a time to make new friends, and in Lillian's case, it was a time to give her students one final review. She gathered them around her and started throwing questions at them. When not a question was missed, her heart's erratic beat slowed, and her breathing returned to normal.

"Now remember, students, don't just blurt out the answer, because a wrong answer cannot be retracted. Take a few seconds to think before you respond. Remember, you are all winners. Do your best and I know that we will come out victorious. Should we lose, we are still champions if we have truly done our best."

Following their final review, they walked arm and arm to the dance hall. This way they were united not only as a body, but also as competitive spirits, knit together to achieve victory. When they reached the dance hall, they formed a single file line, but still held hands. They broke contact only long enough to take their seats, then they once again became a single unit as hands were again clasped, but this time under the table.

Superintendent McNaught and three judges that he had chosen from each community sat at a table which faced the contestants. Each judge was given a printout of the contest questions and answers.

The superintendent had asked three educators from the state to submit sixty history questions each. These educators were teaching from the same history books used by the student contestants in their classrooms. When he received all of the questions, he wrote 20 questions of his own to be used as tie-breakers if they were needed, then asked the *Frisco Times* editor to print them so that there would be no misunderstanding on the part of the judges when they read them to the contestants.

The teachers did not sit on the tables with the students, but sat off to the side in separate chairs. Lillian desperately wanted to sit with her class and add her strength to theirs by being part of the chain they had formed with their tightly clasped hands, but she knew if she broke the rules of the contest by getting too close to her students, they would automatically be disqualified. She breathed deeply. *One hundred and eighty questions! It's going to take all afternoon. Please, Heavenly Father, help them to remember what they have been taught,* she prayed.

When she lifted her eyes, they focused on the doorway and the familiar figure who had just entered to sit down on the back row. If the floppy slouch hat and beard wasn't a clue as to who he was, the piercing warmth coming from the dark brown eyes was. *Charles! What are you doing here? You weren't suppose to come until a week before the wedding, and that's more than a month away!* But there he was, his smile conveying just how happy he was to see her.

Lillian had to restrain herself from leaving her seat and flying right into his arms to give him a proper welcome, but she told herself, *Lillian, you've got to concentrate on one thing at a time. Charles, you'll have to wait! Right now, you must focus all your energy and emotion on this competition.* Reluctantly, she took her eyes from Charles and determined to focus on her students until the competition was finished.

Superintendent McNaught stood and faced the audience. "Welcome to the first History Contest ever held in this school district. Because of Miss Lewis and her creative teaching methods, I was prompted to schedule this event. I had no idea when we decided to do this that it would develop into the exhilarating activities that took place this morning. It's been wonderful to bring the three communities together for such an enjoyable day!"

The superintendent then introduced the three judges, explained how the questions had been gathered, and explained that he himself would be responsible for tabulating the total points for each school.

He then explained that there would be six rounds to the contest. The Milford School would go first and would be asked the first ten questions. The Minersville School would follow with each of their students being given one of the next ten questions. Then the Frisco School would end the first round as they stood to answer their ten questions. At the end of each round, the running score would be taped to the three tables, hopefully adding excitement and anticipation to the event.

It was clear from the very beginning of the contest that all schools had taken the time to prepare well. Each student at the Milford and Minersville tables stood and answered all of their questions without hesitation–all of them correct. It was now Frisco's turn to end the round. The audience was given no warning for what happened next.

Billie was the first to stand as the first judge asked, "What was the Native American civilization called that thrived from about 300 A.D. to 900 A.D. in Southern Mexico and Guatemala?"

Billie did not hesitate as he loudly stated, "The Mayas." He could have sat down and been finished with that correct answer, but he started drawing imaginary lines in the air. The judges and audience stared at him, thinking he had lost his senses. "May we ask what you are doing, young man?" the judge asked.

"I'm drawing some of the symbols and images that represented Mayan ideas. They were called glyphs," Billie proudly stated as the judge, awestruck, remained silent for a few minutes, then firmly said, "By Jove, young man, you're correct on both counts," after which Billie finally took his seat, pleased with his performance.

He's demonstrating how we learned this part of history, thought Lillian. *Way to go Billie!*

Melissa was the next to stand. When Billie squeezed her hand tightly to ease her fears, her lips parted in a tiny smile. "Who was the early American who wrote Poor Richard's Almanac?" asked the second judge.

Melissa's lips quivered ever so slightly before she answered, "Benjamin Franklin," then she straightened her back and looking the judge directly in the eye continued, "in which he said, 'When you incline to have new clothes, look first well over the old ones, and see if you cannot shift with them another year, either by scouring, mending, or even patching if necessary.'" Melissa then pointed at the audience as she finished her extraordinary answer, "Those of you in the audience remember this,–Mr. Franklin said, 'Remember a patch on your coat, and money in your pocket is better and more creditable than a debt on your back and no money to take it off.'"

When Melissa sat down, loud applause filled the hall, and a bone-crushing hug from Billie caused a wide smile to break out on Melissa's face.

"You are indeed correct, Miss Cottrell. I think we could all heed that advice," the judge commented.

Jessica's long, blonde hair literally shone, and her blue eyes sparkled as she stood to answer her question.

"Jessica, who was the leader of the Sons of Liberty?" asked the third judge.

Jessica hesitated only a few seconds before she answered, "Samuel Adams." Then she continued, "The Sons of Liberty were formed to protest the Stamp Act which levied a tax on all printed matter."

"Young lady, you are absolutely correct," stated the judge.

Again applause filled the hall, and Jessica showed her pleasure in their response by coming from behind the table and dropping into a deep curtsy.

Stacy, who had found it extremely difficult to remain quiet since the contest began, literally jumped up from her seat to answer her question.

"During the Battle for Boston, Patriot Americans were atop what two hills?" asked the judge.

"This one's just like churning butter–It's so easy! Bunker Hill and Breed's Hill." Stacy then demonstrated shooting in rapid succession as she yelled at the top of her lungs, "Don't shoot till you see the whites of their eyes!"

"You are correct, Stacy, right down to the exact words of the quote," said the judge.

Uncontrolled laughter broke out in the audience, and the freckles on Stacy's nose literally sparkled.

Clarence had taken extra care with his black hair today, but the pony contest had caused the cowlick on the back of his head to stand straight up. His eyes were bubbling with life as he awaited his question.

"Clarence Wood, Thomas Paine promoted his Patriot cause in a pamphlet that he produced. What was that pamphlet called?"

Clarence shifted his weight from side to side, then slowly and deliberately answered, "That pamphlet was named by a name that Ma says I don't have any of–'Common Sense'." A few suppressed chuckles could be heard, but Clarence was not through. He motioned with his hands for the crowd to give them his attention. One part of this pamphlet said, 'Government even in its best state is but a necessary evil; in its worst state, an intolerable one.'"

"Impressive, young man," said Superintendent McNaught. "You are absolutely correct."

Silence fell over the audience as they realized the hours of study time that must have been spent by this eight-year-old so that he could have such a quote on the tip of his tongue.

Richie slowly stood for his question. Lillian said a silent prayer for him because learning for Richie didn't come easy, and often he had to go through extra reviews to remember the subject matter.

"What English General surrendered to mark the end of the Revolutionary War?"

"Corn..." Richie paused and Lillian held her breath. She remembered a day in class when Richie had answered, "General

Cornpone" and sent the entire class into hysterics. But Richie was all business and a smile broke out on his face as he stated soundly, "General Cornwallis," then added, as he went through the motions of signing something, "The Treaty of Paris, signed shortly after his surrender, gave America its Independence."

"That's my Richie" yelled Richie's mother as she stood to be recognized, holding up both her arms. At this point, every Frisco citizen stood to join her as loud applause and whistles filled the hall.

Superintendent McNaught moved his hands up and down in front of the audience so that they would take their seats and let the contest continue.

Jamie stood at attention, then slapped his hands down to his side and loudly stated, "Jamie Parker here. Ready for my question, sir." With a face that showed no emotion at all, he then saluted the audience.

Trying to suppress a giggle, the judge asked, "Well, Jamie, The Articles of Confederation granted the new American government the right to do certain things. Name one of these things."

Jamie reached into his pocket and pulled out a nickel. "Without the Articles of Confederation, I wouldn't have this nickel to buy some stick candy at The Mercantile because these articles gave the colonists the right to borrow and coin money." At this point instead of sitting down, he moved his hands back and forth over his lips and let out a bloodcurdling war whoop that could have come from the fiercest Indian.

Somewhat shaken, the judge asked, "What in the world was that for, Jamie?"

"To remind me something more about these articles. The Articles of Confederation also set forth a policy towards the American Indian." Once more laughter filled the hall.

When he could once more be heard, Superintendent McNaught stated, "You are absolutely correct, young man."

Mary's straight, blonde hair had been tied into two ponytails which stuck out on both sides of her head and jiggled to and fro with the slightest movement of her body. She stood and shifted from one foot to the other as she said, "Mary Nelson, contestant from Frisco."

"Miss Nelson, could you please tell me what practice the Northwest Ordinance banned?"

Mary took her harmonica from her pocket and began to play a lively rendition of "Dixie."

When she had played for about a minute, she placed the harmonica in her pocket and simply stated, "The Northwest Ordinance banned slavery, sir."

"That is correct, Miss Nelson. You may be seated."

Curt stood and bowed deeply to the audience as if he had just finished an award-winning play. In a deep, resonant voice he projected, "Friends, Romans, and Contest Goers, lend Curt Smithson your ears."

The audience was too stunned to react to this dramatic display, so silence reigned until the judge gently ventured, "Mr. Smithson, can you tell me one freedom that the First Amendment guarantees us?"

"Freedom of religion, speech, and the right to assemble," stated Curt. He then pointed to the editor of the *Frisco Times* and motioned for him to stand. Without the First Amendment, our newspaper editor, Mr. Groover, would be out of work because this amendment also guarantees us freedom of the press."

"Correct, young man," was the judge's firm response.

The last student contestant to stand for Frisco was Laura. *Please, Heavenly Father, help her to take this contest seriously. Now is not the time for one of her dares,* thought Lillian.

Laura's red curls seemed to be sticking out in every direction as she began a most unusual introduction: "My name's Laura Johnson; I look just like a queen, and way down deep inside my head, my brain is pretty keen. When it comes to answering questions, I'm the very best, so let her rip, old Judgie Boy, and put me to the test." She then stepped in front of the table and did an amazing dance with intricate footwork, ending with her hand extended towards the judge.

Another dare! Please don't be offended, Judge, anguished Laura.

But praises be, the judge was all smiles. "That's quite a performance, Miss Johnson, but do you think we can get you to take your place behind the table so that we can end this first round.'

"I'm ready, Judge," said Laura as she and her curls literally bounced to her place.

It took a few minutes for the judge to regain his composure, but finally, he turned to Laura and asked, "Ten years ago the greatest historical event in transportation history occurred at Promontory, Utah. What was this historic event?"

Laura's smile nearly popped all of the freckles off her face as she formed an operatic pose and began to sing her answer as if she were the lead soprano in a famous opera. Loud, melodious notes filled the room as Laura burst into song.

"Bang! Bang! and clickety-clang, the final spike was driven. To connect two mighty railroads–the Central and Union Pacific.The first transcontinental railroad was formed with the driving of this spike.Now travelers can travel across our whole land, and not have to use their bikes."

Laura ended her dramatic song with a long, drawn out, resonate, "T-r-a-n-s-c-o-n-t-i-n-e-n-t-a-l R-a-i-l-r-o-a-d!!"

When Laura had completed her performance, she gave a low bow to the audience. Thunderous applause filled the hall as the audience stood to show their pleasure at Laura's performance.

Lillian was delighted to see that the judge was standing and clapping with the rest of the audience. When the audience had taken their seats, the judge once again addressed Laura.

"That is correct, young lady. Your lyrics were a bit strange for a normal operatic song, but what you sang was indeed correct. You may be seated."

The judge turned to Superintendent McNaught and said, "The Frisco School has just answered their first ten questions correctly, making the contest so far a tie between all contestants."

Excitement crackled through the air as rounds 2, 3, 4, and 5 ended in ties also. It seemed beyond comprehension that not one contestant had missed a question.

And during each round, the audience looked forward to Frisco's answers because the Frisco contestants not only gave the correct response, but their innovative way of answering the questions repeatedly entertained the crowd, and those in the audience marveled at how these young students always had extra information at the end of their answer to prove their expertise in the subject.

At the beginning of the final sixth round, the tension was so thick that it could have been cut by a lumberman's saw. It was announced by one of the judges that the questions for this final round were going to be the most challenging of the contest.

Challenging was a good term for the final questions. During this round, the rules changed somewhat. If any contestant missed a question, that same question would be given to the next team. If that team missed the question, it would be given to the next team. The first team to answer the missed question would get double points for their answer, and if it was the first question of the round, the team that answered the missed question correctly would be declared the winner.

Milford's second question was, "Which state was the last state to ratify the Constitution?"

The contestant whose turn it was to answer thought about it for a full two minutes then hesitantly said, "I believe it was New York."

"That is incorrect said the judge. Minersville, can you give us the correct answer?"

The Minersville contestant shifted from foot to foot, and then answered, "Delaware."

"That's incorrect, also. Frisco, what is your answer?"

Billie's freckles literally popped out of his face as he firmly stated, "That would be Rhode Island, Sir. They ratified it May 29, 1790, almost 2 1/2 years after the Constitution was written."

"That is correct..." No one heard the rest of the judge's comment because at this point all the Frisco residents in the audience and the Frisco contestants on the stage stood up and let out cheers that were loud enough to cause the dead in the Frisco cemetery to rise from their graves and shout, "Hallelujah!" Kerchiefs were taken from necks and twirled over heads, and ladies threw their hats in the air with little thought as to where they would land.

Superintendent McNaught stood up and raised his hands for order, but it took a few minutes to quell the exuberant winners. After he had motioned for about two minutes for everyone to be seated, some brave soul in the back of the room drew his gun and sent one bullet through the ceiling. It was then that order reigned and everyone took their seats. In a loud voice the superintendent proclaimed, "I declare the Frisco School the winner of the History Contest and also the overall winner of the entire day!"

Loud applause, cheers, and whistles filled the air. Once again the Frisco men waved their large handkerchiefs or unwrapped the kerchiefs from their necks and waved them in the air. Some of the Frisco ladies who had found their hats, detached the scarves from their bonnets and joined the men in this waving spree.

Lillian, who was now surrounded by ten children, all wanting hugs and some jumping around the stage like jumping jacks was suddenly enclosed in strong arms and dragged behind the curtain of the stage by a bearded gentleman who demanded a proper welcome home. The element of surprise only added to the static electricity of that scorching kiss which would have continued a few seconds longer if they had not heard Superintendent McNaught say, "Miss Lewis–wherever you are– would you please step forward and receive the History Contest Trophy."

Lillian gave Charles a parting hug and stepped from in back of the curtain with cheeks the color of the wild chokecherries that she often used to make jelly. Laughter filled the hall as

Charles jumped from the stage a few seconds later, his slouch hat tipped crazily to the side.

Holding forth the large History Contest Trophy to Lillian, the superintendent said, "I am proud to award the History Contest Trophy to Miss Lillian Lewis, the most creative history teacher in the entire territory of Utah, and perhaps the entire country. Loud applause and cheers ripped throughout the room, and Superintendent McNaught had to motion for order so that he could call forth the Mayor of Frisco to award him the Overall Trophy for the day.

In the midst of yet another uproar on the part of the crowd, tears filled Lillian's eyes as she motioned for her students and the Frisco Mayor to join her. They formed a semicircle around her as she made a final statement to the audience. "Never has a teacher been blessed with such students. They won this award through their dedication and their desire to pursue academic excellence."

She was now literally smothered by small bodies who were all eager to show her their appreciation. Tears were flowing freely down all the girls' faces, but the boys just gave her a hug then jumped around with their right hands in air yelling, "Frisco's number one!"

She and her students and the mayor now formed a line in front of the stage while people from all three communities came forward to congratulate them for their accomplishments. Billie stood by her side in the line as long as his fidgetiness could stand, and then tugging on her hand whispered, "Teacher, do you think I could go talk to Pa?" Lillian smiled and nodded her head, giving him the signal to leave. Tears filled her eyes as she witnessed the joyful reunion between father and son. There was a huge hug which lasted for a few minutes. Then she saw Charles get down on his knee, take Billie's face in his hands, and do something that she had rarely seen him do–talk earnestly with his son. After the conversation, she witnessed a joyful Billie holding firmly to his father's shoulders as he planted a kiss square on his pa's forehead.

After what seemed like an eternity to Lillian, people started to gradually filter out of the hall. She noticed Nettie taking Billie by the hand and heading him out the door, taking him home so that Lillian could have the privacy that she would soon need. Finally after the last well-wisher had shaken her hand, she was able to join Charles who had been patiently waiting for her by the back door.

When she reached him, she was warmed by the love that permeated from his face as he took both of her hands in his and simply stated, "Lillian Lewis, there is no way I can wait until July to start our life together. How about becoming Mrs. Charles Anderson this Friday?"

Even though Friday was just five days away, Lillian's warm hug gave Charles the answer that he wanted.

Chapter 39

Lillian would later look back on the four days before the wedding and marvel at how everything just seemed to fall into place. Since school was dismissed for the summer, she had plenty of extra time to plan and organize for the festive event.

When the Mayor of Minersville, Samuel Gillins, had congratulated her by shaking her hand following the contest, he had asked if he might hold Sunday services for the Minersville Mormons the next day in her schoolroom. He told her that he was a Mormon bishop of the Minersville Branch and that the Saints wanted to hold a sacrament meeting Sunday before they headed for home.

Lillian did not hesitate to give her consent to the meeting, as long as he didn't mind meeting at eight o'clock so he would not interfere with other scheduled church services.

Later that evening, while she and Charles were eating supper with Nettie, Ben, and Billie, they talked about who they wanted to officiate at the marriage ceremony. Bishop Gillins's face entered Lillian's thoughts, and she suggested the possibility of him performing the ceremony if he could be talked into staying.

Ben and Charles expressed their approval for having Bishop Gillins perform the ceremony, but Nettie had some reservations about the idea.

"You know how much I love the *Book of Mormon*, Lillian," she said as she began to clear the table. "I received a witness of its truthfulness each day that we read together. Why, I'm even reading it now with Ben, and he has a good feeling about it, too, but have you stopped to think that we're living in Frisco where hostility towards the Mormons is still present? You've hidden the nature of your faith ever since you've been here. Do you think it's wise to let the truth come out now?"

"I think now is the very time for everyone in the community to know how much my faith means to me," said Lillian. "It's fitting and proper that on the most important day of my life nothing is hidden."

"Then, so be it!" exclaimed Nettie. "They can't do any more than drive us out of town, and you're leaving the day after the wedding."

When the dishes were washed and the table cleared, Lillian and Charles went to visit Bishop Gillins at the Minersville camp to ask him if he would possibly consider staying a few days so that he could marry the two couples.

When the kindly bishop saw how much these two young people wanted him to marry them, he said that the rest of the Minersville wagon train was leaving Monday and that he saw no problem in sending his family with them while he stayed behind to perform the marriage ceremony.

"I think it would be an experience of a lifetime to perform a double wedding ceremony in Frisco. But, can you guarantee that I'll leave this town in one piece once the Frisco ruffians find out that I'm really a Mormon bishop?"

Lillian smiled as she patted the bishop's arm. "I can't guarantee anything, Bishop Gillins, but I'm convinced that there's more good than bad in most of the people here. Besides, I don't want to brag, but you're looking at the Little Lady who played a major part in their victory yesterday. I don't think that even the most rip-roaring ruffian would want to spoil my wedding day."

The question of wedding finery was also taken care of without a pinprick of worry. Since Nettie and Lillian had known about their wedding for months, their wedding dresses were hanging on nails in the shanty, covered carefully with fine cotton bags. They had spent hours pouring over patterns at The Mercantile, and then the new milliner had carefully measured them and ordered the material from Salt Lake. When it arrived, the seamstress lost no time in creating their dream dresses.

The lace veils which were hanging with the dresses were ready to be attached to a circle of fresh wild flowers and placed on the brides' heads just minutes before the ceremony.

Melissa's mother was an excellent seamstress, and when she heard of the upcoming weddings, she had volunteered to sew the bridesmaids' dresses. The Mercantile had given Lillian and Nettie a large discount on some beautiful calico that they had been unable to sell because it was actually too fine for everyday use. There was enough of the material to make dresses for the bridesmaids and matching shirts for the boys. Mrs. Cottrell's sewing machine had been making a whirring sound for months. Just two days before the contest, she had informed Lillian and Nettie that the shirts and dresses were finished.

The day following the contest, Ned stopped by, and his eyes twinkled as he motioned to Mabel and Lizzy and jokingly remarked, "You know, ladies, these two critters are going to be highly insulted if you don't include them in the festivities." Mabel and Lizzy at this point curled their lips, shook their heads up and down, and set up such a commotion with their loud "Hee Hawing" that Ned and Lillian had to scratch behind four fury ears before they could be quieted. Ned then tried to cover his face with his sternest look as he put his hands on his ample hips and continued, "And tarnation and chicken feathers, I'll never speak to you again if you ain't plannin' on letting me give both of you away!"

Lillian's and Nettie's laughter filled the spring air as Lillian managed to say, "Ned, it was just a few hours ago that we discussed that we would like you, Lizzie, and Mabel to drive us to the meadow where you would lift us from the wagon and escort us to where our prospective grooms will be waiting."

Deep chuckles rumbled from Ned's throat, and his belly shook with pure happiness. "And we will do a proper job of giving you away, by thunder! You'll both have reason to be proud when our part is done." He patted his two mules on their heads, climbed into his wagon, and turned to smile and wave as he rode off to unload the pile of lumber that jostled around in the wagon's bed.

The matter of food was taken right out of their hands and the worry of supplying it right out of their minds when Beatrice, Molly, and Sally came to the shanty Monday morning to inform Nettie and Lillian that they insisted on catering the whole affair with the help of the ladies in the town.

"You kept our spirits up in that dreadful mine, Little Teacher, and it's the least we can do. I have a strong notion that I would never have survived if it hadn't been for that strong goodness that shines inside you and seems to just enter everyone who comes in contact with your perfect personage," Beatrice added as she stomped off to her establishment. She turned to add, "Don't worry. I'm the best cook in these parts, and between me, Sally, and Molly and some of the best cooks in Frisco, we'll treat you to a feast like nothin' that's ever delighted your taste buds before."

"Beatrice is right," said a soft voice that before the mine accident had been strident and shrill at times. "I never would have made it out of that mine without you," said a humble Molly. "My husband said just the other day that ever since the accident I hadn't yelled at him once. I guess when you come that close to meeting your Maker, you come to realize what's really important in your life. Lillian, the way you acted in that mine, concerned about others, not once thinking of yourself, gave me a whole new perspective on life. Don't worry about the wedding fixings. I'm actually becoming a rather good cook," smiled Molly as she headed in the direction of her home.

"What Molly said about being a changed person goes for me, too," said Sally. "Thanks so much for putting up with that gossipy snippet who entered the mine. Your example made us all look at ourselves and see how very self-centered we really were. I like to think I'm a little more concerned about others since the accident. Thanks for being the example that I needed to turn my life around."

Lillian and Nettie gave Molly a hug–a proper "Thank You" for dismissing one more worry from their busy schedule.

Now as Lillian sat on her bed, reminiscing over the past four days, it was hard for her to believe that today was her wedding day. She moved around in a daze, helping with breakfast and going through the motions of packing her belongings that she would take with her to Hay Springs. An hour before Ned's arrival, she carefully dressed in her wedding finery. When she caught a glimpse of herself in the mirror above the washstand, tears filled her eyes when she saw a beautiful bride looking back at her, reminding her that in two hours' time she would be Mrs. Charles Anderson.

Lillian placed the flowers and veil on Nettie's shining blonde hair, then Nettie did the same for her. Their wedding attire was complete and not a moment too soon. Loud "Hee Haws" reverberated from outside the shanty door, announcing that it was time for the wedding procession to start.

When they opened the shanty door, their eyes were treated to a spectacle of creativity never before seen in the town of Frisco.

Riding in the back of the wagon were the children, dressed in their crisp calico shirts and dresses. Every curl was in place, and the boys' hair was slicked down to perfection so that no cowlicks dared to rear their ugly heads. Even the freckles on the shining faces seemed to give off a special glow that seemed to say, "I'm part of a special celebration. Notice me!"

Ned was a sight to behold. He had on a new white ten gallon hat that made him look a little like an ant under a cabbage leaf. A spotless homespun shirt and a new leather vest covered his square chest, and a bright red bandana, crisp and new, was knotted at his neck. His mustache was something to behold. It, along with his hair and beard, had been carefully trimmed, and some sort of pomade had been rubbed into it so that it curled up on each end, making him look a little like an Old-West Santa Claus.

But no matter how pleasing the children and Ned looked, it was clear that it was Mabel and Lizzy who were going to steal the show. The mules had been sponged down with soapy water, then rinsed and combed until they literally shone in the sunlight. Atop each head was a beautiful lady's hat, adorned with flowers. Holes had been strategically cut so that furry ears could sticks through, thus attaching the beautiful creations to the mules' heads. Their tails were visions of beauty. They had been carefully braided by some brave person who had entwined beautiful ribbon inside the braids. The tails swayed back and forth as if in time to some soft music, which indicated the contentment of the fuzzy duo.

Lillian and Nettie were carefully helped into the wagon by Ned. Both brides were visions of loveliness in their wedding dresses made of satin and lace. The dresses were both made in princess style, accenting the lovely shapes of the brides, but lace had been used to decorate each dress in a different manner. Lillian's dress had a lace inset which was attached to the satin bodice and rose to underneath her chin, accenting her long neck. Nettie's dress had a lace collar which softened the effect of the round neckline.

The wedding party drove in complete silence to the meadow, and Ned stopped at the appointed place. The children left the wagon and began the wedding procession. Mary and Curt were the first to begin the march as Mary played "Oh Promise Me" on the accordion. The children were all business with their eyes straight forward, trying to keep in step with the music.

Charles and Ned were waiting with Bishop Gillins about 50 feet from where Ned had stopped the wagon. The grooms made a fashion statement in beige double breasted vests worn over dark brown shirts and new brown pants. Large Stetson hats, made from a new fashionable suede, sat atop their heads and matched the brown of the shirts and pants. The children formed a semicircle on each side of the bishop and turned to face the audience as Mary began to play, "Here Comes the Bride," prompting the audience to respectfully stand from their benches which had been carefully arranged on the grass.

With a bride on each side of his portly frame, Ned and the brides were now the center of attention as they walked in time to the music the final 20 feet to a flower-strewn archway where the grooms stood patiently waiting.

Charles and Ben, in perfect time with the music, stepped forward to claim their brides, eyes glowing and warm with the love that was part of this solemn occasion.

Bishop Gillins began the wedding ceremony by saying, "As a bishop of the Mormon Church, it is a pleasure for me to unite these two couples in holy matrimony this day." Lillian expected a commotion of some sort following these words, but not a murmur came from the crowd, even though a few eyebrows were raised and more than a few eyes were widened.

And so they were united in marriage, surrounded by the beautiful wild flowers in the meadow and warmed by the spring sun.

The ceremony proceeded with all the beauty and solemnity that attends most marriage ceremonies until Bishop Gillins signaled the end of the nuptials by saying, "You may now kiss your brides." At this point, the fireworks began. Before the grooms had a chance to properly kiss their new wives, a high-pitched female voice began singing, "Put on your lace bridal veil with the wild flowers on it, while I hitch Mabel and Lizzie to the wagon, and through the fields of clover, we'll be married in Frisco on this special wedding day."

All eyes left the bride and groom and became riveted on Laura who was singing that same song over and over again at the top of her lungs as she wound her way through the crowd, showering everyone with rice. Ladies ducked and tried to avoid the rice onslaught, but to no avail. Laura was a dead aim, and many a wedding goer was hit square in the face by the flying, oblong missiles. The rice had been camouflaged in Laura's basket by a cover of wild flowers. Now to everyone's dismay it was plain to see that the basket was full of rice, and it was a very large basket.

At this rate, the wedding was about to end on a sour note with more than one Frisco citizen upset at the state of affairs when Laura passed Lizzie and Mabel and just happened to accidentally touch Mabel's tail. That did it! Mabel began caterwauling like she had been killed and started kicking her back feet. All those who were watching this spectacle could not believe what they saw next. Mabel's left hoof sent Sally Reynold's large, elaborate hat, which was adorned with peacock feathers, sailing through the air. It traveled 20 feet and landed as softly as you please on the bald head of Superintendent McNaught.

The superintendent got a startled look on his face and just sat there stupefied for a few moments, then decided to join in the hilarity of the moment. He rose from his bench and formed a pose as if he were a famous model walking down a fashion runway, showing off her creation to the interested spectators.

That's all it took! Laughter reverberated throughout the meadow as the grooms finally got the opportunity to kiss their brides. When Lillian lifted her head from the bridal kiss, it did not surprise her to see Laura collecting something shiny, which looked suspiciously like coins, from the rest of her students.

Then the bridal couples were suddenly surrounded by well wishers whose well-meaning hugs and kisses were meant to give them a proper sendoff as they began their married lives together. When Laura came through the line, she hugged Lillian and whispered in her ear, "I'm so sorry, Miss Lewis. I can never turn down a dare—especially for money. Please forgive me."

Lillian grabbed Laura and gave her a bone-crushing hug. "You're forgiven, Laura, but be sure to invite me to your wedding. This little stunt calls for payback!"

The warm spring sun seemed to give its blessing on the events of the day as it shone down on the dinner that followed. The dishes set out on the large tables were veritable treats to the taste buds. Then fiddlers struck up some lively tunes to end the celebration in some spirited dances. As Lillian waltzed with the man who would be her companion for the rest of her life and hopefully for eternity, his brown eyes gave a promise of love, loyalty, trust, and devotion. Within herself she pledged at that very moment to give him those same things.

Chapter 40

Ben had given Lillian and Charles a spacious room in The Southern as a wedding gift. They would pack the wagon and head for Hay Springs in the morning, so it was very important that this first night following their marriage would be a private, special one.

Lillian sat on the feather bed and smiled as she reminisced over the events of the day. She was alone for a few moments, for Charles had gone to the washroom in the hotel to take a hot bath. The bath that she herself had just returned from had been liberally scented with perfumed bath salts. She had come back from it smelling very much like the roses that she had loved to smell in her mother's flower garden.

She opened her mother's carpetbag to take out her new nightgown. She was instantly comforted as she felt its smooth fabric, for it somehow brought her closer to the mother she had lost. Looking at it, she had a strong feeling that her mother was nearby, giving her blessing on this union. As she slipped the new white gown over her head, she was suddenly overcome, not with the scent of roses, but with the strong scent of lavender which appeared to be coming from the carpetbag.

As she looked at the bag and ran her hands over every inch of it, her gaze fell on a loose thread on the bottom of the bag. That simple loose thread seemed to mar the beauty of the bag, so she pulled on it, trying to break it off. Instead of the thread breaking off, her efforts released an entire row of stitching, and a secret compartment was now visible. Lillian reached her hand inside the space and retrieved a sealed envelope.

The front of the envelope was addressed to William Anderson, Address Unknown. The return address had simply one word–Marian.

The squeak of the door announced Charles's entrance. The expression on his wife's face as she looked first at an envelope that she held in her hand and then back at him caused him to hurriedly sit beside her on the bed, wrap his arm around her, and hold her close.

"Charles, I just found this envelope in a hidden compartment in my mother's carpetbag. It's addressed to William Anderson. Isn't that your father's name?"

"William Anderson was my father's name. This Marian in the return address must be the mother you've often talked about who died in the fire."

"Yes, my mother's name was Marian," said Lillian as shaky fingers carefully opened the envelope and drew out a letter. She held the paper so that Charles could see the writing as she read aloud,

My Dearest William,

I know that you will never read this letter, but I must put my thoughts and feelings down on paper. It is almost as if I am compelled to do so.

Tomorrow is my wedding day–the day that I will be joined in matrimony to Jeramiah Lewis. He is a good man, but I can never love him as I have loved you.

Choosing between you and the Church was one of the most difficult decisions that I have ever had to make, but I can see that nothing I can do will sway you from the road that you are determined to travel. I know that road will only end in your destruction, and I love you too much to see you destroy yourself.

I have a strange feeling in my heart that somehow, some way, the paths that we take in life will be joined, and that true happiness will be the result of that event. I will never stop loving

you and will work toward this final happiness, if needs be, even after my death.

I will always love you,
Marian

The bride and groom gazed into each other's eyes as the scent of lavender that swirled around them testified that the joining of the two paths talked about in the letter had occurred today with their marriage.

As Lillian and Charles kissed for the second time as husband and wife, the scent of lavender departed from the room. Having accomplished her purpose, Marian Lewis could now rest in peace.

Epilogue

June of 1920

A gentle breeze caused ripples to form on the pond in front of the Anderson home and sent the reeds and rushes that surrounded the water to rustling softly. The ducks and geese on the pond weren't bothered by the soft gusts as they went about their business of snatching bugs from the water's surface or snapping them out of the air. The buffalo in the west pasture were bedding down for the night, and their massive heads rested on the soft grass. To the east of them their neighbor's herd of sheep was also preparing for the close of the day as lambs suckled their mothers who were methodically chewing on young alfalfa sprouts.

Lillian and Charles sat with clasped hands on their front porch swing, finding peace and serenity as they gazed at the white granite peaks of the Mineral Mountains. As the sky began to darken, signaling the end of the day, Lillian rested her head on Charles's shoulder as her thoughts traveled back in time over the last forty years.

Expressive green eyes, long, blonde hair, and blazing guns filled Lillian's thoughts. Mandy and Will's letters were frequent and filled with news about how their cattle ranch had grown from fifty head to thousands. Will had learned how to develop a new strain of Herefords that were in demand all over

Utah and the surrounding states. His guns had been retired and laid to rest the second he left Frisco and were now replaced by five rambunctious children–two boys and three girls. One of his letters told of the plastic surgeon in Salt Lake City who had transformed Mandy's scarred face back into some of its original beauty. The last letter brought the news that Will had run for Mayor of Heber City and won in a landslide. He said he'd always wanted to try his hand at politics. He wrote, "If this mayor thing works out, I might even considering working towards moving Mandy into the Governor's Mansion."

Lillian thought that he was joking about the Governor's Mansion but knew that if the former sheriff of Frisco set his mind to something, it would take a herd of raging buffalos to stop him.

Memories of freckles, cowlicks, a dead rat, and a squawking pig next entered Lillian's thoughts. The students that she taught in that first Frisco School–they were branded in her memory with a deep imprint that could never be erased. She smiled when she remembered how they had come trickling into Hay Springs, one family at a time, until all of her students were once more around her, pleading for her attention.

It seems that when their teacher left, they had done everything in their power to convince their families that they needed Miss Lewis like they needed the very air that they breathed. They pleaded and cried until one by one the seven families that were involved showed up at Hay Springs to settle down. Some of the children's fathers found work on the ranch, and some of them traveled to Minersville or Milford and worked in the mines during the week and then returned home to Hay Springs on the weekend.

With all of her students around her, the logical thing for Lillian to do was to start a school in the front room of her home and continue her students' education until they had graduated and were old enough to be on their own. Children from other Hay Springs families had joined them, and Lillian had continued her teaching, sometimes with one of her four children perched on her hip as she supervised the lessons for the day.

After those first ten Frisco students left her care and the haven of Hay Springs, her students faithfully wrote to her, telling her of their accomplishments.

First, there was Billie, whom she considered to be her own. He had become Charles's right arm and full partner in the business that they had begun here in Hay Springs. Charles had bought Hay Springs from Mr. Reed, and he and Billie had sold most of the horses and started a buffalo ranch. In 1905, the American Bison Society was formed with the purpose of building up a few herds and saving the bison from utter annihilation. It was this society that funded the buffalo ranch at Hay Springs by sending Charles and Billie a monthly check to build up the herd which had grown from 25 buffalos to over 500.

Billie spent most of his time repairing the fences on the ranch. Buffalos did not respect any fence, and if they were determined to go beyond that fence, their sheer brute power enabled them to just bowl it down and go where their fancy took them. Taking care of these cantankerous critters took a lot of work and effort, but each new buffalo calf that was born brought in new revenue for the ranch.

Billie had married his beloved Melissa and was now raising a boy and two girls of his own. When their son Charlie threatened to drive them insane one Fourth of July by setting off firecrackers and almost stampeding the buffalo herd, Lillian simply reminded Billie that he had done far worse things at that age. Melissa became Lillian's right arm as she helped with the Hay Springs School. Being married to Billie had instilled in her more patience than most people accumulate in a lifetime. Her quiet, sweet manner won over many a difficult student.

Curt's letters told of his new job as the star reporter of the *Deseret News* in Salt Lake City. When he wrote Lillian about ending up in jail overnight because of a controversial editorial that he wrote on polygamy in the state and how he had talked the inmates into keeping the guards up all night by singing songs as they accompanied themselves by tapping their cups on the bars, Lillian laughed so hard that tears came to her eyes. She was so proud of his accomplishments, but she could see that he would always be the mischievous Curt who had organized Lincoln's funeral.

Bright red curls bobbing in the breeze brought thoughts of Laura who had married a Beaver rancher and become a mother of four children, all redheads. For the past twelve years Laura had been the manager of the Beaver Opera House in Beaver, the center of cultural life for the lower half of the State of Utah. Laura organized the dances which were held on the bottom floor of the white, stone building and arranged for vaudeville acts to perform on the stage on the second floor.

The vaudeville acts always opened to a full house, but it wasn't vaudeville performances that the audiences came to see–Laura was always the center of attention. Whether it was riding her pet donkey down the aisles as she belted out the lively song, "My donkey is a weird duck," or pretending to be a spirited gypsy as she roamed the audience telling fortunes, she was the star attraction. She often earned more money from dares than she took in from actual ticket receipts. Laura had found her niche in life and was just overjoyed doing whatever was outrageous or bizarre.

Then there was her Mary, whose name passed every mothers' lips reverently. Mary was the area midwife. Doctors were few and overworked, and traditions and customs were such that women and husbands were often adverse to using the services of a male doctor during a delivery. Mary was noted for her skill in bringing healthy children into the world. She had spent some time in Salt Lake City where she received special training in childbirth and other medical techniques.

When she heard that the local blacksmith, who was often called upon to extract teeth, was causing his patients undo pain, she stomped into his shop, took away his pliers, kicked him in the rear, then marched home to put up a new sign on her house which read, "Baby Birthing and Teeth Pulling." Those patients who went to her with abscessed teeth swore that their bad teeth were out seconds after they sat down, and no laughing gas was needed, for the jokes she told them sent them from her office in hysterics, their pain forgotten.

Every time Lillian saw a wooly sheep she was reminded of Richie and Clarence Wood. Their letters told of their sheep shearing business at Black Rock, just 30 miles to the north of Hay Springs. When Lillian thought of the Wood brothers, her heart swelled with pride. They had the largest sheep shearing corrals of any place in the Western United States and had also set up a small store near their operation. Sheep men trailed their sheep to Black Rock from miles around and bought supplies at the Wood's store. The brothers' operation could shear as many as 5,000 sheep in one day, and they often ran 30 to 40 thousand head through their shearing corrals in one shearing season. The Woods had built a dam across the Beaver River bed at Black Rock which now stored water for use during the dry part of the season. Many sheep men who got into trouble during dry years knew where they could come for good sheep range and plenty of water.

High praise and kind words continually reached Lillian about Stacy and Jessica. They had married Milford ranchers and started families. The girls had studied at the Beaver Academy when they left Hay Springs, and since teachers were in demand in Milford, they began a team-teaching operation. Since both girls had small children the first ten years of their married life, one would teach one week, while the other stayed home to take care of the children, then they would change jobs.

When their children were grown and out of the house, they filled two permanent positions at the school where they taught history and English, using Lillian's creative methods, producing many plays and musicals for the community. They were well-known for their creative physical education classes where they taught modern dancing, something that was unheard of in the State of Utah at that time. No one ever complained about being bored in one of Stacy or Jessica's classes because they were too busy catching the excitement of their teachers' creative ideas. Larger high schools in Salt Lake had tried to entice them to come and teach at their schools, but the sisters were happy in Milford and started a dance program that was envied throughout the state.

Lillian still couldn't get used to the gold star on Jamie Parker's suit whenever he stopped by the ranch to say hello. U.S. Marshall, the badge said, and Jamie was the best. A tough lawman, Jamie had chased after his cousin, LeRoy Parker, now known as Butch Cassidy, for years until Butch went to South America. He almost foiled Butch when the Wild Bunch attempted to rob the Union Pacific Railroad, but his illusive cousin got away. He was known for his fast gun and his fair way of administering the law. During his frequent visits with Billie at the ranch, his exciting stories about chasing well-known Western outlaws kept them entertained for hours. Lillian thanked her Father in Heaven every day that Jamie had chosen the right side of the law for his profession.

She had lost her beloved Ned ten winters ago, but Lizzy and Mabel were given the royal treatment each day–their residence the Anderson's large, red barn. Though they were old and full of arthritis, they had lost none of their high-spiritedness.

And what of Frisco? Lillian still remembered the night of February 12, 1885. She was awakened when some of her windows shattered, sending glass over her entire bedroom. The next day she found out from a passing traveler that there had been a massive cave-in at the Frisco mine. Luckily it was between shifts and no one was hurt. The greedy owners had stroped the mine so quickly that the crews could not keep up with the support timbering. According to the traveler, at twelve midnight, a group of men had just begun their shift at the 800 foot level when movements in the mine frightened them so badly that they asked to be hoisted to the surface. A massive cave-in occurred at the very moment that the last cage with six men in it was being hoisted to the surface. The cage with the men in it was caught and held at the 200 foot level by the cave-in, and the six men had to be pulled to the surface one at a time.

Lillian was relieved to hear from the traveler that not one injury occurred from the accident. Lillian later read in a Salt Lake Tribune article, "All-in-all the cave-in of February 12, 1885 could have been a complete disaster. Not only could the mine have been completely destroyed but there could have easily been a loss of life. Again the Horn Silver Mine had dodged a bullet. Again the God of miners had protected all the souls in the mine."

That cave-in might well have been the beginning of the end for the Horn Silver Mine, Lillian thought. Even though a new shaft had been sunk to the 1,600 foot level and a concentrator with a 20-stamp mill had been constructed to treat low grade ore, just last year Lillian had learned that production in the mine had fallen off and that the mine had operated at a loss for the first time since it opened. *It's dying,* Lillian thought, but she couldn't help but give a thankful sigh of relief that she had made it out safe and sound from a cave-in many years ago.

Then her thoughts turned to another change that had taken place in Frisco after her departure. A smile covered her finely-lined face as she reminisced about the change in Frisco's religious atmosphere over the past forty years.

Not long after she had left, the Mormons in Frisco became brave enough to come out of their closets and stand in the sunshine of a new religious dawn in the Frisco community. Many of them seemed to say to themselves, "If our beloved Miss Lewis can stand on her wedding day and proudly proclaim her beliefs by being married by a Mormon bishop, then we can be brave enough to let the community know what rests within our hearts."

And so the religious reformation in Frisco began, moving through the community like a slow-moving river. Ben and Nettie, who had stayed in Frisco to run The Southern, had been baptized into the Church shortly after Lillian's departure, and the baptism was a proud event to which all the community was invited. Other Frisco businessmen suddenly started talking to Milford businessmen who were Mormons about their beliefs. As a result, some of these businessmen were also baptized. One saloon owner, Silas Hatch, joined the Church, closed his saloon, and remodeled it into the finest eating establishment in Frisco and the Southern part of the state.

Benjamin Bennett was called by the Church to move to Frisco to preside over the local Mormons. In 1881, the first Frisco Ward was organized, and from all reports, the Church continued to grow little by little in the once anti-Mormon community.

Yes, Lillian had much for which to be thankful. Her love for Charles seemed to just keep growing. He and Billie had been baptized in one of the Hay Springs ponds just six months after their marriage. A year later she and Charles had made the journey to St. George to be sealed for time and all eternity in the St. George Temple. An excursion that the entire family looked forward to almost yearly was a trip on the Union Pacific Railroad to attend General Conference in Salt Lake City. Charles had become a soft, gentle man, even though his crusty disposition still erupted from time to time. He was a devoted, loving father and grandfather to his children and grandchildren.

As the sunset faded in the west and darkness began to fall, Charles helped Lillian from the swing for their nightly walk around the ranch. The cool breeze from the ponds and familiar song of the crickets brought with them a sense of peace. The hand that held Lillian's was gentle and loving. As was their custom each night, they halted their walk for a few minutes when they reached their field of lavender which had seemed to spring up of its own accord shortly after their marriage. As Lillian gazed into the dear face of her husband in the half-light of the retreating day, the scent of lavender swirled around them as a feeling of caring, happiness, and a very special love enveloped them, sending a warm, glowing shaft to their hearts.

A Thought From The Author

We are all pebbles in the river of life, swirling in the river bed that was cut by the creator's own hands. Some of us roll along with the rushing torrent, affecting nothing around us, but there are others that over time become large rocks, even boulders that change the very course of the river, giving it a better, more effective path–those who truly make a difference.

References

Horton, George A., Jr., <u>A Personal View of the History of Milford up to 1914–The Town that Could!</u>, Printed by BYU Print Services, Provo, Utah, 2002.

Brown, C. J., "Someone Should Remember," self-printed.

<u>The Salt Lake Tribune</u>. February 17, 1885.

Margaret W. Miller

About the Author

Margaret W. Miller has lived in Milford, Utah most of her life. She attended Brigham Young University for three years and Utah State University for one year where she earned her BA degree in Business Education and English.

Following college graduation, she was hired to teach English and business in the Beaver Country School District. During her 34 years of teaching, she earned many honors. In 1998 she was selected as one of the three finalists for Utah Teacher of the Year, and her business and English students earned many awards as they represented their school in various competitions.

Following retirement, Mrs. Miller was called back a number of years as a long-term substitute whenever she was needed. She is presently a part-time librarian at the Milford Public Library and enjoys working with the young people during story hour. She sharpens her writing skills each week by writing a column for the local newspaper, The Beaver County Journal. Since her husband has built and maintained hundreds of guzzlers (water holes for animals) in the desert, she acts as his personal secretary to record the data he collects.

She considers her greatest accomplishments and joys in life to be her daughter Denise Bradshaw, her son-in-law Dwayne Bradshaw, and her four grandchildren, Dallon, Dalton, Danielle and Dailey.

Made in United States
Troutdale, OR
03/14/2024